Reviews for the original 1993 edition of
The Element of Fire

"A rich fantasy debut ... Skillfully ble
delights with deft and sympathetic ch
for adventure."

— *Publishers Weekly*

"Fans who appreciate ingenious plotting, witty dialogue, and fascinating characterization will find this tale a truly wonderful adventure in reading."

— *Rave Reviews*

"The Element of Fire is a powerful fantasy."

— *Locus*

"A fascinating read ... I had to finish it up in one fell swoop, staying up until 2:30 to do so, and hadn't known I'd spent that much time in her world!"

— Anne McCaffrey

"... a lively swashbuckler perfectly integrated with a thoughtful, down-to-earth character study—not just a fantasy homage to Errol Flynn movies, but to high Shakespearean drama as well ... A remarkable new book from a remarkable new writer."

— *Dragon Magazine*

The Element of Fire

Martha Wells

And New Philosophy calls all in doubt,
The Element of fire is quite put out;
The Sun is lost, and th'earth, and no man's wit
Can well direct him where to looke for it.
– John Donne
"An Anatomie of the World"

This is a work of fiction. All the characters and events portrayed in this book are fictitious, and any resemblance to real people or events is purely coincidental.

Cover Design by M. Wilson
Typesetting by Katya Loney

ISBN 978-0-6151-3571-7

Original edition published by Tor:
Hardcover July 1993
Mass Market Paperback July 1994

www.marthawells.com

Introduction to the Revised Edition

The Element of Fire was my first novel, written around 1990, when I was 26. It was published in hardcover in 1993 and paperback in 1994, by Tor Books. It was published in Italy in 1995, Russia in 1997, Poland in 1998, in France, by l'Atalante, in 2002, and will be published in Spanish by Bibliopolis. It was a finalist for the 1993 Compton Crook/Stephen Tall Award and a runner-up for the 1994 Crawford Award. The French edition was on the ballot for the 2002 Imaginales award.

It was the first Ile-Rien book, before I knew there were going to be any other Ile-Rien books. Since then Vienne, altered by time, war, and general rough usage, has been a setting for *The Death of the Necromancer* (nominated for the Nebula Award in 1998 and also becoming impossible to find in the US) and *The Wizard Hunters*, *The Ships of Air*, and *The Gate of Gods*, available in paperback from HarperCollins. Kade Carrion also appears in the short story "The Potter's Daughter" in the Tsunami Relief anthology *Elemental*, edited by Steve Savile and Alethea Kontis, published in 2006 by Tor Books.

The text posted here does not match the original US edition; I've edited it to make the prose a little smoother and more in line with my current style, but haven't made any substantial changes to plot, storyline, or characterization.

CHAPTER ONE

THE GRAPPLING HOOK skittered across the rain-slick stone of the ledge before dropping to catch in the grillwork below the third-story window. Berham leaned back on the rope to test it. "That's it, Captain Sir. Tight as may be," the servant whispered.

"Well done," Thomas Boniface told him. He stepped back from the wall and looked down the alley. "Now where in hell is Dr. Braun?"

"He's coming," Gideon Townsend, Thomas's lieutenant, said as he made his way toward them out of the heavy shadows. Reaching them, he glanced up at the full moon, stark white against the backdrop of wind-driven rain clouds, and muttered, "Not the best night for this work." The three men stood in the muddy alley, the dark brocades and soft wools of their doublets and breeches blending into the grimy stones and shadow, moonlight catching only the pale lace at the wrists or shirt collars of Thomas and his lieutenant, the glint of an earring, or the cold metal sheen on rapiers and wheellock pistol barrels. It was a cool night and they were surrounded by failed counting houses and the crumbling elegance of the decaying once-wealthy homes of the River Quarter.

Thomas personally couldn't think of a good time to forcibly invade a foreign sorcerer's house. "The point of it is to go and be killed where you're told," he said. "Is everyone in position?"

"Martin and Castero are up on the tannery roof, watching the street and the other alley. I put Gaspard and two others at the back of the house and left the servants to watch the horses. The rest are across the street, waiting for the signal," Gideon answered, his blue eyes deceptively guileless. "We're all quite ready to go and be killed where we're told."

"Good," Thomas said. He knew Gideon was still young enough to see this as a challenge, to care nothing for the political reality that sent them on a mission as deadly as this with so little support. Glancing down the alley again, he saw Dr. Braun was finally coming, creeping along the wall and uncomfortably holding his velvet-trimmed scholar's robes out of the stinking mud. "Well?" Thomas asked as the sorcerer came within earshot. "What have you done?"

"I've countered the wards on the doors and windows, but the inside... This person Grandier is either very strong or very subtle. I can't divine what protections he's used." The young sorcerer looked up at him, his watery eyes blinking fitfully. His long sandy hair and drooping mustache made him look like a sad-faced spaniel.

"You can't give us any hint of what we're to find in there?" Thomas said, thinking, *This would have been better done if I hadn't been saddled with a sorcerer who has obviously escaped from a market-day farce.*

Braun's expression was both distressed and obstinate. "He is too strong, or... He might have the help of some creature of the fay."

"God protect us," Berham muttered, and uneasily studied the cloudy darkness above. The others ignored him. Berham was short, rotund, and had been wounded three times manning barricades in the last Bisran War. He claimed that the only reason he had left the army was that servants' wages were better. Despite the little man's vocal quavering, Thomas was not worried about his courage.

"What are you saying?" Gideon asked the sorcerer. "You mean we could fall down dead or burst into flame the moment we cross the threshold?"

"The uninitiated so often have ill-conceived ideas about these matters, like the fools who believe sorcerers change their shapes or fly like the fay. It would be exceedingly dangerous to create heat or cold out of nothing..."

"So you say, but..."

"That's enough," Thomas interrupted. He took the rope and tested it again with his own weight. The first floor of the house would be given over to stables, storage for coaches or wagons, and servants' quarters. The second would hold salons and other rooms for entertaining guests, and the third and fourth would be the owner's private quarters. That would be where the sorcerer would keep his laboratory, and very likely his prisoner. Thomas only hoped the information from the King's Watch was correct and that the Bisran bastard Grandier wasn't here. He told Gideon, "You follow me. Unless, of course, you'd like to go first?"

The lieutenant swept off his feathered hat and bowed extravagantly. "Oh, not at all, Sir, after you."

"So kind, Sir."

The brickwork was rough and Thomas found footholds easily. He reached the window and pulled himself up on the rusted grating, balancing cautiously. He felt the rope jerk and tighten as Gideon started to climb.

The window was set with small panes of leaded glass and divided into four tall panels. Thomas drew a thin dagger from the sheath in his boot and slipped the point between the wooden frames of the lower half. Working the dagger gently, he eased the inside catch up. The panels opened inward with only a faint creak. Moonlight touched the polished surface of a table set directly in front of the window, but the darkness of the deeper interior of the room was impenetrable. It was silent, but it was a peculiar waiting silence that he disliked.

Then the window ledge cracked loudly under his boots and he took a hasty step forward onto the table, thinking, *Now we'll know, at any rate.* Dust rose from the heavy draperies as he brushed against them, but the room remained quiet.

"Was that wise?" Gideon asked softly from below the windowsill.

"Possibly not. Don't come up yet." Thomas slipped the dagger back into his boot sheath and drew his rapier. If something came at him out of that darkness, he preferred to keep it at as great a distance as possible. "Tell Berham to hand up a light."

There was some soft cursing below as a dark lantern, its front covered by a metal slide to keep the light dimmed, was lit and passed upward. Thomas waited impatiently, feeling the darkness press in on him like a solid wall. He would have preferred the presence of another sorcerer besides Braun, the rest of the Queen's Guard, and a conscripted city troop to quell any possibility of riot when the restive River Quarter neighborhood discovered it had a mad foreign sorcerer in its midst. But orders were orders, and if Queen's guards or their captain were killed while entering Grandier's house secretly, then at least civil unrest was prevented. An inspired intrigue, Thomas had to admit, even if he was the one it was meant to eliminate.

As he reached down to take the shuttered lamp from Gideon, something moved in the corner of his eye. Thomas dropped the lamp onto the table and studied the darkness, trying to decide if the hesitant motion was actually there or in his imagination.

The flicker of light escaping from the edges of the lamp's iron cover touched the room with moving shadows. With the toe of his boot Thomas knocked the lantern slide up.

The wan candlelight was reflected from a dozen points around the unoccupied room, from lacquered cabinets, the gilt leather of a chair, the metallic threads in brocaded satin hangings.

Then the wooden cherub supporting the right-hand corner of the table Thomas was standing on turned its head.

He took an involuntary step backward.

"Captain, what is it?" Gideon's whisper was harsh.

Thomas didn't answer. He was looking around the room as the faces in the floral carving over the chimneypiece shifted their blank white eyes, their tiny mouths working silently. The bronze snake twined around the supporting pole of a candlestand stirred sluggishly. In the woolen carpet the interwoven pattern of vines writhed.

Keeping hold of the rope, Gideon chinned himself on the window ledge to see in. He cursed softly.

"Worse than I thought," Thomas agreed, not looking away from the hideously animate room. Unblinking eyes of marbleized wood stared sightlessly, limbs and mouths moved without sound. *Can they see? Or hear?* he wondered grimly. Most likely they can. He doubted they were here only to frighten intruders, however effective they might be at it.

"We should burn this house to the ground," Gideon whispered.

"We want to get Dubell out alive, not scrape his ashes out of the wreckage."

"How?"

Good question, Thomas thought. The vines in the carpet were lifting themselves above the surface of the floor like the tentacles of a sea beast. They were as thick around as a man's wrist and looked strong, and metallic glints that had been gilt threads in the weaving were growing into knife-edged thorns. It was only going to get more difficult. Thomas caught up the lantern and stepped down into a chair with arms shaped into gilded lampreys. They were struggling viciously but were unable to turn their heads back far enough to reach him. From there he stepped down to the hardwood floor and backed toward the doorway.

Gideon made a move to climb into the window but the viselike tentacles were reaching up above waist-height and groping along the edge of the table. Thomas said, "No, stay back."

At the sound of his voice the vines whipped around and stretched out for him, growing prodigiously longer in a sudden bound, and Thomas threw himself at the door.

The latch was weak and snapped as his weight struck it. He stumbled through and caught himself, just as something thudded into the dark paneled wall in front of him. He dropped the lantern and dove sideways, scrambling for cover between two brocaded chairs and the fireplace.

Embedded in the wall, still quivering, was a short metal arrow; if he had come through the doorway cautiously it would have struck his chest. The lion heads on the iron firedogs snapped ineffectually at him as he pushed himself further behind the chairs, thinking, *Where the hell is he?* The sputtering candle sent shadows chasing across crowded furniture and everything was moving. Then in the far corner he saw the life-sized statue of a Parscen archer. Naked to the waist and balancing a candleholder on his turbaned head, he was drawing a second arrow out of the bronze quiver at his side and putting it to his short bow.

Rolling onto his back to make himself a smaller target, Thomas dropped the rapier and drew one of his wheellocks. He'd loaded both pistols down in the alley, and now as he wound up the mainspring, an arrow thudded into the over-stuffed chair seat. The other chair began to edge sideways using the clawed feet at the ends of its splayed legs; without thinking Thomas muttered, "Stop that." He set the spring, braced the pistol on his forearm and fired.

The plaster statue shattered in the deafening impact. The shot scarred the wall behind it and filled the room with the stink of gunpowder.

Thomas got to his feet, tucking away the empty pistol and picking up his rapier. *Now the whole damned house knows I'm here.* He hadn't planned to do this alone either, but the vines filling up the first room and curling round the doorway into this one committed him to it.

Avoiding the animate furniture, he went to the door in the opposite wall and tried the handle. It was unlocked, and he eased it open carefully. The room within was dark, but the archway beyond revealed a chamber lit by a dozen or so red glass candelabra.

Thomas pulled the door closed behind him and moved forward. The dim light revealed stealthy movement in the carvings on the fireplace mantel and along the bordered paneling. In the more brightly lit chamber beyond the arch, he could see an open door looking out onto the main stairwell.

He stopped just before the fall of light from the next room would have revealed his presence. There was something... Then he heard the creak of leather and a harsh rasp of breath. It came from just beyond his range of sight, past the left side of the arch. They knew Grandier had hired men to guard the house; it was the only way the King's Watch had been able to trace the sorcerer, since there was no one in the city who could identify him. The man in the next room must have heard the shot; possibly he was waiting for the protective spells to dispose of any intruders. Thomas had planned on something to distract the sorcerer's human watchdogs, to send them down to the lower part of the house, if Gideon would just get on with it...

From somewhere below there was a muffled thump, and the floorboards trembled under his feet. Thomas smiled to himself; shouts and running footsteps sounded from the stairs as the hired swords hastened for the front door. In theory, he wasn't disobeying the King's orders to keep the raid on Grandier's house secret. Placed correctly, a small charge of gunpowder could blow a wooden door to pieces while making little noise, and the houses to either side of Grandier's were empty anyway.

The waiting guard did not take the bait with the others, but went forward to stand at the doorway into the stairwell, his rapier drawn. He was big, with greasy blond hair tied back from his face, and dressed in a dun-colored doublet. Thomas had already decided to kill him and had started forward when the man turned and saw him.

The hired sword's shout was muffled by the clatter of his comrades on the stairs and he rushed forward without waiting for help. Thomas parried two wild blows, then beat his opponent's sword aside and lunged for the kill. The man jerked away and took the point between the ribs instead of under the breastbone, dropping his weapon and staggering back. Cursing his own sloppiness, Thomas leapt after him, grappling with him and trying to drive his main gauche up under the man's chin. In another moment Thomas was easing the limp body to the floor. There was blood pooling on the rug and on his boots, but hopefully the others were occupied below and there was no one left to follow his trail.

He glanced quickly around the room and noted it was free of the sorcerous animation. There was a closed door on the opposite wall, and it bore examining before he ventured out onto the main stairs. As Thomas was reaching for the handle, he felt a sharp stab of unease. He stepped back, his hand tightening on his sword-hilt, baffled by his own reaction. It was only a door, as the others had been. He reached out slowly and felt his heart pound faster with anxiety as his hand neared the knob.

Either I've gone mad, he thought, *or this door is warded.* Testing it with his own reactions, he found the ward began about a foot from the door and stretched out to completely cover the surface. It was a warning, with a relatively mild effect, more than likely meant to keep the hired swords and servants away from this portion of the house. It could also explain why the dead man hadn't left his post to investigate the pistol shot or to follow his comrades to the front entrance. He had been guarding something of crucial importance.

Thomas stepped back and kicked the center panel, sending the door crashing open. Beyond was a staircase leading upward, softly lit by candlelight glowing down from the floor above.

Bracing himself, Thomas stepped through the ward and onto the first step, and had to steady himself against the wall as the effect faded. He shook his head and started up the stairs.

The banister was carved with roses which swayed under a sorcerous breeze only they could sense. Thomas climbed slowly, looking for the next trap. When he stopped at the first landing, he could see that the top of the stairs opened into a long gallery, lit by dozens of candles in mirror-backed sconces. Red draperies framed mythological paintings and classical landscapes. At the far end was a door, guarded on either side by a man-sized statuary niche. One niche held an angel with flowing locks, wings, and a beatific smile. The other niche was empty. Thomas climbed almost to the head of the stairs, looking up at the archway that was the entrance to the room. Something suspiciously like plaster dust drifted down from the carved bunting.

A tactical error, Thomas thought. Whatever was hiding up there wasn't doing it to be decorative. He took a quiet step back down the stairs, drawing his empty pistol. The air felt warm; beneath his doublet, sweat was sticking the thin fabric of his shirt to his ribs. From the powder flask on his belt he measured out a double charge and poured it into the barrel. He pushed the bullet and wadding down with the short ramrod, thinking that it would be quite ironic if the pistol exploded and ended the matter here.

Thomas wound and set the spring, carefully aimed the pistol at the top of the archway and fired. The fifty-caliber ball tore through the light ornamental wood and into the body of the plaster statue that had perched up on the opposite side of the arch. Thomas shielded his face as splintered wood and fragments of plaster rained down. A sculpted head, arm, and pieces of a foot thudded to the floor in front of him. He climbed the last few steps and stopped at the front of the gallery, which was now wreathed in the heavy white smoke of the pistol's discharge. This next trap wasn't bothering to conceal itself.

Ponderously the angel statue turned its head toward him and stepped out of its niche in the far wall. Thomas shoved the empty pistol back into his sash and drew the second loaded one, circling away from the angel. It was slow, its feet striking the polished floor heavily, plaster wings flapping stiffly.

It stalked him like a stiff cat as he backed away. He wanted to save the pistol for whatever was behind the next door, so he was reluctant to fire.

Then his boot knocked against something that seized his ankle. He fell heavily and dropped the wheellock, which spun across the polished floor and somehow managed not to go off. Rolling over, he saw that the hand and arm of the broken statue had tripped him and was still holding onto his ankle. He drew his main gauche and smashed at it with the hilt. The hand shattered and fell away, but the angel was almost on top of him.

Scrambling desperately backward, he caught the base of a tall bronze candlestand and pulled it down on the angel. The heavy holder in the top struck the statue in the temple, knocking loose a chunk of plaster. It reared back and Thomas got to his feet, keeping hold of the candlestand. As it lurched toward him again he swung the stand. A large piece of the wing cracked and fell away as the blow connected, and the creature staggered, suddenly unbalanced.

Past the stumbling statue he saw movement on the stairs. There were dark writhing shapes climbing the steps, dragging themselves upward on the banisters. He backed away, realizing it was the vines that had sprung out of the carpet in the first room. *Are they filling the entire house?* The situation was horrible enough, it hardly needed that. And he had known he couldn't get out the way he had gotten in, but he had hoped to have the front door as an option. Now that way was blocked. Thomas dropped the candlestand and turned to the other door.

He pulled it open and one quick glance told him the room seemed unoccupied by statues. He slammed the door closed as the angel lumbered awkwardly toward him, bracing against it as he shoved the bolt home. He stepped back as the thing battered against the other side.

Moonlight from high undraped windows revealed shelf-lined walls stacked with leatherbound books, most chained to the shelves. It was a large room, crowded with the paraphernalia of both library and alchemical laboratory, quiet except for the erratic tick of several lantern clocks. There was a writing desk untidily crammed with paper, and workbenches cluttered with flasks and long-necked bottles of colored glass. It smelled of tallow from cheap candles, the musty odor of books, and an acrid scent from residue left in the containers or staining floors and tabletops. He drew his rapier again and moved around the overladen tables, inbred caution making him avoid the stained patches left by alchemical accidents on the floor. He knew he would have to come back to this house at some point: the desks and cabinets crammed with scribbled papers would undoubtedly hold some of Grandier's secrets, but now he hadn't time to sort the vital information from the trash.

Thomas circled the rotting bulk of a printing press and a cabinet overflowing with ink-stained type, and stopped. At the far end of the room, hidden by stacked furniture and shadows, was a man seated in a plain chair. He faced the wall and seemed to be lost in thought. Dressed in a black cope and a baggy scholar's cap, his face was angular and lean in profile and his hair and beard were gray. He didn't seem to be breathing.

Then Thomas saw the shimmer of reflected moonlight from the window and realized the man was encased in an immense glass ball. Wondering at it, he took a step forward. The enigmatic figure didn't move. He went closer and lifted a hand to touch the glass prison, but thought better of it.

As if the gesture was somehow perceptible to the man inside, he turned his head slowly toward Thomas. For a moment his expression was vacant, eyes fixed on nothing. Then the blue eyes focused and the mouth smiled, and he said, "Captain Thomas Boniface. We haven't formally met, but I have heard of you."

Thomas had not known Galen Dubell closely, the fifteen years ago when the old sorcerer had been at court, but he had seen the portraits. "Dr. Dubell, I presume." Thomas circled the glass prison. "I hope you have some idea of how I'm to get you out of there."

There was another heavy crash against the door. The statue, the animate vines, or something else was intent on battering its way in.

"The power in this bauble is directed inward, toward me. You should be able to break it from the outside," Dubell said, his composure undisturbed by the pounding from the door.

It would be dangerous for the old sorcerer but Thomas couldn't see any other way. At least the heavy wool of his scholar's robe would provide some protection. "Cover your head."

Using the hilt of his rapier, Thomas struck the glass sphere. Lines of white fire radiated out along the cracks. The material was considerably stronger than it looked, and cracked like eggshell rather than glass. He hit it twice more, then it started to shatter. A few of the larger shards broke loose, but none fell near the old man.

Galen Dubell stood carefully and shook the smaller fragments out of his robes. "That is a welcome relief, Captain." He looked exhausted and bedraggled as he stepped free of his prison, glass crackling under his boots.

Thomas had already sheathed his rapier and was overturning one of the cabinets beneath the window. He stepped atop it and twisted the window's catch. Cool night air entered the stuffy room as he pushed it open. An ornamental sill just below formed a narrow slanted ledge. Leaning out, he could see the edge of the roof above. They would have to climb the rough brickwork.

He pulled his head back in and said, "I'm afraid we'll have to take the footpad's way out, Doctor." He just hoped the old man could make it, and speedily; the battering at the door was growing louder.

Dubell scrambled up the cabinet easily enough. As if he'd read Thomas's thought, he said, "It's quite all right, Captain. I prefer the risk to more of Urbain Grandier's hospitality." He might have the easier time of it; he was almost a head taller than Thomas.

As Dubell pulled himself carefully out onto the narrow sill, the door gave way.

The sorcerer used the scrollwork around the window casement as a ladder, drawing himself up toward the roof. Thomas swung out onto the sill after him and stood, holding onto the window frame. Broken fragments of brick sprinkled down as Dubell grasped the edge of the roof above.

Thomas boosted him from below and the scholar scrambled over the edge. Digging fingertips into the soft stone, Thomas started to pull himself upward. Dubell had barely been able to grasp the ledge from here; Thomas knew he would have to stand on top of the cornice before he could reach safety.

There was a crash just inside. Straining to reach the edge of the roof, Thomas bit his lip as something gave way beneath his left boot. Fingers wedged between the soft brick, he groped for another hold and felt the mortar under his hand crumble.

Then from above, Galen Dubell caught his arm in an iron grip, supporting him as he found another foothold. For a man who must do little with his hands besides write or do scholarly experiments, Dubell was surprisingly strong. The man's gentle demeanor made it easy to think of him as nothing more than an aged university don and to forget that he was also a wizard.

Thomas scrambled over the edge, his muscles trembling with the strain. "I thank you, Doctor," he said, sitting up, "but there are those at court who won't appreciate it."

"I won't tell them about it, then." Dubell looked around, the damp breeze tearing at his gray hair and his cap. "Are those your companions?"

There was a shout. The two men he had stationed atop the tannery were waving from the edge of the next roof.

"Stay there," Thomas shouted back. "We'll come to you."

Slowly they made their way up the crest of the pitched roof to the edge where the others were throwing down some planks to bridge the gap. The slate tiles were cracked and broken, slipping under their feet. They had just crossed the makeshift bridge to the tannery when Thomas turned to say something to Dubell; in the next instant he was lying flat on the rough planks with the others as the timber frame of the building was shaken by a muffled explosion. Then they were all retreating hastily across the tannery roof, choking on acrid smoke, as flames rose from the Bisran sorcerer's house.

≈≈≈

"So much for keeping this quiet," Thomas remarked to Gideon. The two men sat their nervous horses, watching from a few lengths down the street as Grandier's house burned. There was a crash as the façade collapsed inward, sending up a fireworks display of sparks and an intense wave of heat. The neighborhood had turned out to throw buckets of water and mud on the surrounding roofs and mill about in confusion and panicked excitement. The real fear had subsided when the residents had realized the fire was confining itself to the sorcerer's home, and that only a few stray sparks had lit on the surrounding structures.

Three of the hired swords had been taken alive, though Thomas doubted they would know much, if anything, about Grandier's intentions. His own men had obeyed their orders and come no further than the front hall, so they had been able to escape the fire. There had been one casualty.

Gaspard, one of the men who had been posted in the court behind the house, had been hit by a splintered piece of flaming wood as he tried to escape from the explosion. His back and shoulder had been badly burned and he'd only escaped worse by rolling in the muddy street. Dubell had insisted on treating the injury immediately, and Thomas had been only too glad to permit it. Now Gaspard sat on a stone bench in the shelter of a hostler's stall, his shirt and doublet cut away so Dubell could treat the blistering wound. The servant Berham was handing the sorcerer supplies from Dr. Braun's medical box and Dr. Braun himself was hovering at Dubell's elbow. Thomas suspected that Berham was providing more practical assistance than the younger sorcerer.

"The fire is hardly our fault." Gideon shrugged. "Blame Grandier for it."

"Yes, he's a cunning bastard."

Gideon glanced at him, frowning. "How do you mean?"

Thomas didn't answer. Dubell had finished tying the bandage and Martin helped Gaspard stand. As Castero led their horses forward, Thomas nudged his mare close enough to be heard over the shouting and the roar of the fire. "Gaspard, I want you to ride with Martin."

"Sir, I do not need to be carried." The younger man's face was flushed and sickly.

"That was not a request, Sir." Thomas was in no mood for a debate. "You can ride behind him or you can hang head down over his saddlebow; the choice is yours."

Gaspard looked less combative as he contemplated that thought, and let Martin pull him unresisting to the horses.

Berham was packing the medical box under Braun's direction and Dubell was staring at the fire. Thomas had been considering the question of why Grandier had not killed Galen Dubell. The answer could simply be that Grandier might have wanted to extract information from the old scholar, and his plan had gone awry when the King's Watch located the house. But somehow he didn't think it was going to be simple. *The fire should have started when I broke the glass ball. Yes, it served the purpose of destroying Grandier's papers, but why not kill all the birds with one stone? Unless he wanted us to rescue Dubell.* But why? To announce his presence? To show them how powerful and frightening he was? To make them distrust Dubell?

As Berham took the box away to pack on his horse, Thomas waved Dr. Braun over and leaned down to ask him, "Is it possible for Grandier to... tamper with another sorcerer, to put a geas on him?"

Braun looked shocked. "A geas can be laid on an untrained mind, yes, but not on a sorcerer like Dr. Dubell."

"Are you very sure about that?"

"Of course." After a moment, under Thomas's close scrutiny, Braun coughed and said, "Well, I am quite sure. I had to put gascoign powder in my eyes to see the wards around the house, and a geas, or any kind of spell, would be visible on Dr. Dubell."

"Very well." That was as good as they were going to get without taking the old scholar to Lodun to be examined by the sorcerer-philosophers there, and there was no time for that.

Dubell came toward them. "An unfortunate fire," he said. "There was much to learn there."

"I thought you said it was dangerous to create fire out of nothing?" Thomas asked Braun.

"It is," Braun protested, flustered.

Dubell smiled. "It depends on one's appreciation of danger."

"So much does," Thomas agreed. "They'll have some questions for you at the palace."

"Of course. I only hope my small knowledge can aid you."

"We'll find Grandier," Gideon said, coming up beside them.

Dubell's eyes were troubled. "If he continues his mischief on such a grand scale, he will be hard to miss. He'll also be a fool, of course, but he may not see it that way."

"Oh, I hardly think he's a fool," Thomas said. Castero and Berham had gotten Gaspard mounted up behind Martin, and they began to turn their horses away from the crowded street. As the others went down the alley, Thomas took one last look at the burning house. So far Grandier had shown an odd combination of ruthlessness and restraint, and he was not sure which he found more daunting. The sorcerer had snatched Galen Dubell out of his home in Lodun, indiscriminately slaughtering the servants who had witnessed it. For no practical reason, since Lodun University was full of wizards and scholars of magic who had been able to divine Grandier's identity within hours of examining the scene. Yet the fire that could have been so devastating stuck to Grandier's house like pitch and refused to spread to the ready tinder of the other old buildings. As much as he might wish to, Thomas couldn't see it as a gesture of defiance. He only wondered where, in what corner of the crowded city, the word had passed to watch for a sorcerous blaze in the night, and what to do then.

CHAPTER TWO

"Does the mask fit?" Anton Baraselli looked up at the young woman who sat on the balcony railing, her feet swinging under her tattered red skirt.

Gray eyes stared back at him from the pale features of the distorted half-mask. "It fits. Do I have the part?"

Baraselli sat at his table on a balcony overhanging the main room of the Mummer's Mask tavern, where his acting troupe made its home. He was middle-aged, his dark hair wispy on his nearly bald head, but his plumpness and the newness of his clothes reflected his troupe's recent prosperity. He could barely hear the woman's deep voice over the shouted conversation, drunken arguments, and the competing strains of mandolin and viola that rose up from the rowdy crowd on the tavern's main floor below. The wealthier patrons were drinking in the small private rooms off the second-floor gallery, the shutters propped open so the music could reach them clearly.

"Well, you've no troupe to recommend you," Baraselli said, leaning back. He didn't want to pay her as much as she might ask. His last Columbine had run off to be married, leaving without a backward glance yesterday morning.

Baraselli had come to Ile-Rien from conquered Adera years ago when all forms of the Aderassi theater were despised and confined to back alleys and peasant festivals. Now the war with Bisra was over and Ile-Rien's capital was more cosmopolitan and free with its money. Vienne was a jewel of a city in a rich setting, standing on temperate plains roughly in the center of the country, with rolling hills and olive groves on the warmer coast to the southwest, rich forested midlands, and black-soiled farmland in the terraced valleys of the high country to the north. Baraselli had liked it, and now that Commedia and other foreign theatricals were popular he liked it a great deal more.

The woman took the mask off and tossed it onto the table. Her hair was dirty blond and her narrow face with its long nose and direct eyes was plain, too plain to ever play the unmasked heroines. Her faded red dress was old and well-worn, better than a country woman's but no bawd's false finery either. Whatever the rumormongers thought, whores made terrible actresses.

She looked toward him with a grin. Smoke from the candles and clay pipes below reached up to touch the tavern's high beamed ceiling and spread out like a cloud behind her. It was an interesting theatrical effect, but there was something about the image that Baraselli found faintly disquieting. She said, "I'm not here to make my fortune. I'll take what you paid the last one."

She had good teeth, too. "All right, you're our Columbine. But on sufferance, mind. We've got an important engagement, a very important engagement. It happens when you attract the crowds and praise we have. If you don't give a fine performance, you're out. If you do, well, it's one silver per fortnight and a fair share of whatever they throw onto the stage."

"That's well, I agree."

"Anton! Look out the window." Garin, still wearing the gray beard from his Pantalone costume, came pounding up the stairs.

"What? I'm busy."

Garin pushed past him and threw open the shutters of the window behind Baraselli's table.

"Damn it, you'll let the night air and the bogles in, you fool." Baraselli stood abruptly, jarring the table and slopping wine onto the stained floor.

"But look at this." Garin pointed. The Mummer's Mask stood in a huddle of taverns and old houses on the side of a low hill commanding a good view of the River Quarter. Lying before them were the narrow overhung streets of the older and poorer area, which eventually led into the vast plazas and pillared promenades surrounded by the garden courts of the wealthy. Farther to the west and standing high above the slate and wooden roofs were the domes of churches, the fantastic and fanciful statues ornamenting the gables of the fortified Great Houses, the spires of the stone-filigree palaces on the artificial islands on the river's upper reaches, all transformed into anonymous shapes of alternating black and silver as clouds drifted past the moon. But now, against the stark shadowy forms of the crowded structures of the River Quarter, they could see the bright glow of fire, a harsh splash of color in the darkness.

"Down near Cross Street, I think," Garin said.

More of the troupe had drifted up the stairs in his wake, curious. "Lord save it doesn't spread," one of them whispered.

"Another bad omen," Baraselli muttered. One of the clowns had died of fever last month. Clowns were traditionally good luck in Adera, if not in Ile-Rien, and having one of them die unexpectedly had shaken the other performers. *Gods and spirits, no more omens before this of all performances,* Baraselli prayed.

"Maybe it's a good omen," the new Columbine said, selecting an apple out of the bowl on the table and watching the worried actors with oblique amusement. "Some people think fire is."

Dark smoke streamed into the night sky.

కుఖ

They rode through St. Anne's Gate and into the cobbled court between the high walls of the Mews and the Cisternan Guard Barracks. The façades of the two buildings were almost identical, though time and weather had scarred the dressed stone in different ways. Each was entered by three great archways that faced one another across the length of the court. Now torches threw reflections up onto the mist-slick stone as grooms and stablehands hurried to take the horses or curious Cisternans wandered out to see what the excitement was.

Thomas dismounted and handed the reins to one of the grooms. He took off a glove to rub the horse's nape, then let the man lead her away. This was Cisternan Guard territory, but it was also the closest entrance to the palace, and he wanted Galen Dubell within a warded structure before Grandier made another attempt on the old sorcerer.

The palace wards repelled fay, sendings, and any other form of magical attack. They were fitted together like the pieces of a puzzlebox, or a stained glass window, and drifted constantly, moving past each other, folding over each other, wandering at will over their domain. They would prevent the sorcerous abduction that Grandier had used to snatch Galen Dubell from his home in Lodun, and the palace's other defenses were more than adequate to hold off hired swords.

As Thomas crossed the court toward the two sorcerers, the Cisternan Commander Vivan joined him. The Cisternans were the regular guard for the palace, their ranks drawn from the families of the wealthy merchant classes or the gentlemen landowners. Vivan had held the post of Commander for the past five years, and even though the Cisternans were ultimately under the King's authority, Vivan had no particular political ax to grind, and Thomas found him easy to deal with. The Commander said, "A midnight expedition? How exciting."

"I would have preferred to stay here and help you guard the stables, but duty called," Thomas told him.

Vivan snorted. The old king Fulstan had made the Cisternans his body-guard out of dislike for the Albonate Knights, who had held the post tradi-tionally. When Fulstan's son Roland had taken the throne, his mistrust of anything belonging to his father had led him to demote the Cisternans and return to the Albons. Going from the King's Own to the King's Old had been a great loss of prestige for them and the Queen's Own had never let them forget it. Another sore point was that their ceremonial tabards were dark green trimmed with gold, making them good targets and appropriate decor during midwinter festivals.

Gideon reined in near them and dismounted, asking, "Captain, what orders?"

"Send these gentlemen back to the Guard House." As the lieutenant came closer and Thomas could lower his voice, he added, "Go to Lucas. Tell him what happened and then wait to see if the Dowager Queen has ques-tions for you. I'll see him after this meeting." He wanted to double his share of the guard placements and put a watch on Dubell.

"Yes, Captain." Gideon nodded.

Vivan was eyeing the old sorcerer with grudging curiosity as Galen Dubell and Braun dismounted. He asked, "What were you doing, kidnap-ping scholars out of the Philosopher's Cross?"

"Exactly," Thomas said as he went to join the sorcerers. "I could never keep anything from you."

Thomas led Dubell out of the wet chill of the courtyard and through the inner gate at its far end, passing under the spikes of an old portcullis. Dr. Braun trailed behind them. In the wall beyond, a heavy ironbound door guarded by two alert Cisternans led into one of the corridors that ran inside the protective inner siege walls. The corridor was raw stone, lit by oil lamps and undecorated except for scribbled writings by present and long-dead oc-cupants. Dubell shook his head. "I lived here for many years and there are still parts of this place I have never seen. I am quite lost, Captain."

"We're in the siege wall opposite the south curtain wall. The Summer Residence and the Adamantine Way are behind us at the opposite end of the corridor, and we're going toward the King's Bastion." This siege wall divided the newer section of the palace with its open garden courts, domed Summer Residence, and the terraces and windowed façades of the Gallery Wing from the jumbled collection of ancient blocky bastions, towers, and walls on the west side.

A steep stairway led up into the King's Bastion, which loomed above the Old Courts and the Mews. As they climbed, the surroundings began to show rapid signs of improvement, the rough stone softened by hangings and over-laid by carved paneling. The ancient cracked tiles had been recently scrubbed and polished, reflecting the light from hall lanterns of stamped metal and glass as soft pools of gold. They passed Cisternan guards posted on each landing, and began to hear the bastion's hum of activity, never still at any time of night. At the fourth level, Thomas led them out of the older stairwell and across the landing to the carved-oak Queen's Staircase. They were in the heart of the bastion now, and the men posted here were Queen's Guards.

Dubell paused on the landing, looking up at the wide staircase with its dark wood carved into flowing bands and banisters set with fragments of mirror glass. Then he shook his head as if at his own folly and said, "It has been a long time."

The old sorcerer had been led this way the day of his exile ten years ago, to see the Dowager Queen and to hear his sentence, which so easily could have been death. Thomas acknowledged the guards' salute, and thought it fortunate all around that Ravenna had been lenient with Galen Dubell.

The top of the staircase opened into a vestibule, the first room in the Dowager Queen's State Apartments. The King's State Apartments were on the opposite side of the bastion, and the young Queen Falaise lived in another suite on the floor just below. They passed the young pages waiting in the vestibule and went in to the Guard Chamber, a long richly paneled room lit by several glass drop chandeliers. Gideon was already there and several Queen's guards surrounded him, demanding to know how the night's work had gone. They called greetings as Thomas entered, and he went forward to ask Gideon, "Did you see Lucas?"

"Yes, and he spoke to Ravenna. But the Bisran ambassador came in and demanded to see her. They're in the Privy Council Chamber now."

"Damn. What does he want at this time of night?"

"Who knows?" Gideon shrugged. The ambassador was a diplomat, not a soldier, and the young lieutenant didn't think him a matter of much impor-tance.

Thomas considered a moment. Something to do with Grandier? If it was, then there went all hope of keeping the River Quarter incident quiet.

"Queen Falaise has been asking for me." Gideon looked uncomfortable. "Will you need me anymore tonight?"

Thomas eyed him a moment, but said, "No, you can go on."

As Gideon left, Thomas saw Dubell was taking his leave of Dr. Braun, who had apparently decided not to brave an interview with the Dowager Queen. The other guards were watching the sorcerer curiously, which at least meant that news of their adventure hadn't flown too far ahead of them. There were also two young Albonate squires waiting self-consciously in the corner. *So Renier is already here,* Thomas thought. Whether that was good or bad depended on what mood the King had been in when he had sent him. He said, "We'll wait in here, Doctor," as Dubell turned back toward him, and they went into the anteroom.

Tapestried hangings with a Garden of Paradise theme matched the carpet and table covers, cloaking the large, high-ceilinged room in rich shades of green. Renier stood before the immense marble hearth, abstract-edly watching a manservant build up the fire. He was Preceptor of the palace's chapter of Albonate Knights, which was a military order founded for the protection of the King's person, and the only order of knighthood in Ile-Rien that still meant more than a courtesy title. They were members of some of the highest families in Ile-Rien, brought into the Order as boys, living in monastic discipline until they were knighted by the King. Renier would probably have made a better country bishop than a preceptor, but in his tenure he had kept the Order's tendency toward religious fanaticism under tight control. He had broad shoulders and was muscled like a bear, and still rode to tourney on King's Ascension Day, easily managing the weight of the heavy ceremonial mail. Over his court doublet and lace-trimmed collar, he wore the bedraggled coat of sackcloth and poorly cured leather all Albon knights bore in honor of St. Albon, who had done some wandering in the wilderness before his sainthood.

Renier looked up at their entrance, saw Dubell, and smiled. "Success."

Thomas watched the Preceptor greet the old sorcerer, and wondered just how much Renier had known of tonight's expedition.

The door opened again and Lord Aviler stood there a moment, eyeing them thoughtfully. He was dark haired, dressed in the blood red state robes of the Ministry, and his handsome sallow face was carefully controlled. He nodded to Renier and Galen Dubell, then his gaze shifted to Thomas. He said, "The River Quarter is on fire."

Thomas smiled slightly to himself and went to lean casually against the mantelpiece. "Only a small portion of it." Aviler had followed so quickly behind them that he knew the man must have been lying in wait.

"A stupid mistake." Aviler moved farther into the room, his folded hands covered by the hang of his sleeves. Thomas wondered if the pose was intentionally copied from the High Minister's late father, or if it was only habit. Aviler had recently inherited the post of High Minister of the body of nobles and wealthy merchants who formally advised, or were supposed to advise, the King, and had a great deal of theoretical power. But the Dowager Queen Ravenna actively opposed him, Queen Falaise ignored him except on social occasions, and no one had been able to do anything with Roland one way or the other since he had taken the throne at the end of Ravenna's regency last year. Aviler was statesman enough to resent this and just inexperienced enough to occasionally reveal his feelings.

"Really, my lord, what do you want me to say?" Thomas raised his brows inquiringly. "That the mission was in danger of being found out so I set the city on fire to confuse the issue?"

Before Aviler could reply, Galen Dubell said quietly, "It was unavoidable."

"Dr. Dubell." Aviler acknowledged him stiffly. "It's a pity you couldn't have returned sooner and avoided this consternation."

"That was my intention, my lord, but my plans went somewhat astray when my household was murdered and I was abducted." Dubell said it with such good grace that Aviler was actually caught off guard.

"So Galen Dubell is a diplomat as well as a scholar," Renier said softly to Thomas as Aviler recovered his composure. "He was something of a recluse when I knew him, but I suppose years of academic infighting at Lodun will give anyone eyes in the back of his head. It's good he's returned."

Thomas wasn't about to admit he missed Dr. Surete, who had held the post of Court Sorcerer since he could remember and had died suddenly last month of pleurisy. Surete had been seventy years old, had called every man under the age of sixty "boy," and had been the terror of the court for his ability to use sardonic invective like a bludgeon.

Thomas said, "Let's hope Dubell's not anxious to get back to Lodun soon. We're going to need his help." Dr. Surete's assistant Milam had been killed in an accident before Surete himself had died, and since then there had been nothing but argument over who would receive the appointment while lesser talents like Dr. Braun vied for attention.

Renier looked at him thoughtfully. "Lose anyone?"

Thomas's expression betrayed nothing. "Does it matter?"

Renier said softly, "Forgive him, Thomas. He's a boy and he was angry."

"I thought you'd given up on the priesthood," Thomas answered, thinking, *If His Majesty Roland wants me to die in the line of duty, it's his business, but he could have chosen a better time. If he doesn't see that Grandier is a danger to the state...* At Renier's look he added, "It isn't my place to condemn him or forgive him. But tell me, did Denzil suggest the plan to Roland, or was it someone else?"

Renier stiffened visibly. "I know of no plan."

The double doors into the Privy Council Chamber beyond the anteroom opened and the Bisran ambassador stepped out, his expression grim. He was an older man, with the olive skin and hawklike profile of the Bisran aristocracy. Ile-Rien and its capital and court were alien to him, and his disapproval was evident. The excessive formality of the Bisran Court made it stagnant and stultified, while in Ile-Rien landlaw had traditionally permitted high officers and even personal servants to address kings and queens as "my lord" or "my lady," and to forgo obeisance in informal circumstances. The ambassador's dark plain clothing and simple white collar also marked him as a member of their sect that regarded any kind of ornamentation as a work of Hell; the opulence of the palace must seem almost a personal insult.

The ambassador's hard eyes swept the room, pausing on Galen Dubell's scholar's cope and narrowing in dismayed disgust. Turning to the High Minister, he said, "Another sorcerer for the King's menagerie, Lord Aviler?" In Bisra, the magical as well as most of the philosophical arts were condemned, though the theurgic magic their priest-magicians practiced had been a deadly barrier against outside attack during the war. Sorcery that was not performed under the auspices of the Bisran Church was outlawed, and punishable by death.

Aviler hesitated, his diplomatic smile turning thin with annoyance, unable to find the right words to defend Dubell's honor without insulting the ambassador.

Before the silence could last long enough to give the Bisran a victory, Thomas interposed, "Perhaps that's a subject you should discuss with the King himself?"

The ambassador flicked a resentful glance at him and received only an ingenuous smile in response. As a matter of policy, Roland did not receive the Bisran ambassador, who was not very pleased with this arrangement, since it required him to address his demands to the considerably less malleable Dowager Queen. *But why is he here in the middle of the night?* It could be only obstinate determination to get a hearing no matter who he inconvenienced, but Thomas doubted it. To compound the Bisran's discomfort, he added, "But I'm sure my lady Ravenna dealt with you to her best ability."

The ambassador said, "Her Majesty was most...civil," and favored him with the same cold scrutiny he had employed on Dubell. The Bisran Court did not allow favorites to wield political power, so the ambassador tended to discount Thomas's position and influence, and cordially hated him as well. It probably didn't help either that the shape and tilt of Thomas's black eyes gave his face a naturally cynical slant, and that with his dark hair and beard this effect made him resemble certain popular portraits of the Prince of Hell. If the ambassador had noticed the evidence Thomas's climb on a wet and dirty building had left on his clothing, no doubt he attributed it to some adventure in debauchery. Turning stiffly back to Aviler, the ambassador said, "Another matter. I wanted to make certain you understood that if Ile-Rien offers shelter to the devil's son Grandier, the cost may be more than you are prepared to pay."

Aviler bowed, his reserved manner masking a certain wariness. "I assure you, my lord Ambassador, Ile-Rien has no intention of offering shelter to a criminal sorcerer who has caused your land such pain."

Besides, Grandier hasn't asked for shelter, Thomas thought. *Unfortunately.* And since the Bisran sorcerer had announced his arrival in Ile-Rien by abducting a prominent Lodun scholar of Galen Dubell's reputation, it hardly seemed possible that he would.

But it was likely that the ambassador was only using Grandier's presence in the city as an excuse for a confrontation with Ravenna, and if he was being prodded by the Bisran War College to take a more aggressive stance with the Dowager Queen, it could only mean trouble. Bisra was miles of dry flat plains, and only tribute from its conquered states kept its coffers full. The Bisran Church exercised rigid controls on a populace that was land-poor and half-starved in the country and hovered at the brink of mob violence in the crowded cities. Ile-Rien had its uprisings and city mobs as well, but usually over taxes, and they were scattered outbreaks that were settled within a few days. Bisra seemed to teeter always on the edge of chaos, and with Ile-Rien's rich land and its Church's policy of tolerance toward the pagan Old Faith as a constant irritant, war had been inevitable and frequent.

And now Urbain Grandier's depredations had made them even more desperate.

Thomas watched critically as the ambassador nodded with bare courtesy to Lord Aviler and strode to the anteroom door, the page stationed there barely managing to swing open the heavy portal in time.

As the door closed Aviler shook his head and said softly to Galen Dubell, "My apologies, Doctor. To a Bisran, any man in a scholar's gown is half demon."

Dubell's expression was closed and enigmatic. "And a sorcerer, of course, is all demon."

From the Privy Council Chamber two Queen's guards entered and stepped to either side of the doors as the Dowager Queen came into the room. Everyone bowed and she acknowledged them with a nod and a slight smile. "Gentlemen. Forgive the delay." Her graying red hair was tucked up into a lace cap and she wore a dark informal morning gown. She was over fifty now, and the years hadn't diminished her beauty, but transformed and refined it. Only the faint laugh lines around her mouth and the shadow of strain at the corners of her eyes betrayed her age. She took a seat in the brocaded canopy chair beside the hearth, her attendant gentlewoman settling on a cushioned stool behind her. "Dr. Galen Dubell, I'm glad to find you in good health. Perhaps you can help us in explaining this matter."

"Yes, my lady. You saw my letters concerning Urbain Grandier?" Dubell said, stepping forward.

"Yes. Dr. Surete brought them to me when he requested your return to court. His unfortunate death delayed the matter just long enough, it seems. When the messages came from Lodun telling of your disappearance I had already sent an order lifting the ban and requesting your return." As she spoke she was already unfolding a square of half-completed black-work embroidery and looking for the needle that marked her place. Ravenna always had to have something to do with her hands. It was a habit that disconcerted all but the most resolute of petitioners and foreign ambassadors, but Thomas noted it didn't seem to faze Dubell.

The old sorcerer bowed to her. "I am honored, my lady."

Ravenna gestured that away. "Tell me more about this Grandier. He has an odd name for a Bisran."

Watching the Dowager guardedly, Aviler said, "We have some knowledge about his early life. Urbain Grandier was a Bisran sorcerer and scholar, though it is believed his father was from Ile-Rien, possibly a visiting priest, or even a noble, journeying there during one of the temporary treaties in force in the year of Grandier's birth. This would explain his surname, which is certainly not Bisran. Stubbornly, he refused to take another name, and this probably contributed to the suspicion with which he was regarded there."

She frowned at her embroidery. "His original offense was some outrage concerning nuns, and the Bisran Church removed his sanction to perform sorcery? And then he was arrested by the Inquisition?"

"Yes, my lady. After his escape from the Inquisition, Grandier brought on a plague and apparently made subtle changes in the weather over the Kiseran plain, some of their richest farmland, and destroyed most of their last year's harvest. The Bisran theurgic sorcerers are said to be near exhaustion with holding off magical attacks on Church officials and the War College."

Ravenna smiled tightly without looking up from her embroidery. She hated Bisra even more than she had hated her dead husband, the old king Fulstan. "One might point out that it is nothing more than they deserve."

"One might," Aviler agreed. "But the point is that Grandier has suddenly chosen to come to Ile-Rien."

Thomas shook his head, briefly amused. Aviler's relationship with the Dowager Queen was an acrimonious one.

For her part Ravenna merely studied the High Minister a moment. Her fine long-fingered hands had paused on the embroidery, the gold needle catching the firelight. That might mean anything; Thomas had known her to order an execution, explain to the culprit why it had to be done, and deny the family's fervent pleas for mercy, all without missing a stitch. Then she drew the strand of thread up tight and said, "Tell me about the events at the convent, Lord Aviler." She nodded to her gentlewoman. "Lady Anne knows she has permission to leave the room should she hear anything that causes her to fear for her modesty."

As Lady Anne bit her lip and looked studiously at the floor, Aviler frowned and said, "The original incident took place at a convent in a town called Lindre, in the northern part of Bisra. Grandier was accused of corrupting the nuns, causing them to blaspheme against their own Church, to attack each other, to perform rituals that..."

"According to the Inquisitors General of Bisra," Galen Dubell interrupted gently, "he caused them to corrupt themselves." The old scholar had moved toward the hearth and was staring into the fire, an expression in his eyes that Thomas couldn't interpret. "They found evidence of human blood used in rituals, symbols and books banned for centuries, the darkest magic... There was even some evidence of an agreement with a Lord of Hell."

As the others watched Dubell in silence, Thomas said, "In Bisra they still burn hedgepriests for putting curses on cows. Why do you feel you can trust the Inquisition's reports?"

"True, Captain." Dubell turned back to them. "The Inquisitors were, of course, lying. They manufactured the evidence, or most of it. Scholars who are not even sorcerers may have items in their possession that an evil mind can misinterpret. And Urbain Grandier was a scholar. He studied the stars, as well as the body and its ills and humors. He was also very outspoken in his opinions, and involved in the printing of inflammatory pamphlets. It was for this that he came under the Inquisition's scrutiny. The incident of some hysterical nuns at the Lindre Convent was used against him and he was given the usual sentence of torture and imprisonment."

Dubell's voice had an enthralling quality. It might have been facilitated by the growing warmth in the room or the fatigue that was catching up with Thomas, but the old sorcerer seemed to be painting a particularly vivid picture of the man Grandier had been.

After a moment Dubell shook his head. "It turned him, you might say. He escaped eventually, and began to commit many of the crimes of which they had accused him, but on a larger scale. The plague, for instance. It caused pockets of a poisonous humor to form beneath the skin, which burst when the victim was in death agony and spread the disease to anyone who stood nearby. It caused so much chaos entire cities were disrupted; the sick went untended... Only a man well versed in healing-sorcery could have devised something so terrible, and only a man driven mad with the lust for revenge could have brought himself to implement it." In the firelight, Dubell's face was a mask of pain. Then he sighed. "When I heard that a man calling himself Grandier had become established in the city and was believed to be a sorcerer, I thought it best to bring the matter to Dr. Surete's attention. I only wish I'd acted sooner."

Renier had gone to the round table in the center of the room and was looking through the faded parchment and leather maps stacked there. He pulled one out and found Lindre, then thoughtfully tapped the red cross that marked the town. "You knew Grandier very well?"

"No. His excesses and the motivation for them were much discussed at Lodun, where there is great interest in the natural, as well as the magical, arts." Dubell smiled. "And the printing of an occasional pamphlet."

"We know," Aviler said dryly. He paced a few steps, his face severe and only half-visible in the candlelight. Aviler's late father had made his fortune in trading voyages to the East before he had settled down to take over the Ministry, and the stigma of those origins made Aviler the Younger careful to preserve the proper aristocratic disdain toward the occasional political commentary from Lodun. But the High Minister dropped the subject and only asked, "Why does Grandier come here now?"

Dubell spread his hands. "I don't know. But whatever his reason, he must be stopped and driven away."

Ravenna nodded. "Excesses in Bisra are all well and good, but he cannot be allowed to commit them here. I agree, Doctor. But why did he seek you out? Some special grudge?"

Dubell looked thoughtful. "It has been ten years since Dr. Surete and I last tended to the palace wards. With Surete dead and Grandier rumored to be in the city, I thought it best that I should see to them again. The warding stones that hold the etheric structure of spells in formation around the newer sections of the palace must be examined individually, though in the Old Courts where the wards are tied to the structures themselves such attention is not necessary. But now I realize the situation is even more urgent than I thought. If Grandier meant to keep me from examining the wards after Dr. Surete's death, then he must have some way to circumvent them."

Aviler looked up, frowning. "How is that possible?"

"The wards are not unlimited or infallible. The sorcerers who constructed them directed them to react to certain situations in certain ways. But their creators could not, and did not, think of every situation. If a fay knew where the gaps were that their movement occasionally creates, it could pass through them unharmed." Galen Dubell smiled. "Dr. Surete knew the most about the wards. He could tell you their names."

"I see," Aviler muttered.

"Do you? Good." Ravenna finished part of the pattern and spread the square of needlework out on her lap. "Dr. Dubell, when can you begin this examination of the wards?"

"Immediately," Dubell told her. "It will take several days, as some portions may only be performed during certain hours of the night."

"Good, but we must continue the search for Grandier."

Thomas said, "The King's Watch found that house; they'll find him." The King's Watch was a euphemism for the network of spies set up by the late Aviler the Elder to keep an eye on discontented nobles living in the city and the foreign cults that had begun to appear then. It was they who had been able to find Grandier's River Quarter house when the Lodun sorcerers had named him as Galen Dubell's abductor.

"Very well. That is enough for now. Dr. Dubell must rest before he begins his work and I know you gentlemen have much to attend to." As they made to leave, Ravenna added, "Stay a moment, Captain."

Thomas waited, and when the doors had closed behind the last of the others, she asked, "It was difficult?"

"Fairly."

Ravenna lifted a brow. "That's hardly an answer."

He watched her a moment thoughtfully. That Roland had sent him on a mission designed to cause his death probably rankled her more than it did him. "Is that why you wanted me to stay, to indulge my sense of self-pity?"

"Oh, don't start. Roland could send you to the edge of the earth and I would not care." She smiled for a moment, but her expression became bitter as she smoothed a section of the embroidery. "Master Conadine was sent for today from the Granges to help deal with Grandier. He should be here within the week. It was the worst stupidity not to wait for him and to send you with only Dr. Braun."

"If I'd had the choice, I might have gone anyway," he admitted. "If we had waited any longer Grandier could have killed Dubell."

"And taken a handful of men, and only Dr. Braun?" Her lips thinned. "Never mind. Roland did it to aggravate me, and we know who encouraged him to it, don't we?" Ravenna tested the sharpness of her needle with a finger, then selected another out of the case Lady Anne held ready for her. "And what other mischief has Denzil been up to lately?"

Thomas took a seat on one of the stools near her chair, feeling his weariness as a tight pain across his shoulders. The episode with Grandier had worried Ravenna more than she had revealed to Aviler or the others, but he let her change the subject. He said, "He visited a banker on the Riverside Way yesterday, but that was about a gambling debt. If he's planning something now, he's taking more care with it."

"Perhaps." Ravenna carefully threaded the needle. "Someday he will miscalculate."

Thomas shrugged. "Roland can always pardon him." Denzil was Duke of Alsene, Roland's older cousin on his father's side, and acknowledged favorite. There were men who had more respect for the finer feelings of their dogs than Denzil had for Roland, but the young King still clung to him. It was undoubtedly Denzil who had talked Roland into sending a small contingent of the Queen's Guard to beard Grandier in his lair, knowing Thomas would be bound to lead them, and knowing that it would infuriate Ravenna. Thomas reminded himself there was nothing to be done about it tonight. But he was looking forward to the moment when the news reached Denzil that he had gone into Grandier's house and brought Galen Dubell out alive without losing a single man. "What did the Bisran ambassador want?"

"To accuse us of harboring Grandier." She made a gesture of exasperation, willing to be led away from the subject of her son's favorite. "And also to present a new list of their heretics sheltering in Ile-Rien, so they could be arrested and returned to Bisra to burn for their crimes. That the Bisran Inquisition has no authority within our borders is immaterial, apparently. I wish I knew why the ambassador is so certain that Grandier is here with our blessings." She coughed, and Lady Anne hastily produced a lace-edged cloth for her.

Watching her accusingly, Thomas said, "You're not feeling well." She had caught a lung flux last winter when they had gone to Bannot-on-the-Shore to quell a minor upheaval among the March Barons. Her vitality made it difficult to remember that she was not a young woman anymore, and Thomas still regretted allowing her to ride with the Guard instead of going in an enclosed carriage, even if it had let her surprise the barons in the middle of their secret conference. The disease had weakened her lungs despite the best efforts of apothecaries and sorcerer-healers, and she wasn't up to any more midnight rides over ice fields, whatever she might think. "You didn't have to see Dubell tonight, or the ambassador."

"It is very damp out, and you are not my nursemaid." She tucked the cloth into her sleeve, unperturbed. "I wanted to get this over with as quickly as possible. And if the palace wards are weakening..." After a moment, Ravenna shook her head. "And what do you think of Dr. Dubell?"

Thomas knew she wasn't asking about the old scholar's abilities as a sorcerer. "He's no fool. He handles himself very well."

"Lord Aviler, the old Lord Aviler, not that young puppy of a High Minister, had great faith in Dubell. Despite his past disgrace." She sighed. "But I've kept you long enough."

Thomas stood up, took her hand, and kissed it. She said, "Oh, and I'd almost forgotten." She rummaged in her sewing case, and pulled out a ribbon-tied packet of letters to hand to him.

"What is it?"

"An annoyance for you to deal with."

He accepted the packet with an expression of distaste. "And I was afraid I might have to sleep tonight."

"Oh, it isn't urgent. At least not to me." She smiled. "Enjoy."

Stepping out into the Guard Room, Thomas turned the packet over curiously. Ravenna never forgot anything; it must be something she didn't want to discuss. Before he could untie the bound letters, he saw that Galen Dubell was waiting for him. "A moment, Captain?" the old sorcerer asked.

"Yes?"

"Forgive me if the question is intrusive, but Lord Aviler does not care for you?" The High Minister had already gone, though Renier was still in the Guard Chamber, speaking quietly to the two Albonate squires.

"Lord Aviler is like that." Dubell's expression held nothing but mild curiosity. After a moment, Thomas found himself saying, "He doesn't approve of favorites. He's studied enough history to know what damage I could do if I were inclined to it."

"I see." Dubell smiled. "Does Queen Falaise still have her entourage of poets?"

Falaise had been a princess of Umberwald when Ravenna had chosen her to marry Roland a year ago. At eighteen she was four years younger than the King, and if Ravenna's motive in choosing her for a daughter-in-law had been to pick someone she could teach and influence, she had made one of her few mistakes. Falaise might have been the quiet studious girl that the ambassadors had described when she was a third daughter with few prospects, but once here and safely wed to Roland she had taken to palace life like a beggar child let loose in a bakery. "Yes, she does. City gossip reaches you all the way out in Lodun?"

"City gossip is a treasured commodity. The servants bring it in with the milk every morning. The general opinion, I gathered, was one of relief that she had chosen to turn her attentions to harmless poets, considering what else she could have done."

"She could have had guardsmen."

"Or sorcerers." Dubell's expression turned serious. "I owe you a great debt, Captain."

Thomas looked at him sharply. "I think you've already repaid that debt."

Dubell gestured that away. "Nevertheless, if I can help you in any way, do not hesitate to call on me."

As the sorcerer turned to follow the servants waiting to take him to his rooms, Renier intercepted Thomas. "There's something I have to show you." He looked worried.

Resigned, Thomas followed Renier to a quieter corner of the Guard Room. "What is it?"

"A letter. It arrived today in a packet of dispatches from Portier. The courier's a trusted man who swears he never let the packet out of his sight." The big man unfolded a square of paper. "This is a translation I had a priest do."

Thomas took the paper. "What language was it in?"

"Old Church Script."

Thomas read the first scribbled sentence aloud, "'O Best Beloved'?" He looked up, puzzled. "To whom was it sent?"

"Roland. But the priest said that's the proper way to begin an old riddle-song, which is what this is."

Where the music is not heard,
There was a light not seen,
There are barren hills home to multitudes,
And dry lakes where fish are caught above a city's towers.
Catch the incantation, solve the song.

"The answer is a simple one: the fay," Renier said.

There was only one person acquainted with Roland whose feelings would naturally express themselves in poetic forms of the past. "You know who this is from," Thomas said, looking up at him.

"The country folk are calling her Kade Carrion now." Renier shrugged, uneasy. "I suppose we're lucky; she could have sent something that exploded or told the secrets of whomever picked it up."

Roland's older sister, the bastard princess who had never forgiven anything. Thomas tapped the rolled paper against his palm. "An odd coincidence, with Galen Dubell here. Ravenna decides to pardon the man who first told the bane of our lives that she was a witch, and the witch herself starts meddling again." She had chosen her moment well. *We have more than enough to deal with from Grandier, and Kade is too dangerous to ignore.*

"She's been quiet for almost six months. Why now?"

Across the room, a musician had taken a seat at the spinet and now played the opening verse of a popular new ballad, about a man who fell in love with a fayre queen and was taken away by her. *He couldn't have chosen an air more inappropriate to the moment,* Thomas thought. He said, "One hundred and ninety-seven days. I keep count. She might be in league with Grandier." Though Grandier had killed to protect himself, and Kade was rather like a cat—if the mouse was dead it was no good playing with it anymore. *But people change.*

Renier shook his head. "There's not much else we can do. The sentry positions have already been doubled and tripled for Grandier's sake." His eyes flicked up to meet Thomas's. "Dubell is going to tend the wards."

"Yes, he is, isn't he?"

"We've nothing to go on."

Thomas handed him back the letter. "Watch him anyway."

CHAPTER THREE

AT THE FIRST creak of the door, Thomas was up on one elbow and drawing the main gauche from the belt hung over the bedpost. Then he recognized the man entering the room and shoved the long dagger back into its sheath. "Damn you, Phaistus."

The young servant shrugged and knelt beside the hearth to scrape the ashes out, muttering to the unresponsive andirons, "Well, he's in a mood."

Thomas struggled out of bed. Despite the high ceiling and the natural tendency for drafts, the room was almost too warm; daylight shining through the high windows was reflected dazzlingly off the whitewashed plaster of the walls. His scabbarded rapier leaned against a red brocaded chair and his other three civilian dueling swords hung on the wall, along with the heavier, broad-bladed weapons used for cavalry combat. He ran a distracted hand through his hair, working the tangles out, and said, "What's the hour?"

"Nearly midday, Sir. Ephraim's outside. He said you wanted him. And Master Lucas brought that Gambin fellow in."

"Good." Thomas stretched and grimaced. A few hours of sleep had done little besides give his bruised muscles time to stiffen. While Phaistus banged things on the hearth, he found his trousers and top boots on the floor underneath the bed's rumbled white counterpoint and started to dress. "Clean that pistol."

The servant stood, wiping his hands on his shirt tail and glancing over the draw table where Thomas had left his wheellock and reloading gear. "Where's the other one?"

Thomas grabbed up a pewter jug and threw it at Phaistus, who ducked, grinned, and went on with what he was doing. Phaistus had come to the

Guard House as a kitchen boy, silent and terrified, but had grown out of it before his voice changed. "I obviously don't beat you enough." Thomas went to the table and pushed back his sleeves to splash water on his face from the bowl there.

Undisturbed, the boy asked, "Going to kill Gambin, Sir?"

"It's a thought." Deciding he could wait to trim his beard. Thomas picked up the scabbarded rapier and went into the small anteroom.

Ephraim was waiting for him. He was a little old man, the pockets of his faded brown doublet and breeches stuffed with sheaves of paper, the ballads he sold on the street. His stockings were mud-stained and one of his shoes had a large hole in the toe. He grinned and pulled his battered hat off. "You wanted to see me, Captain?"

"Someone sent a packet of letters to the Dowager Queen through Gambin. I want you and your people to find out who hired him."

Ephraim rubbed his grizzled chin. The best of the civilian spies Thomas employed, Ephraim was discreet enough for the occasional official mission as well as for Thomas's own needs. "That could be difficult, Sir. That Gambin lad hires out to so many there's no telling whose business he's on today, and he mightn't have a reason to go back to the fellow, you know."

"Gambin's here now. I'll make sure he does."

"Ahh. That's a different matter. The usual wages?"

"A bonus if you find out by tomorrow."

"Oh, I can't make any promises." Ephraim looked flattered. "But we'll do our poor best."

Thomas left him and went down the staircase toward the clash of steel and loud talk from the large hall on the lower floor. The old, rambling house stood just inside the Prince's Gate, where it was dwarfed by the bulk of the King's Bastion and the Albon Tower. For seventy years the house had been the headquarters of the Queen's Guard and the property of whomever held the commission of Captain. The carved knobs topping the stairway's balusters were gashed and chipped from practice bouts up and down the steps, and the walls still bore the faint scars of powder burns from more serious skirmishes.

The Queen's Guard were all scions of province nobility or second sons of landed families, with few expectations of large inheritances. The requirement for membership was a term of service with a crown troop, preferably cavalry, and an appointment from the Queen. In general the Queen's Own were unruly and hard drinking, and carried on jealous and obsessive rivalries with both the Cisternans and the Albon Order. They were also the most effective elite force in a country where until a few years ago private armies had abounded; commanding them had been Thomas's only ambition for a long time.

As he reached the second-floor landing, Dr. Lambe was just coming out of the archway that led into the other wing. Dressed in a stained smock, the apothecary was followed by a young boy weighed down with various satchels and bags of medical paraphernalia. Thomas asked Lambe, "Did you see Gaspard?"

"I did, Captain, and I'm not sure I believe it." Lambe adjusted the cap on his balding head. Apothecaries prepared the herbal remedies used by sorcerer-healers, and many, like Lambe, also made good physicians, even without any sorcerous skill. Healers learned in magic were in short supply everywhere but in Lodun, where the university drew them by the dozens.

"What do you mean?"

"The burns are scarred over already." He shrugged. "I knew Galen Dubell had a reputation for healing-sorcery, but what did the man do?"

"Whatever it was, he did it quickly. He used some things Braun had."

"Dr. Braun's not so bad." Lambe caught Thomas's expression and added, "He's not a steady sort, I'll give you that, Sir, but he has the makings of a fine practitioner in him. But this work of Dr. Dubell's... It would be an honor to hand the man bandages."

Thomas watched Lambe go, thoughtfully, then turned into the small second-floor council room where Lucas waited for him.

The dingy walls were hung with old maps and a few tattered remnants of flags, some of which were trophies from the last war, while others were more recent acquisitions from the Cisternan Guard, who would undoubtedly give a great deal to learn where they were. In the glass-fronted bookpress were classical treatises on warfare, manuals of drilling, musketry, fencing, and tactics, *The Compleat Body of the Art Military* and *Directions For Musters*. Lucas, the First Lieutenant of the Queen's Guard, was leaning back in a chair, nursing a tankard, his boots propped up on the heavy plank table beside a wine bottle and another tankard.

Gambin was standing in the corner in an attitude that suggested he wanted to be as far away from Lucas as possible, and his long face was sullen. Gambin was a spy as well, but without Ephraim's sense of professional integrity. He worked most often for the lesser lords of the court, and this was the first time Thomas had considered him anything more than a minor irritant. He was dressed in a red and gold slashed doublet, the peacock finery of a court hanger-on that was particularly hateful to the eyes after a hard night and little sleep. Gambin said, "I've business elsewhere, Captain, if you don't mind." The bravado in his voice was unconvincing.

Lucas raised an eyebrow. Thomas glanced at the lieutenant as he set his rapier down. Ignoring Gambin, he poured wine into the other tankard, tasted it, and winced in disgust. He said to Lucas, "Adijan '22? Are you mad?"

Lucas shrugged. "It wakes me up."

"It wakes the dead." Thomas dropped into a chair and looked at the spy. He waited until Gambin's pale eyes shifted away from his, then said, "Someone gave you a package."

"They do. I'm handy for that," Gambin muttered.

"This was for the Dowager Queen."

The spy licked his lips. "Was it?"

"Was it?" Lucas echoed.

"It was," Thomas said. He drew the rapier from the fine black leather of the scabbard and out of the corner of his eye saw Gambin shift nervously. The hilt was unadorned beyond the inherent elegance in the shapes of the half-shell guard and the blunt points of the quillions, and the metal was worn smooth from use. Thomas ran a finger down the flat of the narrow blade, apparently giving all his attention to the shallow dents and scratches it had collected. "Who gave it to you?"

"I'm not saying I had any package."

Lucas pulled the packet of letters out of his rumpled doublet and dropped it on the table. Last night, after discovering that it was Gambin who had delivered the packet to one of Ravenna's gentlewomen, Thomas had given it to Lucas along with instructions to bring in the spy.

Thomas held the rapier up and sighted along the blade. Despite last night's misadventures, it was still unbent. "Where'd this package come from, then?"

Gambin laughed nervously. "There's no proof I had anything to do with that."

Thomas looked up at him. "A Queen's word is not good enough?" he asked softly. "That's dangerously close to treason."

"I… That's…"

"Who gave it to you?"

Gambin made the mistake of changing defensive tactics. "I can't tell you that."

"'Can't'? Surely not 'can't,'" Lucas pointed out. "Perhaps you mean 'shouldn't'? There is a distinct difference."

"I meant I don't know who it was; he had his man give it to me," Gambin protested.

"That's a pity." Thomas laid the rapier gently back on the table and stood up. "You're no use to us, then, are you?"

"So I'll be on my way, then."

"Yes, do that."

The spy hesitated, started to speak, then made a sudden dash for the door. Thomas caught him as Gambin faltered in the doorway at the sight of a group of guards dicing in the next room. He slung the spy around and slammed him face first onto the table.

Lucas deftly rescued the wine bottle and moved it out of the way.

Gambin yelped, the cry escalating into a scream as Thomas twisted the spy's arm upward at an unnatural angle. He said, "Keep yelling. There's no one to hear you who gives a damn. Now I suggest you consider an answer."

"Look here, I... I'll find out who it is for you. I swear, he... I've got friends that can find him." The spy's voice rose in desperation.

"I think you're lying. Doesn't it seem like he's lying?" Thomas asked Lucas.

Lucas shrugged. "Well, he is handy that way."

"No, no, it's the truth," Gambin panted. "I'll find him."

"Are you sure?" Thomas put a little more of his weight on the man's abused arm bone.

Gambin shrieked. "Yes, yes! I swear it!"

Thomas let him go and stepped back. Gambin fell to the floor, gasping. He staggered to his feet, clutching his arm, and stumbled for the door. Thomas stood his chair upright and recovered his tankard from the floor. He gestured at the wine bottle Lucas was holding protectively. "Are you keeping that all for yourself?"

Lucas passed it to him as he took his own seat. "I thought it woke the dead."

"It does. That's what bad years are for." He poured the tankard full and took a long drink. He resented wasting the time on Gambin, and wanted to get back to the problem of Grandier. The three prisoners they had taken last night had known nothing. The man who had hired them had worn a hood and a mask, which was a common practice for nobles and the wealthy slumming in low taverns, and they had not been able to decide if he was a Bisran. Which might mean Grandier spoke without an accent, that the man who had done the hiring had not been the sorcerer but another confederate, or that the hirelings were too witless to have known him for Bisran if he had been wearing a Bisran cornet officer's tabard. *We know nothing about Grandier,* Thomas thought in disgust, *except rumor and common knowledge.* "I suppose Gideon relieved you at dawn."

"Yes, and he was disgustingly cheery about it." Lucas sighed. "I can't recall being that energetic as a youth. Who's following Gambin?"

"Ephraim, the one that pretends to be a ballad-seller."

"Oh, hiring out, are we?"

"Had to. All the regulars from the King's Watch are still looking for Grandier."

"Grandier's a bad business." Lucas picked up the packet of letters and glanced through it. "So you're having an affair with the Countess of Mayence?"

"A long, torrid affair. I get very effusive about it in the one dated last month." Thomas didn't mind his lieutenant's raillery. Lucas was perhaps the first man Thomas had learned to trust entirely, when with the rest of the Queen's Guard they had been employed as couriers and intelligence-gatherers during the last Bisran War. Since they were both dark enough to pass for Aderassi, the two of them had once spent six days disguised as mercenaries from that small country in a Bisran cavalry encampment on the wrong side of a wide and rising river. The Bisran commander had staged executions of captured officers of the Ile-Rien army as after-dinner entertainment, and the bounty he had offered for Queen's Guardsmen was enough to support a well-to-do merchant family for a year.

"Yes, I particularly enjoyed that one." The older lieutenant spread the letter out on the table to examine the signature. "It's a good forgery. I'd think there were some truth to it if I didn't know you were too proper a gentleman to stand in line with the good countess's grooms and lackeys. I expect it's a lucky thing the Dowager thinks so too."

"It's hardly luck. If Ravenna had asked me if I'd actually slept with the countess, I would've had to tell her I honestly couldn't remember. Most of the court ladies are starting to look alike to me." Thomas and Ravenna had not been lovers for more than a year, since her health had first begun to fail, and she knew that he had had other women since then. It hadn't changed anything between them; their relationship had passed that point long ago. The only woman she would have objected to was Falaise. Not too many years ago palace coups had ignited as quickly as fires in a dry summer; Ravenna could not afford to have the man who commanded her guard become attached to a daughter-queen who in many ways was still an unknown quantity, and who one day might like to rid herself of a dominating mother-in-law.

But even though the letters had failed in their purpose, they were an annoyance at a time when Ravenna needed him free to help her, and not constantly guarding his own back. Thomas tapped the packet. "This was done by someone who doesn't know Ravenna."

Lucas nodded. "Someone who doesn't realize how little she appreciates people who trouble with her personal..." He paused and his mouth quirked. "Matters."

Thomas strongly suspected his friend had been about to say "affairs." He let it pass and said, "It's more the sort of thing that would work with Roland. I wonder if our anonymous schemer plans to try it." If some disgruntled courtier also tried to drive a wedge between Roland and his cousin Denzil in this manner, Thomas wished him luck, but it was far more likely this asinine trick was the brainchild of one of the Duke of Alsene's cronies. Inspired by a few casually dropped hints by Denzil himself, of course.

Lucas looked thoughtful. "I wonder if it's been tried already."

"I'd think the screams would have been audible even over on this end of the court. But there's no way to be certain."

"Surely Renier, the ideal of perfect knighthood, would know."

Thomas snorted. As the ideal of perfect knighthood, Renier was not without flaws. He was a skilled swordsman but tended to depend too much on his weight and size, using his greater strength to bowl over smaller opponents. This technique had some merit: there were many men who unwisely dueled with the Preceptor of the Albon Knights only to end with his footprints down their backs. Renier had knocked Thomas down once in a friendly duel, and when the Preceptor had stepped in close to follow up, Thomas had retaliated by slamming him in the groin with the hilt of his main gauche. Renier didn't seem to hold it against Thomas, and his good humor never seemed to suffer. But Renier had a misguided perception of loyalty, and while he was not a bad influence on the young King, he was not a good one either. He often went out of his way to repeat to Roland what everyone else in his hearing said, without regard for Roland's sensibilities or the safety of those whose careless words were later used against them. Thomas said, "The ideal of perfect knighthood thinks it's his duty to tell Roland every word I say to him, and God knows what His Majesty would make of the question."

"Well, whatever you think." Lucas got to his feet slowly. He was only a few years older than his captain, but he moved like a much older man when he was tired. *The reflexes go,* Thomas thought, looking at the rapier lying on the table. *And that's that.*

Lucas said, "I'm off to a well-deserved rest. Oh, there's that entertainment at court tonight. Will you need me?"

"No, Gideon and I will take it. I've doubled the duty list for it, what with all our other little troubles." The acting troupes brought to court by the Master of Revels didn't ordinarily present much of a problem. Before they reached the palace they were examined for foreign spies or suspected anarchists, and the actors seldom turned mad and attacked anyone. "What sort of play is it?"

"An Aderassi Commedia."

Thomas winced. "Well, it could've been a pastoral." He drained the tankard.

"Oh, there's this. I'd forgotten." Lucas picked up a leather dispatch case from a pile along the wall and tossed it onto the table. It was stuffed with papers.

Thomas looked at it without enthusiasm. "What's that?"

"The King's Watch sent it over. It's some writings and copies of documents from Grandier's heresy trial in Bisra."

"You're joking," Sitting up, Thomas pulled out the papers and thumbed through the pages of faded script. "How did they get it?"

"A Viscondin monk who was traveling in Bisra attended the trial. He asked one of the officiating priests if he could copy the documents, and they allowed it. None of it was considered secret, or important, apparently. The King's Watch said it wouldn't be of any use, but they know how you are about these things so they sent it along."

As Lucas left, Thomas spread out the papers. The Viscondin Order was one of the few brotherhoods that could still cross the border to Bisra freely. The Church of Ile-Rien and the Church of Bisra had declared ecclesiastical war on each other when the bishops of Ile-Rien decided against purging the countryside of the pagan Old Faith. The Bisran Inquisition had started its persecution of sorcerers at about the same time, and the Church of Ile-Rien's objections to it had caused Bisra to outlaw most of the independent religious orders.

The Viscondin monk had copied the court documents in the original Bisran. Thomas could read Low Bisran, but not the elaborate High Script used for their official documents. He doubted the monk had been able to either, and the King's Watch had probably not bothered. He sorted the unreadable documents aside to send to the palace clerks for translation.

It was clear even from the monk's crabbed notes on the evidence that Grandier had been a victim. The nuns' testimony had been confused and contradictory, and the details of how Grandier had enchanted them were vague at best; if they had brought such charges in Ile-Rien a magistrate would have had them all hauled off to gaol for false witness and wasting the time of a law court. According to the monk, one nun had even tried to recant her testimony but the judges had refused to hear her.

Grandier had been tortured with fire, the choking-pear, and the other devices the Inquisition used to obtain confessions of heresy. Despite this the sorcerer had refused to confess, and had been sentenced to the question ordinary and extraordinary. He had been subjected to both strappado, having been hoisted by his bound arms and dropped to a stone floor, and squassation, during which the executioner had attached heavy weights to the victim's feet, then hoisted and dropped him to within a few inches of the floor until limbs had been dislocated. *The scars would be visible on his face, his hands. Even if he's healed himself, he can't conceal that kind of injury. It would be a miracle if he could straighten his back or walk without limping,* Thomas thought.

Grandier disappeared from his cell a few weeks after his torture. A month later the priest who had brought the original complaint died insane. Within another month the bishop who headed the Inquisitorial Committee followed him. The witch-pricker, who had probably falsified the demon marks he had reported finding on Grandier's body during torture, died later in "terrible delirium," as the monk described it. The account ended there, before the plague and the other horrific disasters now attributed to the outlaw sorcerer.

If he wasn't working dark magic before the trial, Thomas thought, *he is now.*

The afternoon at the Mummer's Mask passed slowly as the tavernkeepers recovered from the night before and the acting troupe prepared for the night to come. Baraselli and his assistants sat at a big round table on the tavern's main floor arguing over which characters they would use tonight, while the actors lounged nearby feigning disinterest. Shafts of sunlight from the cracked windows glittered off the dust in the air and the various paraphernalia of the stage that had been hauled out for inspection.

Silvetta, the actress who played one of the heroines, said, "What did you say your name was?"

There was a moment of hesitation before the woman who had been hired for the Columbine mask answered, "It's Kade." She was sitting on top of one of the wine-stained tables, her legs folded beneath her skirt in a position that most women of better breeding would have found difficult if not impossible. The playing cards she shuffled were a tattered pack belonging to the tavern.

"Really? Don't tell Baraselli." Silvetta shuddered, rolling her eyes in a gesture better suited for the stage. "Bad luck, ill omens, that's all he talks about. But they don't give children that name here anymore, do they? Except in the country. Are you from the country?"

"Yes."

"When did you learn Commedia?"

"I traveled around with one for a while and learned the Columbine mask. That was after I got out of the convent," Kade told her.

Silvetta leaned forward. "Why were you in a convent?"

"My wicked stepmother sent me there."

"Oh, you're telling me a tale." Personal questions out of the way, she said, "Do my fortune again."

Kade's brows quirked. "I doubt it's changed any in the past hour."

"You can't tell; it might have."

"You can tell," Kade said, but began to lay out the cards for the fortune anyway.

Corrine, the other heroine, appeared out of one of the back rooms carrying two dresses visible only as tumbled confections of sparkled fabric and lace. "What do you think, this blue or that blue?"

Both women paused to give the matter serious consideration. "That one," Silvetta said finally.

"I think so," Kade agreed.

"What are you wearing?" Corrine asked her.

Kade suspected she was anxious to make sure she wasn't going to be outshone by the woman playing her maid. With a shrug of one shoulder, Kade indicated the loose red gown she wore over the low-necked smock. "This."

"You can't wear that," Silvetta objected.

"I'm playing a maid." She laughed. "What else should I wear?"

The free fortune-telling had won Silvetta over completely. She said, "At least let me curl your hair."

Kade ran a hand through fine limp hair that the dusty sunlight was temporarily transforming into spun gold. Ordinarily she considered it the color of wheat suffering from rotting blight. "With an iron?"

"Of course, you goose, what else?"

"I hate that."

Corrine draped the gowns over a chair and said, "The thing to do is to attract attention to yourself. There's plenty of men there, gentlemen, lords, wealthy men, on the lookout for mistresses. Of course, it's not often you can get something permanent, you understand, but it's worth a go."

"Really?" Kade asked, her tone a shade too ingenuous, but not so much so that the other two women suspected subtle mockery.

"Much better than an actor," Silvetta said, and jerked her head in the direction of the tavern entrance. The actor who played the Arlequin stood there talking to one of the tavern-keeps, having just come in from the street. He was darkly handsome, clean-shaven after the current fashion in Adera, and didn't look at all like the other actors who played clowns.

After a moment, Kade said, "How well do you know him?"

Silvetta answered, "He's new. Baraselli hired him last month when the other Arlequin died."

Kade glanced at her. "Was he an old man?"

"Oh, no, all our clowns are young. He died of a fever. It was very bad luck."

The Arlequin had looked in their direction, and seemed to be staring at Kade. Corrine, who apparently had only one thought in her head, grinned and said, "He likes you."

But Kade, who could read wolfish contempt in those dark eyes, snorted. "Hardly," she said, and by sleight of hand managed to insinuate the card for future wealth into Silvetta's fortune.

ᏬᏬᎷ

Thomas had spent the afternoon checking on the progress of the inquiries he had set in motion last night, but the King's Watch had made little headway so far. He had wanted to sound out Galen Dubell on the subject of his one time student Kade Carrion, but last night hadn't seemed the right moment after the sorcerer's rescue from three harrowing days as Urbain Grandier's prisoner.

Galen Dubell had moved into the late Dr. Surete's old rooms, and Thomas found him there when the afternoon sun was glowing through the windows and filling the high-ceilinged room with light. The old Court Sorcerer had needed this room when his eyes had started to fail; the multi-paned windows in the west wall took full advantage of the daylight. Gold-trimmed bookshelves covered the other walls and a globe still shielded by its protective leather cover stood in the corner. The rest of the furniture was buried under piles of more books and a fine layer of dust.

When the servant led Thomas into the room, Dubell looked up from his writing desk and smiled. "Captain." He was wearing a battered pair of gold-rimmed reading spectacles and open books were spread out on one side of the partners desk Dr. Surete had once shared with his assistant Milan.

Thomas said, "I wanted to thank you for what you did for my man last night. He would have died if you hadn't healed him."

Dubell smiled. "You are welcome, but I don't think that is the only thing you came to speak about. Please be direct."

Well, well. Thomas leaned on a bookshelf and tipped his plumed hat back, finding himself more amused than discomfited. Directness was not something one encountered often at court. "We've had a message from an old acquaintance of yours. His Majesty Roland's half sister Kade."

"So that is it." Dubell took off his spectacles and tapped them thoughtfully against the carved arm of his chair. For the first time he looked like a young man who had gradually grown old rather than the model of an aged wizard-scholar who had sprung fully formed out of the fertile ground at Lodun University. "Indeed, I know Kade."

"She was your apprentice."

"Not quite. I was the first to show her the uses for the talent she already had. A mistake I have already paid for. Ten years is a long time to be banished from the city of one's birth." He shook his head, dismissing the thought. "But you have had a message from her?"

"Yes. It seems to suggest she's about to pay a visit."

"In person? That is odd. She usually sends tricks disguised as gifts, doesn't she?"

"If you can call them that." Kade's tricks ranged from the dangerous to the ridiculous. The goblet that no adulterer could drink from had provided some embarrassing and humorous moments for the entire court. A gift of a necklet that, once clasped, contracted and cut the wearer's head off had been considerably less entertaining. The ancient knight who had arrived last midwinter with his beheading game had been one of the most frightening but the least substantive. Of course, Renier had fallen for it like a sack of rocks off a wall. It had taken the Preceptor of the Albon Knights off on a two-month quest that was notable for its pointlessness and not much else. Presumably the fay sorceress had watched from a distance, laughing her own head off. When violent, Kade was about as subtle as a thrown hammer; when devious, she still preferred to sign her name to the deed. As an enemy Thomas would have preferred Kade over Urbain Grandier; she, at least, was a known danger. "Could she be coming to see you?" he asked Dubell.

The sorcerer got to his feet and went toward one of the windows that looked out on the Rose Court five stories below. Thomas followed him.

The stone paths below formed gray rivers among islands of small red and white fall roses. On one of those shaded rivers were a gallant and a court lady, standing close together in conversation. There was something furtive in the turn of the woman's head that spoke of an assignation. They couldn't know they were being watched by the Captain of the Queen's Guard and the man who would probably be made Court Sorcerer sometime in the next few months, but in the palace someone was always watching.

After a moment Dubell said, "Kade could have seen me more easily at Lodun. Why should she wait until now?"

"I can't answer that, Doctor. She's only half human and I don't understand why she does anything." No one had been able to answer the question "why" when Kade's mother appeared at court twenty-five years ago to captivate the old king Fulstan. No one had known she was Moire, a great queen in her own right from one of the multitude of fayre kingdoms that hid under ancient barrows, deceptively deep lakes, or the disappearing islands that lay off the southern coast. She had held Fulstan's attention constantly, day and night, for one year before departing and leaving behind her a baby daughter like a forgotten piece of baggage and a man who was far worse a king than he had ever been before.

Dubell had a way of seeming to pick up on someone else's train of thought. He said, "I remember her mother. I was a young man then. The King's Company was performing The Fortunate Lands and suddenly she was there, dressed in black and her jewels like stars. The Queen of Air and Darkness." He picked up a book from the window ledge and absently added it to a stack on a nearby chair. "A wiser man might have seen a potential danger in Kade. The fay who appear the most human are often more changeable and vindictive than their monstrous brethren. But I saw only an isolated child with the first stirrings of real power and the wit and the will to use it. I admit I have never felt guilty, Captain. I gave her only an elementary tutoring in the craft. If I hadn't, she would have found someone else. I'm sorry for what she has done with the knowledge since then, but I assume no responsibility for it." He looked back at Thomas seriously. "I suspect that may be *lese-majeste*."

"Perhaps, but it's a mild form of it." *Compared to most of what goes on here.* "And we do need your help." He was sure Dubell realized that until another court sorcerer could arrive he had them over a barrel, and Thomas was curious to see if the old scholar would come out and admit it.

Dubell shook his head. "I took a vow of fealty when I first came here years ago. Whatever differences of opinion have arisen since then can have no bearing on it."

The old sorcerer stood there watching the garden below, his stooped shoulders revealing his bone-weary exhaustion. Galen Dubell spoke so freely it made suspicion difficult, even for someone in whom suspicion was a deeply ingrained habit. *And how many times does a man have to swear undying loyalty before you have to give him the benefit of the doubt?* Thomas thought. *At least until events prove otherwise.*

The couple in the court below had moved somewhere out of sight. Dubell asked, "Has anything been heard of Grandier?"

"No, not so far. He's not going to be so easy to find again. You haven't remembered anything else you heard that might hint of his plans?" Thomas asked without much hope. They had gone over all this exhaustively last night on the way back to the palace.

"No, I saw and heard very little of anyone." Dubell spread his hands. "A thing to be glad of, since I expect that is why they allowed me to live."

"I don't know. This is a very complex game he's playing."

Dubell nodded. "So it is," he agreed. "So it is."

ෆ

With winter on the way, the days were growing shorter, but as night dropped over the city on this particular day, Thomas felt he had done a great deal and gotten absolutely no results for any of it. As he leaned on the balustrade of the Queen's loggia and repeated to his young lieutenant Gideon the last message from the King's Watch commander, he was even more convinced of it.

One of the roofed terrace's walls was open to the night and to a view of the park and the river canal where it ran for a time within the towering bulk of the palace's outer curtain wall. Paintings on oiled silk hung from the edge of the roof, rippling slightly in the sharp coolness of the evening breeze.

"They've lost Grandier's trail completely," Thomas told Gideon. Both were dressed in dark brocades for court, with lace at collars and cuffs and overlapping their top boots. Thomas wore Ravenna's signature color of red in the ribbons on his sleeves and his sword knot. "Which isn't surprising at this point. He was here secretly long enough to establish that house; he could have bolt holes all over the city by now."

"That's not very encouraging," the lieutenant said with a rueful expression. One of Gideon's duties was the command of the group of Queen's guards that formed Queen Falaise's escort, and he had been attending to her most of the day instead of participating in the more exciting search for Grandier.

"That's an understatement." Thomas watched the breeze ripple the surface of the canal. Gideon had been Falaise's lover for the past month, and he wondered if the younger man realized that he knew it. Thomas hoped it didn't become awkward. *I've known him since he was a boy,* he thought. *I'd hate to have to kill him.* Muted music and laughter drifted up the graceful staircase to the loggia. The open doors in the archway below led into the entrance hall of the Grand Gallery where the night's entertainment for the court was being staged. Thomas said, "Grandier's playing with us. I think he wanted us to find him the first time, and the question of why isn't an easy one." He shook his head. "I'll have to talk to the King's Watch commander again tonight."

"Yes. Well, there's one other thing." Gideon lowered his voice. "My lady Falaise wants to see you. I know what you've said about that, Captain, and I have put her off, but..."

"I'll take care of it." *You'd think the woman didn't have any sense of self-preservation,* he thought. Thomas was trying to avoid giving Queen Falaise an opportunity to make him any offers he would be honor-bound to tell her mother-in-law Ravenna about. "Who is she with at the moment?"

"Aristofan, he calls himself." Gideon grinned. "His real name is Semuel Porter."

"Which one is he?"

"The pimply one."

Thomas sighed. "They're all pimply, Gideon."

"The pimply one with the red hair." He hesitated. "Braun's coming this way."

Thomas glanced around. Dr. Braun, dressed for court in a black velvet scholar's gown, was gesturing erratically at them from the landing below the loggia. "He seems to have something on his mind," Thomas said.

Gideon looked down at the young sorcerer with thinly veiled contempt. "He nearly got Gaspard killed fumbling around with the wards at that wizard-house."

"Then perhaps it will offset all the times that Gaspard has nearly gotten himself killed," Thomas said, his voice dry. "Go on back to Falaise. See if you can tactfully encourage her to show up for court."

"Sir." Gideon saluted and headed for the stairway leading to the upper levels and Thomas went down to meet Dr. Braun.

"I have something I need to discuss with you," the sorcerer said hurriedly as Thomas reached him.

Dr. Braun was worried, and his normal hangdog expression had given way to a look of frightened intelligence. Thomas found himself asking seriously, "What is it?"

"Captain!" The voice hailed him from the arched entrance to the Grand Gallery.

Hell, it's Denzil, Thomas thought. He told Braun, "If it can't wait, tell me quickly."

Braun hesitated, his nervous eyes on the approaching Denzil. "It can wait," he said. "I'll come to the Grand Gallery later."

"Are you certain?"

"Yes." The young man began to sidle uneasily away.

"Very well."

Braun nodded and all but bolted out of the entrance hall.

Thomas went to join Denzil.

The Duke of Alsene's father had been a wastrel and little better than a border bandit who managed to lose most of the family properties by the time of his death. Denzil had inherited the Duchy of Alsene at age eight, surrounded by a large family of grasping and impoverished noble relatives. Seven years later when he had come to court and captured Roland's favor, all those properties had been restored, and he had been made generous gifts of land, court offices, and the incomes that came with them. Now he had his own cadre of debauched and worthless young nobles, and he encouraged them to plot and spread rumors and otherwise annoy Ravenna, even though two of his foolish friends had gone too far, and died for it on the Traitor's Block outside the city. Ravenna was continually balked by his influence over Roland, and if Denzil's family had deliberately trained him for the part he played now, they couldn't have done better.

"I've heard some unpleasant rumors about the crown's intentions toward my manor at Bel Garde, Captain," Denzil said, adjusting the set of his gloves and deliberately not looking at Thomas. The King's cousin was the mirror of the perfect courtier. His blond hair was curled to perfection, his beard perfectly trimmed, his handsome features unscarred by the ravages of battle, work, or time, his amber doublet trimmed with aglets and his gold-embroidered breeches the height of fashion. That might be part of the attraction Denzil had for Roland; the King had always been an awkward boy. "Perhaps you can put me right on it."

"I would be happy to put you right, my lord," Thomas said easily.

At that the Duke's eyes lifted to meet his, cold blue and opaque, and very much at odds with the pettiness he was affecting. After a moment he smiled ingenuously. "I've heard that a cavalry officer thinks my manor there is some sort of threat."

That was enough to tell Thomas that Denzil already knew all and was only trying to bait him. Bel Garde was built around a fortified tower over-looking the city. In the last century it had withstood a two-year siege and it would make an ideal staging area for an attack on the city wall. That Denzil should be owner of such a valuable and potentially dangerous property was a sore point with the older nobility and particularly Ravenna. Thomas silently damned whoever had let slip their plans to the young Duke and said, "It isn't a manor, Sir. It's a fortress, and in violation of the edict against private fortifications." The edict helped discourage rebellious nobles, but Roland had managed to avoid the issue of Denzil's property at Bel Garde for the past year. He had finally given in to Lord General Villon's diplomatic prodding, but the difficulty had lain in keeping it from Denzil until they could get a signed warrant from Roland.

"Who has said this?"

"Lord General Villon, the commander of the siege engine cavalry."

Denzil snorted. "He's a fool."

Thomas lifted his brows. "It is possible he was misled by the moat and the crenellated walls."

Denzil fingered one of the tawny stones set into the cup hilt of his rapier, apparently trying to decide if the mockery was worth taking issue with or not. Thomas knew the gesture for an empty one, perhaps put on for the benefit of a group of courtiers now crossing the foyer to the gallery behind them: Denzil was a superb duelist, but Thomas couldn't challenge him because of his loyalty oaths to the royal family. Denzil could initiate a challenge himself, but despite provocation, he seemed to be saving it for a time when Thomas was badly wounded or on his deathbed. Denzil finally said, "And so he will destroy it?"

"Only fill in the moat and tear down the walls. The estate itself will be better for it in the long run. I'm told by those who should know that it presents a golden opportunity to extend the park and put in formal gardens."

Denzil's expression suggested this was the equivalent of prostituting one's children. He said, "Surely this plot did not originate with the King."

"This edict has been posted in the Council Chamber for two years and a great many lords have already submitted to it. I would hardly call it a plot, Sir."

Denzil gestured that logic away. "You would not call it so, Sir," he said stiffly. "I would like to know why you are my enemy, Sir, and despise me so."

It was one of Denzil's best tactics with Roland; he could turn any mild criticism into a personal attack on himself. Thomas said, "I suppose if I ever gave you any thought, I might despise you, Sir, but I can't imagine circumstances in which I would be compelled to give you any notice at all."

The expression of artificial indignance in Denzil's eyes hardened to real anger, and for a moment Thomas was hopeful, but the young Duke was only foolish about things that endangered other people's lives, not his own, and the moment passed.

"We will see, Sir," Denzil said softly.

Thomas waited until the Duke had vanished through the main doors of the Grand Gallery before starting down the steps after him. Denzil couldn't have gotten wind of the plans for Bel Garde any time before this afternoon, at the earliest, or he would have confronted Roland about it when he saw him this morning. Wager then that Denzil had approached Thomas impulsively. Wager then also that he would approach Roland sometime tonight, instead of waiting for a private audience, in the hopes of provoking Ravenna into an unflattering and public argument with the King.

Walking through the oversized double doors of the archway was like walking into a wall of sound. The combination of the music from the musicians' galleries above the raised dais and the babble of conversation echoed off the high sculpted contours of the ceiling and shivered the rock-crystal chandeliers. The room was so immense that what Thomas knew to be a large crowd appeared sparse. Visiting nobles, courtiers, ministers, and wealthy merchants invited out of courtesy or political necessity milled in large groups around the bases of the marble-sheathed columns, the orange trees potted in silver tubs, or the fountains running with wine.

Thomas made his way through the crowds toward the dais, occasionally greeting an acquaintance. In the center of the room, the play had just started on a raised plank stage with wooden classical columns and a painted backdrop of an Aderassi marketplace. A gaudily dressed Pantalone with a pointed beard and a mask with a long hooked nose was in loud mock argument with a grotesque Pulchinella with a humped back, protruding stomach, and a high peaked cap. Some of the crowd were even paying attention to it.

Cisternan guards were stationed at all the entrances to the gallery, though they were armed only with swords. The Queen's Guard and the Albonate Knights were permitted to carry firearms in the royal presence at court, but no one else.

The polished-stone dais supported the three chairs of state for Ravenna, Falaise, and Roland. Roland was surrounded by his servants and a few courtiers who had been called up to speak to him. An Albon knight stood guard at his back. Next to him Falaise's chair was empty.

Ravenna was firmly established on the opposite side of the dais from her son. Four guards were gathered near her and a lady-in-waiting sat on a stool at her side.

Thomas swept off his hat and bowed to Roland who was hidden behind his wall of servants and hangers-on, to Falaise's empty chair as a matter of form, and to Ravenna, who smiled down at him. As he climbed the dais, the guard nearest her caught his signal and stepped out of earshot. Thomas kneeled beside Ravenna's brocaded chair and said, "There's news."

Ravenna put her sewing down. "Elaine dear, come and stand in front of me, there's a good girl. Here, wind this thread back on the spindle." The young woman's full skirt, puffed sleeves, and wide plumed hat effectively shielded them from curious eyes.

"Denzil knows about the plans for Bel Garde. It's likely he'll confront Roland about it tonight. You know what will happen," Thomas told Ravenna.

Ravenna's face set. "Villon's been working on Roland for the past two months. He said he'd give the order." She shoved her sewing into her satchel and started to stand.

Thomas said, "Don't."

She stopped, looking down at him, her hands white-knuckled on the arms of her chair.

"Roland won't listen to you. Or worse, he'll do the opposite."

"He will do what I..."

He regarded her steadily. "Face it, Ravenna; it's a fact."

She sat back down with a thump. "Damn Denzil to hell. Damn you to hell. Hand me that fan, Elaine. Oh, don't cringe so, child; I'm not angry with you, am I?" She fanned herself rapidly, the delicate silk construction somehow holding up under the pressure of her grip. "I want you to kill Denzil, Thomas."

Thomas nodded. "Fine. Is now soon enough? I believe I can hit him from here if Elaine would step out of the line of fire."

"No, no. I'll get him eventually. I'll think of something. You'll think of something; it's your duty."

"My duty is protecting you and Falaise," he reminded her.

Ravenna snorted in disdain. "Damn Falaise to hell. What I mind most is that Denzil's making a fool of the boy. Treating him like a puppy to be petted or kicked as the mood takes him. God, I hate that."

Thomas didn't answer.

She twisted the fan between her fingers, then extended it with a snap. "Well?" she asked softly.

Thomas turned over a couple of options, then said, "Send the order tonight. Tell them to start a breach in Bel Garde's curtain wall."

She hesitated.

He continued, "There was a mistake. You thought Roland had signed the warrant, or was about to sign it. You sent the order yesterday."

"Ah." She bit her lip thoughtfully and the fan's motion slowed. "I will order them to stop work immediately when I realize what an unfortunate mistake has been made. I will be properly apologetic. I will repair it with my own funds."

Thomas waited, watching her as she thought it over. A breach in a supporting section of the curtain wall would be difficult to repair, especially with gentle mismanagement, and could be made to buy them at least six months. It would also keep General Villon, who was away with his troop at the moment, from being compromised.

"It will do," Ravenna said. "Elaine, find me that lapdesk, please."

As the girl brought the flat wooden box with the ink bottle and pen set, Thomas noticed the crowd around Roland had cleared and one of the stewards was presenting Dr. Galen Dubell to the King. As the old sorcerer bowed deeply, Roland said, "Come up here, Sir, and tell me how things are at Lodun."

Roland had wanted to go to Lodun or the smaller university further off in Duncanny, but Ravenna had needed him here during her regency, and before that, Fulstan had refused to even let the boy make a progress there to see the place. *It couldn't have hurt,* Thomas thought as Ravenna's pen scratched across the parchment. *He'd have tired of it in a few months, but it would have made him happy. God knows, they might even have been able to teach him something.* Roland resembled his father, with his curling brown hair and blue eyes, but his features were a good deal more delicate. The King's servants would never have let him out of his rooms looking anything other than immaculate, but he still managed to look incongruous in his cloth-of-gold slashed doublet, and the lace of his falling band was beginning to turn.

Galen Dubell climbed the dais and took a seat on the stool a servant whisked into place for him. Roland asked a question and the sorcerer's answer made him laugh. Thomas looked over the crowd for Denzil and spotted him in deep conversation with a man he didn't recognize. Denzil's companion had dark hair and sharp features, and though he was dressed in the heavy brocades of court finery, he was obviously ill at ease. That might not be due to the lofty company: most of the city's monied class was here, bringing with them all the rivalries and old scores that wanted settling. But something about the way he was standing, the way he turned his head, made Thomas think he was observing the crowd and the room with particular care.

If this was some new advisor of Denzil's, he hadn't been in the last report. And if the spies paid to watch Denzil were taking bribes to leave out certain details, then there were going to be a few new heads adorning the spikes on the Prince's Gate come morning. But in that case, surely the man wouldn't casually wander into a court function. *He might be only an acquaintance,* Thomas thought. But Denzil seemed to draw all of his acquaintances into his plots eventually.

Then Denzil broke off the conversation and started toward the dais. "Here it comes," Thomas said quietly to Ravenna.

When the Duke of Alsene bowed in the Dowager Queen's direction she smiled sweetly back at him and nodded graciously.

The steward caught Roland's attention unobtrusively and stepped aside as Denzil bowed.

Roland said, "Welcome, cousin." He looked pitifully glad to see the older man.

With just the right amount of theater Denzil said, "Your Majesty, my home is in danger."

Caught by surprise, Roland said, "You told me your home was here."

Thomas winced. Roland's reply had the distinctive sound of a lovers' quarrel rather than a sovereign dressing down a lord, and the courtiers near the dais were growing quiet to listen.

Denzil recovered smoothly. "It is, Your Majesty. I was speaking of my home at Bel Garde."

"General Villon has spoken to me about it. It's in violation of my edict because the walls are greater than twelve feet in height." Roland shifted uncomfortably. "They will be careful of the surrounding land, and it will improve the view."

Denzil's expression remained stern. "Your Majesty, it is my ancestral home. Its walls have defended our family for generations, and are a symbol of my allegiance to your crown."

Roland's brow furrowed. "I will give you another manor in compensation. There is an estate at Terrebonne that—"

"My cousin, it is Bel Garde that concerns me." The carefully calculated interruption, the appeal in his expression, were all part of the deliberate assertion of his personality over the younger man's.

Thomas could see Roland waver. The King said, "You are a trusted councilor."

Denzil bowed again. "There is none more loyal than I, my cousin, and I need Bel Garde to defend that loyalty."

Then Galen Dubell, forgotten at the King's side, said something to Roland. The King looked down at him, startled.

Denzil caught a hint of something that worried him. Almost too sharply he said, "What was that, Sir?"

Frowning in thought, Roland said, "It is an interesting point. Why do you need the fortress, Sir, when you are under my protection?"

There was a tension in Roland's voice that quieted the rest of the conversations around the dais and stopped Ravenna's pen. Denzil hesitated, staring at the young King. Then he made a gracious bow. "I need it...to present it to you, Sire."

There was a moment's silence as the surrounding courtiers digested that, then a polite murmur of congratulations and applause. "Oh, how delightful," Ravenna exclaimed loudly.

"I accept it, Sir," Roland said happily. "I'll have my best architect put in magnificent gardens, and then I will return it to you."

There was more applause. Ravenna folded the half-written order and handed it to Thomas. "I shall like Bel Garde a great deal with a new formal park."

Thomas allowed himself a slight smile, and dropped the paper into a nearby brazier. "You'll like it even better with your troops all over it."

CHAPTER FOUR

BEHIND THE WOODEN backdrop of the stage, in the small actors' area curtained off from the glories of the gallery by dusty velvet drapes and a canopy, confusion reigned.

Ignoring the outcries and exclamations from the actors and clowns rushing around in the lamp-lit gloom and musty heat behind her, Kade had enlarged a hole in one of the dark blue curtains and was looking out at the rear of the gallery. The back wall was mostly paned glass, its windows looking out onto the terraces and a wide expanse of garden designed to provide a harmonious view.

She remembered that garden, though she could see little of it now through the glare of candlelight on window glass and the darkness beyond. She could have pointed to the stand of sycamore trees, or the hill with its classical ruins carefully constructed to look aged and abandoned. She had expected to remember the palace, but she had not expected its sights, textures, and scents to press in on her in such an overpowering way. The walls were stained with powerful auras of old battles, old anger, love, pain. They hummed with the revenants of the emotions and magics of long-dead sorcerers. She had left her own marks here, somewhere. She was not pleased at the idea of coming upon one of them suddenly.

Here Kade had learned her first real sorcery from Galen Dubell. He had taught her High Magic, with its slow painstaking formulas that used alchemy and the powers of the astral bodies to understand and compel the forces that governed the universe. Galen had been an excellent teacher, his instruction touching on everything from the simplest healing charms to the architectures of the Great Spells that eventually took on lives of their own. When he was banished for that teaching, Kade had been sent to the Monelite

Convent, where she had learned about herbal poisons and the Low Magic of witchcraft from the village women. Later she had learned what she could of fay magic from her mother, but her human blood kept her from shape-changing and practicing many of the other skills that came so easily to the fay. It had been Galen's teaching that had enabled her to survive. Human sorcery was painstaking and slow, but powerful, using numbers, symbols, carved stones, music, and other tools to explain the unexplainable, to control and direct the astral forces the fay only toyed with.

I shouldn't have come back, Kade thought. Somewhere between here and the Mummer's Mask, her courage had fled, leaving her to pick up the pieces of her plan alone. Not that it was a good plan to begin with. She felt an overwhelming desire to discard it and stay with Baraselli's acting troupe for a few weeks. The gods of the wood knew the actors could use the help. Only one thing stopped her.

I might be able to stand feeling like a coward, but I can't live with feeling like this much of a fool. And it would be foolish to turn back when she had come this far. But the more she thought about it, the more the idea of returning to Knockma or Fayre with nothing solved and facing the same old difficulties seemed worse than continuing on this course.

It had become apparent to her that she needed to go home, to the palace at the heart of Ile-Rien, to face her past. To face her half brother Roland, to see if it was really him she hated or the memories and the father he represented. And perhaps to face Ravenna as well, to show the Dowager Queen what that once-unlovely changeling fay child had become. *To get her approval?* Kade asked herself suddenly. *I bloody well hope not.* She bit her lip, fingering the frayed edge of the curtain. *So it's either stay with Baraselli's troupe forever, or go on with what I came to do, what I said I had to do,* she thought. A group of women passed by in front of the windows, the light glittering on their satin gowns, gems, and starched lace collars, their motions hampered by layers of underskirts, hip rolls, and fashionable puffed sleeves. *Perhaps I'll wait and see how the play does before I decide.*

She turned back to the troupe's frantic clamor as Garin hopped through the curtained stage doorway. He was immediately attacked by three other actors and their helpers, who began to tear off his Pantalone costume and wrestle him into the Brighella outfit. Kade picked the wig and cap off the floor and handed it to them, trying not to get her fingers torn off by their frantic grasping.

Baraselli peered through a gap in the backdrop. "Terrible," he moaned. "It isn't going well at all."

"Damn it, man, I've done my best," Garin snapped, his voice muffled because Uoshe was forcing a new shirt over his head. "If it isn't good enough, then you get out there."

Unlike other theatricals, Commedia had no playbook for the actors to learn. The plot was determined by the characters, and the actors learned only the standard lines for one role and supplemented them by whatever jokes or local gossip came to mind. Garin was doing the unfamiliar Brighella role more ad lib than usual and using the standard lines only when he could remember them; it was confusing everyone else terribly.

Garin had taken the extra role because the worst had happened. The Master of Revels and the Cisternan guards who examined entertainers for the court had refused to allow the clown who played Brighella entrance into the palace. The clown had a cousin who was on a list of participants in an ill-fated Aderassi independence revolt. The officials had been terrifyingly polite about the whole thing, and Baraselli, suspecting them all to be magicians of the blackest kind for knowing about it in the first place, had not dared to speak even a word of protest.

In the prisonlike barrenness of the questioning rooms of the St. Anne's Gate Guard House, the troupe had been kept waiting for hours. Partly, Kade knew, to give those who had reason to be nervous a chance to betray themselves, but mostly to allow the clerks to look through the rolls of "undesirable" names that the King's Watch endlessly compiled.

"And what's your name, darling?" the Cisternan guard had asked Kade when it came her turn.

Kade knew the robed academician in the corner of the whitewashed questioning room was a sorcerer, using spells to search out hostile magic. As the guard asked her the question, Kade felt the sorcerer's spell settle over her like a cold mist, invisible and intangible to anyone not trained in magic. It met the masking spell she had prepared and set around herself hours earlier, then slid across and away without friction. The sorcerer's second and third spells did the same. He stopped there, just as her masking spell was beginning to fray on the edges. He might have cast five or six spells and caught her out; Kade, being Kade, had taken that risk. If the sorcerer had detected either her magic or that she was fay, she would have thought of something else.

In answer to the guard's question, she had said, "Katherine of Merewatch. They call me Kade, short for Katherine." Merewatch was a hamlet near the place she made her home much of the time, and so it was factual enough not to set off the truth spell that blanketed the whole room. It was a complex spell, older than she was, as intricate and detailed as the inside of a Portier clockwork toy. It had the combination of ruthless logic and artistry about it that marked it as old Dr. Surete's work. Despite great temptation, she decided not to tamper with it.

The guard stared at her a moment. She had a minor qualm, wondering if they had really burned the only portrait of her, as Roland had claimed they had so long ago. But the man only said, "You ought to change that, you know. Could make trouble for you."

"But it's what my mum calls me."

"Your lookout then. And how's your mum's family called?"

"She didn't have one that I knew of. In Merewatch they called her Maira." Also true; the deep northern brogue of the Merewatch inhabitants rendered Moire as Maira. Kade sensed a faint tremor in Surete's truth spell, but her statement was on that very narrow line of truth and falsehood, and it didn't betray her.

Neither questions nor spells had shown anything odd about the actor who played Arlequin, and that puzzled Kade.

She had suspected him of something, of what she wasn't completely sure, but she knew the palace's protections to be good ones. She had gotten through them with a substantial helping of fayre luck and the willingness to take a risk, and she knew that having been born inside the wards had let her pass them and any other traps Surete might have laid. It didn't seem possible that an ordinary human sorcerer could accomplish it.

Perhaps he's just an ass, she thought, watching the Arlequin now in the backstage confusion. He was sitting on a props box, watching the others with a grin, cool and unaffected by the frantic activity.

Kade lifted her leather Columbine mask and wiped the sweat off her face. She knew she should be going onstage again soon, but with all the Brighella confusion, she couldn't tell if they were getting close to her part or not. Possibly overwhelmed with relief at sighting the end of the play, the others might skip her last entrance entirely.

Kade moved to where she could glimpse the front of the Grand Gallery through a gap where the curtain met the stage's edge. There was a good view of the dais from here.

If seeing the palace again affected her, it was even more of a shock to see its inhabitants. *Roland has changed—for the worse,* she thought. *Worse still, Ravenna hasn't changed at all.* Despite the new gray in her red hair, the Dowager Queen was still delicate, still lovely, and still ruthlessly self-assured. And every woman at court was still hiding behind a fan while fol-

lowing Thomas Boniface with her eyes. That Kade had joined in this pastime
enthusiastically as a child somehow did not make it any better. She had to
admit, at least in the privacy of her own thoughts, that while he was a touchy
and arrogant bastard, he was still well worth looking at.

She remembered deep-set dark eyes, and a remarkably ironic smile. He
had long been known as one of the jewels of the court, even when blond gal-
lants were more often in fashion. She watched him leave the dais and cross
the crowded gallery until he was out of her view. He must be nearing forty
now, but the years hadn't changed him much and there was only a little gray
in that dark hair. *Don't be an even bigger fool than you already are,* Kade told
herself. He and Ravenna had been made for each other.

Baraselli had given off moaning and was now racing around like a madman trying to collect the props for the finish. He rushed up to Kade and
thrust a gold candelabrum at her. "Quick, hold this."

An instant later she realized it was gold paint over iron and dropped the
thing with a curse. It clanged on the tiled floor.

"What is it?" Baraselli cried out, with the same hysterical urgency he
would've shown if she had fallen to the floor in a dead faint.

"I sprained a finger," she growled at him, tucking her smarting hands
under her armpits.

"A sprain? Oh god, it could've been your foot!" He grabbed up the candelabrum and fled toward the stage with it.

Fayre luck, hell, Kade thought. She could hear Silvetta shouting at one of
the heroes and vaguely remembered she should be onstage for that.

She headed for the curtain. If she hadn't stood there like a dolt and held
the thing... The intensity of her magic could be affected for a short time.

ॐ

When Queen Falaise entered with Aristofan, or Semuel Porter, on her
arm, and Lieutenant Gideon and the rest of her escort trailing her, Thomas
had decided it would be more politic at the moment to leave the dais and
take a turn through the crowd. He also wanted to find Dr. Dubell, and caught
up with him as the sorcerer was leaving the gallery.

They stood in one of the gracefully arched doorways at the opposite end
of the room, just far enough away from the milling groups of guests to be
able to hear each other.

"You may have made an enemy," Thomas told him.

"Possibly, but I certainly didn't intend to provoke all that." Dubell looked
back toward the dais, frowning a little.

Thomas leaned back against the curve of the archway and regarded him thoughtfully. "What did you say to Roland?"

"Well, he asked me what I taught at Lodun besides sorcery, and I told him it was debate and logic, and we spoke a bit about how orators use it. Then Lord Denzil started his speech. Finally I couldn't contain myself. I said, 'It's an invalid argument.' His Majesty said, 'What is?' and I said, 'He seems to be claiming that he needs the fortress to protect you, but under landlaw of course you're his protector.' The King quite liked that idea, I think." Dubell shook his head, ruefully amused. "It's almost the right phase of the moon to start the crucial work on the palace wards, and I'd hate to be distracted. At Lodun we're all very experienced in how to give each other the cold shoulder at dinner, but I've been away from court so long I'm out of practice dealing with quarrels of this kind."

"The thing to do would be to bring it to my attention, at least in your case," Thomas said.

"Would it?" Dubell met his eyes seriously.

"It would."

"Then I will remember to do that." Dubell inclined his head. "Goodnight, Captain."

Dubell left, and Thomas turned back into the gallery. He had never offered either support or protection to anyone at court lightly, and he wasn't really certain what had prompted him to do it for Galen Dubell. Except perhaps that the old sorcerer had survived decades of court intrigues and still seemed to have retained both his optimism and his honesty, and Thomas didn't want to see that change. He looked back toward the dais where Denzil now sat at Roland's feet, making his King laugh at something, all ill feeling apparently forgotten. Apparently.

Thomas turned away from the dais and looked around for Dr. Braun, but if the young sorcerer was here he was lost in the crowd.

The Commedia was almost over. Thomas hadn't paid much attention to it, except to notice that it was a little better than the farces performed almost nonstop for market-day crowds. This troupe had apparently altered its performance to accommodate a more sophisticated audience. He stopped near the stage beside a group of outland nobility to watch two of the clowns performing the climactic sword duel. Instead of uncoordinated acrobatics that would have bored most of their audience, with its connoisseur's appreciation of dueling, they did it in exaggeratedly slow motion, allowing them to perform intricate moves that would otherwise have been beyond them.

Thomas had also noticed the masked actress who was playing Columbine. She was standing within about twenty feet of him on the opposite end of the stage from the other actors and was the apparent instigator of the duel for some reason that he assumed would make sense if he had seen the entire thing. With tousled blond hair and a red dress that would have been more appropriate on a disreputable wood nymph, she was hardly as glamorous as the two demure heroines, but she had her tattered skirts kilted to the knee for the acrobatics and undoubtedly had the most attractive legs.

Oddly, the actor playing the Arlequin was standing behind her in the shadow of a painted scenery column, not quite off the stage but not on it enough to be a part of the action. There was something in the man's stance that kept Thomas's attention. The Arlequin seemed to be focused on the actress a few feet in front of him, and not on the mock duel. His half-mask was dark and trimmed with coarse false hair, with deep scarring wrinkles around its pinhole eyes and snub nose. His brown baggy clothes were patched and torn, and there was a bedraggled rabbit tail on the top of his cap. Then the Arlequin took a half step forward and the air around his bare feet seemed to blur. The shadows near the column were pooling around him as if they were solid.

Thomas swore, turned and brushed past the spectators, heading toward the Cisternan guard stationed at the nearest archway. He grabbed the guard's pike and said, "Get Galen Dubell; get him now."

The guard stared. "Sir...?"

"He should be on his way to the North Bastion. Tell him we're under attack. And give me that."

This settled the Cisternan's hesitation at taking orders from another officer. He surrendered the pike and slipped back out of the archway. "What is it?" The Cisternan Commander Vivan was coming over from his post.

Thomas said curtly, "The actor playing the Arlequin is in the process of transforming into something. Get ready to contain it or we're all going to be dead."

Vivan looked toward the stage, startled, then headed toward the next Cisternan guardpost at a run.

Thomas took the pike and started toward the Arlequin, ignoring the curious stares. His pistols weren't loaded and there wasn't time to do it. He came up behind the Arlequin at an angle, out of its line of vision. Through the breaks in the scenery he saw more Cisternans moving up behind the stage. A murmur of unease grew as the crowd saw the guards moving and began to sense something wrong.

The change was so quick it was moments before the panic started. Suddenly the Arlequin's exposed flesh turned mottled and patchy and the actor's leather mask and rough costume seemed to enlarge and meld with its face and body. Then it was twice the size of the man it had been and its legs were taking on the demon-shape of a goat's hindquarters.

A woman in the crowd screamed, and up on the stage the Columbine actress whirled and saw the Arlequin just as the creature rocked forward to leap at her. Not close enough yet to do anything else, Thomas threw the pike.

The weapon struck the Arlequin's arm, staggering it. Wailing, it jerked the pike out and tossed it away, scattering yellowed bits of flesh. The crowd and the actors were scattering in panic and the Cisternans were fighting their way through the rush.

Trying to push past the panicked spectators himself, Thomas saw the Arlequin strike one of the actors who hadn't fled quickly enough, slamming him through the wooden backdrop. It pushed a column aside, knocking another actress down, then charged the woman playing Columbine. Incredibly, she waited until the last moment, then ducked out of the way and leapt off the stage. Its own momentum carried the Arlequin to the end of the platform before it could stop itself and turn.

Thomas broke free of the crowd and picked up the fallen pike. The Cisternan guards were circling the stage, pikes leveled at the snarling creature. Thomas moved to join them, noting that some of his own men were coming up to help. He hoped Gideon was getting Ravenna and Falaise out of the gallery, but he couldn't spare a look over his shoulder.

A shot went off from somewhere behind them, then another, echoing thunderously against the marble facings, but the Arlequin wasn't affected. Thomas knew there were some creatures of Fayre immune to gunfire and silently damned Galen Dubell for not being here. The Arlequin made a darting motion at one of the Cisternans, testing them. It seemed reluctant to face the pikes again. Thomas shouted, "Steady, we can hold it!"

He glanced sideways and saw the masked Columbine actress, a little to the side and behind him, watching the Arlequin.

Everyone else with any sense had long since fled. "Get out of here," he yelled at her.

She glanced at him and obligingly backed up a few steps. *Madwoman*, Thomas thought.

Abruptly the Arlequin rushed forward, moving with sudden and blinding speed. It slammed into two Cisternans, knocking both men aside with a force that must have broken their necks, then changed course and darted toward Thomas.

It caught the top of his pike before he could brace the butt against the floor. He let go and dove out of the way. The Arlequin overshot and crashed into a brandywine fountain in an explosion of plaster and brass pipes. Dripping with brandywine, it struggled out of the debris and turned to come at him again as he rolled to his feet. A guard threw another pike at the creature and caught it a glancing blow as Thomas drew his rapier. The Arlequin pounced forward and was almost on top of Thomas when he shoved the sword into its chest.

The creature's forward motion against the rapier sent Thomas falling backward, his back striking the hard floor, momentarily knocking the breath out of him. Then the Arlequin was straddling him, falling forward on top of him. Its smell was foul, like rancid milk. Desperately he twisted the hilt and pushed, the creature's own weight helping to drive the rapier through cartilage and muscle. He felt the vibration through the hilt as the blade snapped, then the Arlequin shrieked and leapt away from him.

Thomas scrambled back and shoved to his feet. One of the Cisternans tossed him a sword, but the Arlequin had leapt backward onto the stage. At least the thing was slowing down—and still dripping brandywine. Thomas glanced around and spotted one of his men. "Martin, go get a torch."

The Arlequin paced around on the creaking wood of the stage, snarling at them. As Thomas looked back he saw that the actress who had been struck down in the first attack was on her hands and knees and trying to crawl toward the edge of the stage. Before he could move to distract the Arlequin, it whirled and saw her. She screamed and the Arlequin grabbed up a section of one of the painted columns and hurled it at her.

Suddenly Columbine was on the stage and shoving the other woman out of the way. The wooden missile hit her in the back and knocked her off the stage, sending her crashing to the floor in a heap of splintered wood.

Damn it, Thomas thought. *Damn brave madwoman.* He looked around as Martin ran up with the lit torch, a makeshift affair of a chair leg, a torn piece of someone's underskirt, and lamp oil. Thomas took it and moved forward slowly. The Arlequin shifted away, wary, ready to charge again.

Thomas's first thought was to lure it away from the wooden stage, knowing the stone and marble facings in the rest of the room would give them time to put the fire out. But he suspected the Arlequin's instinct would be to take as many people with it as possible; when it was racing around like a monstrous torch, it would have plenty of opportunity.

In the pile of shattered wood, the Columbine actress stirred. She pushed herself up, shaking her head dizzily as her actor's mask fell away. Thomas was thinking, *She must have a head as hard as a brick...* Then she looked up and saw the Arlequin just as it turned and saw her.

Instead of rushing her, it gave that wailing cry again. Thomas took the moment of distraction to run forward and hurl the torch.

He saw the actress struggling to her knees, her hands a flurry of motion. Thinking it over later, he thought she had scraped up a handful of splinters, spat on them, and tossed them at the Arlequin. They flew further than their weight allowed, blown by some invisible wind to scatter around the creature's feet.

The torch struck the brandy-soaked fur on the Arlequin's chest, which caught fire as if it had been dipped in pitch. The Arlequin wailed and battered at the air around it, fighting an invisible wall. There was something containing it, a hardening of the air that the heat of the flames shivered against.

The Arlequin dissolved into a cloud of thick black smoke. Its wails ceased and it curled up like a roll of paper kindling. Thomas saw Dubell arriving through the arched doorway leading from the long hall, and realized the fight had lasted only a short time.

Actors and guests who had scattered around the room behind columns or furniture began to emerge from hiding.

The guards were beginning to look around for wounded and dead. Thomas walked slowly over to where the Columbine actress still sat in a pile of scrap wood. She was watching the monster burn with a grin of undisguised triumph.

He already knew who she must be, but it still took him what seemed moments to put together the direct gray eyes and the long straight nose with a forgotten portrait in an upstairs hall, and with the wildness of the magic she had just performed.

Kade looked up at him, met his gaze, then winked.

CHAPTER FIVE

THOMAS SAID, "MAY I congratulate you on a spectacular entrance?"

The sorceress looked up at him from the floor. After a moment, her lips twisted ruefully. "It was one of my best."

Dubell moved to Thomas's side. He looked at what was left of the Arlequin, at the destruction in the gallery, and down at Kade. "Was this your doing?" His voice was incredulous.

For a moment her expression was that of a small boy caught stealing an apple. "No." As she got to her feet, Thomas saw there were wood chips in her hair from the broken column the Arlequin had thrown at her. She looked defensive. "It followed me here."

Thomas moved a few paces away from them. The Cisternans and his own men were scattered, collecting the wounded and the dead. There were still courtiers milling around toward the end of the room. Now would be a terrible time for a pitched battle.

Dubell met Kade's eyes a long moment, then he said thoughtfully, "Did it really?"

"Well, in a way it did." She began to pull the splinters out of her hair. "But it joined the troupe before I did, and I think it killed one of the clowns to get a place. I would have stopped it sooner but I'd touched some iron, and it took a bit to wear off."

Renier and a group of Albon knights burst in through the archway and started toward them. The hide and sackcloth coats they wore over the lace and velvets of court finery made them look like ancient barbarians arriving to loot a city. Thomas went forward quickly to stop Renier. "Let Dubell handle her," he said in a low voice.

Renier signaled his knights to halt. "Who is she?"

"Kade Carrion."

Renier stared. "My God, we've got to…"

"No," Thomas said pointedly. "If he can get us out of this without a bloodbath, we've got to let him try."

The big knight considered a moment, then nodded tensely. "Very well." He signaled the other knights to move back.

Thomas nodded, thankful that while Renier wasn't a particularly brilliant statesman, he wasn't a bloodthirsty idiot either.

"Did she cause all this?" Renier asked, looking around at the chaos in the gallery.

Thomas glanced back at Kade and Galen Dubell. She was watching them, wary and a little angry. Her brows were darker than the pale blond of her hair, so the effect was that when she was looking at you, you knew it. He thought about her leaping to push the other actress out of danger and said slowly, "I don't think so."

Then Kade's eyes focused past them and her expression changed. Thomas followed her gaze and swore. Roland stood in the archway the knights had come through. Thomas said, "Renier…"

"What?" The knight looked around and gasped, "Damn that boy." He sheathed his sword and strode toward Roland, deliberately placing himself between the King and the sorceress.

Thomas looked back toward Kade, aware that the other guards in the room had held off on his order. He would have to decide what he minded more, dying or behaving this stupidly.

Galen Dubell was watching Kade thoughtfully. With gentle firmness he said, "Kade, don't."

She looked up at the older man, her eyes losing some of their intensity. "I didn't come here to kill anyone—even him."

Renier, as Preceptor of the Albon Knights and the only man in Ile-Rien allowed to touch the King without his permission, seized Roland's arm and hustled him out of sight. Dubell watched as they disappeared, then turned a worried eye on Kade. "Then why did you come here?"

She smiled. "For an audience with my dear brother, of course."

And that, Thomas thought, *is not going to help matters at all.*

The gallery smelled of ash and sour wine. Many of the chandeliers and lamps had gone out, throwing the upper half of the huge chamber into shadow. The court had been dispersed, and Ravenna, Roland, and Falaise had retired to a nearby solar with watchful guards. A breeze, created by an open door or window somewhere up one of the long galleries, swept gently through the huge chamber, lifting the heat and the stench for a moment.

"How long had he been with the troupe?" Thomas asked Baraselli.

The Aderassi actor-manager moaned and would have sunk to his knees again but for the two Queen's guards who were struggling to hold him up. The Master of Revels hovered worriedly nearby; it was on his responsibility the troupe had passed the final check at the gate.

"No one's done anything to you, and no one will, if you just answer the question." Thomas kept his voice mild, despite his growing irritation. It was easier to question recalcitrant anarchists under torture than someone who was so busy collapsing that he could hardly stay coherent enough to speak.

"Only a month. Only a month. I didn't know." Dubell had moved quietly up behind the actor-manager. His lips moved soundlessly for a moment, then he looked up at Thomas and nodded. Baraselli was telling the truth.

"Who recommended him?" Thomas nodded to the guards, who cautiously released their hold of the man and stepped back.

Baraselli swayed on his feet, but stayed upright. "It was his first mask, he told me. He'd learned it from an old actor he lived near. He did it well, and he came to us just after Derani died…"

"Who was Derani?"

"He played the Arlequin until he died of fever."

Dubell asked, "What were the symptoms?"

Baraselli whipped around, staring up at the tall sorcerer in fear, but something in Dubell's expression and mild demeanor calmed him and he said, "He… His skin was hot to the touch, and his wife said he couldn't keep anything down, not even water, and he had blood in his, pardon, piss, and… We paid to have the apothecary in to him, but he just died."

There was something familiar about that. And convenient, for the Arlequin. Thomas asked, "When was this?"

"Last month. Well, a month and a fortnight ago."

Thomas shook his head, pressing his lips together. There was a pattern here, a deadly one. He looked up at Dubell. "About a month and a fortnight ago Dr. Surete's assistant Milam fell down a stairway in the North Bastion and broke his neck. A week after that Surete himself died of pleurisy. It came on suddenly, and by the time anyone realized how serious it was, he was dead."

Dubell's brows drew together as he considered it. He said, "It's the easiest of dark magics to bring sickness, and the hardest to detect. It's simplicity itself to send a bookish and uncoordinated young scholar down a staircase. If one has the stomach for that sort of thing, of course." He nodded at Baraselli. "He's telling the truth, and I doubt he can reasonably be held responsible for Kade's actions. What will be done with him?"

Even without the confirmation of Dubell's truth spell, Thomas was inclined to believe Baraselli. He had observed enough people under stress to read the sincerity in those hysterics. He told the Master of Revels, "Give him his money and tell him to take the others and go away." Baraselli sobbed and tried to fall to his knees in thanks. The Master of Revels gestured sharply to the Cisternans waiting nearby, who intercepted the actor-manager in mid-grovel and hauled him away.

"It's either a hell of a coincidence, or a hell of a plot," Thomas said quietly to Dubell. He knew which he favored.

The old sorcerer sighed. "There are no coincidences."

Thomas watched him thoughtfully. "I would have thought it difficult for a wizard to hex another wizard, especially someone like Dr. Surete. He was the Court Sorcerer for two decades."

"If a sorcerer is in fear for his life, he might test every object he is about to touch with a sprinkle of gascoign powder or some other preparation that reveals the presence of magic." Dubell made an absent gesture. "But Surete and Milam were not in fear for their lives. The spell could have come to them on anything—a forged letter purporting to be from a friend, an apple sold to them by a street vendor..."

As Dubell stood lost in thought, Thomas watched the sorceress. Kade Carrion was pacing around the remains of the stage which the servants were dismantling. As she walked around the painted panels scattered on the floor and the stacks of singed planks, he had two distinct impressions of her. The first was that she was only a young girl with a tangled mop of hair and a tattered red dress, not oblivious to the consternation she was causing but not particularly worried by it, either. The other was that here was a creature ephemeral yet solid and real, who walked with the night and the wild hunt. *Dubell is the only one who really knows her,* Thomas thought. *And even he isn't certain what her game is now.*

If she hated her brother and the rest of the royal family as much as she claimed, she wasn't without motive. Their father Fulstan hadn't been much use as a king: he had neither Ravenna's head for finance and diplomacy nor the ability to listen intelligently to advisors who did. The fayre queen Moire had drained him of what vitality and strength of character he possessed, leaving him bitter and old before his time. He had taken out his anger at

Moire's abrupt departure on anyone in his reach, especially on Moire's daughter. No one directly in his power had mourned his death.

Urbain Grandier, however, had no motive, at least not one that Thomas knew.

Kade might be in league with the Bisran sorcerer, but discovering what she knew wasn't going to be easy. Dubell was looking toward the center of the stage platform, where what was left of the Arlequin had burned down into a heap of some foul-smelling dark powder. "Be careful not to step in that black powder," he called to the servants who were warily clearing away the debris. Then the old sorcerer turned and saw Kade, whose curiosity had already led her ankle-deep into the black powder. She lifted her head, surreptitiously rubbed a stained bare foot against her calf and looked the other way. Dubell shook his head irritably.

The Albon knights had by now arrived in force. There were about forty of them in the gallery now, guarding the arched doorways and the terrace windows, pacing the musicians' balconies, and watching the sorceress. The rest of their number were patrolling the palace with most of Thomas's men and the Cisternans.

Behind the dais, Renier emerged from the wide oak door inset with panels of stained glass. It was the gallery entrance to the solar where the royal family had retired to fight things out. He walked up to Thomas and said softly, "Roland wanted to put her under arrest, but Ravenna has talked him out of it. Apparently she's in favor of giving the sorceress the audience she wants, and trying to settle it quietly."

Thomas thought wearily, *Yes, Renier, tell me all about how the anointed King still can't win an argument with his mother.* He said, "Really."

Renier either did not recognize the sarcasm or ignored it out of habit. "My guess is they'll give her the audience."

Thomas eyed him. "Very likely. I suppose, in the long run, it is better than going to war with her in the middle of the palace, killing everyone who stumbles into the way."

As Galen Dubell turned back to them, Renier asked, "Dr. Dubell, could you tell what that creature was?"

The old sorcerer nodded, gesturing back toward the ruin of the stage. "It wasn't fay. It was a construction of wood and animal bone, animated by a very powerful spell, called a golem. I'm not sure, but I imagine it was designed to resist anything the weight and size of a pistol ball. It's a relatively new technique which I believe will come in quite handy on the battlefield once it's perfected. Doesn't help at all for cannonballs, though. The combination of the weight and size…" Dubell recollected himself and shook his head. "But that is neither here nor there."

"How did it get past the wards?" Thomas asked, looking at the heap of black powder.

Dubell met his eyes frankly. "I've done some work with the wards, nothing that should weaken them. They shouldn't have let this creature pass through. I believe something has affected the ward structure, making the gaps their continual movement creates larger, making those gaps appear in locations predictable to someone. It would take an intimate knowledge of the construction of the wards, at least as great a knowledge as Dr. Surete had, but it would be possible. And, perhaps more disturbing, the spell that caused the golem to shape-change from the appearance of a man to that of the creature we saw here would have to be actuated by someone close at hand."

Slowly, Thomas said, "You mean the sorcerer was here, in the gallery."

"Or an assistant, who carried in the charm designed to trigger the golem. I have looked for Grandier's power-signature, but the ether in this room is free of it." Dubell nodded to himself. "Yes, I believe it was only an assistant who was here tonight."

"What a chance to take," Renier said sourly. "There was a Parscen witchman who tried to cause trouble last year. Surete said there was a disturbance in the wards, and had some of us come with him while he tracked it to the source. We found the witchman hiding in an empty house in the Philosopher's Cross, sitting on the floor and crying like a baby. Surete said he must have tried to do a sending against someone in the palace, but the wards stopped it and followed his magic back to him and took his mind away. We knew that he tried something because he had more witch-poisons and hair amulets on him than you can imagine, but it didn't help him at all."

Dubell's attention had gone back to Kade; his expression was worried. *As well it might be,* Thomas thought. Had the golem been activated by a confederate of Grandier's or by Kade herself? He nodded to Kade, who was still wandering the stage. "Did she tell you why she wanted an audience with Roland?"

"No." Dubell was silent a moment. "Her abilities here, in the mortal world, are not as great as when she is in Fayre, and it is difficult to fatally wound her with anything other than a weapon of iron, but… It appeared the creature was attacking her?"

"Yes," Thomas admitted.

"I hope so, for all our sakes."

The door to the solarium opened and one of the stewards emerged, look-ing harried and somewhat the worse for wear. He hesitated, then ap-proached Thomas and Renier. He said, "His Majesty will see the sorceress now."

Thomas said, "Good. Go and tell her."

The steward blanched visibly.

Thomas relented. "Very well, I'll tell her."

As Thomas approached Kade looked up, a strange creature not at all like the child he barely remembered, or the fifteen-year-old girl in the portrait. He said, "His Majesty will see you now."

She lifted her brows. "Will he?"

"Yes."

"And I thought he would be so glad to see me he'd have run out into my arms long before this." There was a bitterness underneath the light irony in her voice.

"You were mistaken."

"I suppose." She shrugged, abandoning repartee with a disconcerting abruptness.

Thomas turned and walked back toward the solarium's door without looking to see if she followed.

After a moment she caught up with him. "This isn't turning out right at all," she muttered.

He glanced down at her. "Oh? Who did you plan for the Arlequin to kill?"

She snorted. "You don't really believe that. And I don't know who sent it so you won't find out from me." Her mouth quirked. "Oh, was I supposed to pale and let something slip at that point? I'm sorry, I was thinking of some-thing else."

Thomas didn't slam the door of the solar open with any more force than necessary, and bowed her in with elaborate courtesy.

The old solar wasn't used much, and the three huge windows covering the further wall had already been shuttered by painted panels in preparation for winter. The scene on the panels was a lurid traditional hunting landscape, subtly at odds with the other paintings on the oak-sheathed walls, the hang-ings of brocaded satin and striped silk, and the delicately carved furniture. Thomas remembered that this room was one of those that had been redeco-rated after the death of Roland's father; the painted panels reflected the old king's taste, and had probably been left unaltered by mistake. He thought

Ravenna might have chosen the room for that rather than its convenience to the gallery.

Roland was slumped in his chair in a sulk, Denzil seated beside him. Falaise's face was still a little reddened under the powder, as if she had been weeping from anger rather than hysteria. She had chestnut hair and blue eyes, and her natural prettiness had been transformed by her coiffure and costume into fashionable beauty. She wore a blue gown trimmed with gold ribbons and seed pearls, and against the somber colors of the rest of the room she looked like an orchid thrown into a dirty alley. Ravenna was the only one who appeared calm. Her hands were busy on her embroidery and she didn't look up at their arrival. There was a stiff silence in the room and the dregs of a bitter argument lay heavy in the air.

Thomas realized it was his duty to announce Kade, the steward having apparently seized the opportunity to escape. Sensing that calling her "the evil fay sorceress" would probably please her no end, he said, "The Princess Katherine Fontainon," then moved to take his place at Ravenna's side.

Kade's fair skin made her helpless against a sudden blush. Ravenna looked up and said, "How lovely to see you again, dear child."

Kade curtsied in what had to be an intentionally graceless fashion. "I'm sure it's just as lovely for you as it is for me, stepmother."

"I'm not your stepmother, dear," Ravenna reminded her calmly. "Your mother did not bother with the travesty of marriage with your father, and it would hardly have served the purpose if she had, because he was already my husband at the time. You know this, but it seems to please you to hear me repeat it."

In a whisper plainly audible to the rest of the room, Denzil said to Roland, "Cousin, this is all too dull."

Ravenna snapped, "Roland, send him away. This is private."

Roland glared. "I could ask you to send your paramour away too, mother."

In the ensuing moment of silence, Kade snickered.

Thomas glanced briefly heavenward. Denzil looked at Roland in irritation as the implication in the unfortunate phrasing of the King's retort sunk in.

Realizing what he had said and reddening faintly, Roland continued defiantly, "This is a family matter and he is the only one of my family who is truly fond of me."

"What a sad thought," Kade added helpfully. "Sad, but true."

Roland stared at her, meeting her eyes for the first time since she had entered the room. "What do you want here?"

Kade ignored the question. She looked to Ravenna, who had gone back to her embroidery. After a moment the Dowager Queen said, "And how is your dear mother, child?" as if her prepared greeting had never been interrupted.

Ravenna's expression was as polite as a judge passing sentence; Kade looked ironic and amused. "She's in Hell," she said.

Ravenna's brows lifted. "Wishful thinking, certainly."

"Oh no, she really is," Kade assured her. "We saw her go. She lost a wager."

"My condolences," Ravenna said dryly, as the rest of the room digested that. Kade had just reminded them all of her strangeness, and Ravenna had taken the point. "Now tell us why you've come here in this unseemly fashion, as an actress of all things, bringing an enemy with you and disturbing our peace."

"What are you more worried about, that I brought you a battle or that I was with an acting troupe? Never mind." Kade shrugged, playing with the frayed threads on the edge of her sleeve. "I have quite a few enemies; I can't help it if they follow me about. As to why I'm here…" She paced a few steps, not looking at them, hands clasped behind her back and the dingy lace of her petticoats swirling around her feet. "I just wanted to see my family, and my dear younger brother."

The slight emphasis on the word "younger" made Roland sit up and flush.

Kade looked from Ravenna to Roland, her gray eyes passing over the quietly watching Falaise.

This isn't turning out right at all, she had said outside, Thomas remembered.

Ravenna just watched her, until Kade said, "I want to make an agreement with you."

"Was it agreement you wanted when you sent my court those cursed gifts?" Roland demanded. "How many of us have you tried to kill?"

"Then there's the death of King Fulstan," Denzil added helpfully, before Kade could answer. "His illness was very sudden, was it not?"

"I see no point in resurrecting either the dead, or the rumors of years past." The gaze Ravenna turned on Roland's cousin should have transformed him into stone. He only nodded politely at her. "Kade, what agreement are you—"

Unable to contain himself, Roland interrupted, "Why would we want to deal with you, sister?" Contempt twisted his voice. "You've threatened us, ridiculed us—"

"Threatened? Oh, what a King you are, Roland." Kade clasped her hands dramatically and said mockingly in falsetto, "Oh, help, my sister is threatening me!" She looked down at her brother, lip curled in disgust. "If I wanted to kill you, you would be dead."

Roland shoved to his feet. "You think so?" he said. "When you cursed the name of our family—"

"You mewling idiot, so did you," Kade shouted, her sarcasm abruptly giving way to rage.

"You're lying; I never did. It was you who—"

"Silence, both of you," Ravenna said, but something in her tone told Thomas she had rather enjoyed the argument. Brother and sister stared at each other a long moment. Kade's hands were at her sides, curling into fists, uncurling.

Damn it, he's too close to her, Thomas thought. The Albon knight nearest Roland had eased forward, ready to snatch him out of his sister's reach.

Then Roland turned away from her and threw himself down in his chair. Kade turned her back on him and walked stiffly to the other side of the room, her hands shaking.

Into the silence Ravenna said, "You haven't said what agreement you want to make, dear."

In a voice almost a whisper, Kade said, "You make me wish I never..." She stopped, shook her head. "Landlaw and courtlaw, stepmother. Landlaw favors the first-blooded child of the female line. That's Roland. But courtlaw favors the first-blooded child of the male ruler. That's me." Kade stopped to watch them a moment, their silence, their concentration.

She shrugged. "Roland's little ass is planted firmly on the throne. That gives him the advantage. And you base your power on landlaw, stepmother. You founded your regency on the rights it gave you. You keep your guard by its traditions." She met Thomas's eyes a moment. He returned her gaze imperturbably. She went on, "But there are still those who think I should have been the heir."

Without looking up from her embroidery, Ravenna said, "Do you want to be Queen, dear? When you were fifteen you said you didn't. You spat on the throne and said it was a foul thing and you wouldn't have it as a gift. And yes, there are still those who would put you on it, or at least long enough to secure the succession for a more manageable candidate."

Kade shrugged. "It's caused you no more trouble than it has me."

"Then what is your solution, dear?"

"I'll sign an agreement formally giving up my claim on the throne and any Fontainon family properties. Have your counselors draw it up." She gestured eloquently at the King. "And I'll even stop 'threatening' Roland."

Ravenna frowned. "And what do you want in return?"

Kade was deliberately silent until Ravenna looked up at her. "The freedom of my old home," the sorceress said softly.

"That's impossible," Roland said, his voice low and harsh.

"Oh, it's hardly that," Kade told him.

Ravenna still looked thoughtful. "And what has brought this change of heart about?"

"I have my own reasons." Kade smiled thinly. "You don't have anything I want enough to make me tell you what they are."

"But why, dear?"

"Because I want it."

Ravenna lifted her brows. "That isn't much of a reason."

Kade made her a half-bow. "It's always been enough for you."

Have to give her that one, Thomas thought. *Good shot.*

Ravenna's hands paused on the fabric and she stared at Kade. Her voice hardened. "You don't know enough to judge me, Katherine."

Kade tilted her head. "Don't I? You've always thought yourself fit to judge me. It's only fair."

"You are young, you know nothing, and life is not fair."

"I know enough, and life is what you make it."

There was a pause.

Ravenna said quietly, "If you are to stay here, there are proprieties that must be observed…"

"No conditions. I haven't made any." Kade smiled. "It's only fair."

The whole idea was so unlikely it took Thomas a few moments to realize that Ravenna was seriously considering it. In a low voice, he said to her, "It isn't worth it, my lady. It's too dangerous."

"Very likely," Kade agreed, idly twisting a lock of her pale hair.

Thomas knelt beside Ravenna's chair so he could see her face. "Don't do it."

Ravenna looked at him, then regarded Kade for a long moment. Her opaque blue eyes betrayed no emotion. She said, "I accept your proposition, dear."

"No," Roland said, his voice unsteady. "I forbid it."

Ravenna turned a basilisk gaze on her son. He trembled, whether from anger or fear it was difficult to tell, but said, "I won't have her here."

For a long moment the outcome was in doubt. Thomas realized he was holding his breath. The room was silent in suspense, as if they observed someone poised on the brink of a chasm. Even Denzil had lost his expression of detached amusement and watched the struggle in fascination.

Then Roland's nerve broke. He pounded his fist on the chair arm and shouted, "I don't want her here! Damn you, can't you listen to me?"

It was a retreat. A shadow crossed Denzil's face that might almost have been disappointment. Ravenna started to speak but Kade interrupted her. "Oh, come now, Roland." The sorceress smiled. "You have more to worry about than my presence here."

He looked at her uncertainly. "What do you mean?"

She said, "The palace wards are still in place. I felt them when I came in." She frowned thoughtfully and laid a hand flat on the marble veneer of the fireplace. She curled her fingers, drawing something out of the stone that was gray and wriggled.

It came out with a shower of stone chips, but without leaving a hole in the mantel. Kade held it between thumb and forefinger like a boy with a rat, a spidery, boneless thing that struggled frantically. It was hard for the eyes to fix on it. "This is a frid. It's harmless. It lives in stone and eats crumbs spilled on the floor. But it shouldn't be here."

She dropped it. It hit the hardwood floor with a splat, hopped once to reach the hearthstone, and disappeared beneath the pitted gray rock like a duck diving under water.

"I'd say the wards aren't proof against the fay anymore. You have a problem, stepmother." Kade bowed to the room in general and was out the door before anyone could react.

Roland leapt up and moved to stand over Ravenna's chair. "You have overreached yourself this time, mother," he said. The protest convinced no one. His face was red with thwarted anger, but he had lost his chance to defy her.

"Have I? What would you have done, Roland?" she asked, as if not terribly concerned with his answer.

"Arrested her!"

"And if she didn't want to go with the guards? Power is relative, my lord." Ravenna let heat creep into her voice. "I thought I'd taught you that if nothing else. Tell me you understand."

She looked up at him, waiting, while Roland stared at her. Lounging back in his chair, Denzil said, smiling, "Really, cousin, it's beneath your notice."

Roland looked back at him. After a moment he nodded. "Perhaps you're right." He turned back to Ravenna, lips twisted with contempt. "Do what you like, mother; it doesn't concern me."

Then Roland turned and stalked toward the door, his page scrambling to open it for him and his knights smoothly surrounding him.

Denzil stood and bowed to Ravenna with an ironic smile. "Congratulations, my lady. Very well played."

Ravenna looked up at him, her eyes opaque. "How old are you, Denzil?"

"I am twenty-six, my lady."

"And do you intend to be twenty-seven?"

Denzil's smile widened. "I depend upon it, my lady." He bowed again and followed Roland's departing retainers.

"What a good idea," Ravenna said to the room at large. "Why doesn't everyone go?"

When Ravenna phrased an order as a question it was a good indication that her temper had reached the boiling point. Falaise started to speak, reconsidered, and stood up to let Gideon conduct her out. Ravenna's guards and attendants all moved hurriedly to wait for her outside.

Thomas had started for the door when Ravenna said, "Stay here, Captain."

Unwillingly he stopped, his back to her, waiting until the others had filed out before turning around.

Ravenna had shoved her sewing aside and was resting her face in her hands. The flicker of light from the hearth played about the red highlights in her hair and the metallic threads in the embroidery of her gown. Without moving, she said, "Don't look at me like that."

He folded his arms. "I am not looking at you in any particular way."

"The hell you're not." She lifted her head and rubbed her temples. "If she had been my daughter I'd have married her off to the God-King of Parscia. Civil war would have been the least of his worries."

Thomas gave up pretense and let her see how angry he was. He leaned on one of the flimsy rosewood tables that looked so out of place next to the blood-splashed hunting scenes that dominated the room and said, "Civil war may be the least of your worries now that you've let her in here. Before this she was taking out her revenge in small pieces, which was a damn sight better than what she could've chosen to do. Now she wants something more."

Ravenna sat back and looked up at him. "She may well get it, whatever it is," she said seriously. "Did you see the way she dealt with me? And I think there was a moment when Roland actually forgot Denzil was in the room. She makes a fine enemy."

"She could be a deadly enemy. She's grown now and she doesn't want a child's revenge anymore," Thomas told her. Ravenna was single-minded and ruthless in a way that would have been devastating had it not been for the lack of any sadism. She had been born to be an absolute ruler as some men were born to paint or write music. She wanted to bring Kade back into the fold, to direct the sorceress's powers and talents to her own ends. He didn't think Ravenna would understand the bitterness of wounds that had never healed.

"A child's revenge," Ravenna said, looking into the fire. "I wish I had a child's revenge. Fulstan wore away at them, both of them. When I discovered all he had done... And I didn't realize it until he'd made my son a coward."

Fulstan's treatment of Roland and Kade had been at its worst when Kade was fourteen and Roland twelve, at the time when Ravenna was away on the borders during the last Bisran War. Thomas had been a lieutenant then, traveling with Ravenna and the rest of the Guard. There had been no one at the palace with the courage to inform the Queen that while she was managing supply lines and browbeating her generals into cooperation, Fulstan was destroying Ile-Rien's future through its heir. Thomas had long wondered if Fulstan hadn't known exactly what he was doing. If he wasn't striking back at Ravenna in the only way open to him. God knew she had been indifferent to anything else he'd ever done.

At this time it had also been an open secret that Thomas was Ravenna's lover. Most of his conversations with the late king had been limited to details of the execution Fulstan had planned for Thomas the day Ravenna died, or grew tired of him. *He did have a gift for words. Perhaps he would have been happier as a poet than a king.*

Ravenna was saying, "Had my children been bastards I think all of us would be the happier for it."

Thomas let his breath out, suddenly weary. "Very eloquent. Now what are you going to do about it?"

She stood up and flung her sewing to the floor. "Sixteen years ago when I approved your appointment into my guard, I knew I was making a mistake," she shouted.

"Probably," Thomas agreed. "And I suppose that bit of misdirection, while admirable, though not quite up to your usual standards, is the only answer I'm going to get."

She stared at him a moment, then shook her head, her expression turning wry. "If I had an answer, I wouldn't need misdirection." After a moment of thought, she asked, "Can we trust Galen Dubell?"

And that was that, even if he stood there and argued until he fell down dead of old age. Thomas rubbed the bridge of his nose. It wasn't the first time Ravenna had given him a headache. He said, "I think so."

"Really?"

"I don't think he knew she was coming here." Thomas shrugged. "But he's genuinely fond of the girl, and there are people who are going to mistake that for collusion. It would be against your best interests to be one of them."

"Yes, we need him. Braun and his little apprentices are no good for serious work like this. The sorcerers we sent for from the Granges and Lodun haven't even reached the city yet. That's suspicious in itself. I'll tell Renier to send more messengers." Ravenna paused, her back to him, her slender form silhouetted against the light of the fire. "I want you to watch her, Thomas."

"I gathered that," he said dryly. "I've already arranged for it." There was a discreet tap on the door, and Ravenna irritably called, "Enter."

It was the steward who had made his escape from the solar earlier. He said nervously, "My lord High Minister Aviler is requesting an audience, my lady."

"Oh, he is? Well, I'm in the mood for him, as a matter of fact. Tell him he may enter, and don't think I didn't notice when you disappeared earlier, Saisan. Let's not make a habit of that, hmm?"

The steward bowed. "No, my lady."

As the servant withdrew, Thomas said, "Fond as I am of Aviler, I have some things to attend to."

"Thomas?" she said quietly.

"Yes?" He stopped halfway to the door.

"You're the only man I know who doesn't hate, dislike, or fear me, and it is a blessed relief simply to speak to you; did you know that?"

Because the High Minister was already coming through the door behind him, Thomas swept off his hat in his best formal court bow and said, "My lady, it is my very great pleasure."

On his way back to the Guard House, Thomas took the immense circular stairwell that led up from what had been the main hall of the Old Palace two centuries earlier and now linked the wing that held the Grand Gallery with the older defensive bastions. The gray age-old stone of the banisters and the central supporting column were carved into flowing ribbons and bands that ended in the heads of gryphons, lions, and unrecognizable animals from the artisan's imagination. The lamplit twilight of the stairwell was cool, and echoed faintly with the humming activity of the rest of the palace.

Thomas wondered what Kade Carrion the fay sorceress was doing now.

The first time Kade had used her power against the court had been on a Saints' Day ten years ago. It was held on Midsummer Eve because combining the Church's holy days with the Old Faith's festivals made it easier for the priests to get a respectable turnout for the services, especially in the country where most of the population still considered themselves pagan. Outside, the city streets had been packed with costumed entertainers, traveling merchants, and celebrating crowds, while in the High Cathedral the bishop was saying the Saints' Day Mass before the royal court. At the culmination of the service, pandemonium had erupted. Objects levitated and smashed into walls. Candlelamps, altar vessels, and stained glass windows shattered. It had been a display of raw uncontrolled sorcerous power.

Dr. Surete had been Court Sorcerer then, and he had immediately sensed the cause of the disturbance. It was Kade.

Galen Dubell, who had been at court working with Surete, admitted that for most of the past two years he had been secretly teaching Kade the rudiments of sorcery. This in itself was not much of a crime. But Kade was the illegitimate daughter of the king. She was older than Roland and courtlaw gave her a claim on the throne. She was also half fay, and elements at court and in the Ministry had been advising Ravenna that Kade was dangerous almost since the girl's birth. The next day Ravenna had banished Dubell to Lodun and sent Kade out of the city to the Monelite Convent, perhaps knowing she would not long remain there. Many had wondered at the time why Ravenna had shown the daughter of her husband's mistress that much mercy, when no one in Ile-Rien except the disgraced Galen Dubell would have objected to Kade's execution. But they knew that Ravenna did everything for her own reasons, and asking for an explanation when none was offered was useless.

In the solar, Ravenna had unintentionally said "my children" and Thomas didn't think she was including the two stillborn girls buried in the High Cathedral's crypt. Ravenna had wanted Kade to be the canny beautiful daughter she had never had, and in some ways she still wanted that. But that was exactly what that brave, daft, strange-eyed sorceress would never be.

There was a clatter as Martin appeared on the landing above and called, "Captain?"

"What is it?" Martin had been sent with the other Queen's guards to see that the palace was secure after the Arlequin's disturbance. Thomas suspected the expression of relief on the young man's face indicated that he was about to pass a thorny problem on to someone else.

"Trouble, Sir," Martin said as Thomas reached him. The young guard led the way off the landing to a short pillared hall. "We just found him. It's Dr. Braun."

On one side of the hall an oaken door stood open. Thomas followed Martin into a small room furnished as a salon which had been used as a waiting room for foreign ambassadors when the Old Hall had been an audience chamber.

Braun lay crumpled on an eastern carpet whose rich color was distorted by his blood. He lay as if he had been sitting on the stool at the high writing desk when he had slumped to the side and fallen to the floor.

Two more Queen's guards waited there, Castero and Baserat. Both were looking at the corpse as if trying to decide what to do with it. Thomas went past them and knelt beside the body. The carpet was soaked with blood and squished unpleasantly underfoot. Carefully he lifted the young sorcerer's head and saw that his throat had been cut. The edges of the wound were straight, not ragged. It had been done smoothly, with a very sharp knife. The body was cold and beginning to stiffen. "Who found him?" he asked.

"I did," Martin said. "We came past this room earlier on the first quick search and missed him. You can't see the body from the door since the secretaire is in the way. When we were working our way back just now doing it thoroughly I walked all the way in and saw him."

"He's cold, so he must have been here before that, Sir," Baserat added.

"Yes, and he must have been killed here," Thomas agreed. The carpet was evidence enough of that. Braun had been leaving from the gallery, going back to the King's Bastion, and must have stepped into the little room to speak to someone. Someone who had come up behind him at some point during the course of the conversation and skillfully slit his throat.

"What is this?" Thomas looked up to see High Minister Aviler standing in the doorway, watching them suspiciously. It wasn't surprising that the High Minister's audience with Ravenna had been a short one; in her current mood it would have been succinct, to say the least. Thomas answered, "At first glance it appears to be a dead man."

"I realize that." Aviler stepped into the room, his long state robes brushing the floor, keeping a wary eye on the other guards. *As he well might,* Thomas thought, if this were really the murder in progress the man obviously half hoped it was. Martin and the others, who were probably still uncertain whether they had neglected their duty and didn't appreciate Aviler's presence as a witness to it, were no doubt helping this impression by their obvious attitudes of belligerence and guilt.

The High Minister came to the edge of the blood-soaked carpet and stopped, frowning, as it became apparent the death was some hours old. "Braun," he said in surprise, recognizing the young sorcerer. "Who did it?"

"That's a good question." *Why? is another good question,* Thomas thought, though he could guess at least part of the answer. *Poor bastard. He said it wasn't important...*

CHAPTER SIX

THE AIR SMELLED like rain. Kade sat on the ledge of the fourth story of the North Bastion, leaning on a stone porpoise and watching the sky. The clouds were gray and heavy, though sunlight broke through in occasional patches. Across the maze of paved courts and formal gardens below were the high walls and steeply pitched roof of the Gallery Wing, more modern and airy in its design than the blocky bastion at her back. It was a cool day, and a damp breeze tore at her hair.

She could feel the wards. They stretched from the bottom of the outer walls to a point high above the palace, forming an invisible, constantly shifting dome. Years ago Galen Dubell had shown her how to use gascoign powder made from hart's horn and crab's eyes to see the corona of light that marked their presence, and to use ash or flakes of charcoal to track their movements. Bad weather tended to push them closer to the earth; perhaps that was why they seemed to be intruding into her thoughts today.

The frid must have slipped in through one of the naturally occurring gaps between the individual wards. If it had blundered directly into one, the harmless powerless creature would have been eaten in an instant. If the motion of the wards was slowing, then the frid—and the golem for that matter—might simply have been lucky enough to slip through. The new sorcerer Braun might have been as incompetent at tending the wards since Dr. Surete's death as he had been at defending himself from whoever killed him. Galen Dubell had only been back a day: not much time to make up lost ground with as complex an etheric structure as the wards.

However it had gotten in, Kade was fairly sure the golem had been sent for her. She had enemies enough among the courts of Fayre, without even considering those among the mortal sorcerers. There were many fay who wanted Moire's strongholds, especially Knockma, and Kade was determined not to give them up.

Someone moving through the garden below reminded her that she was being followed, but the passerby did not glance up. Kade had dodged the men who were watching her, though they probably knew she was somewhere in this bastion. It didn't matter; all she needed was a few moments' privacy.

Seeing Roland and Ravenna again had stirred a whole nest of unpleasant memories. *He stood there and said I cursed the name of our father, as if nothing had ever happened. As if I hadn't held him while he prayed to the Church's God for our father to die,* she thought. Roland was only two years younger than she; he couldn't fail to remember.

Fulstan had always been a frightening presence in their lives, but during Ravenna's long absences from court in the last years of the Bisran War, he had been at his worst. Kade's memories of those times were particularly vivid. The day Fulstan had beaten to death one of Roland's servants, a boy no older than the ten-year-old Prince. *Gods, how can Roland forget that. Those little bones breaking—* In sheer terror Roland had sent away his other young servants, and even his pages, sons of high nobility meant to grow up with him and become his companions and advisors. Fulstan had permitted this, because it had left Roland alone.

Except for me, Kade thought. Looking back, she could see that they should have spoken to someone, that Roland could have sent a letter to Ravenna... As the daughter of the king's supernatural and despised leman, Kade had had fewer options, but neither she nor Roland had been able to believe that a world existed where help was available.

Landlaw expected even a sovereign to be responsible for his behavior, even if courtlaw did not, but Fulstan had been careful. He had made the Cisternans his personal guard instead of the Albon Order, thereby ridding himself of the interfering presence of an Albon Preceptor. He had never done anything to Roland that would leave an outward sign. He had surrounded himself with sycophants and cronies, and he had been a terror to the palace women.

For a long time he had been wary of Kade, perhaps half hoping, half fearing that her mother Moire would return to claim her. He had treated his daughter with contempt, reviled her, held her up to the court as an object of ridicule, but he had never touched her. Until that day of her fifteenth summer, when he had pinned her in a corner of her room and told her that as she grew older her looks were almost passable...

The next day had been Midsummer Eve and the Saints' Day episode in the cathedral. She had been banished to the convent, and six months later Fulstan was dead.

Kade cursed softly to herself, coming back out of the past to the cloudy day and the breeze lifting her hair. *It's no good to think about it; it's over. If Roland hates you for leaving him, that's his decision. You were a prisoner escaping a cell, and you took the first chance you had.* At least that was what Galen Dubell had told her, two years ago at Lodun.

From the open window a few paces along the ledge to her left came the sound of a door squeaking open, then a moment later the muted thump of something heavy being shifted. *That's Galen,* Kade thought, easing herself up the wall to stand on the ledge. The servants never moved anything.

She stepped around the elaborately figured window casement and onto the wooden sill. Galen Dubell was in a corner of his room, piling stacks of books atop a stout wooden chest. He finished and straightened his back with a sigh, turned, and saw her. "Kade."

His expression was disturbingly neutral. She wondered at his lack of reaction. Even though she had never fallen off anything high enough to hurt herself, he hated to see her walk on ledges. She said, "I wrote and told you that I was coming back. Didn't you get the letter?"

"No, I never received it," he said slowly. "I would have tried to dissuade you."

"You told me I should face my anger and that would help me get rid of it. I take it this wasn't exactly what you meant." Kade spoke with a sinking heart. And she had thought her decision to return to the palace to confront her past was sensible and wise.

"Perhaps I didn't know what I meant." He almost smiled. "Perhaps I've become too used to dealing with old men who would rather talk than act. But if this is the way you must do it, then I wish you luck."

"But you don't want me to involve you," she said, and thought, *How calmly that came out.* The wooden window frame was rough against her hand and she realized she was gripping it very tightly.

He held her gaze gravely. "That might be for the best."

It was not what she had wanted to hear. She had wanted him to look exasperated and say, *That wasn't what I meant at all, you little fool; now stop feeling sorry for yourself and come down out of that window.*

"Something is going to happen here, Kade," he was saying. "I don't know what it is yet, but I have to be free to deal with it."

And not be banished again because of me. She said, "I know. It's someone called Grandier."

He frowned. "What do you know about him?"

"He tried to kill you." Kade shrugged.

"He failed."

She shook her head, trying to put the anger away. "The lesser fay won't even speak his name. They're more afraid of him than they are of me. The ones from the higher courts say they've never heard of him, but it's pretense. They wouldn't tell me the truth anyway."

"He's in the city, perhaps closer than anyone realizes. Dr. Braun was killed last night. I'm certain Grandier had something to do with it, and that means he must have someone inside the wall already." Galen let out his breath, his face weary. "I could use your help, but I dare not take it. Do you understand?"

"Yes, well, I suppose I do." She managed not to say it with too poor grace.

He watched her carefully. "And you must give me your word that you won't harm anyone here, no matter what provocation."

Kade couldn't look at him anymore. Her voice was more bitter than she intended. "You know I can't promise that." She slipped out of the window and began to make her way down the ledge to an unused balcony. Behind her, he called with a trace of his old exasperation, "Be careful, damn it."

The guards spotted her again when she had reached the ground floor and was coming out of the entrance into the Rose Court. Kade picked up her skirt and bolted down one of the stone-paved paths between the rosebushes. As she reached the wall of the court, she heard heavy bodies crashing into the thorny and not-so-delicate hedges. The wall was rough and pitted and she scaled it easily.

Reaching the top, she crouched amid the tangled vines and took a quick glance around. As she had seen from above, the area between the bastion and the high walls of the Gallery Wing was a honeycomb of intersecting gardens and courts, some old and familiar and others that were recent additions. She ran lightly along the wall, jumped to a narrower intersecting wall, and ran along its length. She heard a yelp and a crash as the vines on the first wall gave way on someone. As she spun around to look, her lace underskirt caught on a lionhead spout on the wall's rain gutter, throwing her off balance and forcing her to jump down.

She landed heavily in a pile of raked leaves. She was in a long and irregularly shaped garden, with a clipped lawn and overflowing flower borders, most of it rambling out of sight behind the wall and sheltering hedges.

Kade got to her feet and strolled toward the mossy fountain just around the curve of the wall, prepared to be mildly amused when they caught up with her.

In the fountain, water spouted from pitchers in the hands of stone nymphs. Kade wriggled her toes in the cool grass. The garden widened out from this point on, becoming larger and more grand than she had first supposed. In the wide area of lawn were yew bushes shaped into a scaled-down battlement with towers half-circling a large round mosaic of a massive sundial. Distracted, it was moments before her eyes focused on the man and the woman seated on a bench beneath a honeysuckle arbor only a few yards from her; the play of the fountain had covered their voices. It was Queen Falaise and Denzil.

Falaise saw Kade at almost the same moment. She stood, jerking her hand free of Denzil's grasp, and hurried toward her. Kade, who was more used to catching people unawares than being caught, stood there and stared.

The Queen stopped a few feet from her, said uncertainly, "My lady Katherine...ah, Kade?" She wore a dress of rose and pearl and was clutching a small book in a white-knuckled grasp. Like most aristocratic women would have been, she was out of breath from the exertion of walking quickly across the garden. Falaise hadn't been crying, but there was something stricken in her blue eyes that amounted to the same thing.

Kade felt herself looking stupid. She said, "Yes?" hoping to provoke an explanation.

A little desperately, Falaise said, "We had an appointment."

Kade realized that the Queen was not seeing her as a sorceress or as her husband's mad sister, but only as another woman. "An appointment," she repeated helpfully, nodding.

Denzil reached them and caught Falaise's arm again. The Queen flinched and dropped her book, which barely missed the fountain. Kade stooped immediately to rescue it from the damp ground.

Denzil said, "Another appointment, my lady?" His smile was confident and amused. A brief glow of sunlight breaking through the cloudy sky touched his blond hair, the powder blue of has doublet, the gems ornamenting his sword. He and Falaise made a beautiful couple.

Falaise hesitated. "Yes, I..."

"I was late," Kade said, brushing dirt off the little book's sheepskin binding.

"Yes, she was," Falaise agreed instantly. She stepped away from Denzil, the movement stiff and awkward.

He chuckled and bowed slightly to make the point that he was allowing her to escape. "Then I'll leave you to your appointment."

His arrogance was too obvious for Kade to leave well enough alone. "Do that," she said.

Amused and ironic, he met her eyes and bowed. "My lady."

They watched him cross the garden toward the gate behind the hedges. Kade didn't know Denzil very well. He had been presented to court shortly before she had left. He had attached himself to Roland shortly thereafter.

There was nothing she hated more than people who didn't take her seriously.

Falaise sat down on the edge of the fountain, heedless of what the moss would do to her silk damask skirts.

This near to the Queen, Kade was suddenly conscious that the climb on the bastion's ledge and her fall into the leaves hadn't done her dress any good. But her grubbiness was bound to aggravate Ravenna, and she resolved to let her clothing degenerate as far as modesty allowed. "Where are your guards?" she asked Falaise.

Falaise shook her head slightly. "This is my private garden. When I give audiences here they wait beside the gate. I bribed my ladies to go down to the grotto."

"Why didn't you call them back?"

"That wouldn't do any good." Her face was bleak.

Falaise had the calm of someone who has been miserable for a long time and expects to go on being miserable. Kade shifted uneasily. "It's difficult for someone to make advances when there are a lot of men standing around looking at him as if they want to kill him. They're Queen's guards; even Roland can't order them away when they're protecting you."

Falaise looked away wearily, the wind playing with her curls and ribbons. "It isn't that sort of advances."

"It doesn't matter what sort of advances. It always worked for Ravenna's ladies when..." *When my father...* "when they needed it," she finished, but Falaise didn't notice the lapse.

"He wouldn't let me call them."

Kade snorted. "Do it anyway."

"It's easy for you to say." Falaise gestured helplessly, the puffed sleeves of her gown almost hiding the movement. Kade watched her a moment, then sat on the fountain rim beside her. "Not always."

But Falaise opened the book on her lap and turned the pages distractedly. By craning her neck Kade could see it was written instead of printed, and by a hand not as fine as a professional clerk's. Poetry, she guessed, and it would hardly be from Roland. Falaise slammed the book closed and said abruptly, "What do I call you, Katherine or Kade?"

"Kade."

"Kade. Did you ever turn yourself into a bird?" Her expression was wistful.

Kade lifted her brows. "I thought about it, but I decided I wanted to live." It came to her that Falaise wasn't really much of a coward. Denzil must have browbeaten her thoroughly. Possibly most men in authority over her had browbeaten her thoroughly. "Human sorcerers can't shape-change, not if they ever want to turn back into themselves. Most fay can, but I never had to badly enough to make the experiment."

"That's a shame." Falaise fingered the book again. "It would be wonderful to just turn into something and fly away."

They sat in the quiet a moment, with not even birds to interrupt the fountain's bubbling. Then Kade remembered something and asked her, "What did you mean when you said Denzil wasn't making that sort of—"

A man came running around one of the yew hedges toward them. He threw himself at Falaise's feet so enthusiastically Kade had to scramble out of the way to avoid being tumbled into the fountain.

More graceful than the sorceress, Falaise kept her balance and said in exasperation, "Aristofan, please—"

The young man kneeling at her feet was handsome with russet hair and eager brown eyes. He was dressed for court in blue and gray and had lost his feathered hat in his run across the lawn. "It was him, wasn't it? That was why you didn't want me to come to you today. You must tell me what he wants from you."

Kade looked down at herself to make sure she hadn't inadvertently faded from sight.

"No, I can't, I told you." Falaise spoke firmly, but then she stroked his hair. "Really, it's all right."

"Don't mind me," Kade said. "I'll just stand over here, shall I?"

Aristofan clasped the Queen's hand ardently. "Don't you trust me? I'd do anything for you."

Falaise smiled fondly. "Sometimes I almost think you would."

One of the men following Kade appeared at the top of the wall, spotted her, and waved back to his companions. "Well," Kade said, "I have to leave before they decide I'm holding you prisoner and roll in a couple of cannon."

"Please." Falaise looked up at her. "You won't say anything?"

"I don't know anything." Kade started away, then stopped and looked back at the other woman. "If you're going to tell someone, tell Ravenna."

Falaise looked down at Aristofan's head, her expression drawn and troubled.

To avoid Falaise's guards, Kade left the garden by going over the wall behind the battlement hedge. She was still not quite ready to be followed again, and she rejoined the path that led away from the Queen's garden only when she was out of sight of the garden gates. The path wandered past walled herb gardens then abruptly opened out to the paved area below the terraces of the Gallery Wing. The smooth stone of the Gallery Wing's walls was butter colored and would glow like gold in the full sunlight. She climbed the steps and walked along the terrace, looked at the view of the rolling lawn, the trees, and the artificial temple ruins, and wondered about Galen Dubell.

I'm not going to sit like a lump while he fights this Bisran bastard Grandier single-handed. Does he honestly expect me to do that? No, he couldn't, she decided. It was incredible. If she were going to behave in that ridiculous fashion to one of the few friends she had, then she might as well have stayed in the convent and saved years of trouble. *Galen isn't an idiot. Grandier trapped him once; he might do it again. He knows he needs help; he just can't ask for it.*

She stopped, drew a toe meditatively over a pattern in the paving stone. She was tired of being followed.

Kade closed her eyes and pulled glamour out of the damp air and the dew on the grass, wove it with the afternoon sunlight filtered through the clouds, and drew it over herself like a concealing blanket. If anyone saw her she would appear as another courtier, a servant, whatever they expected to see.

She would help Dubell, and she had an inkling of how to go about it.

⁙

"Well, that's been a waste of time," Thomas told Lucas.

They had just finished questioning the last of Dr. Braun's apprentices and servants and had elicited nothing but a tearful confession from the sixty-year-old chamberlain about a few pennies' worth of misappropriated household funds.

During the questioning, Lucas had been entertaining himself by flipping a small boot dagger from hand to hand, and now he sent it into the table with a thud. "So, who killed the poor bastard? The chamberlain?"

The room was damp and too warm, despite the open window. Thomas stood up from the table piled with papers and moved restlessly to the room's little balcony, unbuttoning the top of his doublet. From here he could look down onto the hall where servants wandered, off-duty guards gathered, and the main life of the Queen's Guard House was concentrated. He leaned against the rough pillar in the corner of the balcony and said, "He's too short. Braun was sitting at a clerk's writing desk and the stool was a foot or so taller than an ordinary chair. Whoever cut the good doctor's throat was at least my height. The way that old man's back is bent he'd never have been able to reach him."

On the stone-paved floor of the hall below, some of the men had discarded their doublets to practice swordplay on wooden targets and one another. Constant work was required to keep in top form for the real duels, which usually lasted no more than a few moments, depending on the relative skill of the opponents, and often ended with a death or a crippling. All used their regular dueling swords rather than the blunt-tipped weapons often employed for practice, and it was only due to the skill of the combatants that so little blood was being shed. There were not as many men off-duty as usual; all the guardposts and duty shifts had been doubled since last night.

All this morning Thomas had noted a tension on the wind that hadn't been there yesterday. Everyone knew the danger of dark and deserted places, but the palace had always been safe ground from any but human opponents. Two Cisternan guards had been sent back to their families in boxes today, the first casualties in a new and uncertain war. The rest of the court had also finally bothered to notice the danger, and today there were complaints, mild hysteria, and loud questions about why someone wasn't doing something.

"If you're going to be clever about it, we won't be able to arrest anyone," Lucas pointed out.

The pillar Thomas leaned against still bore the nine-year-old bullet hole that had signaled the end of his predecessor's career. He picked at the splintered area thoughtfully and said, "We're looking for a throat-slitter who takes an unprepared man from behind but who still scruples at robbery." Braun had been wearing a respectable amount of court jewelry, including a diamond-studded presentation medal from Lodun and several gemstones given to him by past wealthy patrons. All had been left on the body. "That eliminates most of the servants but certainly throws suspicion on every member of the nobility in the palace. And Grandier."

Lucas tipped his chair back against the yellowed plaster wall. "Always Grandier. What did Braun have that Grandier would want to kill him for?"

"Information." And thinking of information, Thomas wished the clerks would hurry with the translation of the documents chronicling Grandier's trial in Bisra. They knew so little about the man, and he wanted to take advantage of every resource, no matter how sparse it might be.

Lucas nodded. "You think Braun saw something someone preferred he didn't..."

"Or remembered something. He tried to talk to me last night but we were interrupted by Denzil."

"Coincidence?" Lucas lifted his brows in speculation.

Thomas glanced back at him. "Which coincidence? Braun wanting to tell me something or Denzil interrupting at the opportune moment?"

"We're not going to get anywhere if you keep inventing new questions." Lucas glanced briefly toward the window, which opened onto the narrow alley between the house and the stone wall of the old armory. "Half the palace is saying that it was the sorceress."

"Not a bad suggestion, except she was already in the gallery performing bad Commedia in front of everyone who matters in the city when I saw Braun alive. The body was long cold by the time she left." Thomas shook his head. She was also too short. "Today she lost her guards in the Queen's garden. One of them reported it an hour ago."

"What was she doing there?"

"Talking to the Queen, apparently."

"Odd." Lucas frowned, looking puzzled at the idea that anyone might want to talk to Falaise. Possibly because they were all so used to discounting her influence, it was hard to remember that she had any power in her own right at all. "What's going to come of that, do you think?"

"Not much." Thomas smiled. "They can't banish Falaise."

Lucas was silent a moment, watching Thomas. "Your great friend High Minister Aviler is implying it was a Queen's guard."

Thomas's lips twisted in annoyance. "What a helpful suggestion. How in hell did he come up with it?"

Lucas shrugged uneasily. "The usual way. There was some loud muttering about Braun, some of the men blaming him for his incompetence when you were trying to get Galen Dubell out of Grandier's house. Braun was never half the help old Dr. Surete was."

"So one of them takes it on himself to remove the irritant? It's unlikely." But Gideon had said something about Braun last night. And Lucas clearly believed it was a possibility, though he wouldn't say it outright.

Thomas was struck by an unpleasant image. Braun, unable to find Thomas in the crowded gallery, stopping a faceless Queen's guard on a deserted stair. Asking him to take a message to his captain, stepping into a quiet parlor to use the writing desk... But Thomas had always seen Braun as a pitiable figure, and the young sorcerer had been coldly eliminated in a way that didn't agree with the theory of a guard murdering him in sudden anger. Then again, Braun was a sorcerer and would surely have had some means of defending himself; he would almost have to be taken from behind...

The door creaked as a servant opened it to usher in Ephraim, the ragged ballad-seller and professional spy. "Good news?" Thomas asked as the old man grinned and bowed to both of them.

Ephraim pulled off his cloth cap and began to knead it conversationally. "In a manner of speaking, Sir. It's quite a tale. The Gambin lad's dead, you see."

If he had his throat slit around the same time as Braun did, I'm going to retire, Thomas thought, and kept the surprise off his face. "What happened?"

"From the beginning it was that a couple of my own boys followed Gambin to see if he would lead us to the fellow who hired him, and he led them a merry way, Sir, but he ended up back at the palace quarter and entered Lord Lestrac's house." Ephraim hesitated. Not from trepidation, but more as if he were still trying to sort things out in his own mind. "After a bit he came out, and the boys followed Gambin on a wandering way back to his home ground, and waited outside his house, as they hadn't any instructions to do otherwise. Before dawn this morning a young woman arrives, and she goes in and starts to scream. The boys figured they should go in and see what the matter was, and as Gambin didn't know either of them they could say they were passersby. Well, they didn't have to say much at all, because Gambin was dead, you see, without a mark on him.

"When I got there I sent for a lady who lives down in the Philosopher's Cross and knows a bit about these things, and in her opinion it had the look of a wicked sending about it, though I never heard of Gambin to trouble with sorcerers before. She said it was most likely in something he was given, some token, that was enspelled to murder the lad whenever the master was finished and didn't want the likes of anyone asking questions. It cost extra for her to search for the token, and I thought you'd want your own people to do that, so I locked up the house and came on here."

"You've done your best," Thomas told him, preoccupied. This was another piece in the puzzle. And it was a damn good thing he had set Ephraim on this job; without him, it might have been days before news of Gambin's death reached Thomas, and the evidence of sorcery in the killing might have been gone by then. "Tell them to get you a drink, and the Paymaster has your fee."

Ephraim's bow was unpolished but sincere. "Oh, that's very good of you, Captain."

When the spy had left, Lucas grimaced. "Well, well. Lord Lestrac is our nameless letter-forger, and Gambin is silenced the same way you think Dr. Surete and Milam were. Another connection to Grandier?"

"Maybe." The attempt with the letters was the sort of unsubtle ineffective trick Denzil's friends were famous for in their attempts to please him, and of which the Duke unconcernedly let them suffer the consequences. "It almost seems as if there are two different men, or factions, at work. Grandier with his sorcery, and then someone else plaguing us with little distractions. Gambin was hired by the second man, and when he was compromised, Grandier killed him."

"If they're working together. They might not be." Lucas worked his dagger out of the table, frowning at it. "There's no way to tell."

Thomas bit his lip thoughtfully, considering his options. He said, "I want you to send men to search Gambin's house and pick up the body; I'll want an opinion on it from Dubell."

"How lovely for him," Lucas said dryly, getting to his feet. "You know, if I'm not mistaken, Lestrac is also a friend of Denzil's. I think the good Duke of Alsene maintains that house for him."

"He does. And it was searched by the King's Watch about two days ago. They didn't discover anything." Lestrac's house was one of a group of manses for royal dependents that were built up against the outside of the palace's west wall. Lestrac was a landless dissipated young nobleman, useful occasionally as a tool for Denzil but not much else. He had never been implicated in one of Denzil's plots deeply enough to send him to the traitors' graves outside the city, but he assisted Roland's cousin in the spreading of rumors and lies. Thinking it over, Thomas shook his head. "Even if we did connect a friend of Denzil's to Grandier, it won't prove anything to Roland. To convince him we'd have to catch Denzil standing over the royal bed with a drawn sword, and even then I'm not sure he'd believe it."

"Lestrac was supposed to have dabbled in black magic in his wilder days, and bargained with demons, like Grandier. The letters might have been his own idea, and he could have killed Gambin himself," Lucas pointed out.

Thomas wasn't convinced. "I heard he dabbled, but I never heard he dabbled all that successfully. Finding the token should settle it. Have them be especially careful of anything valuable on Gambin's body. If I were Grandier, I would have put the spell on the payment that was given him." He paused. "I'll see Lestrac myself."

Lucas frowned. "Will you take Dubell with you?"

Thomas shook his head. "He's still a target for Grandier and I'm not sure I want to risk him. He may be the only protection the palace has."

Lucas eyed him, not happily. "So you go to Lestrac's house where Grandier is hiding and he kills you because Galen Dubell is safe back here. Does that make sense?"

Thomas had to concede the point. "It's not a perfect plan, I'll admit. I'll take one of Braun's apprentices. They aren't completely useless."

"Or take me."

Kade Carrion was sitting in the window, perfectly composed, the ragged hem of her dress tucked under her feet. How she had gotten there without either one of them hearing her was incredible; from her attitude she might have been there for the past hour.

"What are you doing here?" Lucas asked, so startled he dropped a hand to his sword.

Her look said she suspected his sanity. "Listening. Next you'll ask me how much I heard, to which I'll very likely reply 'enough.' Can't we dispense with all that?"

Lucas looked at his captain and raised an eyebrow inquiringly. Thomas shook his head minutely, and asked Kade, "Take you where?"

She made an impatient gesture. "To what's-his-name's house where you think Grandier is."

Thomas leaned back against the pillar and folded his arms. "Why do you want to go?"

She rolled her eyes in exasperation. "I'm offering to help."

"And in such a touching and spontaneous way. If I refuse your help?"

She appeared to seriously consider the question. "I might follow anyway. I'm good at that. Or not. I might do a lot of things; the day is young."

This was ominous. "And I'm expected to trust you?"

Apparently outraged, she sat up straight against the window casement and said, "I gave my word."

"No, you did not." Thomas was fairly certain he would have recalled that.

"I did."

"When?"

He saw her hesitate, then she gave in and grinned. She said, "So I didn't. Come on, you know you want me to go. I'm lucky."

"Lucky for whom?" Lucas muttered.

"This isn't a game," Thomas said, wary. She had her own brand of charm, that was certain. And Thomas realized that even against his will he was tempted by that charm. *Because she's different, or because she's dangerous?* he asked himself, irritated. *Stop being ridiculous and concentrate.* "You've said you want to help, but you haven't told me why. And you haven't been terribly helpful in the past."

"The past is the past." Kade tilted her head to one side, watching him with those very direct eyes. "Grandier would have killed Galen Dubell, who is my oldest friend." She finished lightly, "I can't have that, can I?"

Trusting her was a decided risk, but if Grandier was in that house, or had been there and left more traps, Kade would be their best hope. And so far Thomas had come across nothing to suggest that she was the Bisran sorcerer's ally. *And this is certainly one way to find her out if she is.* He said, "Very well."

CHAPTER SEVEN

THE HOUSES THAT clustered against the palace's west wall presented blank stone façades to the public, most of their life and wealth turned inward. The clouds had closed up overhead and a light rain had started, settling the dust and washing away the habitual stench of the street, preparing to turn it into a river of mud. Street vendors who sold ribbons, trinkets, foodstuffs, and amulets to protect against night-dwelling fay were gathered in damp clumps around the pillars of the promenade that faced the line of houses. Coaches splashed by, trying to reach their destinations before the storm started in earnest; few of the wealthier residents were abroad at this hour, and most had retreated into the rich shops further under the sheltering roof of the promenade. The street was mostly unobserved, for which Thomas was glad. He hated an audience for this sort of work.

Lestrac's house was four stories topped by a steeply pitched red tile roof, set between the towering residence of a ship owner and the winter home of a minor noble.

Rain dripping off his hat, Thomas stepped back to look up at the barred windows while Castero banged on the door. Another Queen's guard tried the double carriage doors while the others spread out in front of the house and attempted to look innocuous. There was no back alley and no other exit. He had brought twenty men, which was overkill if this was Lestrac's own plot. If Grandier himself was in there despite the earlier search by the King's Watch, the entire troop might not be enough.

There was no answer at the door. Thomas started to tell Castero to break it in when he glanced down and found Kade Carrion at his elbow. The water that was beading on his dark cloak was dripping from her hair and her dingy red dress. She had appeared so suddenly it was possible that she had simply risen out of the mud. She had been investigating the street on her own, wandering about in a random fashion and poking around doorways. "There's someone in there," she said positively.

Thomas eyed her. "Is it warded?"

She stared at the door, brows drawn down in concentration. "No. It should be."

"Open it," Thomas told Castero.

The guard drew his pistol and used the heavy butt to pound the lock. The wood around it cracked and Castero used his shoulder. As he struck the door it swung backward and came off its hinges.

Kade slipped past Thomas almost before the door gave way. As she ducked inside Castero jumped back and muttered, "Pardon me."

If it's a trap, she's determined to spring it first. Thomas signaled Baserat and another two guards to stand watch outside and followed her, drawing his rapier.

Inside was a high-ceilinged area with a stone staircase curving up the wall to the second-floor entrance. The floor was stone paved, and a black coach with polished brass fittings stood in front of the carriage doors. Light came in through high narrow windows in the outside wall. There was stabling beneath the stairs, and Thomas nodded for one of his men to investigate it. Kade was halfway up the steps. Thomas called to her, "Give us a moment, please." She threw her arms up in exasperation, but stopped, tapping her foot impatiently.

The guard flushed a couple of frightened grooms out of the stalls where they had been attempting to hide. From the number of horses stabled there, Lestrac was indeed home and entertaining.

Thomas put two more men to watch the servants and to keep any fugitives from escaping behind them, then headed toward the stairs, the others following him. Kade was off again as soon as he started up. Behind him, Castero whispered, "Captain, should we let her go first? I mean, she is a woman."

"Presumably she knows that," Thomas told him.

At the top of the steps, just before the wooden doors, Kade stopped them with an outflung arm. After a moment of intense study of the dirty stone of the landing, she tore a scrap of cloth from her skirt hem, licked it, and stooped to rub it over some invisible spot on the flagstones. Something came away bright blue, and Kade flicked the cloth over the edge of the landing.

"A ward, but it wasn't working anymore. It was old," she admitted, and stepped up to push the door open.

It was the first room of a suite of salons, the dying embers in the hearth revealing landscape paintings, papered walls, heavy oak cabinets, and brocaded chairs. Sprawled around on the fine furnishings and all drunk into unconsciousness were three young men Thomas recognized as sprigs of nobility and two women whose elaborate and revealing costumes proclaimed them upper-class bawds. A bottle had broken on the floor and wine had seeped into the carpet. From the smell, they had been lacing the stuff with syrup of poppies. Some of the candles were still lit, their holders half-buried under bizarre shapes of dripped wax.

"We've interrupted a party," Thomas told Castero, who grinned, and tipped one of the unconscious young men off a couch.

"A dull one," Kade said, looking around with a puzzled expression.

Thomas considered her a moment, suddenly recalling that she was a member of the royal family and had spent some of her youth in a convent, then decided to let it go. If he had known Lestrac was going to be hosting an orgy, he would have reconsidered allowing Kade to accompany them into the upstairs rooms, but he was damned if he was going to say anything about it now.

"A livelier brood in here, Captain," one of the guards called from ahead, and Thomas followed him into the next room.

There were five of them in a central parlor, and they had leapt up from a card table, overturning their chairs, fumbling clumsily for swords. They were all drunk, though not quite to the advanced stage of their companions in the other room. "What is this?" one of them demanded muzzily. Thomas thought he might be the second son of the Count of Belennier, though he wasn't certain. He ignored the question and nodded to the guard who was covering them with a pistol, who immediately said, "Drop your swords, gentlemen."

While they disarmed, Thomas quietly told Castero, "Leave a few men down here to watch this lot, and take the others on ahead to search the rest of the house. Lestrac is the one I want."

"What about me?" Kade whispered, standing at his elbow again.

"You go with him," Thomas snapped.

"Why?"

"You're here to spring sorcerous traps, not to stand about and be entertained by me."

"Oh. My mistake." She didn't sound particularly chastened, but she followed Castero and the others.

Turning back to the group held at bay, Thomas suddenly recognized what he had thought at first to be a completely unfamiliar face. It was the dark-haired stranger he had seen with Denzil at the disastrous court last night. There was nothing unusual about him; he had the same pale bedraggled look as the others, the early lines on his face that came from too much drinking. But there was something about his eyes... Guarding a queen of stubborn and definite opinions in the crowded courts had made Thomas preternaturally sensitive, and people who were hiding something usually betrayed it in some way, either in look or gesture or simply by the way they stood. This man was hiding something.

The object under scrutiny seemed to realize he was being watched, and swayed a little against the table. Thomas smiled to himself. *He's also not as drunk as he's pretending.* "Where's Lestrac?" Thomas asked the group in general.

"He's about somewhere," answered the second son of the Count of Belennier, who seemed to have elected himself the spokesman. "You'll pay for this, forcing your way into a gentleman's house—"

"I'll discuss that with the gentleman in question."

"Well, he's about somewhere." The young man stared around blearily, as if expecting Lestrac to suddenly appear.

"How long have you been here?"

"Oh, all day." Recalling he was outraged, he protested, "And you've no right to question us, if it's Lestrac you're after."

And he's about somewhere. That would be all Thomas could get out of them until he actually produced Lestrac, but the chances were they hadn't been here yesterday when Gambin had visited the house. At least, if Lestrac had any sense at all they wouldn't have been here.

"Don't let them talk to each other," Thomas told the guard with the pistol, and moved on after the others.

They went from one well-appointed room to another and up the central staircase to the third floor, the guards spreading out to search more thoroughly as Kade flitted before them checking for magical traps.

After a short while, it became apparent that the only inhabitants were those they had already discovered and that Lord Lestrac was nowhere to be found. Thomas and Castero met back in a central parlor on the second floor.

"He must be on the run, Captain." The young guard absently kicked a chair.

"Unfortunately." Thomas looked around, one eyebrow lifted in an ironic appraisal of the empty room. It seemed clear. Lestrac had used Gambin in a minor plot against Thomas. When it failed to have the expected result, Lestrac had panicked, used magic to dispose of Gambin, and fled. "How very neat and tidy." The other guests had been herded into the next salon under guard. A few had families influential enough that they would have to be released, but Thomas hated to do it before he knew where Lestrac had gone. Each one was a potential accomplice.

Kade wandered into the room from the stairwell. She looked around, apparently in a state of deep consternation. "It's here. I don't know what, but it's here. And it's not." She moved around the room, touching things, stooping to look under the furniture.

Madwoman, Thomas thought. But the longer he was in the house the more suspicious it seemed to him. There was more here than appeared, or something out of place, and he wasn't willing to leave until he found what it was.

Kade straightened suddenly. Her examination of the parlor had led her to the far wall. "How many rooms on this floor?"

Castero stared at her. "Nine."

"Eleven upstairs." Thomas saw what she was getting at, and suddenly realized what was wrong about the place. It was the position of the stairwell in relation to the second floor. He went to stand beside the sorceress and ran a hand across the paneled wall. "Look at the way the top of this meets the ceiling. It's a false wall. There must be a moving panel or—"

Kade said, "No, not a panel." She placed a palm on the center of the wall and leaned in, whispering to it. Thomas stepped back as the shape of a door slowly formed out of the dark wood, as if a sculptor were molding it out of clay. Grinning with triumph, Kade stepped back as it solidified.

As she was reaching for the handle, Thomas caught a handful of her tattered smock and hauled her out of the way. He stepped to one side of the door, motioning for Castero to take the other. Castero stepped hastily into position, winding his pistol. At Thomas's elbow, Kade was silently bouncing with excitement.

Thomas twisted the handle and flung the door open.

It was a banqueting room with a long table and sideboards, lit by a dripping candelabrum and chandeliers. There was a man seated at the end of the table, slumped over forward.

Thomas advanced cautiously toward him. There was a half-empty wine bottle on the table, two more on the floor beneath it.

Thomas used a handful of the man's unkempt blond hair to pull him upright. It was Lestrac. The lean, dissipated features were slack and sickly red.

His eyes didn't focus, and the pupils were so wide they seemed to cover most of the white. His breath was quick and panting, as if he were running for his life. *It's poison,* Thomas realized. *Belladonna or henbane, something that the Aderassi are always using to put each other out of the way.* Holding the young lord up, he could feel his burning skin. "Who did this to you, Lestrac? Was it Grandier?"

The dying eyes seemed finally to focus. "No, no, not him..." Lestrac shuddered weakly, the effort of speaking almost too much.

"But you know him. Was he here?"

"No, he's... He told me he'd teach...power. I should have known."

"Where is he now?"

"It was Dontane, on Grandier's orders," Lestrac said suddenly, his voice growing stronger. He made a convulsive movement and caught the front of Thomas's doublet "Captain Boniface, you've got to get that bastard Dontane." Lestrac started to slide out of the chair and Thomas caught him and shoved him back. The nobleman's head lolled and his eyes were wide open and staring, though he still breathed. Thomas let him go and stepped back. That was it, Lestrac would stay like this, impossible to wake, until he died in a few hours. *But they've made a mistake, perhaps their first,* Thomas thought. Someone, perhaps Lestrac himself when he hired Gambin, had acted out of turn, revealing that Grandier had the help of others who could come and go inside the palace. *And if Denzil isn't involved somehow...* He told Castero, "Send someone for the men from the gate watch. We're going to tear this place apart."

As Castero left, Kade did a quick circuit of the room, checking the walls for more concealed doors. Watching her, Thomas knew that at least to some extent she was enjoying herself, and that she certainly didn't give a damn for the fact that Lestrac had all but expired a few moments ago. He didn't know why that should bother him, since he didn't care either and knew that if even half of what he suspected was true, Lestrac would have been executed anyway. And to some extent he was also enjoying himself. Perhaps her reaction annoyed him because it was so much in tune with his own.

Kade had drifted back to the table and now took the wine bottle and emptied the last of its contents onto the polished surface. She stirred the pool twice with a finger and stared into it intently.

Unwilling to ask, Thomas stepped up behind her to see what she was doing.

Without looking up, she reached out and grabbed his wrist. Before he could pull away, he saw a shadow come over the wine pool and something move within it. It was a man. At first the image was shifting and muddy like a poor mirror, but abruptly it cleared, revealing the face of the man in the other room, the man who had been with Denzil at court last night.

Kade said quietly, "I thought so. He was in here, and they fought, or at least argued. Violent emotions always make the strongest impressions."

She let Thomas go and he stepped back, and the pool became only spilled wine again. He hadn't realized until then how the sounds of his men searching the next room and the occasional drunken protests of Lestrac's friends had temporarily faded as the picture appeared in the pool. "Is he a sorcerer? Did he conceal the door?"

"Maybe. But that one might have done it, too." She nodded toward Lestrac's still form. "You said he knew some of the art, and it wasn't a very powerful illusion, though it was tricky."

Thomas nodded to himself. "He brought Dontane in here, Dontane killed him, then walked out through the unconcealed door on this side. He stayed with the others to make sure Lestrac didn't come staggering out gasping accusations. He must have known how long it would take to die from the stuff. Any later and we would have missed him."

Kade looked thoughtful, then turned for the door, remarking pointedly, "Well, I'm certainly glad I bothered to come."

After considering Lestrac's slumped body a moment more, he followed her.

Later, Thomas had the guards carry Lestrac out past the group gathered in the parlor. Leaning on the billiard table, which was extravagantly covered in green velvet and lit by candleholders mounted on its raised sides, he watched the nobles react with varied degrees of befuddled shock. Including Dontane, whose reaction was perfectly in keeping with the rest.

"When do we carry out this lot, Captain?" Castero asked.

"Now. Take them to the Cisternan Guard House for the present." He touched one of the silver bells fitted above the billiard table's goal. "All except Dontane."

Dontane looked up, but if he was startled he concealed it well. As Castero and the other guards herded Lestrac's guests out, Thomas waited patiently. When they were gone, that left Dontane, three watchful guards at the door, and Kade, who was sitting on top of a sideboard and swinging her feet. As Thomas looked at her and started to speak, she announced, "I've been a help, and shown quite a bit of restraint, and I think I should be allowed to stay and watch."

It was harder than Thomas would've thought to conceal his smile. He said, "Well put."

Watching them with contempt, Dontane said, "I assume there is some reason for my being singled out." He swayed slightly and steadied himself on a chair.

"You assume correctly." Thomas watched him a moment more, wondering how long the playacting would last. "How long have you known Lord Lestrac?"

"Not long. But I am a friend of the Duke of Alsene."

"That puts you in the minority, then, because no one else here is." It would have been foolish to deny the connection; Dontane must realize he would've been seen at court last night. *And why attend court at all, except to activate the golem so it could attack a certain sorceress.* Thomas folded his arms, deciding on a more direct attack. "I know you poisoned Lestrac."

Dontane drew himself up. "That is an insult, and I will challenge you for it." He stiffened resentfully as one of the guards at the door chuckled.

The man was certainly presenting a good performance of a foolish young noble. Thomas said, "You were in that room with Lestrac. Were you discussing a spy named Gambin, perhaps?"

"I don't know what you're talking about."

"He's lying," Kade interrupted.

"Yes, thank you, I know," Thomas told her patiently.

"I suppose I should be flattered that you find it necessary to have your pet witch here to deal with me," Dontane sneered. But he had lost a little of his pretense of drunken nonchalance. Thomas thought Kade's presence was making the man uneasy. *As well it might.*

"'Pet witch.' I like that," Kade said, apparently addressing the blue faience vase sitting next to her on the sideboard. "I'm going to put a curse on him."

"If you can't be quiet you'll have to leave, pet," Thomas said.

Kade turned a look of narrow-eyed reproach on him, then regarded Dontane with so much sly malice it had to be artificial.

Thomas studied him thoughtfully a moment, then asked, "Are you a sorcerer?"

Dontane's expression was calm. "I am not."

"Then are you a dabbler in magic, like Lestrac?" He hadn't forgotten the young lord's last words: *he said he'd teach power.* If one had a taste of power, enough to hide a door by illusion, or to witch a useless spy dead, the temptation to learn more at the hands of a master like Grandier might be over-whelming.

"No, I am not," Dontane said, looking away in disgust.

Had he hesitated, deciding how to answer? "Is he a sorcerer?" Thomas asked Kade.

She dug a moment in the pocket of her smock, and when she drew her hand out her fingers were covered with a dark powdery substance. She touched her forefinger carefully to the corner of each eye, then looked up at Dontane.

He smiled, scornfully. "Well, witch?"

She held his eyes a moment, then said, "I think he knew what I was doing."

Dontane snorted derision and looked away. Watching him carefully, Thomas asked, "And what was that?"

"Putting gascoign powder in my eyes. If he had been using a spell, or if there had been a spell on him, I would see it. It doesn't prove he isn't a sorcerer."

Dontane smiled. "Alchemical powders are hardly a secret."

"Maybe," Thomas agreed. He had heard of gascoign powder as well, but that explanation for Kade's actions hadn't immediately leapt to mind. If Dontane wasn't trained in the craft of sorcery, he had at least been much around those who were. "Where's Grandier keeping himself these days?"

"Who? I don't know the name." It was said admirably, with just the right amount of confusion.

Thomas smiled. "Then you must have been under a bushel. Everyone else knows it." After Dr. Braun's murder, rumor had spread out of control in court circles and Urbain Grandier's name had been prominent, though with-out any real detail.

Dontane's expression froze and for a moment he looked dangerous, and not at all like the drunken puppies that Castero had herded out.

Dangerous, Thomas thought, *but weak, like Lestrac. Someone's useful tool.* He said, "You will be glad to know that I am extending the hospitality of the pal-ace to you."

"You'll regret this." Dontane had gathered up the remains of his façade, and spoke with drunken arrogance.

"I'm sure one of us will," Thomas agreed.

It was evening by the time they returned to the palace. The rain had stopped but the clouds still obscured the stars and the waning moon. Thomas had seen the prisoners settled in the Cisternan Barracks, with Dontane in one of the cells specially warded against the use of sorcery. Then he set off through the corridor within the outer wall toward the King's Bastion. He wanted to find Lucas and hear what they had found at Gambin's house, though he suspected it wouldn't be much. The answers he needed would have to be pried out of Dontane. It was pure luck they had managed to catch him at all.

Pure luck, and Kade, who had disappeared again after they passed through the Prince's Gate, taking her confused motives with her. She couldn't be here simply to cause trouble. Thomas might have realized Lestrac's hidden room was there without her help, but he would never have gotten into it in time to question the dying noble.

He climbed the rough-cut stone staircase that angled up into the King's Bastion. The tapestry-concealed entrance on the third floor gave onto a long central mirror-lined gallery, which was unusually crowded and noisy for this time of night.

Thomas made his way past a group of loudly talking courtiers and saw the cause of the excitement.

Denzil was dueling with Aristofan, Queen Falaise's poet-companion. They had stripped to their shirts and were stalking each other up and down the length of the candlelit room. The young poet was intent but breathing hard, and was obviously having the more difficult time. Denzil, his blond hair tied back, was moving with easy grace and confidence. It was the social event of the night, the women watching from behind fluttering fans, the men commenting on the performance and quietly placing wagers.

Thomas joined Lucas, who was watching from the sidelines with the old Count of Duncanny and a few other bystanders. "How did it start?" Thomas asked him.

Lucas shrugged. "The boy accused Denzil of insulting the Queen in some way and Denzil challenged him. It's all very mysterious. Neither will say exactly what the insult was."

Arms folded and eyes critical, the old count said, "I don't think they know."

Most duels were sparked by boredom. Courtiers and city-dwelling nobles with little to do except drink, gamble, and argue fought over everything from their wives' honor to the score of card games. This one had a certain impromptu look; there were no seconds and they were fighting in the flickering inadequate light of the long gallery.

Face shining with exertion, Aristofan was quick to take advantage of the openings in Denzil's guard, but his blade never seemed to connect. After a few moments, Thomas recognized Denzil's technique, which was one he had often used himself for training inexperienced swordsmen. Denzil was completely controlling the fight by maintaining a constant distance between himself and the young poet. Denzil was the taller man, and with his longer reach and better control, Aristofan hadn't even a chance of wounding him.

The Duke of Alsene was using a special dueling sword with a black metal cup hilt that matched his main gauche. Thomas noticed Aristofan was using a businesslike dueling rapier. "Where did he get that sword?" He looked at Lucas.

Lucas shifted uncomfortably. "You should have seen the one I took away from him. The boy was going to try to defend himself with a piece of jewelry."

Thomas snorted. "Getting sentimental in our old age, are we?"

"Won't help," the count said quietly.

Thomas sensed movement near him and looked down to find Kade Carrion at his elbow again, watching the fight with a faint look of contempt. He was beginning to wonder if the woman was intentionally following him. As if aware her presence had been noted, she asked, "What's this about?"

Several nearby watchers looked around at the shabby figure of the sorceress in surprise, having not realized she was there until that moment. Thomas said, "Possibly the Queen's honor, possibly nothing. Public opinion is divided at the moment."

She glanced up at him suspiciously. "Oh."

Denzil was continuing to play with Aristofan, turning the duel into a cat-and-mouse game Thomas began to find repellent. *He should end it. Bastard.*

Kade asked suddenly, "Are the rumors about Denzil and Roland true?"

Thomas automatically glanced around to see if any of Denzil's tale-bearing friends were within earshot. Roland had a morbid fear of idle talk, and what the gossips would make of Kade's innocent question would reach his ears in no time. Her presence had cleared the immediate vicinity of everyone except himself, Lucas, and the Count of Duncanny, who was a staunch supporter of Ravenna's faction, and Thomas didn't see any real reason not to answer her question. "If they are, it isn't because of any affection or desire on Denzil's part, at least." He had always seen Roland and Denzil's attachment as a strange sort of parasitic relationship on both sides, and he found himself searching for a way to explain it. "And I don't think it matters. Denzil's real control over Roland is the friendship they had when they were boys. If Roland had other favorites, or even if he managed to notice Falaise's existence for once, it would mean taking his attention away from Denzil, which Denzil can't allow. Roland must know how easy it is for a king to attract admirers; Denzil doesn't want him to discover how easy it would be to use a rival against him."

Denzil was apparently finding the fight as it was boring. He stepped back, tossing away his main gauche and drawing a second one from his sash. The hilt on the long dagger was over-elaborate and the blade looked oddly heavy.

A moment later this was explained as Denzil pressed a hidden catch on the weapon's hilt. Two metal rods popped out of the central blade and snapped into positions at acute angles to it. Their movement revealed that the center blade had a serrated edge.

The Count of Duncanny shook his head in disgust and walked away.

Kade squinted, frowning. "What is that?"

"It's for breaking blades," Thomas explained.

"I thought that's what quillions were for."

Thomas said dryly, "Obviously we were all mistaken."

Aristofan shifted his stance and adjusted his grip on his rapier. The weapon was obviously heavier than what he was used to, but it still wouldn't hold up against the main gauche's serrated edge. Aristofan and Denzil circled each other.

"You're about to lose a blade," Thomas told Lucas.

"I've been doing this twenty years and I never needed anything like that," Lucas said, exasperated. "This isn't a duel; it's a murder. That young idiot ought to give over."

"It would look bad. People would talk." Thomas's voice was heavy with irony.

Lucas made an impatient gesture. "He'd be alive to hear them. He's only a poet; why should he care what people say?"

"Everyone does," Kade said.

Thomas looked down at her and saw the tension in the way she was standing, the intent look in her gray eyes, and realized what she was about to do. He decided to let her.

Aristofan attempted a desperate parry and Denzil trapped the boy's sword in his elaborate main gauche and snapped the blade. The Duke's first slash opened a long cut on Aristofan's cheek; his second never landed.

Kade slammed into Denzil from the side. He staggered and twisted away from her, landing heavily. Before she could leap on him, Thomas caught up with her from behind and pulled her out of the way. Denzil leapt to his feet, threw down his sword, and started toward her.

Thomas shoved him backward and said, "Temper, my lord. Take them one at a time."

They were treated to a good view of Denzil with the veneer of civility stripped away. "How dare that bitch interfere with me?" he shouted.

Aristofan had fallen to the floor and was pressing his arm to his face, trying to staunch the blood flow. A couple of watching servants ran forward to help him.

"I'll do more than interfere with you, posturing monkey," Kade sneered at the infuriated Denzil. "Why don't you take on someone with a chance against you?"

"There's a thought," Thomas remarked pleasantly.

Denzil focused on him and his expression changed. He smiled and gestured back toward the fallen poet. "Is that the problem, Captain? Am I usurping your duty?"

They regarded each other for a moment, long enough to realize the entire chamber had fallen silent. Thomas turned and saw Roland standing in the doorway at the far end of the room, his attendants grouped around him. After a moment of angry contemplation, the King strode forward and shouted, "What is this?"

"What do you think it is?" Kade asked him with withering contempt.

Roland turned a slightly darker shade of red, embarrassment added to anger, and said, "You will all stop this immediately."

There was some shuffling among the spectators as they tried to look as if they were obeying. The main figures in the drama simply stood there and stared at him.

Roland looked at Denzil and started to speak, then abruptly wheeled and stormed out of the room. Denzil recovered his sword and went after him without even a glare for anyone else.

⟡

As Thomas expected, Lucas and the others had found nothing incriminating at Gambin's house that had any bearing on Urbain Grandier. They had brought the body and its effects back to the palace and Galen Dubell had promised to examine them.

Thomas had gone out to the portico that extended off the third floor to take a shortcut across to the main part of the building when Kade caught up with him.

She asked loudly, "Why did you stop me?"

He turned to face her. The threatened afternoon storm had never produced more than a light rain, but the evening breeze was damp and strong, rocking the lamps hanging from the columns and tearing at her hair. He asked, "Why did you let me?"

He watched her mentally back up to begin again. She demanded, "What did Denzil mean by 'usurping your duty'?"

She could hear it from anyone, and was perfectly capable of badgering him about it for hours. He said, "Queen Falaise had a lover, a young stupid man like Aristofan, nearly helpless with a sword. He became too arrogant, she sent him away, and he insulted her in front of important witnesses. I killed him."

Kade turned that over for a moment. Her eyes narrowed. "You wanted to stop the duel."

"Yes." In spite of everything, he was surprised. For someone who leapt to conclusions as often as she did, her leaps were fairly accurate.

She stared at him. "You bastard, if you want to kill Denzil, have the guts to do it yourself; don't use me for it."

It was foolish to be angry with her, but Thomas found himself saying tightly, "If you don't want to be used, then don't open yourself to it by behaving stupidly and leaving other people to pick up the pieces. You can't play the spoiled witless child all your life."

"Well it's better than what you're playing at, isn't it?"

"I wouldn't know, having never been so lacking in initiative that I had to act like a raving idiot to get what I wanted."

As Kade was drawing breath to answer, there was a crash beneath their feet as a glass-paned door was flung violently open on the balcony of the floor below. Both of them flinched.

"My lord—" Denzil's voice said.

"Don't call me that, not while we're alone." It was Roland.

Thomas remembered that this terrace was directly above the balcony of one of Roland's private solars. He and Kade regarded each other in silence. They could hardly object to each other's eavesdropping, Thomas supposed, having just come to the mutual conclusion that they were both too despicable to live in polite company anyway.

Denzil asked, "Are you all right?"

"You ask me that?"

The voices below had grown softer. Thomas took a silent step forward to the railing to hear more clearly. After a moment Kade joined him.

"What? Were you worried?" Denzil's voice had a laugh in it. "That was barely worth the effort."

"You take too many chances. But you should have left that boy alone. He's nothing." Roland was oblivious to the fact that Aristofan was perhaps a year or two older than himself.

"He insulted me. And you should thank me for ridding you of him. He's your wife's lover."

"He's nothing. All the married women in the city have lovers. My mother has lovers. God knows my father had worse habits—"

"Don't. If your honor means nothing to you, it means something to me."

And how is Roland's honor affected by an insult to Denzil, Thomas wondered. Where was Dr. Dubell to ask the pertinent question?

"Sometimes I think you're the only one."

Denzil did not dispute this. "I'm sorry I upset you. That bitch of a sorceress—"

"Is my sister."

At his side Thomas sensed Kade stiffen.

"And where was she when you needed her?"

"She ran away. I loved her and she left me behind without a second thought."

Kade shivered once, a slight movement with all the intensity of a restrained convulsion. Thomas found himself unwillingly sympathetic. Roland had been the Crown Prince; his exiled sister could hardly have taken him with her, as if they were farm children escaping a harsh master. And the choice to stay with him in the city had been taken from her by Ravenna's command.

Kade drew back as if to leave. Impulsively, Thomas put a hand on top of hers on the railing and she froze. At that moment an army probably couldn't have kept her on that balcony by force, but that gentle touch seemed enough to hold her there.

"Who stayed with you?" Denzil asked.

"You did. I'd have died without someone."

"Then it's a good thing she wasn't all you had." There was silence, then a creak as one of the men below opened the door.

Thomas released Kade's hand, and she vanished back through the archway.

CHAPTER EIGHT

KADE FOUND HERSELF in need of company. Falaise was the only person she could think of who might possibly be willing to put up with her, and Kade was in such a mood that she was willing to put up with moping, which was probably what Falaise was doing at the moment.

The Queen's apartments were on the fifth level of the King's Bastion, but when Kade came up the stairs to where she could see the doorway of the first antechamber, it looked like a disturbed anthill. Gentlewomen and maid-servants were running in and out, and Queen's guards were stalking around outside the door. *That doesn't look promising,* Kade thought. She didn't par-ticularly want to start another sensation, so she crept back down the stairs and out of sight.

The next stairwell gave onto the cathedral-like entrance of an old gallery, and she stopped in front of the oaken doors carved with willows and birds of paradise. This was the hall where the royal portraits were kept, "where the family was interred," as some long-ago courtier had referred to it.

After a moment, Kade went inside.

It was cold with the chill of marble, fine wood laid over stone, and gilded frames, and it felt barren as rooms that have never been lived in feel. The hall lanterns illuminated ancestors, distant relations, and the notables of this or other ages, which Kade passed by without more than a cursory glance. There was only one set of portraits here anyone ever came to see. They were the Greancos, the portraits of the royal family.

Other painters had done royal portraits which were scattered about the palace or presented to favored nobles, but Greanco had been a seventh son of a seventh son, with half his mind in the Otherworld. Having a portrait done by him was to take a chance at having one's soul revealed. Fortunately for

Greanco, this held a fascination for Ravenna and her family that had kept him at court longer than anyone else would have put up with him.

Knowing the effect and having felt it before didn't help; shivers ran up Kade's back as she stood beneath those canvas eyes. She had to fight the conviction that there were people watching her who disappeared when she turned to face them.

She stopped before the portraits of the old kings: Ravenna's father and grandfather. Their hard eyes stared down at her. Both men had been beleaguered warrior kings, and the primary impressions the portraits gave were those of guile and strength. Undoubtedly they would have found Ravenna a proper daughter; her strong features were echoed in theirs. But what would they think of Roland, Kade wondered. Or herself, for that matter? *Probably not much,* she decided. Why Ravenna's father had chosen to settle the ruling right on Fulstan and not on her was a mystery. Perhaps he had not entirely trusted her, or perhaps he mistook independence for willfulness. Kade had heard that Fulstan had always put on a good show for his father-in-law. It hadn't mattered in the end, and Ravenna had had the kingdom in reality, if not in name. *We all make mistakes,* she told the portrait silently, as she moved on. *But some of us have to live with them.*

There were solemn representations of other relatives, and courtiers she should have known, generals or statesmen who had walked these rooms when she was a child and had since died. But like the children she had played with until her father found reasons to send their families away, she only dimly remembered their faces and couldn't quite recall their names.

Then she circled a pillar and found herself facing the portrait of Fulstan in his prime. Surprisingly, Kade could look at it without emotion; Greanco had painted an empty slate, a weak vessel that had not yet been subjected to the stresses that would deform it. He had faithfully depicted the handsome features, the full brown hair, and the wide-set blue eyes but had managed to give the impression that the beauty was transitory, and not something that grew out of character, that would last through age. The later portrait that revealed the older bitter man was said to hang in Ravenna's bedchamber, there only because the Dowager had reportedly said that she couldn't think of a better place for him than nailed up there on the wall, watching.

After the Arlequin's attack, Denzil had brought up the subject of Fulstan's suspiciously quick illness and death, and Kade had felt an odd mingling of triumph and guilt. She had been almost certain for years that she had caused Fulstan's death with that same unskilled power that had smashed the cathedral's windows, that she had wished him dead all the way from the Monelite Convent. But she was a little afraid of those thoughts, too. She wanted to think her sorcery had some control, that it wasn't as wild as her fay magic. But study was the only cure for lack of control; she should be studying in the quiet peace of Knockma instead of stirring up trouble here.

The next portrait was of Roland as a child. The better-known and inferior portrait by Avisjon hung in a more prominent location downstairs. Despite the trappings of royal tunic and mantle, the scepter and the Hand of Justice, Greanco had captured Roland's frightened eyes all too well.

She wandered down the wall a little and unexpectedly encountered her own portrait.

I should have known, she thought, staring. Ravenna wouldn't have let Roland burn the rags Greanco used to wipe his brushes, let alone one of his paintings.

When it had first been painted so long ago, Kade had been upset that her awkwardness and anxiety had been so well revealed. Now she saw what had really been there. It was pain.

So that's what it was like, she thought. *It seems I might have forgotten.*

Kade now understood why Ravenna had had the portrait put away after it was complete. It was also a reproach. How it had found its way up here she couldn't imagine.

She stepped back to where she could see both her own and Roland's portraits and thought, *Did I run away?* At the time it had seemed a glorious escape. *What would have happened if I'd stayed? Nothing or everything.* She couldn't remember being angry at Roland when she left for the convent. She felt like a contributor to that expression on Roland's young face which Greanco had captured so well, and she didn't like the feeling. *I should leave, tonight, now,* she thought wearily. *This isn't turning out the way I imagined and I'm just in the way. Now that they've seen me again they probably won't even be afraid of me anymore.*

Kade remembered that hot Midsummer Eve's day when the power had come flowing out of her as if she were a bottle shattered from pressure within. She hadn't had any grudge against the cathedral itself; in fact, she rather regretted the destruction of those stained glass windows. She had done simple magics under Galen Dubell's tutelage, but that had been the first time the ability had risen in her with such strength, the first time she could focus it at will. It had been marvelous. But it was the first and only time. She would not reach that peak so easily again. The only road to that kind of power was the one of hard study, and she had dedicated the years since to mastering her abilities, though it had never been easy. And perhaps she had let the more painstaking magics of sorcery take second place to the easy power of fayre.

She turned to go, but she had missed the paintings on the other side of the gallery and now one caught her eye. It was an informal portrait of a younger Ravenna with an elite group of her Queen's Guard and the officers. She sat in the center, dressed in a mantua of black velvet and flame silk, a rose of diamonds on her breast. A younger Thomas Boniface leaned on the chair at her side and slightly behind her, with the rest of the guards grouped around, all handsome and all with a pronounced air of danger.

Kade didn't remember seeing it before. It must have been done after she had left, to commemorate the recently victorious Bisran War, when Ravenna had brought the years of fighting to an end. It was odd that it wasn't somewhere downstairs, but Kade supposed that it had been scandalous for an independent queen with a useless husband to have her portrait done with a group of young men. But then that was Ravenna down to the bone, and Greanco had conveyed that, too. During that war, Ravenna had traveled extensively around the disputed borders with her guard and one or two maidservants. Knowing Ravenna, she had probably chaperoned the maidservants more than they had chaperoned her. A few bishops had spoken out against her, but the rest of the country thought the Church poked into other people's morals too much as it was; landlaw barely took notice of adultery, and queens had traditionally taken lovers among their personal bodyguard.

It was the tacit rules of landlaw that allowed Ravenna to keep command of the Queen's Guard when she should have passed it on to Falaise as the younger woman was crowned. Under landlaw, a personal bodyguard could not be inherited or given away without the liege's permission. If there was something Ravenna was good at, it was manipulating laws and circumstances to her own ends.

I should learn to do that, Kade thought, bitterly amused at herself. But fayre had few laws, or at least few that made sense. Like the court, the denizens of the Kingdoms of Fay fought, plotted, and stabbed one another in the back to excess, but they were soulless creatures and their passions were short-lived and shallow. The outcomes of their games didn't really matter to them, and there was nothing like the solid trust that was reflected in this portrait…

You are getting sentimental, you idiot.

The next portrait was of Thomas Boniface, also in informal dress. Even for a Greanco it was dark and elusive. Though Thomas was more than ten years the elder, he and Denzil had much the same presence in person: arrogant and sensual and well aware of their own worth, both wolves in lapdogs' clothing. The portrait suggested that in the Captain's case the arrogance might be tempered by irony.

Tradition dictated that the Captain of the Queen's Guard as well as the Preceptor of the Albonate Knights renounce all familial connections so their whole loyalty would be to the crown. Nepotism and interfering relations could be permitted with other nobles who served in the palace, but these positions were seen as too important. Renier had been Duke of something, Kade remembered, when he handed the whole thing over to a younger brother and took his post for Roland. Thomas had been Viscount Boniface.

Both court offices came with a huge amount of wealth and some land, but gave up the right to leave that wealth to any heir other than the next man appointed to the position. If the Albonate Preceptors lived to retire they were usually created a duke and awarded estates and income. It was assumed the same thing would be done for the Captains of the Queen's Guard, but in recent history all of them had died at duty.

Kade realized abruptly that Thomas Boniface probably expected the same to happen to him. If he outlived Ravenna his position at court would not be a good one. Roland and Denzil were both against him, and Falaise seemed helpless to protect anyone including herself. That was what the portrait conveyed, Kade knew suddenly. It was the face of a man who took service with the crown accepting the possibility of eventual betrayal and a violent death, but not one who enjoyed having to kill people whose main crime seemed to be stupidity.

Kade turned away and started resolutely for the stairs, telling herself, *I don't know why I care; I don't even like him anymore anyway.*

Then the nagging restlessness that had plagued her coalesced into dread, and she stopped in the doorway. Her heart was fluttering. She took a deep breath, her hand pressed to her chest, and tried to think what it could be.

Something's gone wrong; something's happening. She forced herself to move forward, to start down the stairs. *I've got to get to Galen.*

ﮑ

"What kind of a man is Grandier?" Thomas asked.

Kneeling on the floor beside the wall niche, Galen Dubell paused to give the question serious consideration. "He is driven," he said finally, looking up at Thomas seriously. "And in pain. The worst sort of opponent to face."

They were in one of the deep cellars of the Old Palace, the rough stone walls glistening faintly in the flickering light of the candlelamp. Stone pillars as wide as draft carts stretched up into darkness to meet the arched ceiling somewhere overhead. The dirty straw-dusted floor was littered with broken or empty barrels, boxes, and odd pieces of ironwork. Battered and forgotten siege engines, lowered through traps in the ceiling sometime in the dim past, looked like the metal skeletons of beached sea monsters in the half-light. Wandering at the edges of the light were the three Queen's guards Thomas had assigned to watch Dubell when the old man's work took him into deserted corners of the palace. They were fighting both boredom and nerves and trying to look unaffected.

In an effort to discover what was wrong with the wards, Dubell was examining the warding stones buried in various locations around the palace. He was also planning on moving the keystone. He could remove it with Thomas and the guards present, but he would have to convey it to its new resting place alone. Thomas wasn't happy about Dubell moving about the undercellars of the palace unguarded, but the keystone was kept safe by being hidden away among the hundreds of other warding stones. Dubell was the only one who would know its exact location.

After carefully examining the dull-colored egg-shaped warding stone, Dubell replaced it in its wall niche and sealed it up with clay, handing the bucket back to the unwilling servant boy who had been drafted for the task.

"Driven by what?" Thomas asked, though he wasn't sure why he was pursuing the subject. Though if it provided no insight into Grandier, it might reveal something about the way Dubell thought.

"By his convictions." Dubell climbed to his feet awkwardly and they started toward the pillars in the center of the cavernous room, the boy trailing behind.

The cellar was damp, but the air was neither too hot nor too cold, and not at all stale, as if the airshafts within the thick walls of the Old Palace overhead might have openings somewhere in the cellar's ceiling.

Thomas had followed Dubell down here to ask him what he had found out about Gambin's death, but Dubell hadn't been able to discover what the spy had been killed with or how it had been done. Now that Thomas was down here, he might as well wait until Dubell was finished; the old sorcerer might be helpful during Dontane's questioning. Thomas said, "I don't understand why his convictions would lead him against us. This isn't Bisra. If a sorcerer steals or kills his neighbor, he's hanged just like anyone else, but not for practicing magic."

Dubell gestured with his trowel. "That, of course, is the difficult point. Why is he here at all? In Lodun we believe he has never been across our borders before, even though his father was from Ile-Rien. He has certainly never been accused of a crime, justly or unjustly, by our crown. Which leads me unfortunately to believe that his grudge against this land or this city is ideological, in which case there is little that can be done to deter him."

Thomas shook his head. "I can't agree with that. There's a member of the city Philosophers' Academy who has invented some kind of clockwork that can add figures when he turns the knobs on the outside. The Inquisitors General in Bisra heard about it and have declared him a devil's servant, and if he ever crosses their border they'll kill him. If Grandier considers himself such a scholar, why isn't he still over the border giving hell to the Bisran crown?"

"It would certainly seem more sensible of him. Unless," Dubell paused as the idea occurred to him, "he has been offered money by someone to persecute us."

"That's been considered." In Bisra, mobs surrounded the churches where the Inquisition held court, accusing each other of witchcraft and seeing demons under every bush. If it came out that the Bisran crown had employed a man who had escaped the death sentence for black magic, there would be riots it would take them weeks to put down. Thomas kicked a pillar thoughtfully. He would have to consider ways to let the appropriate rumors slip across the border. "Grandier might do it, if they offered him something he wanted badly enough."

Dubell shook his head, brow furrowed. "If I were him, I think my quarrel against them would run too deeply."

"There are several possibilities as to who could have hired him." Thomas had no wish to discuss the possibilities who were nearer at hand than Bisra; not with Galen Dubell, at any rate. "And you have never heard of this man Dontane?"

"Not in connection with Urbain Grandier. Not at all, in fact. The poison that the poor fellow Lestrac was given tends to cause hallucinations and delusions before the sleep that soon turns to death. He might have accused the man falsely."

Thomas didn't think it had been a delusion. Lestrac had been too certain, too angry in his betrayal. "Kade seemed sure that he was the one in the room with Lestrac. She made his likeness form in a pool of wine."

"That is not entirely a tried-and-true method. Kade is," Dubell hesitated, "quite brilliant in a peculiar way. But she also tends to let her imagination get the best of her."

Thomas, who also thought of Dubell as brilliant in a peculiar way, didn't comment.

Dubell stopped at one of the huge pillars and pointed to a square section near the base that had been carved out and refilled with clay. "This is where the keystone is buried. I've already prepared the new location for it, and it will only take me a short time to convey it there. Not long enough to cause any degeneration in the wards."

Frowning, Thomas knelt to look at the clay seal more closely. "This is recent. Have you looked at it before?"

"No." Dubell stooped anxiously, and started to pry out the clay. "Perhaps Dr. Surete... God, if it's been this all along..."

The explosion was like a cannon going off directly over their heads. The stone pillars trembled with the shock of it, releasing a rain of dust and rock chips from above. Thomas stood, then staggered as the floor slipped suddenly under his feet. Deafened by the noise, he waited for the thousands of tons of stone to come crashing down on top of them.

The walls shuddered back into stillness.

For a moment Thomas and the other guards stared at each other. "What..." whispered Baserat.

Dubell had rocked back on his heels with the concussion but he kept digging away at the clay seal. It broke under the pressure and he shoved his hand back into the niche. "It's empty," he said, and began to curse Grandier.

Thomas hauled Dubell to his feet. "Come on," he said and led them at a run toward the stairs. *It might have been the city armories,* he thought. The two long stone buildings housed stores of gunpowder and stood on the opposite side of the inner wall from the Gallery Wing. But even if both had gone up at once... No, there was no accidental cause for an explosion like that; the palace was under attack, from outside or from within. He tried to remember who had been on duty in the building overhead, and where Ravenna was likely to be at this time.

They reached the staircase at the far end of the shadowy darkness. Thomas took the lamp from the guard who had had the presence of mind to bring it and held it up. The narrow stairs spiraled upward, unblocked as far as the light reached.

Thomas said, "Load your pistols."

Dubell took the lamp and moved to peer uneasily up into the stairway as the guards loaded their weapons with the swiftness of long practice. By the time Thomas closed the cover over the priming pan of his second wheellock and tucked it back into his sash, he had calmed himself enough to think clearly. If the few of them were going to do any good, there could be no mistakes. He started up the stairs, the others following behind him. The four-story climb might have stretched to infinity.

They had reached the second flight when there was a yell from behind and Thomas turned back. Treville was slumped on the stairs, clutching his side. The figure standing over him was nightmarish; it looked like a man, but its skin was gray and foul, its clothes in brown tatters, its hair a torn greasy mop. It seemed as though they froze there, staring at the apparition, for moments, but it must have been only half a heartbeat because the creature never had another chance to move. On the stairs below, Baserat struck upward at the same time that Martin fell on it from above, almost succeeding in impaling himself on the other guard's sword.

Dubell flattened himself back against the wall so Thomas could get past. The two guards were standing back from the creature now, looking down in shock. Thomas had to put a hand on Martin's shoulder and move him out of the way before he could see it.

Its narrow features twisted in death, it looked like a man who had been held prisoner in a dark place for a very long time and starved. The wound in its chest where the point of Baserat's rapier had emerged was bloody but also burned, as if the metal blade had been red-hot.

Dubell had edged down past them and was helping Treville to sit up. Thomas picked up the weapon the creature had used. It was a bronze short sword, with a narrow blade and wickedly sharp edges. Not much protection against a steel weapon, but it did its job well enough on human flesh.

"It was up above us, perched there, Captain," Baserat said, his voice a little unsteady.

"What is it?" Thomas asked Dubell.

"Fay, but I don't recognize what sort." He finished staunching Treville's wound and looked up at them. "With the keystone removed from the matrix for more than a few hours, the wards would begin drifting away from the outer walls of the newer sections of the palace. The creatures must have been waiting for a large enough opening."

Thomas felt everyone's eyes on him. He had known it must be an attack, but he had assumed the enemy was human. Ignoring the cold dread creeping up his spine, he looked down at Treville. "Can you walk?"

"Out of here I could run." The man grinned weakly.

"Good." Thomas looked at the others. "Let's go, gentlemen."

Dubell helped Treville to his feet, then reached back to collar the servant boy and pull him further up the stairs. "Here, boy, carry the lamp, and don't fall behind."

The boy took the lamp in a shaking hand and whispered, "Yes, Sir."

The air in the stairwell was growing warmer. It might mean the entrance above them was blocked, or the building overhead had caught fire, or collapsed entirely. *It might have been Kade. It might have been her plan all along,* Thomas was thinking. He had no idea why that thought made him so angry. She had never promised him anything.

The final turn brought Thomas to face the wooden doorway at the top of the stairs, which still stood open as they had left it earlier. The darkened corridor was blocked by the collapse of its wood and plaster ceiling. Dim lamplight shone down from the resulting gap in the passage above.

Thomas climbed the debris and took a cautious look through the opening in the ceiling. Above them was a passageway, its floor and one wall wood while the rest was the original stone. The source of the light was hidden around a corner further up the way. He thought about the layout of the Old Palace and decided they were near the lower kitchens and storerooms. There were many ways leading out into the rest of the structure from here; some would have to be unblocked.

"All right," he said to the others, "this is our way."

It took some moments to get Treville up into the passage, his wound making their efforts to help difficult and painful for him. Just as Thomas gave Dubell a hand up, Baserat signaled them hastily for silence. "Hear that?" he whispered.

In another moment they all did. There were people further down the passageway. For a moment Thomas found it a relief that they were not the only survivors of some immense disaster, then the faint sound turned into a tumult as shouts and a woman's scream echoed down to them.

"Save your pistols," Thomas told them. The unspoken thought was on all their faces. *Because we don't know what we'll find upstairs...*

Thomas ran down the passage and burst through an archway into a large low-ceilinged storeroom. A group of men and women dressed as servants was trapped in a corner, half-surrounded by a dozen or so of the sickly emaciated fay. The servants were fighting the creatures off with torches and makeshift clubs and whatever else they had been able to find. The fay rushed their new attackers as they entered the room. The first leapt at them, waving its sword over its head, and was disemboweled by Thomas's rapier. A bronze sword swung at him from the side and he swept it away and punctured the owner's chest.

One of the fay kicked over a lamp, sending the room into near darkness. *Obviously the creatures can see in the dark,* Thomas thought, parrying another thrust. *Pity we can't.*

Dubell shouted something and clapped his hands. Immediately a small bright ball of pure light appeared over his head and hovered there, flooding the room with a stark white illumination.

From behind, something grabbed Thomas's arm and swung him around. The strength was astonishing for a creature so apparently delicate. He slammed the rapier's heavy hilt into its face and it fell away from him with a shriek.

As he turned, Thomas saw that three more fay had come at them from the door to the passageway. *Hell, they must have been following us up the stairs.* One had attacked the wounded Treville from behind, and he was now sprawled bleeding on the floor. Martin leapt over his wounded friend to knock the creature away from him; as it staggered back he drove his rapier through it.

Nearby another fay was grappling with Dubell, trying to plunge its sword toward his face, but the old sorcerer was holding it off. Dubell managed to shift his weight and shove the creature up against the wall. Thomas stepped up behind Dubell, said "Pardon me, Doctor," and finished off the creature.

All the other fay in the room were down. The spell light above Dubell's head died away as the servants relit their lamps, and the strange unwavering white light was replaced by the familiar flickering yellow.

"Captain," someone gasped at his side, and Thomas turned and saw Berham. The servant had armed himself with a crude but effective iron club. "Captain, there's fighting in the hall by the round stair. We could hear the shots. That's where we was making for."

"Good." As an afterthought, Thomas asked, "Do you know what's happened?"

"No, Sir, I couldn't say that." Bertram's story was like their own. He had been visiting nearby when the explosion had occurred. As a veteran of the last war, his instincts had taken over and he had gathered survivors, armed both men and women with what was available, and set off to join the organized resistance.

Martin came up to them as Berham finished, saying bitterly, "Dr. Dubell said Treville's gone, Sir. The bastards go for the wounded like wolves."

"Aye," Berham said softly, looking back toward the bodies of his companions who had not survived the ambush. "I noticed that."

"Take his sword and give it to Dr. Dubell. Let Berham use the pistols. We'll come back for the bodies when we've secured the palace," Thomas told him, and thought, *I sound like a bloody idiot of an optimist.*

But it was what the other two men wanted to hear. As they moved to obey, Thomas went to where Dubell was still kneeling beside Treville. Dubell looked up at Thomas and said, "I'm sorry."

"It wasn't your fault," Thomas said automatically.

Dubell's face was drawn. "The fay are attacking in force. This is no raid. It's another damned war, Captain."

Another damned war, Thomas thought. *But the Bisran army fought us for two decades and they never got as close as this.*

As they returned to the others, Baserat was leaning over the fay that Thomas had disemboweled, poking the entrails experimentally with the tip of his sword. "See, it looks human to me."

"You're right. I wish I had my glasses." Dubell peered down at the creature, then said, "As I thought. The Unseelie Court, or the Host, as they are more commonly called. On their nightly rampages they seize human captives whom they will use to attack their fellows." He paused as Martin came up and handed him Treville's rapier. Dubell looked at the weapon as if he wasn't sure what it was, then said, "Yes, of course."

"What makes men turn into that?" Thomas nudged the corpse with the toe of his boot. He couldn't believe it, though he knew Dubell must be right.

"Prolonged exposure to the influence of the Host. Their captives become like them. Iron becomes poison to them. They gain some powers of the fay, but they lose their souls in the process."

The room had grown silent as the others listened. The servants were watching them with white bruised faces and apprehensive eyes.

Something bumped his elbow and Thomas looked down to see the servant boy who had somehow managed to survive so far, peering interestedly down at the fay's corpse.

"Berham," Thomas said. "Keep this one with your lot."

"Yes, Sir," Berham said, gesturing sharply to the boy. "Come away from there, boy, before you get in the way."

There would be far too many people wandering about without Berhams to organize them. Unarmed retainers and servants, children who could not fend for or protect themselves, women who would not think to pick up a weapon. "We have to get moving," Thomas muttered.

Kade was on the stairs in the King's Bastion when the explosion shook the Old Palace. She held onto the balustrade as the walls trembled in sympathy with the adjoining building. A stiff breeze poured up the stairwell; the stink it carried made her wince. The shaking stopped and the beams supporting the stairs gave an uneasy creak before deciding to hold. Kade started down again, stumbling occasionally because her legs were trembling for some reason. The inexplicable wind had ceased with the reverberations of the explosion, but it had left the air smelling of mud, stale water, and death.

It can't be the wards, Kade told herself uneasily. *It can't be.*

She found the bottom of the stairway blocked by a panic-stricken crowd of palacefolk and servants and she had to go back up a flight to work her way around by back passages. She could smell smoke now, from fires that had caught when candles and lamps were knocked over.

When she reached the long gallery that connected the bastion to the Old Palace, it was badly lit and in chaos.

Albon knights were milling around the doors and Renier was shouting orders. Over the noise, someone was yelling, "If you don't send them to help us fight the fire, they won't have anywhere to retreat!"

Kade ducked into the crowd, slipping past a mailed arm before it could stop her. She emerged onto the wide balcony of the great spiral staircase that led down into the main hall of the Old Palace.

It was a pitched battle.

The main hall was on two levels and the wide sweep of steps leading down to the lower portion of it was where the battle line had been drawn. Furniture, boxes, and other debris had been piled up at the top as cover for the defenders. Queen's guards and a few Albon knights and Cisternans were manning the barricades along with disheveled courtiers, retainers, and servants who had either taken up weapons or were crouching back behind the defenders and reloading pistols. The lower half of the hall was walled away by a palpable unnatural darkness. Missiles flew out of that darkness, bronze-tipped bolts of a deadly effectiveness demonstrated by the number of corpses sprawled on the floor.

Kade started down the staircase, one hand on its wide banister. The zoomorphs carved on the stair's central column leered out of the shadows as they were briefly illuminated by torches, adding to the nightmare quality of the scene. Refugees struggled past her, palacefolk and wounded guards.

As she fought her way closer, she began to see past the curtain of shadow in a way the others defending the barricade below could not. There was movement in that darkness, mangled faces, shifting forms, distorted or partly human. *The wards must be gone, at least over the Old Palace and the Gallery Wing; that's how this mess got in*, Kade thought, and forced herself to keep moving down the stairs toward that chaotic darkness stretched across the hall. *But what drove them here?* It was the Unseelie Court, the rulers of the dark fay and the other creatures who fed on blood and terror, who rode the night in the form of the Host, preying on humans and destroying every living thing in their path. They traveled the sky on dark windy nights accompanied, the church priests claimed, by the souls of the dead and wreaking havoc wherever they went.

At the bottom of the stair, Kade started toward the barricade, dodging running forms, ignoring startled glances of recognition. As she reached the hastily erected wall of broken furniture and tried to peer through it, she heard, "If it isn't the Queen of Air and Darkness."

The voice was sibilant and soft and came to her quite clearly over the noise. She looked down slowly and saw the face through a gap in the barricade. It was Evadne, one of the princes of the Unseelie Court. His narrow features might have been called handsome by someone less picky about character, even if his skin was powder blue. But though his expression was that of a wistful fay child, his eyes were gloating and entirely adult. Kade said, "Your eyesight is as bad as your sense of humor." She had never truly accepted her mother's title, which Evadne must know.

He grinned up at her, revealing pointed teeth. "Why don't you join us, my sister? What has the Seelie Court ever given you that you should risk your life to side with them and battle us?"

Kade ignored the growing knot of coldness in her stomach and laughed at him. The Seelie Court was the highest court of the Otherworld. Titania and Oberon ruled it, but spent little time in governing the fay who swore allegiance to them, and occupied most of their days in fetes, rades, contests, or other unreal pastimes of Fayre. The fay loosely attached to the Seelie Court loved daylight and music but were often dangerous to humans, either through acts of mischief or simple lack of concern over human frailties.

The Queen of Air and Darkness was not truly a member of either court, and Kade did not like to think about what would happen to the balances of power in the Otherworld, which she only vaguely understood herself, if this were to change. Evadne must be very confident to risk making that offer. She said, "The Seelie Court has given me nothing, which is far better than the trouble you've given me. What makes you think I'd throw my fortune in with either of you?"

His features drew into a pinched sneer. "The Host grows in power by the moment. The mortals' pitiful protections are scattered and you can't stop us. I'll destroy you myself."

"Promises, promises. Who's your master? Is it Urbain Grandier?"

The eyes hardened. "We have no master."

"I'll tell him you said that when I meet him."

Evadne stepped back, fading away into a darkness even Kade's sight couldn't penetrate. "I expect," he whispered, "that you will…"

Kade dropped to the floor and used the hem of her dress to wipe a clear spot. Evadne had given her an idea. *Those were powerful wards; they couldn't simply dissolve.* They must be about somewhere. If she could find one…

"Hey, come away from there." She looked up to see a man in a Cisternan officer's colors, who started back when he recognized her.

Kade said, "I need chalk, wax, and some burnt coal." At his expression she shouted furiously, "Do you want help or not?"

ᴋᴪ

An unblocked corridor leading out from the storerooms led Thomas and the others into the main hall.

Wounded guards and refugees were climbing the huge spiral stair up into the King's Bastion and a thick white pall of smoke from pistols and muskets hung in the air. Out of the confusion, Thomas spotted the Cisternan Commander Vivan. He stepped forward and caught the other man's arm. "What did we lose?"

Vivan ran a hand through his dark hair and didn't seem to notice when it came away bloody. He said, "They're in the Gallery Wing, and probably all of the east side."

Thomas kept the shock off his face. "What about the King's Bastion?"

"Secure. Everything inside the inner wall is secure, They didn't come through there."

"The wards," said Galen Dubell, who was suddenly standing beside them. "They have drifted away from the newer structures of the palace, but the foundations in the older sections act as keystones themselves and are holding the wards in place there."

Thomas nodded. "Good, it'll give us breathing room." What he wanted to do most was slam Vivan up against a wall and demand to know where Ravenna and Falaise were, but there was no time, and no sense in it. He knew Lucas and Gideon were on duty and for now he would just have to trust that they had gotten both Queens to safety. He said to Vivan, "You're trying to push them back so you can close the siege doors at the top of the stairs?"

"Yes, If we fall back now, they'll push forward and we'll all go, but the sorceress said—"

Thomas stared. "Who?"

"The sorceress said if we gave her some time she could keep them back long enough to let us retreat."

"Where is she?"

"At the barricade." As Thomas started away, Vivan called after him, "Thomas! They're throwing elf-shot."

That explained the ominously still forms that bore no visible wounds.

Thomas spotted Kade's tattered form crouching near the center of the barricade between two Cisternan guards firing muskets. He began to make his way over to her.

She had drawn some kind of design on the floor and was dripping wax from a lighted candle onto it. She was muttering continuously at it and Thomas thought she was saying a spell until he was close enough and realized she was cursing.

He crouched beside her and said, "How much longer?"

She tossed her head to get the hair out of her face and said, "Hours, days, weeks, how should I know?"

A bronze crossbow bolt shot through the barricade and clattered off the stone floor between them. They both hunched their shoulders instinctively and Kade said, "Close," in a conversational tone. She tossed her hair back again.

Thomas reached over and tucked her hair into the back of her smock for her.

She muttered, "Thank you," without looking at him, a slow flush spreading up her cheeks.

He said again, "How much longer?"

"Not long. I'm almost done. Listen, what I'm doing is calling a ward." She stopped, grimacing as the barricade shuddered under another onslaught. "Impatient bastards."

"Calling a ward?" he prompted.

"Yes. Its name is Ableon-Indis and it's supposed to be over the St. Anne's Gate but it's lying across the top of the King's Bastion now. I don't know why."

"Someone's taken the keystone."

"Damn. That would be the reason, then. The newer wards float away from their places without the keystone in the etheric structure, but the King's Bastion has the strongest warding spells in the old parts of the palace. It's drawing the drifting wards over to it. Not that it's helping much." Her expression was grim. "Anyway, when I finish this the ward should fall toward us here. If I'm lucky it will come to ground right here along the barricade. When we leave, the Host will surge forward, run into it, and get an unpleasant surprise. But Ableon-Indis will start moving upward again almost immediately. What I'm doing here isn't as strong as the warding spells still drawing it to the King's Bastion."

Thomas nodded. "So we'll have only a few moments at best?"

"Yes."

"It'll be enough."

She looked up quickly and grinned.

Berham made it over to them and knelt beside the barricade. "Albons are holding the doors in the bastion, Sir," he reported.

"Which officers are up there?"

"Just Sir Renier that I could see, Sir. They said if I came in they wouldn't let me go back because the idea was to get everyone out, you see."

"All right." Thomas looked around and saw Martin nearby. He waved him over and said, "Find Commander Vivan and spread word that when I give the order to fall back everyone's to stop firing immediately and head for the stairs. We'll have our retreat covered but not for long." As Martin hurried off he told Berham, "You tell the reloaders to make sure they get the wounded out of here before we have to move."

"Yes, Captain," Berham said, pushing to his feet. "By God, this might work."

As Berham made his way back to the reloaders, Thomas saw a disturbance on the other side of the hall. Soot was pouring out of the great hearth in a dusty cloud. Thomas stood and started toward it. There was something coming down the chimney.

Closer, he could see that the head emerging from under the stone mantel was like a horse's in size and shape. But its eyes were glazed over and white and it looked as though its coat had been removed with a dull knife. It had teeth like a lion. Thomas drew his pistol, but before he could wind the mainspring, the creature plunged out of the fireplace and fell on a group of men who had been reloading muskets. It swung its great horse's head from side to side, its teeth tearing as the men scrambled to get away.

Reaching it, Thomas drew his rapier and slashed at its side. As it turned toward him with a scream of rage, he drove the point through its neck. It teetered, then fell toward him, dragging him down as it slumped onto the floor.

A second creature was emerging from the fireplace. Thomas dropped the rapier and wound the pistol's spring, then braced it on his forearm and fired. The ball hit the creature in its broad chest along with three other shots fired from different areas of the hall and a fourth ball that all but shattered the mantel of the hearth. The creature dropped like a stone.

Galen Dubell appeared at Thomas's side, pointed at the fireplace, and gestured. The creature's body caught fire as if it had been dipped in pitch and flames shot up the chimney. "That should hold them for awhile," Dubell said with satisfaction.

Thomas shoved himself upright and went to put a foot on the fay-horse's neck to work his rapier free. He asked, "Can you help Kade?"

"No, anything I could do might only counteract the effect she is attempting to create and then we would be dead." Dubell smiled grimly. "But I can harry the enemy and perhaps give her more time."

As the sorcerer strode off Thomas looked after him, a little nonplused. *Disasters agree with you.*

As others ran up to carry the wounded, more fay charged the barricade and Thomas joined the defenders.

Nightmare images flung themselves out of the darkness and were driven back by pistol balls or pikes wielded over the barricade. There were hideous animal-shapes with distorted bodies and wicked intelligent eyes, creatures with oddly human faces and bodies that were marked with startling deformities, and other things that vanished so quickly the mind discounted what the eyes saw. Their shrieking and keening mixed with the blasts of muskets and pistols was deafening.

Thomas had lost track of time when Vivan grabbed his arm and said, "She's ready."

Thomas looked around. The wounded and the refugees had vanished up the stairway and Commander Vivan had already sent the reloaders after them. Thomas said, "Pass the word: when I give the order, stop firing and fall back into the bastion." He stepped back where he could see Kade and waited for the word to pass down the line.

When the guards at each end signaled ready, Thomas looked at Kade. She nodded, and he yelled, "Fall back."

Discipline held remarkably, even among the Albon knights, who didn't think themselves obliged to listen to anyone.

The shrieking din from their attackers rose in a crescendo. Thomas moved with the others to the foot of the stairs and looked back for Kade, not seeing her among the crowd.

She was still crouched beside the barricade. Thomas saw what she had been waiting for. The Host surged up toward the barricade and met a wall of hostile air. Some dissolved into myriad colors that shrieked toward the ceiling and away like fleeing ghosts. Some popped like soap bubbles and disappeared while others fell backward, marked by horrible wounds.

Kade smiled tightly to herself, leapt to her feet, and ran.

Thomas waited for her to reach the stairway before starting up. She was a little ahead of him halfway up the second tier when she was thrown back against the banister as if something had struck her.

The Host started to pour over the barricade. Thomas reached Kade and lifted her up. She was unconscious but still breathing and weighed practically nothing.

The third tier passed in a blur with the fay on the stairs below. Then the Albon knights were closing the siege doors behind him, foot-thick oak panels sheathed with iron. They slammed them to and shoved the heavy locking-bolts home. The foyer was crowded with wounded guards and refugees, and the light was dim and smoky.

Kade let him know she was awake and wanted to be put down with a sharp elbow in his ribs. He set her on her feet and she staggered slightly. "What happened to you?" he demanded, his breath coming hard from the climb.

"I don't know. Ow." She felt the side of her head gingerly. "Where's Galen?" The old sorcerer was already on the other side of the gallery, helping with the wounded. As Kade turned away to go to him Thomas said, "Wait."

She paused, wary, and he asked, "Did you know this was going to happen?"

"No." Her voice was scornful. "That is the Unseelie Court, the Dark Host, the enemy of light. I wouldn't have anything to do with them. They were the ones who tricked my mother into accepting a wager she couldn't possibly win. I wasn't much fond of her, but no one deserves— And they would just as soon do the same to me."

He had to be sure. "You didn't mention you knew how to manipulate the wards."

"I wouldn't have been able to call that ward down if the keystone had still been in its place. Removing it destroyed the etheric structure that held the wards in their courses." She winced and touched her head again, then continued more calmly. "Galen taught me how to track wards in a puddle of ash, and the way I called Ableon-Indis to me was only a variation on the spells used to temporarily hold a ward in one place, which every apprentice knows. Ask him if you don't believe me."

There was a muffled thump from the other side of the siege doors, then an echoing roar, as some thwarted creature expressed its displeasure. If Kade had not bothered to aid the defenders, they would have been on the other side of those doors now. Thomas thought, *She didn't have to do it, and it certainly wouldn't serve her purpose if she meant us any harm.* He said, "It won't be necessary to ask him."

Kade hesitated, as if she was just as inexperienced at accepting trust as he was at giving it, then she turned without a word and slipped into the crowd. Renier pushed past the other Albons clustering near the siege doors to reach Thomas and said, "The doors are holding."

Thomas asked, "What started it?" It had occurred to him that he still didn't know exactly what had exploded or where, except that it was somewhere in the Old Palace or the Gallery Wing.

The big knight looked like he had been run over by a wagon. The final touch was a perfect black eye. He said, "I only know we've lost half the Cisternan Guard and anyone who was posted past the main hall of the Old Palace. Including one of your lieutenants. I saw him going that way just before it happened."

Gideon would be with Falaise in the King's Bastion. "Lucas Castil?"

"Yes, that's him."

"God damn." Thomas leaned back against the wall and used the full sleeve of his shirt to wipe the sweat off his forehead. He could still smell the fay-horse's acrid blood. "Where's Ravenna?"

"She's here in the bastion; I've seen her. Roland was in the Gallery Wing when it happened. We got him out barely in time." Renier hesitated, then said, "I have to talk to you in private."

Thomas looked up at him. With Kade on the other side of the gallery, there was no one to eavesdrop except for their own men, who were standing or lying about in various positions of pain or exhaustion, but Renier's expression was deadly serious.

As they moved off a little, Thomas asked, "How did you get that eye?" Considering everyone else's wounds, it was oddly minor.

"The King was a trifle upset at certain developments," Renier answered with a noticeable lack of expression.

"Well, he's a great comfort to all of us," Thomas snapped. *We've given our lives for an idiot child.* And Lucas was dead.

Renier didn't seem to notice the comment. He seemed almost dazed. "Thomas, I'm not sure about this but…"

Renier hesitated such a long moment Thomas had to take a better hold on what was left of his patience. "Go on," he said in a level tone.

"A knight stationed on the Prince's Gate Tower reported to me a short while ago. He said they could see fires and fighting in the streets. It's not just the palace quarter; it's the city."

CHAPTER NINE

RENIER SPREAD THE gilt-edged map on the table and indicated a spot with one calloused finger. "The Cisternan Barracks were overwhelmed in the first few moments." He cast a worried glance at Commander Vivan, who was slumped in a chair by the fire.

"They came through St. Anne's Gate, then?" Thomas asked.

"No. Mind, the reports we have come from grooms and stableboys who were able to seal off the Mews to keep the creatures out of the Old Courts, but they said the attack seemed to come from the inner gate into the palace, not the outer gate. As to how that was managed..." Renier shook his head.

They were in the Queen's Guard House, in one of the small rooms adjacent to the practice hall. The walls were hung with leather and parchment maps and the door was open to the hum of talk from the hall. They knew the human, or once-human, members of the Host had been used as cannon fodder in the initial attack, and that the fay had come after, but Thomas felt they still did not have an accurate picture of how the invasion had taken place. He said, "We still don't know what that explosion was."

"It wasn't the city armories. You can see them from the top of the inner wall. But that's what everyone thought. The off-duty Queen's guards were heading that way to repel what they thought was an attack through St. Anne's Gate when they were stopped at the Old Hall. My men were right behind them."

Thomas saw Gideon drawing breath to make a comment, and cleared his throat. Their eyes met and the younger man subsided with disgruntled reluctance. Most of the guards felt that the main body of the Albon Knights should have followed them down into the Old Hall, instead of staying in the relative safety at the top of the stairs. Thomas was willing to concede that someone had to hold the siege doors; whether the task had required almost the entire Albon troop was another matter. But it had been an act of disorganization rather than cowardice, and he wanted to keep the trouble among the two troops to a minimum. Looking back to Renier, Thomas said, "In the cellars it sounded as if the explosion was almost directly overhead; it must have been somewhere in the Gallery Wing."

"But there's nothing there to explode, not with that sort of force, not unless they brought it with them," Renier protested.

"Maybe they did." Vivan's voice startled them.

Only an accident of history had placed the Queen's Guard House in the area protected by the ancient wards of the inner walls. They had lost far too many men as it was, but the Cisternan Guard, and their families living within the barracks and adjacent to it, had been nearly destroyed.

After a moment, Renier cleared his throat. "We should hear from the commanders of the city levies by morning."

Thomas shook his head. There were over six thousand city volunteers, half musketeers and half pikemen, organized into regiments based on their neighborhoods. Both the crown and the Ministry had the right to call them out, but in the chaos of this night that would be impossible. "The city levies won't be able to form; they'll be too busy defending their own homes and it will be suicide to go out into the streets tonight."

Renier regarded the map again. "The Host has never attacked in force before. It has harried travelers, solitary farmsteads, but never... Well, the gate garrisons will be trapped inside until daylight at least. The Host can't attack when the sun's out."

Thomas had been told by Kade that the main body of the Host was composed of powerful quarrelsome spirits from the Unseelie Court, who could agree on nothing but revelry and fighting the Seelie Court, their opposites in Fayre. In their wake would be fay predators: hags, bogles, spriggans, things that haunted lonely places or preyed on travelers. Thomas said, "They can't attack in the kind of organized force they used on us in the Old Palace, but there's a mob of dark fay following them like scavengers after an army. They aren't organized, but they can stand the daylight and they will attack at any opportunity."

Renier pursed his lips in disapproval. "You heard that from Kade Carrion, I assume. I'd prefer another source for that intelligence."

Thomas controlled an inexplicable surge of irritation, and without too much acid in his voice asked, "Who else did you have in mind to question?"

Frowning, Renier shook his head. "Still... There's no help for it, I suppose. Does she know if Grandier is aiding them?"

"No, but he must be involved somehow." Thomas considered a moment. "The Host was depending on surprise, and they had help. Someone knew to go down into that cellar and take the keystone, and whoever it was is probably still here with us." Dontane might have known who that traitor was, but he must have died with the other prisoners and the guards in the Cisternan Guard House.

Renier looked up. "Perhaps the man who killed Dr. Braun got the location of the keystone out of him before he died."

Thomas managed not to roll his eyes. "Braun was killed instantly; he wasn't tortured for information."

"If we could get the keystone back—"

"It could be hidden anywhere." Thomas shook his head, frustrated. "We can't count on that."

"Well, we can't beat our heads about it now." Renier leaned over the map. "The corridors in the outer walls have been sealed. The rooftops and the open areas of the Old Courts are protected by the wards, and the iron-shod siege doors are keeping them from coming through the King's Bastion to us. The only thing we can do now is wait it out."

If Renier wanted to "wait it out" with a traitor in their camp it was his business. But Thomas had no reason to argue the point while he still had a few more preparations to make.

Lord General Villon and the siege engine cavalry were posted at the Granges, a royal fortress about fifty-five miles to the south. It was the mobile force closest to the city, except for Denzil's small private garrison still in residence at Bel Garde. The fay might be able to take the city, but they couldn't hold it. They couldn't close the iron-hinged gates, use the cannon mounted on the walls, or the stockpiles of arms. Villon had proven troops and a populace that would rise to aid him as soon as they saw his flags.

Renier rolled up his map and went back out into the hall. Thomas caught Gideon's arm and said softly, "If anyone's going to offer to hold Renier's sword while he falls on it, it's going to be me; is that clear, Sir?"

Gideon smiled reluctantly. "Yes, Sir, it's clear."

As the others left, Thomas hesitated a moment over Vivan, but he had no idea what to say to him.

He walked out through the hall, where things were beginning to calm down as the night wore on without attack. The refugees in the house were mainly palace servants and retainers who didn't mind bedding down on a clear space of floor as long as there was a roof overhead and plenty of iron lying about. They were stretched out on blankets along the walls or huddled in groups telling each other their horror stories from the last few hours. Their children played on the second-floor balconies with nerveless unconcern, but no one apparently felt secure enough to put out any of the lanterns, despite the number of people trying to sleep. The only real disturbance was an old woman kneeling in the far corner praying at the top of her lungs, while a nervous young girl anxiously pleaded with her to stop.

Queen's guards and the few remaining Cisternans were prowling the house like caged cats, checking their weapons over and over again and alert for anything. The refugees of higher class were crowded in the Albon Tower and the Gate Bastion, with the King's Bastion being kept as a buffer area between the fay in the Old Palace and the fortified court. Thomas had preferred this arrangement, knowing that if he had to have a large group of civilians under his protection in a battle, it was better to have ones who were trained to take orders without question. Ravenna and Falaise and their entourages were safely ensconced on an upper floor.

In the entrance hall he found Phaistus, standing before the partly open doors and looking tentatively up at the cloudy night sky. "What are you doing?" Thomas asked him.

Phaistus jumped, then shifted the heavy coil of rope tucked under his arm. "Berham wanted this in the tower, Captain."

His reluctance was understandable. On the open roads of the country, the Host traditionally attacked from above, swooping down on men like hawks on mice. Except that hawks were unquestionably kinder in dispatching their mice quickly than the Host would be with human captives. The wards still clinging to this side of the palace were supposed to protect them while outside, but the wards had failed before.

"Well, come on then." Thomas hauled him out into the open court.

The night air was chill, the court lit only by light seeping through cracks in shutters and closed doors. The Albon Tower high above them was only a dim shape in the darkness, clouds streaming swiftly across the moon. Phaistus hurried along in Thomas's shadow, casting worried glances at the sky.

The first level of the tower had become an infirmary, and the sick familiar odor of cauterization hit Thomas as soon as he went in.

The wounded lay on pallets along the walls of the high-ceilinged hall. There were women and children among them, far too many. They had been hacked up by the bronze blades of the human servants of the Host, burned in the sporadic fires that had broken out from overturned lamps, or bitten and clawed by the fay. There were no victims of elf-shot. If someone was hit by one of those tiny harmless-looking stones he fell down and never moved or spoke again, no better than breathing dead, and was lucky if starvation or thirst killed him before the stone found his heart. Anyone struck by elf-shot had been left behind, or smothered by Dr. Lambe or one of the other apothecaries.

Fires had been lit in the two great hearths, and dozens of lamps and candles added their stains to the smoke-blackened rafters. The furniture had been pushed aside to make way for more pallets, and Thomas had to climb over a couple of tables to reach the other end of the room. It brought back less-than-pleasant memories of the Bisran War, of border villages overrun and taken before the inhabitants could scatter into the forest, and of the aftermath of battle.

Dr. Lambe stood near the long draw table where bags of instruments and jars of medicinal herbs were laid out. He looked exhausted and considerably the worse for wear. He looked up at Thomas's approach and said, "Captain, when can we leave?"

"As soon as it's daylight. The Host won't be able to form then." Thomas made himself sound sure despite his own doubts.

Lambe didn't look reassured. "And how sure are we of that?"

"I have it on fairly good authority." He had to admit, "What might be wandering the streets is another matter, but they won't be after just anyone."

Lambe glanced upward. The King was on one of the upper floors, guarded heavily. "You're right about that."

The palace was a trap, and they couldn't afford to be caught in it. Ravenna and Roland would have to be gotten to safety. *Whether Ravenna likes it or not,* Thomas thought. His first choice was to get them out of the city and to Villon at the Granges—and they would have to be together. Roland would be swept under by the chaos and lose his throne to the first opportunist with a troop. Ravenna could ride the storm.

Galen Dubell crossed the room toward them. Like Dr. Lambe, the hem and sleeves of his robe were stained with dried blood. "What sort of protections are we employing for the evacuation?" he asked.

Before Thomas could answer, an Albon knight stepped up to them and said, "His Majesty requires an audience, Captain Boniface."

Thomas looked at him, but the knight's face betrayed nothing. After a moment he said, "Very well," and turned to Dubell. "Doctor, could you send a message to my lady Ravenna and let her know I'll be unable to attend her for a short time?"

Startled, Dubell looked from Dr. Lambe's stricken expression to the other Albon knights who had suddenly appeared in the room. He said, "Yes, of course."

Thomas followed the knight to the bottom of the narrow stairwell that led up into the tower, where there were two more Albons waiting for them. He took in their appearance without comment and they started up the stair.

It was a long way up to the fifth level of the tower, the many lamps that illuminated the stone steps making the air smoky and close. There were knights standing guard at each level.

On the landing there were two more Albons at the wide oaken door. The knight who had come after Thomas smiled and said, "His Majesty has requested that you disarm before coming in to him."

Thomas met his eyes. As a member of the Queen's Guard and an appointed officer he had the right to go armed in the royal presence, and he also knew what any sort of protest to that effect would mean to Roland, and what would happen if they searched him inside and found a concealed weapon.

In silence he handed over both pistols, his main gauche, boot dagger, and unbuckled the rapier from his baldric.

One of the knights opened the door and they went inside.

The room was far too warm and too crowded. The gold threads in the red tapestries caught the candlelight and cast it back. There were more Albon knights, all showing signs of the past battle. Some of Roland's younger courtiers were playing cards at a table in a corner, and somewhere out of sight a musician played a soprano recorder. Renier wasn't present. Roland was seated in a tapestry-draped armchair, Denzil at his side.

As Thomas bowed, Roland said, "Kneel, Sir."

Even though he was hearing the latch of a trap snap shut, it was second nature to make it look like an easy gesture.

Denzil smiled lazily and said something inaudible to Roland that made the young King giggle and redden with embarrassment. Thomas realized Roland was not drunk yet, but he was definitely well on the way, and he would have bet anything it was Denzil's doing.

Roland fiddled with a torn piece of lace on his cuff, his eyes large and dark. "What is my mother doing now?"

"She's resting, Your Majesty." Thomas kept his expression even and his voice level. The room had quieted, and the courtiers were watching with a fascinated intensity that combined sly amusement at someone else's misfortune and fear for their own necks.

"And my Queen? My cousin has said she refuses to attend me here."

Thomas wondered if Falaise knew she had refused to attend Roland. Probably not. "She isn't well, Your Majesty, and your mother required her to stay in her rooms." This was a lie, but he wasn't going to throw the young Queen to the wolves to save his own skin. *If the matter doesn't become academic in the next few moments.*

Roland said, "Oh." Even at this time, he realized Falaise was not likely to ignore a direct order from Ravenna. But Denzil nudged him with an elbow, causing the knight standing guard behind their chairs to tighten his grip on his sword-hilt. Thus prompted, Roland said, "And my sister?"

"She's in the Guard House, Your Majesty."

Denzil idly twisted one of his rings. His hands were trembling slightly, probably from excitement. He said, "She was seen smearing blood on the lintels and cornerposts of the Guard House. Now why was she doing that, we wonder?"

How the hell should I know? "I don't know, Your Majesty." Thomas directed his answer to Roland, just to see Denzil's expression tighten with anger. It was hardly likely to be anything detrimental; even Kade wouldn't put a curse on a house and then settle down in it for the night. And she obviously hadn't made a secret of what she had done. It sounded more like a feast-day practice one of the foreign cults in the city performed.

Roland absently rubbed the carved arm of the chair, thinking over his next move. Denzil leaned toward him familiarly, watching Thomas out of the corner of his eye, and whispered something. Roland giggled and looked guilty.

Thomas allowed himself to look just slightly bored. Denzil's attempts to prey on his nerves were having more effect on the Albon who was standing behind him and could hear what he was saying.

Finally Roland said, "Perhaps you told her to do it."

"Why would I do that, Your Majesty?" Thomas had always known that if he had to die to please a royal ego, he wanted it to be as scandalous, messy, and politically inconvenient for as many persons as possible. Disappearing into the depths of the Albon Tower was not a scenario he preferred.

Roland didn't answer immediately. He bit his lower lip and looked at his cousin.

Denzil stood and strolled around the room, behind Thomas and out of his sight. He said, "We don't know what part she had in this attack."

Thomas kept his eyes on Roland. "She was almost killed in the retreat from the main hall." Defending her this way could be dangerous for both of them, but he wasn't sure what Denzil was after.

Roland looked surprised. "She was?"

Standing too near him, Denzil brushed Thomas's hair aside to reveal the pearl drop in his right ear. "That's a gift from the Dowager Queen, is it not?"

The door opened and a knight bowed his way in. "Pardon, Your Majesty."

Denzil stepped away from Thomas. Roland shifted in his chair nervously. "What is it?"

"The Queen... The Dowager Queen has sent a messenger requesting Captain Boniface's immediate presence."

All eyes in the room went to Roland as most of those present realized the implications of this. Thomas thought, *Don't provoke her, boy, not now.* Ravenna was exhausted and angry and sitting on top of the best-organized force left in the palace with an armory at her back. But if Roland pushed her into a civil war just because he could, then he didn't deserve to be King, let alone to live.

Roland stared at the knight. Denzil started to speak but abruptly Roland waved him to silence and said, "Fine, then, go on. I'm tired."

Thomas stood, bowed, and left the room. He collected his weapons in complete silence from the knights on the landing, then went down the stairs. Martin was pacing restlessly near the outside door.

Reaching him, Thomas said, "Tell her you saw me outside and I'll be there in a few moments."

Martin said, "Yes, Sir," and bolted back across the court. Thomas went the other way, along the tower's wall, until he came to a place in deep shadow but with a good view of the door.

He pulled his cloak around him and stood with folded arms, watching the cloud-strewn sky. The cool wind lifted the hair off the back of his neck, and he thought for a few moments about treason and murder.

But he had learned more from Denzil than the Duke had from him. *He thought he had me. He was sure of it.* He had tried to provoke Thomas to fight. He wanted Ravenna and Roland at each other's throats; he wanted the palace in chaos.

Denzil was confident. He had expected the attack.

He took the keystone, or he ordered it done. Never mind how he knew where it was; I'll work that out later. He may have killed Braun himself. And I don't have a shred of proof against him.

There was only one thing Denzil could want in return for treason of such a magnitude.

The young Duke of Alsene had so much already from Roland. Would he abandon a secure existence on a chancy bid for the throne, based on such infirm ground as the help of a foreign sorcerer? *But is Denzil's existence secure?* Thomas asked himself. *Or more importantly, does he think his existence is secure?* Roland was still Ravenna's son, and Fulstan's. He could have Denzil killed on a whim, at any time. And he was still a young man; he could become as changeable in later life as his father had.

As a patch of moonlight illuminated the court, a swift smooth shadow crossed it. Something large enough to be flying above the wards yet throw a man-sized shadow on the pearl gray paving stones.

Thomas leaned back against the wall, his dark clothing blending into the rough stonework. A reminder from the Host.

As it passed out of sight and the clouds crept back over the moon, the Albon knight he had suspected was following him stepped quietly out into the court from the door of the tower.

Thomas waited until the man gave up and disappeared back inside, then started back to the Guard House.

Denzil was in league with Grandier, and regardless of the consequences, he was going to have to die.

తుం

In the Guard House, Kade was sitting on the floor near the stairs. She turned over another card from the deck she had found, winced, swept the scattered cards together, and reshuffled them. Something was happening in the Albon Tower, something interesting, and no one would tell her about it. *Who can I pry it out of,* she wondered, looking speculatively around the quiet hall and laying out the cards again.

No one seemed to find her presence objectionable. The refugees had brought her everything from amulets to prayer books to bless for luck, and she had collected several apples, an egg, a few ribbons, and a battered daisy as propitiatory gifts. The guards were all nobles and so less superstitious, but treated her as a sort of mascot, which was better behavior than she had had from anyone connected with the crown in a long time. They knew who had been on the wrong side of the bastion's siege doors with them, and were acting accordingly.

Falaise had sent her a pair of boots. The woman who had brought them had said they were a boy-page's boots, made for a masque last month and brought along accidentally in the trunk the Queen's ladies had hastily packed before leaving the King's Bastion, but the Queen had "thought they would suit best." *She meant they looked big enough,* Kade thought. Falaise and her ladies had small perfect feet, not ugly long-toed things better suited for walking on tree branches. But the boots were soft, blue-stamped leather with gold stitching, and she liked them immensely.

She rubbed the bruised lump on her head thoughtfully. That is, no one objected to her presence openly. She still didn't know what she had been hit with in the retreat to the King's Bastion. An object that small of wood or stone would have certainly startled her, but not knocked her reeling and half-conscious against the banister. No, the object had been cold iron, and no fay had cast it at her.

And Thomas Boniface had carried her up the stairs.

That had triggered a memory, a tactile child's memory. She had been six or seven, playing on the warm dusty stones of a palace court with servants' children, and suddenly found herself among a forest of sharp hooves and tall equine legs, horses snorting and dancing around her. For a moment she had found it wonderful. But just as fear had time to set in, a strong arm had caught her around the waist and lifted her out of danger with a muttered "And what do you think you're doing." She had been deposited on the side of the court out of harm's way, and left with a memory of a deep voice and a masculine scent combined with the musky sweat of horses.

Her father had heard about it somehow. He heard about everything somehow. He had called her a whore. When she had told Galen about it, he had slammed things around his small study and muttered to himself for an hour, but he was not quite worldly enough to realize what was bothering her and explain it away. It wasn't until weeks later when a scrubwoman had explained to her what a whore was that she understood she couldn't possibly be one. *A whore,* she thought, old stale anger rising again. At that age and about as alluring as an awkward puppy. *It's a wonder that I'm not mad as a wool-dyer.* It was a wonder she wasn't as helplessly at sea in the world as Roland was.

"Excuse me, my lady?"

She looked up to see a nervous dark-haired gentlewoman on the stairs above, looking down at her hesitantly. Kade thought her one of Falaise's ladies, but she wasn't the one who had come before. Then the woman said, "My lady, the lady Ravenna would like to speak to you in her chamber."

"Oh," Kade said. She collected the cards and stood up.

She followed the woman up the lamplit stairs to the third floor. The rooms Ravenna and Falaise had taken were in a single suite. There was a group of Queen's guards and two Cisternans standing in the anteroom having a low-voiced, intense, and agitated conversation Kade was sure would have been quite interesting, but the gentlewoman opened the inner door to Ravenna's chamber for her, curtseyed, and fled.

Ravenna sat alone near the shuttered window, head turned to look down at the empty hearth. A few carved chests stood open, and richly embroidered robes and rugs were tumbled about and piled in the chairs. Kade fought a surge of anxiety that suddenly welled up in her gut; she was not a child anymore.

"I wanted to know your intentions." Ravenna turned to look at her, finally. "Why you are still here."

Kade looked down and noticed her feet again. She said, "Why shouldn't I be here?"

"'Why shouldn't I be,'" Ravenna mocked. "Your wit astonishes me. Of course, everything I've built with my life and my blood is tumbling down around my ears; why shouldn't you stay and watch?"

"If you already know then why are you asking?" Kade said it quietly, and looked up to deliberately meet Ravenna's eyes. *That was good. I did that well.*

"Oh, never mind." It was Ravenna who looked away. "I suppose if you actually had some sort of motive, you would give me an answer."

Kade sighed, then realized the old Queen's sharp eyes were on her again and felt a chill that didn't come from the air. Ravenna had set a trap for that telltale expression of relief. "Well," Ravenna said slowly. "Do you still want the throne?"

"No! I just said that; I didn't mean it." *I should have known that would come back to haunt me.* "Can't you just leave me out of your idiot power struggles?" But it was easy to talk about the throne. Ravenna couldn't understand how little it meant to her.

Ravenna's mouth hardened. "No, I cannot. I'm old, and frightened. I get angry when I'm frightened and your brother does not know when to stop pressing me. Or rather, he lets Denzil tell him that it is all some sort of game, and that his mother will forgive him anything, because she wants him on the throne. Well, I'm having second thoughts about that."

"Don't bother having first thoughts about me, because I won't do it."

Ravenna's hard eyes came back to her again, cynical and doubting. Kade said, "I'm serious. It's hard enough being a queen in Fayre, but this is...real."

"I wish Roland knew that. I tried to teach him to rule, but he doesn't understand. Our people aren't serf-slaves, like Bisran peasants. They'll riot in the cities and rebel over the vine-growers' excise in the country. The balances of power that must be maintained among the nobles of this city alone…" She tapped her fingers on the chair arm and shook her head. "I push Roland, to test him, to make him strong, but he backs away. Then he lets Denzil goad him into pushing me too far."

Kade looked at her curiously. Even in the soft candlelight Ravenna was all glinting sharp edges, her sharp profile, her jewels, her eyes. She wondered if her brother understood that someday his mother would be gone, and there would be nothing to cushion him from the battleground of the court. "If not Roland, and not me, then who?"

Ravenna seemed to ignore the question. She said, "I planned it so carefully. I let the Ministry gain power. The nobles," she invested the word with considerable contempt, "clung to each other in salons all over the city, alternately whining and shouting about it, but they couldn't stop me. I reduced the walls of their private strongholds, took away their private armies, so if the flower of nobility wanted to rebel against Roland they'd have a damned hard time doing it. And Aviler has some concept of how a state should function; he would have been able to keep Roland from making too bloody a fool of himself. I made an enemy of Aviler, even though his father was one of my closest friends, because if I had ever shown him favor Roland would never have listened to him. Of course, Roland never listened to him anyway. And now we don't know where Aviler is, or if he's alive." She stopped and looked away. "If not you, then no one."

Kade anchored her eyes on the floor. *She is already speaking of Roland in the past tense.*

After a long moment of silence Ravenna said, "I'm rather an all-or-nothing sort of person when it comes to violence. Roland doesn't understand that." There was a returning quality of strength and calculation in her tone that made Kade look up at her.

The old Queen was watching her carefully again. "Thomas is rather an all-or-nothing sort of person when it comes to loyalty. I don't think anyone at court understands that, excepting myself and the Guardsmen. You could come to understand it."

Kade stared at her, feeling completely transparent under that gaze. A slow flush of heat reddened her cheeks.

Ravenna said, "Are you sure you won't reconsider my offer? The benefits are considerable."

She said, "Listen, you dried-up old bitch—"

Ravenna smiled.

Kade took a deep breath to give herself enough air to get the words out. "If you want my help in pulling your fat out of the fire, then you can damn well keep your offers and your speculations to yourself, because I don't want to hear them and I won't, do you understand?"

"Quite well, thank you, dear." Ravenna nodded pleasantly.

Kade stalked out the door and slammed it behind her.

The anteroom was empty. *Why do I stay here?* Kade raged at herself. *I meant to cut off all these old ties, say what I wanted to say, and forget about all of it. To get some peace at last. But I've done nothing but get into stupid arguments with Roland and make Ravenna think she can put me under her thumb again. How dare she even imply... Imply what?*

She paced a tight circle in the anteroom, remembering Ravenna's smile at her angry response. *Did I just make a mistake?*

The door to the hall opened and Thomas walked in. Kade jumped guiltily.

"Did you put blood on the lintels and the cornerposts of this house?" he asked her, keeping his voice low.

She held her hand out, to show him the fresh cut across the white skin of her palm, and thought, *He has such dark eyes, like velvet.* She was starting to blush again, for no accountable reason. To distract herself, she asked, "What happened while you were gone?"

He regarded her for a moment. "What is it for?"

God, can no one answer a direct question? She folded her arms and looked at the floor. "To keep fay out. To let them know I'm in here, and that I'm not receiving visitors."

"Will it work?"

She shook her head. "Not that well. The ones it will keep out wouldn't be that difficult to deal with anyway. But it's something."

"Why did you choose here, and not one of the other buildings?"

Not wanting to answer, she began to tap one foot in growing irritation. He waited. Finally she looked up and said, "I like it here. There, are you happy?"

He said, "Delighted," and went into Ravenna's room.

Well, I handled that brilliantly, Kade thought. A soft noise made her glance back and she saw Falaise standing in the doorway to her room. She was wearing a pale blue heavily embroidered mantua and her hair hung like a chestnut curtain. She looked like a startled fawn. "What is it?" Kade asked her, temporarily distracted.

Falaise made a noise like a strangled gasp and vanished back into her room. Kade followed her. Inside was the tumbled splendor of a parlor attached to a small bedchamber, three ladies-in-waiting looking up at them in surprise. Falaise stopped in the middle of the room and shrieked, "Out! I want to be alone." It wasn't the full-throated bellow Ravenna was capable of but it worked well enough. As the gentlewomen scurried for the door, Kade stayed where she was, correctly surmising that the order had not been directed at her.

As soon as the door closed behind the last woman, Falaise seized a wine glass from the table and dashed its contents onto the polished floorboards. As Kade stared, the Queen shoved a chair away from the wall that adjoined the Dowager Queen's quarters and crawled under a table, placing the glass to the wall and her ear on the glass.

"What are you doing?" Kade asked, baffled.

"There's a weak board here. I can hear through to Ravenna's room."

"Brilliant!" Kade climbed onto the table and pressed her ear to the wall, but couldn't hear anything but muffled voices. "What are they saying?"

"Shhh."

Short of dragging Falaise out from under the table by the ankles and taking her place, which would cause them to miss some of the conversation, there was nothing to do but wait. Kade paced, tangled her fingers in her hair, and tried to contain herself.

Finally, as doors slammed out in the anteroom, Falaise crawled out from under the table and sat back on the floor with a sigh.

Kade bounced with excitement. "Well?"

Falaise scrubbed wine out of her ear with the sleeve of her mantua. "It was a terrific fight."

"About what?"

"He has a plan for leaving the palace because we're going to be attacked by the fay again. He said they're just waiting, they have a traitor inside helping them, and that when they can come through cracks in the walls, we can't hope to keep them out forever."

"He's right."

Falaise sat back on the floor, hugging her knees, looking up at her quizzically. "Are the wards working?" The question was anxious, but not panicky.

Kade decided to tell her the truth. "They're working up above us. But most of them aren't touching the ground anymore. It's only the siege doors and the gates keeping the Host out."

"I see." The Queen bit her lip.

"But what did they fight about?" Kade demanded.

"We're going to be leaving in the morning. But Ravenna doesn't like some part of the plan, and it made her very angry. She yelled and threw things, and said she didn't intend to die alone."

"Really?"

"Yes, and he told her she was too mean to die at all, alone or in company, and if she thought he was fool enough to fall for these mock hysterics then she should think again and she was going anyway if he had to tie her to a horse." Falaise shook her head, an irritated kitten. "Something happened in the Albon Tower, something to do with Roland and Denzil. But she already seemed to know what it was, and they didn't discuss any details."

"Hell, that's not much." *Maybe I can find out more downstairs.* As Kade reached for the door Falaise said, "If you find out anything else, will you come and tell me?"

"All right."

"Thank you."

Leaving the room, Kade wondered if Falaise had heard her own conversation with Ravenna, and if it mattered. *It might. She is full of surprises.*

〰

Thomas crossed the hall and went into the map room. The fire burned low behind the grate and Vivan was gone; he was unsure if that was a good sign or not. He stood for a moment contemplating a faded parchment map of the city on the table. He needed to go back up to Ravenna, but he didn't trust his temper quite yet.

He knew she would agree to his plan. She wouldn't let emotion get in the way of necessity for too long, and it was only his part in it that disturbed her. And whatever she did, he didn't intend to give in to her this time.

"Captain! Captain, look!" someone shouted from outside the room. Stepping toward the door, he saw Gideon surrounded by a noisy group of guards and conducting another man across the hall in an apparently friendly headlock.

Thomas started forward as Gideon released his captive with an affectionate shake, and felt an idiot grin spreading over his face as he saw who it was.

Lucas and a younger guard named Gerard, whom they had also given up for dead, staggered into the room under the enthusiastic greetings of their comrades. Lucas grinned back at him. "What are you gaping at?"

"Why aren't you dead?" Thomas caught the older man in an embrace. "And where the hell have you been?"

Lucas dropped onto a bench at the table. "I've been banging on a bloody gate, trying to get the idiot on the other side to let us in. Before that we were crawling through the streets on our bellies. Look, God bless that man for a saint!"

Anticipating the request, Phaistus was bringing in an armful of wine bottles and tankards.

As the wine was passed around, Lucas said, "It's a wonderful story; do you want to hear the version where I climbed the St. Anne's Gate in a hail of heathen arrows with my sword in my teeth and a fainting Gerard slung over one shoulder?"

"You lying bastard!" Gerard objected, slamming down the tankard that someone had just handed him, spraying everyone around him with the contents.

"We got out the Postern Gate, actually," Lucas admitted more soberly. "It's a ruin, no sign of anyone. We couldn't come along the outside wall; there's a lot of somethings-or-others congregated along it that we didn't want too close a look at. We had to go several streets over to get around and back to the Prince's Gate. There's a very large hole in the park side of the Gallery Wing. I couldn't get very close but it looked as though something erupted out of the floor in the Grand Gallery."

Thomas knew Lucas well enough to recognize the fear in his eyes. That fear was masked by bluff, as it was in most men, and the louder the bluff the greater the fear. It was very loud in that room right now. "Out of the floor?" he asked. "Are you certain?"

"Yes. Don't ask me what it was; I've no idea. If we hadn't been in the portico and halfway outside already when it happened, we'd be dead." Lucas turned his tankard around thoughtfully. "As it was we lost Arians, Brandon, and Lesard." He looked up. "That I know of."

Thomas told him. "Twenty-six altogether, not counting you two."

"That many." Lucas looked away.

"What's it like in the city?" Gideon asked softly.

"It was hard to tell. We saw some houses broken into and burned out, but others locked up tight. No one's out on the streets anymore that we could see. There was ten or so palace-folk that crept out after us, but they decided to chance it in the city. We thought we'd try to make it back here so we could die with our friends like gentlemen." He looked around at everyone. "So? How have you lot been keeping busy?"

CHAPTER TEN

THOMAS AWOKE KNOWING what it felt like to be a corpse—stiff and cold. The fire had burnt down to coals, and seemed to be emitting nothing but a dim red glow. Any heat produced was lost in the frigid air. He eased out of the chair and started pulling wood out of the stacked pile beside the hearth. His hands were numb.

The kindling he dumped on the coals caught and he started to add the logs. After a timeless wait the heavier wood started to burn and he began to feel alive, and only two or three times his age.

Sitting on the floor in front of the fire and still shivering, he heard the timber frame of the house creak protestingly against the onslaught of a harsh wind. It was an oddly sudden cold spell for this time of year.

They should be due for two to three more months of fall rain before winter set in. It never got this cold until after midwinter.

He climbed to his feet and found his cloak on the floor across the room and bundled up in it, then went out into the hall. Only two lanterns were lit there now, and it was as cold as a saint's bed. An old house with this many restless bodies crowded into it could never be entirely silent, but all the sounds—footsteps of patrolling guards creaking the boards on an upper story, the fitful stirring of sleepers on the hall floor, a child's frustrated crying—were oddly muted. Shadowy forms wrapped in blankets stumbled around the dark cavern of the hall's huge fireplace, building up a fire in the hearth that had been scraped clean and unused since last winter. Once they got the blaze going, warmth from the chimney would help heat the upper floors, though not nearly enough for comfort.

Thomas started upstairs, buttoning up the sleeves of his doublet.

There was a small window looking out into the court from the second-floor landing. Ice was starting to form on it already. Clouds still streamed across the sky, allowing the shrinking moon to briefly illuminate the court one moment, leaving it in pitch darkness the next. He could hear the wind howling, and the front wall protesting faintly in response.

He didn't hear Kade's footsteps but was somehow unsurprised when he noticed her standing beside him.

She said, "Grandier had to work on this for days."

He looked down at her but there wasn't quite enough light to see her expression. She looked like a fanciful drawing of a gypsy with her hair flying in all directions and a torn piece of petticoat dragging the ground. She wore a blanket over her shoulders and the night muted the red of her dress, making her look very human and solid. He asked, "How did he do it?"

"A shift in the wind one day, gather clouds from over the sea the next. Very slow work, and very subtle. Oh, it might have made it a little cooler than it should have been, or there was less rain or more rain. But who would notice?" The slender moon peeping through a gap in the swift-moving darkness above revealed clouds like monoliths, black streaming giants crossing the sky.

Thomas watched the clouds. This was obviously meant to be the last nail in their coffin, trapping them within the city, forestalling aid. "Can you do anything?"

She shrugged. "The spells to do this were set and done months ago, when the forces were favorable. Now the planets aren't in the right houses for influencing the weather, and they won't begin to favor atmospheric magic for another month at least. His timing of its arrival is excellent, and there's no saying how long it will last. Galen might know of something to try, but I don't. I'm only the Queen of Air and Darkness by inheritance, and I don't have a degree in philosophy from Lodun."

They stood there quiet for a time. The wind's fury made the timber and stone wall of the house seem flimsy, as if they were separated from a vicious animal by only a thin layer of decorative fence. Thomas found himself watching Kade. He was no longer certain what to think about her, and that disturbed him far more than it should, considering everything else there was to worry about. *I always try to understand my enemies,* he thought, *but it's time to admit that the one thing she is not is an enemy.* Finally, he asked, "What does it mean to be the Queen of Air and Darkness?"

Her brow furrowed, she said, "I don't have a kingdom, except for the castles my mother kept. Some of them are in little pockets of the Otherworld, some are in this world, but protected by spells. But in a way... From knowing

Titania, Oberon, the other rulers of Fayre, I have the sense that what I am somehow defines what they are. I might exist to balance them, the way they exist to balance the Unseelie Court. But it isn't good and evil, either. I'm not particularly evil most of the time, and they aren't particularly good hardly any of the time, at least not by human standards." She shivered, and the moonlight brought silver to her hair. "The Unseelie Court doesn't approve of balance, and they're always scheming to upset things. My mother Moire accepted a wager from them, that she could steal all the grain from Oberon's stables without missing a single seed. She got past the fay guarding the stables by changing herself into a beautiful white mare, and she made all the grain vanish—except for one flax seed. The Unseelie Court had suborned a flower sprite that lived in the stable, and it hid the seed in the bell of a flower, so Moire couldn't find it. So she lost the wager, and they sent her to Hell. They seemed to think I should be grateful for it. She wasn't a nice person and we didn't exactly live in a state of joy together, but she was my mother." After a moment she seemed to shake off the recollection and pulled her blanket more closely around her. "The weather will be worse tomorrow. Grandier wouldn't have spared us the snow."

Thomas hadn't missed the hurried change of subject. He wondered why she had told him so much. He asked, "Spared us?"

Kade looked up at him.

"When did it become 'us'?"

She turned from the window and started to walk away, but stopped after a few steps. "Do you remember me?" she asked.

Because of the intimacy of standing here in the shadows watching death come out of the north, or just that he was becoming used to her way of speaking, he knew what she meant. He said, "Not the way you looked, not really. Not very well."

"I remember you."

He didn't reply. The silence stretched, and Kade faded back into the shadows. Thomas turned away from the window and went down the stairs and back to the map room. The weather was one more thing to worry about, one more factor to take into account. At least a freeze would put off the possibility of a plague brewing up among the unburied dead in the east quarter of the palace, and the rest of the city.

As he neared the open door of the map room, he saw an outline of a long cloak or robe silhouetted by the edge of the firelight. Someone was there. Thomas stopped in the doorway, feeling an inexplicable chill that had nothing to do with the cold.

But a flare-up from the fire showed him it was only Galen Dubell warming his hands near the hearth, his stooped shoulders shivering faintly underneath his heavy robe.

Stepping into the room, Thomas said, "You're awake early, Doctor."

The sorcerer looked up and smiled. "It's a trifle cold for my old bones." He shook his head. "I'll begin work on counter-measures against this weather as soon as it's light. You realize it is not natural."

"Kade told me." Thomas lit the candlelamps with a twig from the fire, and began to go through the maps stacked on the table, looking for the one of the city walls and the solid paths through the water meadows. Under the maps, he found the pile of translated Bisran court documents instead. They had been sent over the night of the attack, and he had never had the chance to look at them.

Dubell took the armchair near the hearth that Commander Vivan had occupied some hours ago. "I must admit, Kade is not the same girl I once tutored," he said.

Thomas sat down on the bench and began idly paging through the trial documents. He said, "I would hope not." The list of questions and answers was much the same as the monk's account had been. Grandier had refused to name accomplices, which must have cost him a great deal. Thomas also thought the Inquisition showed an unhealthy degree of interest in sexual relations with demons.

After a long silence Dubell said, "I find myself wondering at her motives."

Thomas looked up. The sorcerer's expression was vaguely troubled. "I don't think it's as complicated as it seems. She has unfinished business with Roland and Ravenna." Thomas had been younger than Kade was now when he had had the devastating and final confrontation with his father, when he had left to pursue the commission of Captain that would allow him to legally and permanently disown his entire family. The urge to try to settle old arguments and angers had been strong, and his attempts along those lines had turned out just as badly as Kade's seemed destined to.

"Perhaps you're right." But Dubell didn't seem convinced.

Thomas turned over the last page of the trial transcript and glanced over the next closely written document. A note at the top described it as a Bisran priest's description of Grandier's confession during his questioning.

Thomas skipped through most of a page of unconvincing preamble as to why this disclosure wasn't violating the sanctity of confession. The rest of it read:

> *...and he confessed to me quite freely. He had not dealt*
> *with the darkness, or at least the Evil One as we recognize*

it. He had been approached by the aspects of the fay, who had offered him powers beyond the reach of mortal sorcery in exchange for mortal souls, which they must annually tithe to Hell to preserve their soulless immortality. He had refused these offers, but our ill treatment (I but repeat his words) had caused him to reconsider. They had offered him swift travel and flight, but what he would bargain for was the terrible ability to alter his physical form, that no wizard of human blood had been able to accomplish. This would cause great pain to him, and once done he would never be able to resume his own shape, nor any other shape that he would assume and abandon, and it required that he could not assume a shape in an image worn by a living man, he must destroy its original before he could assume it...

...before he could assume it. Thomas found himself wiping his hands off on his trouser legs. It had the ring of truth about it as nothing else in the Bisran documents had. It was far too realistic for a Bisran priest, who had been trained to find evil influence in every lung fever and to hate magic like a mortal enemy, to fabricate. *This is true; this is what he told them after they drove him mad with torture and accusations. And if you were Grandier, which shape would you choose...* He looked up at Galen Dubell.

The sorcerer was sitting absolutely still and watching him with an expression of thoughtful speculation. He was no longer shivering from the cold. "What are you reading, Captain, that has apparently been so revealing?"

"Nothing in particular. A dispatch from Portier." Thomas' rapier stood against the wall near the hearth perhaps four steps away. He started to stand.

"I don't think so."

The gentle contradiction held no anger, but Thomas stopped. He had betrayed himself somehow, but Dubell had always shown a talent for guessing at others' thoughts. *I can't let him kill me now. If he burns these papers and walks out of here no one will ever know until it's far too late. It may already be too late.*

The old sorcerer said, "Perhaps the time for the masquerade is over anyway. But I think I've been found out."

"It's a priest's report of Grandier's...of your confession during your trial." Thomas slid the document across the table, but the sorcerer didn't take the bait and reach for it. Thomas kept expecting the mask to drop but it didn't. It was still Dubell's face, Dubell's eyes. Dubell's look of regret.

"Indeed," Urbain Grandier said softly. "I didn't expect to have anyone take it seriously. Not in Bisra, at least. They all believed I was hand in glove with the Prince of Hell, you know. As to how the incriminating document followed me here, I suppose I can credit the Church's league of brotherly spies."

The fire popped loudly in the silence. Thomas felt the extreme danger that lay in carrying on this conversation but was unable to stop. Knowing and believing were two different things. If a weapon had been in reach, there was a good chance he would have hesitated with it, and that would have been fatal. *And he looked up at me over Treville's dead body and said, "I'm sorry."* He said, "Did you do it when you kidnapped him from Lodun?"

Grandier looked mildly surprised. "Oh, no. It was long before that. I kidnapped myself, you see."

It would have had to be that way. Dr. Surete's death, and Milam's. *It was simplicity itself, he told us, if one had the stomach for it.* Grandier watched him with a dead man's eyes. Thomas said, "Why haven't you let the Host in yet? That's part of your bargain, isn't it? Your payment to them."

"The Unseelie Court did me a great service," Grandier agreed. "I owe them much. The first shape I took was that of the man who served as the secular judge at that farce the Inquisition deemed my trial. He was so cold, so forbidding even to his own family that aping his manner presented no challenge. He was powerful, and I took my revenge as I liked. I lived as him for nearly half a year, before I tired of it. Then it was a young servant in his house, for I needed to move about without drawing attention to myself..." Grandier gestured the memory away, his expression wry in the firelight. "But my plans do not always coincide with those of my associates, a fact they fail to understand."

A log shifted in the fire and as Grandier reflexively glanced toward it Thomas rolled backward off the bench, grabbed his sword from where it stood against the wall, and whipped off the scabbard. Grandier leapt out of the chair, his hand moving as if he were gathering something out of the air and tossing it. Thomas saw the sorcerer's quick motion and scrambled sideways, coming to his feet as a blue blaze of light struck the wall where he had been. It splashed on the bricks, sizzling and smoking like acid. Thomas threw himself at Grandier with a suicidal lack of caution. But Grandier dodged backward with surprising agility and the tip of the rapier only slashed a yard-long hole in the hanging fold of his sleeve.

They both saw Kade standing in the doorway at the same time.

Thomas's first thought was that faced with the situation the only reasonable conclusion she could come to was that he was attacking Galen Dubell. But it was Grandier she was staring at.

She looked at Grandier with a kind of growing incredulous fury, a combination of wounded pride at being fooled and all-too-human betrayal. The sorcerer looked back at her, and his eyes held all of Dubell's intelligence and wit and the gentle humor he employed on those who pleased him. He said, "No, it wasn't your fault."

The fury flared and ignited and she took a step toward him. But Grandier's hand came out of his robes and he tossed something at her. It wasn't a deadly flash of sorcerous light. It was a handful of iron filings.

Iron wouldn't harm Kade as much as it did other fay, but it would interfere with her ability to do magic. Even as Thomas started forward Kade leapt back to avoid the filings and Grandier pushed past her and out the door. As he crossed the threshold, the candles and the fire were extinguished with a hiss as if all had been doused with water, plunging the room into shadow.

Thomas banged into the heavy table that had somehow moved into his way, shoved it aside, and ran out into the hall.

Grandier was halfway to the outside door, Kade running after him. The few lamps that were lit extinguished as the sorcerer passed them. Thomas shouted for the guards in the hall to follow him, but in the confusion and darkness he couldn't tell if any heard.

Thomas caught up with Kade in the entry hall and together they slammed out the door and into the frozen mud and cold of the court. The clouds had opened up again and the moonlight was stark white, the wind a tearing force, and Grandier was nowhere to be seen.

Kade spun around, trying to look in every direction at once. Thomas did a quick circuit of the court, but found nothing.

"Damn it, where is he?" he muttered. Grandier, loose in the confusion of the palace...

As he reached Kade's side again, she looked up and said, "Oh, no." Thomas followed her gaze. A shadow had appeared and now grew on the moon's narrow face, becoming larger and larger. It was a blot of greater darkness dropping toward them out of the night.

She said, "He's opened the wards."

Without having to discuss it they both went for the nearest shelter, the lee side of the wellhouse. They were too far from the Guard House, from the entrance of any building. The winged fay plunged toward the ground, then seemed to hover above the courtyard, as insubstantial as a shadow.

The wellhouse's door was on the far side, Thomas knew. They could edge around to it if they were lucky, if the fay beast was half-blind.

Thomas started to slide along the wall and Kade grabbed his arm and whispered, "Don't move." He hesitated, thinking, *Does she know what she's doing?* Then he noticed the quality of the light change as the moon's sparkle on the ground around them became almost palpable, and remembered Kade's ability to eavesdrop without being seen, and that one of her fay powers was supposed to be illusion.

The creature that touched ground lightly in the courtyard was a living shadow, the moonlight seeming to bend away from it. In the jumble of dark shapes that composed it, Thomas could see only a snakelike motion and the pointed delicate razor-outline of a claw held at an unlikely angle.

Kade was whispering, "Moonlight, shadow, moonlight, shadow..."

Thomas thought, *Thank God we're downwind.* Then he saw Grandier, walking toward the bizarre thing. A moment later the creature was aloft, soaring upward at an incredible speed.

Kade slid down the wall to sit in the mud.

The illusion around them dissipated into tiny sparkling droplets of light that fell to the ground like beads of dew and disappeared. Fayre glamour, Thomas realized. He said, "Very good," and gave Kade a hand up.

Kade swayed a bit as she stood, not bothering to brush the mud and dirt off her dress. She shook her head frustratedly and ran a hand through her hair. "He let the wards move back into place, after he was past them. Why did he do that?"

Thomas assumed it was a rhetorical question. At least, he had no idea how to answer. The door to the Guard House swung open and torchlight poured into the court. There were shouts from the direction of the Albon Tower. The timing was too good. He wondered if Grandier had cast another spell besides the one to extinguish the candles, a spell to create confusion and keep everyone else inside.

Then Kade demanded, "What did he do with Galen?"

She was looking up at him, those clear gray eyes angry and beginning to be afraid. Not having read the priest's document, she would not have understood that part of the conversation. He said, "Galen's dead."

᾿ᴕᴕ᾿

"Mother, this seems like cowardice," Roland said. He stood huddled in a heavy fur cloak, attended by Renier and two servants, all dressed for hard riding in frigid weather. The other knights charged with guarding him paced about warily, a short distance away. It was barely dawn, and the sky was a solid gray roof, low and threatening. A half hour ago the wind had died and the snow had begun to fall.

Ravenna pulled her hood up over her tightly braided hair and adjusted her gloves. "No, dear, it seems like survival." She turned to Elaine, who stood quietly at her elbow. "Wrap your scarf more carefully, child; this cold could ruin your skin."

Thomas folded his arms and tried not to show his frustration; it was just like Roland to balk at the eleventh hour. Staying in the palace, at Grandier's mercy, was impossible.

They stood in the court below the Albon Tower, an island of relative calm amid the bustle of preparations for the evacuation. Under his cloak Renier wore a gold-embossed gorget and back- and breastplates as many of the Albon knights did. Thomas and most of the other guards preferred the heavy leather buff coats which offered almost as much protection as the awkward armor pieces and allowed more freedom of movement. In the dim morning light servants ran past, coaches and wagons were being loaded, horses saddled or harnessed, all in apprehensive haste. Nothing had been said about last night's confrontation in the Albon Tower, and nothing would be said, unless Roland was an utter fool. *Which is not entirely out of the realm of possibility*, Thomas thought.

"I'm not deserting my court," the King muttered stubbornly.

"Roland," Ravenna said with a sigh. "You are the court, the crown, and the throne. This place has only symbolic value; you can rule just as well from Portier or the Granges. But only if you're alive."

The King looked away, a little mollified. "I dislike having them say we ran, that's all." He hesitated a long moment, and Thomas silently contemplated the gray sky and braced himself to let Ravenna handle the next objection. But Roland said, "Is it really true about Dr. Dubell?"

Panic and rumor had spread through the crowded halls, and Thomas had spent most of the night trying to quell it. Ravenna's eyes went hard and she said, "Yes, it is true." The news had not sat easily with her; she had hated the thought that she could be deceived along with everyone else.

Roland bit his lip, not meeting her eyes, then nodded. "I see." He turned abruptly and went back toward the tower, the snow crunching under his boots, his servants and knights trailing him. Renier shook his head and followed.

Ravenna smiled ruefully. "A pretty speech I gave about symbolic value, don't you think? One might imagine I believed it." She eyed Thomas with mild annoyance. "I'm still angry with you. I didn't enjoy being coerced into this, but you've got your way, and I suppose that's the height of male ambition."

"That's amusing coming from you," Thomas said without rancor. They had been through this all last night, when he had finally persuaded her to accept his plan for the retreat.

"Perhaps." She watched him a moment, a flicker of something other than cool control in her eyes. "For all your faults, I trust you'll come out of this alive." She started across the court without waiting for a reply.

Though he needed to be elsewhere now, Thomas found himself pausing to watch her. Occasionally he was surprised anew by the idea that someone so frail could also be so strong.

"Captain."

He looked up. Denzil stood only a few steps away, dressed in heavy brocades and a fur-trimmed cloak, snow collecting in his hair. Ravenna and Roland's presence in this section of the court had for the moment cleared it, and the servants loading wagons near the Guard House were making enough noise to cover their voices. Though, undoubtedly, eyes watched them from most of the surrounding windows. Thomas said, "Are you sure you don't want to save this performance until you have a better audience?"

The Duke acknowledged that with a smile, but said, "At times your impatience with Roland is ill concealed. From your manner one would be tempted to think you despise your King."

"I don't despise him, I pity him. He actually loves you."

"Of course he does." Denzil's smile widened, and for the first time Thomas felt he was being allowed to see the man's real face, the truth behind the sham he put on for Roland, for the court. The petulance, the pretense of shallow vanity, were gone, replaced by intelligence and an amused contempt for those the mask had fooled. "And it was well done, wasn't it?"

"It furthers your purpose."

"Whatever that is." Denzil paced a few steps. "I can say anything I want to him, do anything I want to him, cause him to do whatever I want"—he looked up, his blue eyes mocking—"I can tell you about it with perfect impunity. And I have made him love me for it."

Thomas looked away, seeing and not seeing the wounded being helped into a wagon near the door of the tower. He felt stupidly, irrationally angry for Roland's sake. *Why? You'd think I'd know better than to give a damn about the feelings of a boy-king who spits on me.* He was as block-headed as Renier, who actually believed in his oath of knighthood. But he said, "And what a conquest it was. A boy whose father taught him to take abuse. Undoubtedly he believes he deserves you."

"Perhaps he does. Weakness is its own reward."

Denzil was just as crippled as Roland, but in his own way, with his hate turned outward instead of festering within. *But Denzil's intelligent enough to see it. Probably he does see it. And probably revels in it.* Thomas said slowly, "You are a piece of work."

"Yes, but it's my own work," Denzil answered easily, sounding pleased. "And I've gotten nearly everything I've ever wanted."

And now you're getting a reaction from me, something else you've always wanted. Thomas put a little bored doubt in his voice and said, "Have you?"

"Nearly everything. I wanted you, once, before I realized how much it would have harmed my cause with Roland."

Still watching the wagons, and inwardly a little amused, Thomas said dryly, "How flattering."

"My pride demanded it, because I could sense how you hated me."

A flurry of wind tore through the court, scattering snow around their boots. Thomas searched for the words that would deal the deepest wound, and after a moment he said, "I know. I found your motives transparent." He looked back at Denzil, and was rewarded by the ill-concealed anger in those cold blue eyes.

"Words," the Duke said softly. "Ravenna is growing old, Thomas. Take care that when she falls, you don't fall with her."

"You take care. When I fall, I'm taking you with me," Thomas said, and walked away.

ର

The Prince's Gate yard, the buffer area between the smaller inner gate and the towering bulk of the outer gate, was closed in by a wall and the south side of the Gate Bastion. Queen's guards and Albon knights manned the walls, last night's tensions forgotten among this morning's fears.

Thomas's horse danced sideways in the churned mud and snow, glad to be out of the stables, and he reined her in. Fifty of the Queen's guards, with Vivan and most of the surviving Cisternans, sat their horses with him, waiting for the lookouts on the walls to give the clear signal. Snowflakes caught like crystal in their hat brims, hair, and the fur of their cloaks. Renier waved from the top of the wall, then the main gate swung open and they rode out.

Many of the wealthy houses along the row had been caught by surprise. The doors and windows had been smashed through, revealing dark empty openings, snow blowing freely in. They would prove perfect daytime lurking places for the fay. A few houses across the way were still tightly shuttered and bore no outward sign of invasion, but nothing stirred as they rode out into the street.

There were a few bodies half-buried in the snow. Their horses, battlefield trained to ignore such things, would have walked right over the first had Thomas not guided them around. The Unseelie Court could not appear while the sun was visible, even when it was dimmed by the gray snow clouds. They would not be faced with the power that had driven them out of the Old Palace unless the clouds grew considerably darker, blocking out most of the light. But the dark fay that followed the Host were not so handicapped. There would be things that flew, that traveled beneath the snow, that would leap down at them from the rooftops and the broken windows of the houses around them. So Kade Carrion had told them.

Thomas wondered where Kade was, if she was watching or if she was back in Fayre. After Grandier's escape they had gone into the kitchens attached to the Guard House to talk. The servants had fired the ovens and it was almost warm. It was not deserted either; men and women were packing supplies for the journey. Along the side where the stores were kept, among barrels of apples, flour, and barley and shelves stacked with rounds of yellow and white cheeses covered with wax, they had stopped. Kade sat on an apple barrel, fixed her eyes on the rubies in his cloak pin, and said, "How do you know he's dead?"

He had brought the copy of Grandier's confession, and handed it to her.

She read it through twice, her eyes bleak. He said quietly, "He wanted us to be completely dependent on one sorcerer, and he chose Galen Dubell. He killed Dr. Surete and Milam after Surete had convinced Ravenna to let Dubell return. He told me how himself, after the golem attacked you in the Grand Gallery. He said it would have been simplicity itself to give either the Court Sorcerer or his assistant an enspelled object, especially if it seemed to come from a friend. So they died, like Dubell himself, his servants at Lodun, that clown in your acting troupe, a spy called Gambin, and Lord Lestrac, who knew too much of their plan and was prone to dangerous mistakes. Maybe there were others. We'll probably never know.

"I thought Denzil was Grandier's agent in the palace. That he'd taken the keystone. But Denzil didn't know where it was kept—only Dr. Braun and Dubell knew that. The night Braun was killed he must have thought of something or found something that he believed important, and he was afraid to tell me with Denzil so nearby. He was on his way back to the King's Bastion. Dubell was coming along the same way toward the gallery. They met, and Braun must have decided to tell Dubell what he had meant to tell me. They went into that salon and… Braun idolized the man and had no reason to be suspicious. He would never have thought twice about turning his back on him. Neither would I, for that matter, and I don't do that lightly. Grandier played his part very well."

Kade turned the paper over, and studied the blank back of it.

Thomas said, "You told him you were going to get into the palace with an acting troupe, didn't you?"

She nodded. "He said he never received the letter."

"But he did. You were right when you said the golem was after you. All Grandier had to do was find out which troupe was likely to get the invitation to court and plant the golem among them. You were the one who knew Galen Dubell the best; you were the one most likely to expose an imposter.

"I think it was Denzil who brought him here. Lestrac and Dontane were the contacts between them, so Denzil wouldn't know that Grandier had taken Dubell's place. That way Grandier could talk Roland out of leaving Bel Garde its walls, and we'd think of Dubell as his own man and no friend to Denzil. Denzil's antagonism would be real, and no one would suspect the link between them. It was the only way for him. Grandier was scarred and crippled by torture, and it would've been impossible to go unnoticed with his own appearance. He used this to move around undetected in Bisra and have his revenge on the priests in the Inquisition, to cause the plague and the crop failure."

For the first time Kade met his eyes. "Why did he let the wards close again? He could have held them apart and let the Host down on us. He could have done that at any time."

"I don't know. I don't know why the man does anything," Thomas confessed. He remembered the burning house in the River Quarter, and how the magical fire had considerately failed to spread to the other buildings on the crowded street. He had noted it at the time, the equal portions of viciousness and restraint, and he understood it no more now than he had then. "Why he would help Denzil of all people… I don't think it was malice against Galen Dubell. It was just that he was perfect for Grandier's purposes. He was trusted, well-known, but he'd been a recluse for ten years. He was living alone at Lodun, without family…"

She interrupted, "He stopped taking students last year. He said he was working on a treatise on…" She stopped, and buried her face in her hands.

He stepped close and pulled her hands away from her face. She wasn't crying. He might have expected grief and rage, but this wounded silence was pain itself. "I'm going to need your help."

Kade seemed to realize he was holding her hands and pulled free. Standing up, she moved away a few steps. Not turning to look at him, she said, "I'm leaving. That's what I was going to tell Galen when I heard you call him Grandier."

"Why?"

She looked back at him. This time there were tears streaking her face, but her expression was that familiar one of exasperation. "There is nothing for me here, especially now."

But he had still told her what the plan was, how he had intended for Dubell to cover the escape to Bel Garde, the closest defensible position that could be reached before nightfall. She had listened without comment. Before leaving he had said, "There's a difference between running away from your fears and walking away from your past. For your own sake, make sure you know which is which."

And that was a damn pompous thing to say to her, he thought now.

The first of the six wagons carrying the wounded who had survived the night left the shelter of the gate and trundled down the frozen mud of the street. They were guarded by about half the surviving Cisternans and a large party of servants and retainers—men, women, and children. Thomas would rather have kept the Cisternans together, but he knew they would obey his orders whereas there was no guarantee of that with Albon knights. Vivan and the other few remaining Cisternans would come with his group.

It was a relief to be outside, to be moving. Inside the walls, it seemed everything was held together by threads which were beginning to unravel. Thomas looked back at his men grouped around the gate. Baserat was checking the set of his pistols in the holsters on the saddlebow. Thomas also had two long wheellock pistols in saddle holsters and was wearing a rapier with a wide cavalry blade. A dueling rapier was slung over his shoulder.

One large armed party, mounted with only one wagon for supplies, left the gate and headed down the street in the opposite direction. It was the Count of Duncanny, who had chosen to lead away his family, retainers, and some of the other nobility who could not be counted on to keep up in a hard ride. They had some Albons with them, and Thomas could only guess what their chances might be.

The count did not turn around as they rode away, but he lifted one hand to them in farewell.

Thomas noted the similarity to a funeral procession.

The men on the palace wall had vanished. He hoped the fay, and Grandier, didn't guess the significance of that for another few moments at least. The last wagon passed out of the shadow of the Prince's Gate and Thomas nodded a signal to one of the guards waiting there.

Thomas spurred his horse and they were off. The crash of two coaches barreling through the gate signaled the eruption of the quiet street into pandemonium.

Surrounding the coaches were Lucas and about twenty Queen's guards, the other Cisternans, and a few volunteer Albon knights. Behind them rode the rest of the Queen's Guard and the Albon troop.

Grandier would anticipate their escape. He knew they would have to move now, before the snow choked the streets. Thomas hoped he hadn't anticipated any further.

The promenades and tall houses of the palace quarter flashed by. Out of the corner of his eye, Thomas saw a horse stumble and go down. He couldn't tell who its rider was.

The attack came. A large dark-winged creature struck the top of the first coach, leaping away immediately as its claws encountered the iron nails embedded in the roof. But the coach swayed under the weight and fell sideways, two of its wheels crushed beneath it. The driver tumbled free and the horses screamed, staggering and fighting their harness. The second coach shuddered to a halt beyond it as more fay leapt off rooftops and sprang up out of the mud and snow in the street.

Thomas wheeled his horse, leading the escort group of Queen's guards and Cisternans to surround the two coaches. They fetched up against the dressed stone wall of a fortified town house.

Thomas looked back toward the second company. If Renier didn't follow his instructions... No, the Albon troop and the rest of his men had split off with the wagons as the fay had attacked the coaches. They were heading up the Avenue of Flowers, riding pell-mell for the gate out of the city. But even as he saw them go, an illusion of a confused roiling mass of horsemen settled in their place.

She's here, she's done it. A moment later he saw Kade leap off the back of the coach that Berham had driven and disappear into the illusion she had created. He had intended for Dubell to cover the retreat of the second troop with illusion, the plan he had fortunately not had time to reveal to the old sorcerer. Kade could do it with fayre glamour, which neither the fay nor Grandier would be immune to. Until this moment he had not thought she would.

The coaches had been empty but for their drivers. Ravenna, Roland, and Falaise were on horseback in the midst of the Albon troop, the wagons carrying the supplies and the wounded, and the rest of the Queen's Guard.

Ravenna had ridden under conditions almost as desperate during the war, it was one of the few things Roland did well on his own, and Gideon was under orders to keep Falaise on her mount if he had to tie her there. If Grandier was watching, Thomas knew his own presence with the coaches would add verisimilitude to the deception.

Then the fay were on them and there was no more time for worry about the others. Thomas emptied both pistols at the flying creature that had struck the first coach as it stooped on them again, then used the heavy cavalry rapier to slash down at the fay that clustered about his horse. A gunpowder blast erupted somewhere nearby, with the shriek of wounded men and horses—the barrel of a too hastily loaded wheellock exploding.

The horses were trained to kick in battle and their iron-shod hooves kept the fay back at first. Then Thomas saw Baserat go down and an instant later something struck the side of his own horse, knocking it sprawling. He managed to fall clear and the horse tore itself free, staggered up, and bolted. As Thomas struggled to get to his feet, a fay leapt on him from behind and slammed him to the ground. He twisted and shoved an elbow back into it, expecting a bronze blade in his vitals, then the hilt of the rapier that was still slung across his back touched the thing's head. He heard the creature's flesh sizzle and it yelped as it leapt away.

Thomas stood and cleared a path through the creatures with his cavalry blade and put his back to the wall of the house. Blood was slicking his swordhilt—his own possibly, though he couldn't remember being wounded. He saw the second coach collapse and the misshapen dark fay swarming over it, and grimly anticipated their disappointment at its empty interior. He wished Kade had not come with them after all. He hoped she was controlling the illusion from a distance, or had gotten herself away by now.

Above the screams and shouts of men, horses, and fay, he heard the crash of a door slamming open from further down the side of the house. He thought to work his way down there in case someone had found a way inside where they could retreat, but one of the humanlike servants of the Host came at him, swinging its sword wildly. He stepped forward and neatly speared its throat with the rapier's point, then something struck him in the leg just above his right knee. For a moment he felt only the slight pain of a bee sting. Then the ground was rushing up at him, then nothing.

CHAPTER ELEVEN

As KADE TRIED to reach the partial shelter of the wall of the house, a clawed hand caught her hair and the back of her cloak, hauling her around. It was a bogle, a short squat ugly thing with muddy gray skin and harsh yellow eyes, and it was grinning at her. She pulled a handful of glamour out of the cold air and flung it into its eyes, giving it an all too temporary blindness, and it fled away shrieking. *Damn things,* she thought, dodging one of the coaches and its plunging horses. *Why anyone allows them to exist is beyond me.* If she ever got back to Fayre she would consider dedicating the rest of her life to removing its inhabitants from the face of the earth.

Kade fetched up against the wall of the house, just as the carriage doors slammed open and men poured out. Private troops... No, there were sprigs of white and red tucked into some of their hatbands, the colors of city service. A trained band.

She could feel the iron mixed into the mortar of the wall behind her as a distant heat. The proximity of so much iron made her wary, but she hadn't felt any real emotion she could identify since early this morning. She hadn't been able to leave. The idea of returning to Knockma and being alone with her thoughts was difficult enough to face, and the lump that had been in her throat for hours seemed to be keeping her from any decisive action.

Men came to the aid of the small group formed into a defensive knot between the two wrecked coaches and the house, and the fay began to disperse. The bulk of the house was probably what had saved many of the Guards. The flighted fay large enough to carry off humans had not been able to reach them. A thick haze of white smoke from pistols and muskets hung over the street now, but Kade could see that the glamour that formed her illusion was beginning to dissipate. The reflective quality of ice and snow had produced glamour in abundance. A trick on Grandier, that his foul weather produced material for her illusions.

Kade slipped inside the door with the others as the house troops withdrew. In the large stone-floored room within were half a dozen coaches, stabling for many horses, and the confusion of wounded and dying men.

She made her way across the chamber. Nearly to the bottom of the stair into the main house, she saw a dead man on the floor in Cisternan colors. She recognized him as their commander, Vivan, who had helped her in the palace hall battle. She hesitated, but there was nothing to be done, and in another moment the crowd pushed her on.

She couldn't see any of the Queen's guards, or Thomas, anywhere. With nothing else to do, she decided to look for them.

She made her way up the stairs and into the maze of rooms on the second floor. From outside, faced with only the one uncompromising gray wall, she hadn't realized the house was so large. The beautifully appointed rooms were crowded with refugees from the surrounding neighborhood, mostly shopkeepers or members of the more wealthy classes whose homes hadn't withstood the attacks. They were making an awful noise, yelling, screaming, complaining, children crying, though as far as Kade could tell the house had never been penetrated by fay. Surely they were only stirred up by the battle outside. Surely they hadn't been like this since last night.

She fought her way through crowded rooms until she saw a young servant bustling through, carrying an armload of rolled linen bandages. She caught his arm. "Whose house is this?"

He didn't even look at her oddly. It probably wasn't the most witless question he had answered today. "Lord Aviler's house, the High Minister."

Kade let him go. She remembered Aviler a little from the night of the Commedia, but mostly from the conversation between Thomas and Lucas she had eavesdropped on. His position in all this was obscure, at best. *And why do I care?*

She found another stairway and went up. The third floor would hold audience chambers and more private entertaining rooms and salons. It was unguarded, since custom and fear of irritating their patrons kept any of the refugees from venturing up there.

It was mercifully quiet. Then she heard voices raised in argument, and in a sudden silence one familiar voice. *It can't be...* She followed the sound to a carved double door that let her into a large state dining room with a long polished table and candelabra hung with colored glass drops. A group of battered Queen's guards and the lieutenant Gideon faced Denzil and a group of Albon knights while tall sallow Lord Aviler looked on. But seated nearby was Falaise.

Kade stood still a moment, trying to disbelieve her eyes. The Queen was sitting in an armchair, her head down and her hands knotted in her lap. She looked like a prisoner.

Kade started down the room toward them before they saw her. Denzil noticed her first, and Gideon stopped shouting to follow his gaze. She thought, *If Denzil smiles at me there will be trouble.* But the Duke's expression of angry contempt didn't change.

Kade focused on Falaise. "What are you doing here?"

The Queen looked up, her eyes locked on Kade's with desperate intensity. She was dressed for hard riding, in a man's breeches under a plain hunting habit, with a cloak wrapped around her. "We were attacked, and I was separated from my guards. Lord Denzil found me and brought me here." Falaise's voice held suppressed hysteria.

"He abducted her and brought her here," Gideon corrected Falaise, watching Aviler. "She would be safely out the city gates by now if—"

"If you had been competent to get her out the gates—" Denzil interrupted.

"Sorceress," Aviler said. His voice, used to addressing the loud and argumentative city assemblies, overrode theirs.

Kade looked at him. His expression was watchful and carefully wary. A part of her not concerned with death and the present had time to observe: *I must look more than half mad.*

Aviler said, "Lord Denzil told me you had left the city."

She said, "Ask him why he didn't take her after Roland and the others. Ask him why he didn't take advantage of the escape we bought for them." *And when did it become "we,"* she asked herself.

Aviler's gaze went from Kade to Denzil. "He has already explained himself."

Gideon swore in exasperation. "You're in this with him, aren't you?" One of the other guards put a cautioning hand on his shoulder.

Denzil said, "We were separated from the main troop, and the Queen had to be gotten to safety." His expression reflected angry concern, and Kade thought, *He's acting. He's doing it very well, but he's acting. Does Aviler know that?* She couldn't tell. Aviler seemed to be mainly worried over what she was going to do. *I'm not the danger here, you idiot.*

To Falaise, she said, "Do you want to be here?"

As the Queen started to answer, Denzil interrupted smoothly, "Of course she doesn't. She would rather be with her king."

Aviler spared an unreadable glance for him, but kept his attention on Kade. He said, "The Queen must choose for herself whom she wishes to accompany. I offered to let her go with her guards, but—"

"My lady, please," Gideon begged Falaise, going to his knees beside her chair. "For your honor and your safety, you know we'll protect you."

Kade looked down at the Queen. "Or come with me."

Falaise's frightened eyes went to Denzil. She was afraid to accept help from another woman, Kade realized. With that thought came a cold fury, but it was a fury wrapped in cotton wool, like the rest of her reality. Falaise turned back to her and shook her head helplessly. Kade walked out of the room.

She went out into the maze of salons, seeing servants and a few battered soldiers, but no one she recognized. She could have asked for directions, she supposed, but she was not in the mood for questions. Then she saw Berham disappearing into one of the doorways carrying an armload of firewood. She hurried to catch up with him.

It was the antechamber to a suite. Inside were Queen's guards she recognized and two men in Cisternan colors. Several were wounded, and all looked up at her in surprise. Berham stopped as he saw her. He said, "Oh, I'm glad to see you. We thought you'd gone off."

"Where's Thomas?" The words were out before she quite realized it. It crossed her mind that this was the first time she had called him anything but "you bastard."

Berham eyed her a moment, then he opened the next door and stepped back to let her go in.

She stopped in the doorway.

It was a bedchamber, cold and musty despite a new fire in the hearth. Thomas lay unconscious on the bed, still wearing the doublet and blood-stained buff coat from the battle. It took her moments to recognize him. She had never thought to see him so still, so white. A thin elderly man in a velvet doctor's cope sat next to him on the bed. Lucas was standing over him. He was hatless, and looked as if he had been caught too near a pistol blast; his face and the side of his doublet were flecked with powder burns. Martin was standing at the foot of the bed, leaning on the bedpost, and the sleeves of his white shirt were blood soaked. The young servant Phaistus was backed into a corner, trying to stay out of the way.

Kade took a step into the room, Berham brushing past behind her.

She asked, "What is it?" Her voice was unsteady and she hated herself for it. The doctor glanced back at her, but said nothing.

Lucas said, "Answer her."

The lieutenant's tone was even and reasonable but the doctor looked up at him and blanched. He said hastily, "I can't find a wound serious enough to cause this. It has to be elf-shot. There's nothing to be done."

Sensation returned and hit Kade with the force of a hammer. She stumbled and steadied herself against the wall. "Get him out of here," she said.

Martin consulted Lucas with a quick glance. He saw something in the other man's expression that constituted agreement, and caught the doctor by the thick collar of his cope and slung him toward the door.

The doctor had a highly developed sense of self-preservation. He scrambled to his feet and darted out without a threat or protest.

Kade went to sit on the bed. She touched Thomas's face. His skin was hot but his sweat was freezing. Distractedly she noticed that the striped wool of the bedclothes was faded, but the plumes topping the canopy were still pure white and the headboard had a design of twining laurel leaves. It spoke well for Aviler. She knew Denzil would have been too petty to provide his enemy a decent place in which to die.

She found the elf-shot by finding the hole it had burnt through his trouser leg. Elf-shot never appeared to leave a mark, and the tiny fragment was lodged just under the skin of his lower thigh. It must have glanced off the heavy leather of his boot top and entered his flesh at an angle. It was why he was still alive. The stone had not had time to work its way further into his body on its eventual track toward his heart.

She said, "I need a silver knife. It doesn't have to be pure, but it should have as little base metal as possible."

Martin said, "That's an alchemy tool. Where would—"

"Or a piece of family plate," Lucas interrupted. "Berham."

"No sooner said." Berham dropped the wood and hurried for the door. He was limping, Kade noticed. *It's not too bad; he's walking. Worry about him later.*

"Have you done this before?" Lucas asked her.

He didn't ask her if she thought she could do it, and she was so grateful she answered honestly. "No, but I've seen it done." Or at least attempted. Other doctors or sorcerer-healers had tried to cut out a fragment of elf-shot on the rare occasions when it was close enough to the surface of the skin to find, but most made the mistake of using iron rather than silver. And elf-shot didn't lose its power once it was embedded in a human body; if a sorcerer did manage to remove it he was just as likely to have it seek his own heart instead. The fay who cast the shot sometimes removed it for reasons of their own, but those instances were few and far between.

Victims of elf-shot were usually killed to keep them from suffering further, if they didn't die immediately. It was a perfect opportunity for Denzil, or High Minister Aviler. And Thomas Boniface was a disliked favorite whose patron and troop were out of the city by now, if they lived. *The doctor might talk. Maybe we should have killed him.* It was too late for that now. *And why do I care?*

Because from the moment you set foot in the palace, he did not treat you as a child, a fool, or worse, a court lady. He treated you as exactly what you are, whatever that is, and he knew what Galen's death did to you.

She paced the room with rabid impatience until Berham returned. He shut the door hastily behind him and brought a small delicate paring knife out of his doublet. "Will this do?"

Kade took it from him and felt the nearly pure silver resonate through her. "Perfect," she said. "Now all of you get the hell out of the way."

If she had spared enough notice, she would have been surprised to see that they did just that.

She passed the knife through a candle quickly, and that would have to do. It was a little too dull but Thomas would be in no position to notice.

She sat down on the bed and gently probed for the fragment. It wasn't there anymore. It had worked its way deeper already. She cursed, fighting a foolish surge of panic, and thought, *Why can't anything ever be easy?* She knew where it had to be. It hadn't had time to move more than an inch or so down into the muscle. She saw her hand was trembling, and she was glad Thomas was deeply unconscious because he would otherwise have surely said something infuriating at this point. *Now,* she thought, and carefully inserted the knife.

A little blood welled up, and after a long heartbeat she felt the knife vibrate as the elf-shot adhered to it. *My God, it worked.* Gently she withdrew the blade. As soon as the tiny fragment was free she closed her fist around it to keep it from flying at someone, stood, and started toward the fireplace. Then she felt it pushing at the skin of her palm.

She froze, staring at her closed hands. If she let it go, God knew who it would head for. *But I'm fay,* she thought against the rising dread. *It can't hurt me.*

There's no such thing as half human, Galen Dubell had told her once long ago, and she had typically ignored his words. *One drop of red blood is enough.* She whispered a fay charm of warding danger, and felt the elf-shot press at her hand, pushing through the skin. Fighting panic, she hoped the planet of influence was close enough and shouted the Lodun formula for the destruction of dangerous objects.

The sorcery worked where the fay magic had not. She felt the fragment catch fire and hastily scraped it off her hands onto the hearthstone. It burned bright blue for an instant, then disappeared.

She sank down and sat on the floor. All those years that elf-shot could have put her out of their misery and the Unseelie Court had never thought to make the experiment, to test to see if she had the same immunity to it as the other fay did.

Idiots, she thought. Her palm hurt like hell.

She turned back to the bed and saw Thomas move his head on the pillow. Feverishly, but he had moved.

She had forgotten anyone else was still in the room, and was startled to find Lucas standing next to her. He took her hand and turned it over. "God damn," he muttered when he saw the burn. "Hey, Ber—"

Berham appeared with a handful of snow scraped from a window ledge. He slapped it into her palm.

She snatched her hand away, then realized the cold had cut the intensity of the pain nearly in half. She watched Thomas while Berham fussily bandaged the burn, and was rewarded by seeing him move twice more.

※

Much later Kade sat on a stool by the fire and looked at the deep red mark on her hand. It didn't seem inclined to blister, so she supposed it couldn't be too bad. Unlike pure fay magic, the craft of mortal sorcery was a messy business and she was used to hurting herself occasionally. *Messy, but more certain,* she thought.

She had helped the other wounded as best she could, but without the philtres and salves that were so necessary to healing-sorcery, or the ingredients with which to mix them, there wasn't much she could do. She could have made a healing stone, but that only worked for disease, not torn flesh. A well-stocked apothecary box would have saved lives tonight. The charms to give strength and to hold the soul to the body had little efficacy without the herbal preparations that soothed the wounds. The effort had left her cold and dreadfully tired, and she would have traded all her fay ancestry for half of Galen Dubell's skill at healing-sorcery. And she knew that if she had devoted all her attention to study, she would have had that skill by now.

Kade was worried about the wound in Thomas's leg. The spell she had used to knit the flesh together had seemed to work, but the wound was deep and there was no telling how the elf-shot had affected it. By the firelight, his hair and beard were inky black against his fever-pale skin. She resisted the urge to get up and walk over to the bed again. *You thought the world ended when you found out Galen was dead, but when you heard that fool of a doctor say elf-shot...*

She took a deep breath and faced herself. It was idiocy to deny it. How could she not know? But looking back, she couldn't see when it had happened. She was not sure how her childhood passion figured into it, or when her carefully preserved distant appreciation of him had been intensified by intimacy. She was even less certain when the thought *I want this man for a friend* had become *I want this man.*

Simply because she had never felt it before didn't mean she couldn't recognize it, even though it wasn't very much like the poets and books had described it. Some had implied that the depth of the emotion would hurt; they had not said it would be like the blunt end of a poleax in the pit of the stomach.

She had wondered if being fay would make her unable to love; it had certainly made her unable to feel even the slightest fondness for any of her relations. She had thought she loved Roland once, but then had decided that if she really had, she would not have been able to leave him. She had thought herself as cold as her mother Moire and the rest of the fay, who put on a great show of grand passion but who, underneath their shallow surfaces, had hearts as empty as broken wine barrels. To find that she was capable of love, that it was happening now and under less than ideal circumstances, was more than a shock. It was horrific. And worse, like every other bubbleheaded court lady, she had fallen in love with the Captain of the Queen's Guard. When she was a child at court, someone had proclaimed undying passion for him every other week. Trying to guess who he was going to show interest in and who he was going to brush off had been a game with Ravenna's gentlewomen. Kade felt herself a fool, and she had seen too much bloodshed and horror in the last few days to seek the comfort of childishly wishing herself dead.

She would have to think about what to do at some point. *Not right now,* she told herself. *Just not right now.*

∾

Thomas turned his head toward the light. It resolved into a glowing orange fire in an unfamiliar hearth. The room was dark, except for one candle that he could see as a dim glow through the curtain at the foot of the bed. He felt the sweat-drenched heat of a receding fever, and everything ached. Except the wound in his thigh that felt like a hot coal had been buried beneath the skin. He sat up on one elbow and parted the bloody and burned (Burned? he wondered) fabric to examine what looked like an especially clean sword thrust. It was closed over with a new pink scab, a sign of sorcerous healing.

Then he saw Kade sitting on a footstool by the fire, where she had blended into the light and its reflection on the polished stone hearth, a creature of amber, rose, and old gold. One could never tire of looking at her, he decided. There was always something new to see, an effect made even more interesting because she produced it unintentionally and entirely without artifice. They stared at one another for a time, until Kade blinked and shook herself.

"Where are we?" he asked her.

"Lord Aviler's town house. You've been near dead most of the day, because you were hit by elf-shot."

It took a moment for the words to sink in. He said, "I couldn't have been."

"Very well, argue about it as if you weren't unconscious when it happened."

Thomas looked at the wound again. "Did you cut it out?"

"Yes."

"It couldn't have been easy." It was supposed to be impossible.

"I have had a hard day," she admitted with dignity, lifting a handful of sweat-soaked hair away from her forehead.

He saw the bandage wrapped around her hand and asked, "What happened there?"

"Nothing." After a moment of hesitation, she said, "Denzil's here, with Falaise."

Thomas closed his eyes. "No."

"Yes. He got her away from Gideon and the others when they were attacked. They followed him here, but she's too terrified of Denzil to take their help and Aviler stands about like a great idiot saying the Queen must decide who escorts her."

Thomas fell back on the bed and contemplated the underside of the tester for a moment. "You realize that a short while ago I was as good as dead and this was all someone else's problem."

"You're welcome. I think I know why Denzil's here."

He sat up again, taking a deep breath to steady himself as dizziness threatened. "I'd appreciate it if you'd tell me."

"Aviler. If he's in this plot with Denzil and Grandier, that's one thing, but if he's not…he isn't just going to stand there and watch."

The High Minister. A man who would support Roland despite personal differences, knowing he could increase the political power of the Ministry and it would never occur to the young King to stop him. A man with no patience for royal favorites. A man with nothing but suspicion for royal favorites. "You're right." With the help of the bedpost, Thomas hauled himself up and stood carefully, wincing at the tight pain of the wound. Limping around on it wasn't going to do it any good but he hardly had a choice.

Kade was fiddling with her hair again. She said, "Falaise knows something."

Thomas looked down at her. She was obviously reluctant. "Why do you think so?"

"She's afraid of Denzil."

"She should be." He limped to the foot of the bed and found his dueling rapier and main gauche. He drew the sword to check the blade and saw it was nicked and dented but still unbent.

"I know that," Kade said with asperity. "But she doesn't know that, not unless she knows more than she should."

Thomas hesitated, thinking it through. "How much do you think she knows?"

"She won't tell me. She doesn't think I can protect her. But I think she'll tell you."

"She may have tried to already, and I thought she was after something else. I should have listened to her but the woman never gave any sign she could think before." If they somehow escaped the current situation, that might save Falaise's neck. He could say she had confided to him early suspicions of Denzil but had been unable to give him anything definite. That would keep Roland or some ambitious courtier from charging her with treason along with Denzil. *If they got out of this. Damned optimist.* Then he realized the full implication of what Kade had said and looked down at her in surprise. "Doesn't think you could protect her? That's ridiculous. You're not a supporter of Ravenna, Roland, or Denzil; you're the only one who could protect her with impunity."

Kade considered that. "Maybe she just can't trust anyone anymore."

Slipping his baldric over his head, Thomas thought, *That's an idea we could all have sympathy with.*

The door opened and Lucas entered, then stopped abruptly as he saw Thomas. "You're alive," he said, smiling. "And I thought I was about to be promoted."

"Careful, I might take you up on that." Thomas gritted his teeth as he put his weight on his bad leg.

"Oh, I'd have to decline under these circumstances."

"Typical of you. How many are we?"

"Eighteen. Not as bad as I thought it would be for a moment there, but bad. Commander Vivan's dead, and Baserat..."

As he listed the familiar names Thomas shook his head. He would have to deal with it later. Worse that he didn't know if their sacrifice had accomplished anything, if Ravenna and Roland had been able to get out of the city. Lucas finished with, "...and hard as it is to believe, Denzil's here with..."

"I know. I'm about to go and give him the good news about my premature survival. Do you know where Falaise is?"

"Yes, Martin found where they're keeping her. Gideon and some of the others are hanging about outside her rooms, making sure no one makes off with her."

The Queen was ensconced in a suite in the opposite wing. Bloody and ragged, Thomas and Kade drew considerable attention passing through the house. Thomas limped, and resisted the urge to steady himself on the walls. They finally arrived at a suite guarded by five weary battered men with the badges of city service, who were in turn being watched by Gideon and six other Queen's Guards.

Gideon was pacing, and when Thomas and the others entered the anteroom where the guards were gathered, he looked like he was in agony. Stiffly he began, "Sir, I—"

Thomas said, "Shut up," and walked past him into the next room.

The city guards watched with great interest and made no attempt to stop him, but inside were several of Denzil's contingent of Albon Knights, given to him by Roland and sworn to his personal service. Thomas said, "Gentlemen, really."

The knights were well aware that denying a Queen's Guard lieutenant the right to see the Queen was irregular enough, but denying it to the Queen's Guard Captain was practically equivalent to abduction. One of the older knights looked uneasy. "We have our orders—" he began.

Falaise threw open the door and stood there, her eyes wide. She was still dressed for riding and her hair was coming down. She said, "Captain, thank God you're all right."

"I think your orders have just been countermanded." Thomas smiled.

Falaise tapped the knight who was blocking the door on the shoulder, saying in an irritated tone, "Get out of the way."

Thomas thought that if Kade were ever foolish enough to get herself into a similar situation, she would have probably punched the man in the kidney. The knights reluctantly moved aside.

Then from the anteroom Denzil pushed his way in through the city guards, Lord Aviler behind him. The High Minister looked mildly surprised to see them. Denzil stopped when he saw Thomas, and his eyes narrowed dangerously.

Yes, Thomas thought, *how awful that it all doesn't go your way.* He said, "I was looking for the Queen. It seems the King has temporarily misplaced her." He wondered if Denzil would challenge him now.

The air in the room was brittle enough to break.

"She is under my protection," Denzil said.

"Yes, I've heard all about that, but it isn't necessary anymore."

"I have men here—"

"You have twenty armed men sworn to your service, my lord," Aviler interrupted. "And you, Captain, have about an equal number of Guardsmen in any condition to fight. I have a hundred city troops in service to the Ministry, and I suggest we leave them all to their duty of keeping this house secure."

"A very diplomatic suggestion." Thomas inclined his head.

Abruptly Falaise said, "I...thank you for your help, Lord Denzil, but I do not...require it any longer."

Denzil stared down at her a long moment. "As you wish, Madame." He turned away and left the anteroom. Aviler bowed sardonically and followed him.

Thomas followed Falaise into the room and closed the door behind him. It was a perfect setting for her, with light sarsenet hangings and mirror-glass set in the paneling. There was no maid in evidence. He wondered briefly if Falaise had sent her female attendants away, or if she had even been offered any. *Was Denzil on his way here just now because he heard I was, or because he knew Falaise was alone? And was that why Aviler was trailing after him?* He leaned on the back of a tapestry-covered armchair to take the weight off his leg and said, "My lady, I think there are some things we need to discuss."

"Yes." Falaise sat down on the daybed and looked up at him anxiously. "About Denzil."

Kade had vanished somewhere along the way, though Thomas suspected she was nearby and within earshot. He wasn't worried about that. She already suspected most of what Falaise was about to tell him. "How much do you know about the Duke of Alsene's plans?"

"Nothing, not really. He…" Falaise looked away nervously. "Denzil suggested that if my husband were to have to leave the throne, I might consider marrying him."

Landlaw again. The oldest traditions held that by being the King's wife, Falaise took on part of the mystique of the crown, if not its authority. If Roland died without leaving children, and one of the possible heirs married Falaise, it would go far to strengthen his claim in the minds of a great many people. There were a considerable number of families with enough royal blood to pursue the throne, and many technically closer to it than Denzil's. But none of them had tried to suborn Falaise… *It implies he's fairly sure she's soon to become a widow.* "That's treason."

Her expression was earnest. "I know."

Thomas closed his eyes and rubbed the bridge of his nose. "What did you tell him?"

"I didn't answer him." She made a helpless gesture. "I tried to put him off. I was afraid if I said no he would tell Roland lies about me, but if I said yes, even if I didn't mean it, he might go through with what he planned. I didn't know who to go to."

Yes, you did. You just couldn't get me to listen to you. Thomas noticed she had refrained from pointing that error out to him, but it would have been against Falaise's lifelong training to tell a man he had made a mistake. No, she would try to delicately manage him, which would make it all the more difficult to get the truth out of her. Yet that tactic had worked well with Denzil. She must have made a good job of stringing him along, if she had kept it up for several days without the young Duke losing his patience. Thomas could easily imagine Falaise swooning, gracefully weeping, and doing everything a woman about to give in did except actually give in. He looked up. "And he didn't give you any hint of how he was going to accomplish this?"

"No. If he had, would that make things any better?"

"Probably not."

Falaise was knotting the ribbons on the sleeve of her coat. "It is very bad, isn't it?"

"Yes. If we ever get the evidence against him to bring a formal charge of treason, then he can take you to the gallows with him. You could bring the charge yourself, but I doubt Roland would take your word over Denzil's. There are plenty of others who know Denzil and probably would take your word before his, but their opinions won't count." Thomas shook his head wearily. "We'll just have to make sure it won't come to that."

"How?"

It was just one more reason for Denzil to die a hero's death at the earliest opportunity. It might not stop Grandier now, but it would clear up a number of miscellaneous side issues and relieve the feelings of several people, among them Kade, Ravenna, Falaise, and himself. But it didn't make it any easier. They were not under Roland's nervous eye anymore, but with the knights and High Minister Aviler as biased witnesses, it was still a difficult problem. "The less you know now, the better," he told her.

"Wait." She hesitated. "I wanted to tell you that my patronage is yours, whatever happens. I know that Roland is against you, but if the Duke of Alsene is gone he would be so much easier to deal with and if things get back to the way they were... When Ravenna isn't here anymore, when I'm patron of the Queen's Guard, I want you to stay as Captain." Her eyes lifted to meet his for the first time. "My patronage, and my very sincere...regard."

Oh, fine, Thomas thought in annoyance. In the language of the court, her meaning was clear. Regard equaled favor, and favor meant access to her bed in return for his support. He looked at her a long moment, keeping his expression neutral. "I'll remember that, my lady."

இ

Listening in the anteroom, Kade knocked her head ungently against the wall and thought, *And that is the tale of my life.* She slipped out, unnoticed.

இ

When Thomas went out into the anteroom, Lucas was telling Gideon, "—and when he heard about it he went absolutely mad and you're lucky if you're not—"

They both looked up when he shut the door. Thomas said to Gideon, "When this is over we're going to have a talk, but until then we won't refer to it. Now stay here and make sure no one walks off with her."

The young lieutenant winced. "Yes, Sir."

Thomas went out, Martin and Lucas following him. A servant wearing a steward's chain approached them, somewhat warily. "Lord Aviler would like to see you, Captain."

Lucas raised an eyebrow and casually adjusted one of the pistols in his sash, but Thomas shook his head. He followed the man through a small gallery hung with family portraits and to a door at the far end, the others trailing along. As Aviler's man knocked on the door, Lucas dropped into one of the armchairs and Martin leaned on the wall. The servant eyed them nervously, but didn't voice any objections.

Inside was a study warmed by a fire in a pink marble hearth and lit by gray late-afternoon light from two windows in the far wall. The floor was covered with bright eastern carpets probably brought back from the trading voyages Aviler the Elder had made his fortune on. Through chance or careful planning, they managed not to clash with the striped red silk covering the walls. The High Minister was standing with his back to the fire as Thomas stepped in. He motioned for the steward to withdraw, then said, "Lord Denzil's preparing to leave. I thought you might be interested."

Thomas limped to one of the windows. The snow had stopped and the view gave onto the street below where they had fought that morning. The wrecked coaches were still there, though the city troop must have brought in the bodies. The carriage doors below were just opening. Night would fall in an hour or so; it was a nearly suicidal time to be venturing out.

Aviler said, "For a house under siege, there's a great number of people coming and going. I know what you're planning."

Thomas watched Denzil emerge on horseback with his men grouped behind him. They began to pick their way down the snow-choked street before he turned back to the High Minister. "Do you?"

"You're going to take the good Duke of Alsene down. If I hadn't been there, your lieutenant would have killed him in my dining room." Aviler crossed to a long draw table piled with books and papers and sat on one corner, watching him. "I don't mind what you do to each other, and he did put the Queen in unpardonable danger by keeping her from leaving the city." He leaned forward. "But don't do it here."

Thomas watched him thoughtfully. "I don't have that choice anymore, it seems. And he's done more than put the Queen in danger."

"I can hardly believe anything you tell me at this point."

Thomas started for the door. "Then I won't tell you. But if you think he's going to join Roland, you're laughably wrong. Send someone to follow him and you'll find he's taking the street back to the palace. Then ask yourself why."

He went out. Lucas looked up as he shut the door behind him and said, "Well?"

Thomas told him, "We're getting the Queen out of here tomorrow, whatever it takes."

ꙩꙨꙩ

The court had ridden into Bel Garde in the late afternoon, and now in the gateyard Ravenna sat her horse amid the turmoil of servants, courtiers, Albons, Cisternans, and her own men, watching as Renier ordered guard placements. The late Dr. Braun's apprentices already stood before the closed outer gates, working with books, incense burners, and other odd tools to temporarily ward those fragile barriers of metal and wood against the fay. They had been attacked again passing through the city gates, and several parties had been scattered or killed, but the fay had not followed them out. Satisfied with the arrangements being made here, Ravenna let her guards urge her further into the fortress.

Once through the inner gate and the portcullis, Bel Garde's celebrated interior court with its fountains and miniature gardens was visible, though smothered now under a heavy blanket of snow. The stonework on the newer bastion looming over them was as ornate as gilded filigree, with curves, curls, and the faces of classical luck sprites worked into the carving. A gem of a fortress, someone had called this place. *Yes,* Ravenna thought, *but because a sword is jeweled does not mean the blade is no longer deadly.* "Find Lieutenant Gideon and tell him to bring Falaise to me at once," she told the nearest guard.

As he rode off she looked down to see Elaine trotting beside her horse and tugging urgently on her riding skirt. "My lady, if you don't come out of this wind you'll get your sickness again."

Ravenna leaned down to remonstrate with her and found herself coughing helplessly into her sleeve.

Acknowledging physical weakness was not something she did gracefully. Once she could speak again, she cursed Elaine, the guards who came to help her down, and, rather unjustly, her horse, who stood rock steady with well-trained patience throughout the whole episode.

They led her through a wide door into a large, beautifully appointed entry hall. It was too cold to remove her cloak, but Ravenna had to admit the relief from the wind was welcome. She gestured Elaine away impatiently and paced, knotting her fingers together, noting the servants who worked to build up the fire were her own and not those of the fortress. "I want this place searched top to bottom."

"Yes, my lady."

The guard she had sent after Falaise came through the door, letting in a blast of cold air. His eyes were worried and Ravenna tensed. "My lady," he said, "Lieutenant Gideon and the other men who rode escort to the Queen aren't anywhere to be found."

Ravenna stopped, staring at the carved paneling in front of her. "And Falaise?"

"Not with the Albons or His Majesty's party."

Ravenna nodded to herself. "Denzil."

◊◊

Later, Thomas sat in front of the fireplace in the parlor of the suite they had commandeered for a headquarters. Gideon and most of the others were guarding Falaise, and Lucas had led an expeditionary force consisting of himself, Martin, and the two Cisternans down into the kitchens after food. Berham and Phaistus were sitting at a table across the room making bullets, the older man holding the leather-wrapped bullet mold and the younger carefully pouring hot lead from the small crucible.

The most badly wounded guard had died a short while ago. With men Thomas had led and fought beside for years dying and in constant danger, it was foolish to grieve over the death of someone he had in actuality never really known, but he found his thoughts turning to Galen Dubell.

He had never been so completely taken in by anyone, Thomas decided, and that was what disturbed him the most. He had first come to court younger than Roland was now, and had made his way through all the traps and pitfalls alone. Never allowing himself to trust anyone, he had escaped machinations that had ruined others and had learned how to deceive with the best of them. Perhaps he had believed Grandier because the old sorcerer had never asked for anything. Thomas wondered how Dubell had felt when he had realized the trusted friend or servant that Grandier must have pretended to be had been watching, learning, gathering information for an impersonation that would kill its victim. If the old man had even been allowed to realize that, if he hadn't died in complete ignorance of what was happening to him.

Kade wandered into the room with the air of someone waiting for a public coach and settled into the other chair, and he was glad of the distraction. Thomas had not asked her why she hadn't left the city. They had all assumed she had the means to do so, though they had never had any proof of it.

It had occurred to him that he was taking her for granted, like taking gunpowder for granted when one carried pistols much of the time.

And now she was staring at him. He said, "Yes?"

She said, "What do you think Roland will do when he finds out about Denzil and Falaise?"

He had the feeling this wasn't really what was on her mind, but he wasn't willing to pursue that suspicion. He said, "I don't know." At the moment he was too tired to care about a possible outburst from Roland, though he supposed later he would have to manage it. Interesting to think how it was possible to grow out of the need for power, and to desire freedom from the constant wrangling of those who still wanted it. "Roland, Denzil, and Falaise make an interesting triangle. It's a pity I can't confuse the issue any further by pursuing Falaise." The young Queen was beautiful, but so were most of the other women at court. She was also the kind of woman for whom men would continually ruin themselves, and he was past that stage. Did Denzil want Falaise, or was that the only way he knew to approach her? Falaise had evidently not wanted him. Thomas doubted she wanted anybody. Her offer to him had held no warmth. She offered her body because she thought it was part of the process of sealing an agreement.

Was I like that? Thomas wondered. *Was that what I thought when Ravenna first approached me, all those years ago?*

Kade interrupted his thoughts. "Why not?"

He had time to notice that he had spoken to her in the offhand way he might speak to a friend, without any regard for propriety or anything else. He also suspected he had just opened the way for her to ruthlessly question him about whatever subject occurred to her, but it was too late to stop at this point. "If I were going to raise a child, I'd have started before now."

Kade greeted this with another long moment of enigmatic silence, then she said, "Oh." She looked into the fire for a little while, then chuckled to herself.

He glanced at her suspiciously. "What?"

"Nothing." Another pause, then she asked, "How did Denzil get such a hold on Roland? That he can threaten the Queen, of all people, with her too afraid to ask for help?"

Thomas watched the fire for a moment, remembering. "Right before your father died, Roland tried to kill himself by cutting his wrists, but he bungled it. Denzil found him, bandaged him up, concocted a story to explain it. He also kept him from attempting it again."

Kade bit her lip, thinking, then shook her head. "But that almost seems like Denzil must care for him, and I may be odd, but I can't imagine that."

"You can care for someone and hate them at the same time. And Denzil was nothing without Roland's support then. He needed a live prince to at-

tach himself to." He glanced over at her. "Don't look like that. Roland didn't
have to fall into Denzil's clutches. Look at you. You haven't got a Denzil
hanging about somewhere in Fayre, have you?"

"Of course not." She shuddered theatrically. "And I was not looking
guilty, I was looking thoughtful."

Thomas hadn't said the word "guilty," but he didn't intend to point that
out. If she could fall into such an obvious trap then she must be considerably
distracted.

A log rolled to the edge of the hearth, and he stood, somewhat awkwardly, supporting himself on the arm of the chair, to push it back in with
the poker.

Kade winced. "I'm sorry about that."

He dropped back into the chair. "About saving my life? There's a cheery
sentiment."

She refused to be diverted. "What if it never heals?"

She was just as well aware as he was about what it would do to his speed
in a fight. "Well, I'm getting old for a duelist. It probably won't make any
difference in the long run."

"Don't say that; I have enough to worry about." Kade slumped further
down in her chair. "How are we going to get rid of Denzil?"

Thomas wondered how she could sit like that without breaking her back.
He answered, "I'm going to kill him, if I ever get the chance. But I'd like to do
it without dooming Falaise, myself, or anyone else."

"I could do it. Roland hates me anyway, and he can't come after me
where I live."

He snorted. "I'm hardly likely to ask you to do a thing like that."

"It's nothing I haven't done before."

The somewhat airy way she said this caused him to doubt that she was
as indifferent as she pretended, but he answered, "I don't care if you go
about murdering people every afternoon. You'd make me look a fool or a
worse scoundrel than Denzil, and I'd think of some horrific way to retaliate."

She shrugged and rubbed the arm of the chair distractedly. "It shouldn't
matter, even if I am related to him. I wished my father dead."

Thomas frowned. "What makes you say that?"

Her eyes on the fire, Kade said slowly, "I wished it, very hard, with
everything I had, which I was beginning to realize might be quite a bit. And
he died."

"He didn't just fall over dead."

"Yes, he did." She looked stubborn.

"No, he did not. Were you there?"

"No, of course not, but I know what happened because I caused it."

"I don't know why I bother to listen to you argue in circles."

Kade made an exasperated gesture. "Because you can't come up with anything better than 'No, he did not.' How do you know? My magic was wild then, I didn't know what I was doing, I could have caused any amount of harm."

He was silent for a long moment. He said finally, "Does it matter, as long as he's dead?"

"No, I suppose not." She sank further in her chair and stared at the fire.

Thomas glanced back at the two servants. Berham was deep into a story of one of the last battles of the Bisran War, and Phaistus was so engrossed in it he was getting hot lead all over the table. He turned back to the fire. "Fulstan was poisoned."

Her expression went blank. It was hard to tell if she was astonished or not. He said, "Ravenna did it. I got the poison for her. It was foxglove, as I recall."

Kade stood up and walked around the room in a circle. After a few moments she wandered back to the fire and sat down again as if she had just arrived.

Thomas added, "Believe it or not, Ravenna never quite realized what Fulstan was doing to you or to Roland. She's very single-minded. He knew he should be wary of her, but she couldn't touch him under court- or land-law, and I suppose he thought his position was safe. After your little outburst in the cathedral, she began to wonder why you'd become such a terror. I discovered some of the details for her so she sent you out of the city to the convent. You'd been gone a week when Roland botched his attempt to bleed to death, and when she heard about that she made the decision." He shrugged. It all seemed a very long time ago. "There wasn't any dancing in the streets, but most of the mourning was insincere."

She was silent for a long time, and Thomas listened to the fire crackle and Bertram's voice in the background. Finally Kade said quietly, "I never thought anybody wanted to kill him but me. Even Roland thought it was something he did, like not riding well enough or playing games badly."

Thomas leaned forward and added another log to the fire. "Well, it was time you knew."

᠅

It was much later and most of the house was asleep when Kade made her way up to the highest attic and eased up the sash of a window there, mindful of the nails in it. It was cold, bitterly cold, with a patina of frost glittering over every surface and clouds hiding the stars. It was very dark and the moon was in its waning; in the Old Faith, it was the dark time, the death of white magic. The reigning time of the Host. The gray-black rooftops spread around her like an angular un-moving sea. She could just see the palace from here as an odd collection of shapes, some recognizable as towers, another as the dome of the Summer Residence. The faint glow of witch-light flickered over the walls.

She climbed out onto the slate-shingled roof of the gable just below and sat in front of the window, to keep anything from trying to enter the house behind her back. She shivered and hugged her knees, though she had augmented her clothing with a man's shirt Berham had found for her and Thomas's battered buff coat.

I did not kill my father. Her emotions were as tangled as a jumbled collection of beaded necklaces. She wished she could untangle the strands and run them through her fingers one by one. Disappointment, that she could understand. It was not an odd emotion for someone who had believed a lie was the truth, particularly as it was a lie she had told herself. Confusion, anger, remembered fear, all these were explicable, if hopelessly intertwined. It was the strange sensation of release, the sense of freedom that she couldn't understand, that made her face hot and her hands numb with the strength of it. As if something tightly coiled inside her chest had relaxed a trifle. It seemed to make other things possible as well. It seemed to imply that it might be possible to forget, eventually. *Time to stop dreaming like a child,* she told herself with an irritated toss of her head. Time to think and plan. She closed her eyes and whispered, "Boliver, come here now; I need to talk to you." A gust of wind carried the words away.

Nothing happened. *I hate it when he makes me do this.* "As Queen of Air and Darkness, and on my sovereignty of Knockma, I call Boliver Fay."

For a long breathless moment there was no answer, then out of the cloud-covered sky a star fell. It plunged toward her and landed lightly at her feet, then resolved with a flash of light into Boliver, who said, "It's not bloody easy getting here, you know." He was about Kade's height, wizened and red bearded, and his vivid blue eyes were worried. He wore a high peaked hat and a somewhat tattered velvet doublet.

"No, I don't know. That's why I called you. How is Knockma?"

"Not so good. There are members of the Host drawn up on the border to Fayre, though not a sign of them on the mortal side, so far. They didn't like you much to begin with, and now with you taking the human part in this war—"

"Is everyone all right?" Kade had worried about her household. Some of them were human, and none terribly good at defending themselves.

Boliver was offended. "You know I wouldn't let anything happen to them. But why are you doin' this? Have you gone witless? You didn't make up with your brother by chance?"

"No, of course not." Kade doubted she ever would. Roland wouldn't welcome such an overture, and she wasn't certain she wanted to make it anymore. There was too much history between them, and they might only remind one another of things better forgotten. The news that he had tried to take his own life had been an unpleasant surprise, and her thoughts shied away from it. She looked out over the dark dead city again. "I've got a reason for it."

"'A reason,' she says. Oh, joy." Boliver rolled his eyes.

She rubbed her forehead. "I'll hold Knockma for us, don't worry."

"I'm not worried." He let his knees knock and his teeth chatter convincingly. "I'm petrified. I've no wish to vanish down Evadne's gullet. Or watch me bosom companions do likewise."

"Neither do I." She shifted impatiently. "I need your help."

He snorted. "As if I had a choice."

"Well you don't, so be quiet and listen. I need you to fly over the palace and tell me what you can see."

"Fly over the palace? What have I done to deserve it? With all those boglie-woglies everywhere?"

"Yes. I'd do it if I could, but I can't, and that's all there is to it!" Boliver was her oldest friend in Fayre, and she didn't want to risk him, but there was no other way to learn what she needed to know. If there was one thing Kade regretted, it was her lack of the fay ability to shape-change and to fly.

"Yes, yes. I know. You've got your head set on defeating the Unseelie Court and their minions one-handed, I suppose, and there's no dissuading you. Well, wish me luck."

She stood as he vanished into starlight and streaked away toward the shadowy bulk of the palace towers. "Luck," she whispered.

CHAPTER TWELVE

THOMAS WOKE BEFORE dawn, the wound in his leg stiff and sore. Despite the fire, the room was frosty and he sat on the bed and struggled into his doublet. He stood and limped around until he could walk without obviously hobbling, then tried to do a fencer's full extension. He got halfway down and needed the help of the bedpost to get back up.

Phaistus was sleeping in front of the doorway, rolled up in a rug and snoring. He hadn't stirred when Thomas was bumping around the room and didn't wake when he stepped over him and opened the door.

The anteroom was lit only by two candles on the mantel, their soft light making the blue wallpaper dissolve into shadow and hiding the disarray of the fine furnishings. Kade was sitting on the floor with the contents of an ebony trinket cabinet spread out around her. It was probably the silver-gilt curiosities and mother-of-pearl boxes that had attracted her attention, but it was the seashells, the baby's skull, and the ostrich egg that had undoubtedly kept it.

She looked up at him. "Are you going back to the palace today?"

It was too early for this. He dropped into an armchair. "Wouldn't that be an extraordinarily foolish thing to do?"

"I don't know. I don't think about things that way." She held up a seashell with her bandaged hand, passed the other hand in front of it, and the shell disappeared. "I suppose it would depend on why you were going. And who went with you." She pulled the shell out of her right ear. "Do you want to find the keystone?"

Thomas watched her for a moment. She was giving the shell the sort of concentration usually reserved for a deep philosophical problem. He was certain Denzil had returned to the palace yesterday, and he meant to discover why. He had thought the keystone was a lost cause. "Would that do any good?"

"The wards themselves are still there, drifting over the older parts of the palace, and the other wardstones are still in place. If we replace the keystone, it will pull the wards back down into their original courses, and the Host will have to leave or be trapped inside."

Thomas knew Grandier must have taken the stone, probably soon after he had arrived at the palace, but that still didn't leave them a clue of where to look for it. "He could have hidden the keystone anywhere inside the palace. Or more likely, he handed it to Dontane, that night at court when he was there, to hide somewhere in the city. It would be like looking for one certain rock in a quarry."

"But it's a very special sort of rock. If I could get to one of the plain wardstones, and take a chip from it," Kade said slowly, "I might be able to use it in a spell, to find the keystone."

Thomas frowned. "How?"

"Years and years ago when all the stones were placed in the warding spell, they became one. Even when the keystone has been removed, and the matrix isn't there anymore, the stones remember. It's like using a lock of hair to find a person." She stared at the shell in her hand, vexed. "I should have thought of this before we left the palace yesterday."

"There aren't warding stones in the Old Courts. It would have been just as dangerous to go into the other part of the palace then as it is now," he said. *And you had other things to think about.* "If you came with me, you could do this spell while we were in the palace, and discover if the keystone is still there?"

Kade considered this a moment, her eyes moving through the collection of curiosities on the floor. "No. Am I a fool for being honest?"

"No. Am I a fool for expecting you to be honest?" Even as he said it he realized it was true. He had been prepared to believe her answer, even if it had served her purpose.

Kade didn't look up at him, staring instead at the shell lying on her bandaged palm. "So, whatever are we going to do?" She closed her hand, and opened it again. The shell had vanished.

"Don't play coy; it ill becomes you."

She pulled the shell out of her ear again and for the first time looked at him directly. "All right, will you say I can come with you or do we have to have a loud fight about it and attract the attention and speculation of the entire house?"

Thomas sighed and looked at the ceiling. "I don't know, I could do with a loud fight. Gets the blood moving." He had seriously considered asking her to come already. She could escape any danger far more readily than he could and with her help his chances of accomplishing something increased to the point of the almost possible.

Kade made the shell vanish again, stood to lean on his chair arm, and apparently found it in his ear.

This time he saw it come out of her sleeve. "Get away from me," he told her cordially.

Kade smiled. "I'm going with you, am I not?"

He said, "Yes. We'll both be fools together."

ᕀᕀ

Falaise did not complain when told she had another long ride ahead of her. She seemed just as anxious to go as they were to send her on her way.

The Queen's presence had assured them the loan of some of Aviler's horses, and the servants readied them in the large roofed court that held the house's stables. The large chamber was warmed somewhat by the presence of the animals and was probably one of the more comfortable areas of the house. This did not entirely account for the number of city guardsmen who had ostensibly shown up to see them off, probably on Aviler's orders.

Thomas was sending all the guards who had survived the flight from the palace, even the most badly wounded. Aviler would probably interpret this as the basest form of distrust, but at the moment the last thing Thomas cared about was the High Minister's opinion of him.

He drew Lucas aside while Gideon was helping Falaise to mount and said, "I'm not going with you. I'm going back to the palace."

He hadn't thought this would be well received and he wasn't mistaken. Lucas stared at him incredulously. "Why?"

They keep asking me that, Thomas thought. *Do I seem bored, that I have to invent these things to keep myself busy?* "Why do you think? That's where Denzil went. He must realize that we'll get the Queen out of here, and with her gone he's not likely to come back."

"What if he isn't there?"

"If he is, it's the best chance I'm likely to have at him. If he's not, I can at least have a look at what's happening there before I go on to Bel Garde." He didn't know if Aviler had sent someone to follow Denzil or not; probably not, and he didn't want to give his own plan away by asking. It seemed unlikely that Aviler was in the plot with Denzil, but it had seemed unlikely that Galen Dubell was anything other than what he had appeared.

Lucas said, "Send someone else, Thomas. Or I'll go."

"No, it's a fool's mission. I'm not Roland, to send someone off to die on an idiot whim." Thomas glanced around. The argument, though low voiced, was attracting the attention of the city guards who were loitering in the stable and of Lord Aviler himself, who was watching from the narrow second-floor balcony where an arched door led into the rest of the house.

Lucas noticed and made a concentrated effort to appear calm. "You're going alone?" he asked.

Thomas found himself curiously reluctant, as if he were admitting to something. "No, Kade is coming with me."

Lucas winced.

"She's a sorceress, and she can get me back in without a fight."

"I know, I know." Lucas hesitated. He looked toward the other men who were saddling the horses, or waiting half-nervously and half-impatiently for them to get on with it. "She could do it by herself. You don't need to go with her."

Thomas shook his head. "She's not invincible, she only thinks she is."

"So do you." Lucas looked back at him, saying deliberately, "In your condition, you'd probably slow her down."

"Then it's no loss to anyone if I don't come back."

Thomas had spoken with more heat than he had intended, but Lucas seemed to realize that line of argument was not going to get him anywhere. He said, "I'll wait for you here."

"I need you to go with Falaise."

"Gideon can do that. He's not a fool; he'll get her there."

They were both silent a moment. Thomas didn't want to force the issue, not here, not now, and not with an audience. He said, "All right, then, but keep a couple of the men with you. And don't wait too long. If it takes more than a day, we'll have to hole up somewhere for the night, and this place may not be safe much longer. If something starts to happen, get out and ride like hell for the gates."

Lucas nodded distractedly, then without looking at him said, "You know that girl's half in love with you."

"Falaise will keep." Thomas looked over at the Queen, who sat her horse with a kind of delicate ease, a few ringlets escaping from her hood. "If anything, it will make things easier in the long run—"

"I'm not talking about Falaise." He hesitated. "You didn't see her when she thought you were dying. I did."

There was only one other "her" he could mean. Thomas said slowly, "Well, she's the excitable type."

"It was more than just that."

"You're mad," Thomas told him, but couldn't help thinking about a woman who chuckled wickedly to herself at odd moments and offered to kill people for him.

"I'm only telling you to watch yourself, that's all," Lucas said, his expression serious. "She's not exactly an ordinary woman."

"I realize that," Thomas said. *Believe me, I realize that.*

"You think you do, but I've known you a long time and you've got a blind eye when it comes to this type of woman."

Thomas said, "Now I know you've gone mad," and turned and went back toward the others. Gideon was holding the bridle of Falaise's horse and looked up as he approached. Thomas said, "Do you think you can get her back to Roland without losing her somewhere along the way?"

The younger man's eyes lit up at the chance to redeem himself. "I'll get her there safely if I die for it."

"Don't die until she's out of the city."

Falaise leaned down and said, "Captain, remember what I said."

"I will, my lady," he answered, thinking, *Let's all survive the day at least before we start plotting again.*

Kade was waiting beside the sorrel gelding Thomas had chosen for their outing. He had managed to get his buff coat back from her, and she was wearing instead a thick wool doublet that Berham had scavenged for her over about a dozen other layers of assorted clothing. She asked, "What was all that about?"

He checked the girth, then swung up into the saddle. "None of your concern."

"I'll wager it was."

He looked down at her. "Would you like to be left behind?"

"Not particularly," she answered brightly, dropping the matter with an insight that shouldn't have surprised him. She held up a hand and after a moment he leaned down and helped her climb up behind him. Two grooms opened the carriage doors, allowing in a wave of frigid air, and she said, "What a nice day this is, except for the prospects of being killed and freezing to death and all that."

Thomas, feeling the light pressure of her weight at his back, tried to avoid thinking about what Lucas had said.

He guided the horse out onto the street and waited until Gideon, Falaise, and the others had started on their way to the city gates, then turned back toward the palace. The sky was gray, almost the same color as the dingy snow piled deep in the streets, and the wind played roughly over the tops of the houses. He was reluctant to take the direct route they had used to escape, but the first side street he picked was blocked halfway down by rubble and a pile of collapsed scaffolding, some noble's building project that had not withstood the shock of the attack, let alone the test of time.

They backtracked, then cut through an alley to the next street. It was slow going, the horse picking its way through the knee-deep drifts with some difficulty. The town houses towering up on either side gradually gave way to the more dilapidated structures of the trading classes. The shingled roofs became wood instead of slate, the brick façades showed signs of wear, and ramshackle balconies overhung the street. It was hard to tell how much damage had been done here; the windows were tightly shuttered as if for night, and there was no sign of life. Thomas was keeping an eye on the tops of the buildings, and spotted the fay before it saw them only because he noted the unevenness in the spacing of the ornamental gargoyles atop the roof of an aging church. Kade said, "Wait," and he reined in, the horse sidling uneasily. The quality of the light around them changed as Kade covered them with illusion. They moved slowly on beneath the waiting presence, unnoticed.

They had ridden a short distance down the deserted street when Kade said suddenly, "I wonder why they did it."

"Who?"

"The Unseelie Court." He felt her shrug. "The Bisran document said they wanted souls to trade to Hell for their immortality, but that's nonsense. Not even the Host trades with Hell. Besides, you can't just send someone there; they have to go on their own. So what did Grandier give them?"

Once Thomas had known who Grandier was, the plot had started to peel away like the layers of an onion, but there was still much they didn't know. Grandier's motivation for helping Denzil for one; Thomas refused to believe Grandier was acting simply out of madness. "Maybe it isn't what he gave them, but what he's promised them. What would they want?"

"The only thing that stands against them is the Seelie Court. And iron wielded by humans."

"Destroying us isn't going to do anything to the Seelie Court, is it?"

"No, they don't care about anyone."

"So... They can't destroy our ability to make iron. No matter how badly they ravage the countryside, they can't get every blacksmith." He paused as an errant gust of freezing wind whipped down into the street, momentarily making breathing difficult, then continued, "Bisra will invade long before they can get around to that, and they'll have another iron-wielding army to deal with."

Kade sounded thoughtful. "Will the Bisrans come here?"

"No, they'll strike at Lodun. It's closer to their border, and they have to eliminate the sorcerers there before they advance any further. If they move fast, if our crown troops are still trying to retake this city, they just might succeed." Lodun had been a small town before the founding of the university. It had since outgrown its confining and protective walls and depended on the strength of the border garrisons for its defense against possible attack from their longtime enemy. With the capital in chaos and unable to send provisions or fresh troops, those garrisons could be swept away. "There are some powerful sorcerers there, but without troops to back them they can't hold off a large assault. The Bisrans would have to cross a countryside where there would be a peasant in every bush with a matchlock; but of course that wouldn't do more than delay them. They would finish us, then tear through Adera and Umberwald." It would be a long bloody war.

"Human sorcerers," Kade said suddenly.

"What?"

"I was wrong. The enemies of the Unseelie Court are the Seelie Court, iron, and human sorcerers."

"Which Lodun is well supplied with. Grandier could have told them that he would destroy Lodun. And he will. Bisra will do it for him." It was a neat bit of reasoning, but it didn't explain Denzil's position. Could he possibly be bargaining to be a puppet princeling under Bisra's domination? There wouldn't be anything left worth ruling; the Bisran Church would condemn as a heretic everyone from Lodun sorcerer-philosophers to the peasants who kept a sprig of rowan over their doorways. "Right now Grandier has us over a barrel. We're on the defensive, forced to react to whatever he chooses to do. If Bisra invaded again, we would have to forget an attempt to retake this city and use the troops to fortify Lodun and the border."

"But Grandier must hate Bisra, hate it worse than anything," Kade protested.

Thomas reined in. "There's something coming down the street."

Kade leaned around him. "I can't see it."

"It was near the ground."

The horse reared suddenly, and it took Thomas all his strength to wrestle it down. Kade slipped off and staggered in a high drift, and Thomas dismounted. He held onto the reins and tried to soothe the horse as the animal whinnied and jerked its head. Behind him Kade murmured a curse. He looked down and saw white mist rising out of the snow. It was no more than a foot or so above the ground, but it was becoming thick and solid with alarming speed.

The horse made a violent convulsive movement that nearly yanked Thomas off his feet; he let go of the reins to avoid being knocked down. The horse bolted awkwardly away, leaving a trail of blood in the snow. It was only able to make a short distance up the street before it staggered and collapsed, felled by whatever was rising out of the ground.

The nearest building, a three-story stone structure that seemed to be leaning slightly under the weight of the snow, had a staircase running up its side to the roof. Though it looked casually put together and was slippery with ice, it seemed a safe haven at the moment. Kade had already retired to a step above the rising mist, and Thomas quickly climbed after her.

"It's a boneless," Kade said. She was digging in the pockets in her smock and muttering to herself. Above her rough gloves, her wrists were dotted with blood where she had touched the ground to catch herself when she had stumbled. "This may be a problem. It doesn't have eyes to fool, and I don't have a spell that can hold it back, the way it oozes around obstacles."

Thomas said, "Go further up."

They climbed to the second floor and Thomas stopped to see what the creature would do. The mist had taken on a kind of half-solidity, becoming a white undulating form. On the step above him, Kade shifted impatiently.

It reached the stairway and hesitated. A white translucent tendril touched the bottom step, then it flowed onto it and began to climb after them. "I didn't know it could do that," Kade said, obviously taking the thing's action as a personal affront. Thomas gave her a push to get her started and they climbed up to the third floor.

The houses were so close together that the street might have been lined with one continuous structure. The garrets of one hung over the next roof, and the overhanging balconies were awkwardly shoved together. There was a slippery step down to a projection of ice-covered roof, then a brief scramble over the wooden rail to the next house's balcony. Kade climbed like a monkey.

They went that way down the street, balcony to balcony, taking to the icy roofs only when it was absolutely necessary. They were more exposed to the wind up here and the cold was intense. Thomas kept up a good pace, trying to ignore the aching wound in his leg.

They reached the end of the street, which opened into a square with the far side formed by the palace wall and the Postern Gate.

It was deadly quiet. Before the attack, this area had been a small marketplace, crowded with street vendors, musicians, pickpockets, and madmen proselytizing new cults. Now it looked as if it had been run over by a cavalry charge. The ramshackle stalls that had grown like spiderwebs between the pillars of the large countinghouse were smashed, and the statues atop the public fountain were broken off, their naked copper pipes leaking trails of ice.

The last house had partially collapsed, and the nearest stairway to the street level was blocked by wooden debris.

As Thomas wrested the heavy wooden boards aside, Kade said suddenly, "What are you going to do afterward?"

"After what?"

"After this is over."

He stopped and stared at her. She was holding onto the wooden railing and shivering with cold, and had put the question with the same puzzled intensity she had shown during their speculation over the Host's motives. He said, "Don't you think that question is a bit premature?"

"Would you accept Falaise's offer?" she persisted.

There was a smudge of dirt on her nose, which he decided not to mention to her. He said, "Do you have to know everything?"

"I wasn't asking about everything."

He turned back to clearing the stair. "I might have to accept it." It wasn't a decision he wanted to make at the moment.

"Only if you wanted things to go back to the way they were before."

Only if he wanted to hold onto that power he had sentimentally wished to be rid of last night. "Why would I want to change it?"

It wasn't a question but she answered it anyway. "Because there are things you don't like about it, like killing people who get tricked by Denzil or get in the way of someone powerful—"

"Do you mind?" he interrupted her. He shoved the last board aside and they climbed down to ground level.

The Postern was smaller than the huge edifices of Prince's and St. Anne's. It had no gate tower and was much narrower. One of the great doors stood open, the other lay in the plaza. Thomas hoped whatever had rammed into that yard-thick wood now dearly regretted it. "Lucas was right," he said. "The way that door's been flung, something broke out, not in."

They paused in the rubble-strewn shadow of the last house and Kade considered a moment, frowning. "They'll expect us through the Prince's Gate, since it was safe before."

"They'll be watching all the gates."

"They might not. They're not very quick thinkers, most of them, and they might not remember things like that. And Denzil didn't have too many knights with him."

"He may not have any knights with him now. He can't afford witnesses," Thomas said dryly.

They skirted the square, staying close to the buildings, finally reaching the shadow of the wall and slipping through the gate.

To the right of the snow-covered yard there was a high wall, part of the inner defenses designed to trap intruders, and to the left, the three-storied Gate House with gaping holes in its dressed stone wall. Directly ahead was the icy canal, which came in under the north wall and went out under the east, where it was covered over by stone for a mile or so before rejoining the main river that cut through the city. The drawbridge that had allowed access to the rest of the palace compound was a ruined heap, but the siege wall beyond it still stood, blocking the view of the park. Thomas stopped beside a hole in the Gate House wall and took a cautious look inside. "I want to see what's around the Gallery Wing before we rush over there. If I can get up to the second story here, I can see over that wall."

Kade followed him through the gap, saying, "Why do you think Denzil's in the Gallery Wing?"

"I don't know where he is, but that's where the Host seemed to hit the hardest, and that's where the explosion was. I'd like to see just what in hell they wanted there."

Light came down through the torn roof, and the shattered beams had buried many of the defenders. Only the cold kept the atmosphere from resembling a charnel house, and a dull patina of ice hid most of the unpleasant details. The interior staircase had come free of the wall and hung at a crazy angle, but a pile of smashed beams and rubble allowed Thomas to climb to a window on what had been the second floor.

"They might have any reason for doing that," Kade said.

Thomas winced as beams shifted underfoot. "Yes, well, I'd like to know what it was."

"It might have to do with the way they arrived here. However that was."

Something about the way she said it made Thomas wonder for a moment if she had some suspicion she wasn't ready to explain. He considered pressing her about it but he reached the window and found the shutters jammed shut. He had to brace himself and batter the hinges off with his swordhilt.

He pried the shutter away. On the other side of the canal, the park stretched out, an ice field marked by the occasional snow-covered tree. Beyond the park, the Gallery Wing stood, the inner wall and the bastions to the other side looming like monoliths, contrasting dramatically with its graceful outlines. Nearer to the Gate House was the dome of the Summer Residence, which doubled as an observatory for astrologically inclined nobles and scholars. A wall sprouted out of the circular building and met the side of the Old Palace, sheltering the Gallery Wing and the gardens from the public areas on the other side. There was a servants' passage in that wall, and in the thick outer wall of the Old Palace. They could make their way out the opposite side of the Gate House and along the curtain wall, cross the canal where the unused mill bridged it, then enter the Summer Residence and take the passages into the Gallery Wing.

He climbed awkwardly down again, trying to avoid putting weight on his weak leg. Kade, who had been prowling about the place on her own, met him with a worried expression. She said, "The stupid dark fay have used most of the glamour around here. If it's like that all through the inside, I won't be able to hide us from them."

Thomas considered that. He had come too far to go back at this point. "If you want to stay here and wait for me, or start back—"

"Do I look like a coward?" she asked, with an exasperated expression.

"No, you don't look like a coward."

For some reason this seemed to disconcert her considerably, and Thomas reminded himself again to be careful. She tapped one foot impatiently, then said, "Well, all right then. Let's go."

CHAPTER THIRTEEN

KADE FOUND HER warding stone along the passage into the Old Palace. It was cold and silent in the narrow little hall, and only the soft glow of a lamp they had appropriated from the Summer Residence held back the darkness. Thomas waited while Kade dug through the clay seal near the bottom of the wall to pull out the round water-smoothed stone.

He used his dagger to chip a piece off for her, and when he handed the stone back, she said, "That's odd. It's tingling, as if it's still part of the warding spell."

She was staring at the stone in perplexity, so he said, "Maybe it's something to do with the wards over the Old Courts?"

"Maybe. It's very odd." But she replaced the stone in its niche and they moved on.

When they reached the Gallery Wing, the narrow passage opened into a small bare room with a curtained doorway in the far wall. Thomas pushed it open a slit, seeing that they had come out about where he had thought they should. On the right wall was the wide sweep of stairs leading back into the lesser galleries, which would eventually lead to the Grand Gallery with its terrace giving onto the park. To the left was the arched entrance to the Old Palace and the main hall. This area at least was empty, bare of any intrusion except a fall of blown snow across the parquet floor.

They hadn't seen any fay, though twice in their trek across the palace, Kade had steered them around places where she seemed to sense some presence. Most of the creatures who could stand daylight were out hunting the streets. As for the others, and the main body of the Host, they might be hidden anywhere. It had been a cold trail marked by the dead, and the amount of damage was worse than Thomas had suspected. Now he waited until

Kade put out the lamp, then he pushed the curtain aside and went cautiously to look into the entrance of the nearest gallery. At his side, Kade said, baffled, "What is this?"

Light fell through narrow windows high in the opposite wall to illuminate a formal gallery with a vaulted ceiling and delicately sculpted columns with blue and gold inlay. The floor was littered with refuse and debris, most of it looted from other portions of the palace. There were pallets made of tattered blankets, tapestry work pulled from walls, and the heavy damask of curtain material. Gold and silver plate, dented candleholders, and ornaments prized off statues formed glittering heaps. Thomas picked his way through it, thoughtful and wary of anything that might be lurking under one of those piles. Besides the loot, there were more prosaic items such as a scatter of gunflints, green glass shards from a shattered wine bottle, and more of the trash left by military camps. With the toe of his boot, he turned over an empty wooden powder flask and said, "It's a troops' billet."

Kade's nose wrinkled in disgust. "Troops? Denzil's troops?"

"Very likely. Bel Garde is a private estate, and he has the right to maintain a force to garrison it, even if it is within sight of the city." *But where are they now?* Thomas wondered. Plain to see why he had to have them. *You can't take a throne without a private force whose loyalty you can trust, but why aren't they here?* Jewelry that must have been stolen from the bodies of the slain had been left casually about. He picked up a pearl clasp and saw it still held strands of long dark hair from where it had been torn from its owner's head. He tossed it back onto the floor in disgust and looked around, entertaining the idea of torching the place. Broken furniture would provide plenty of kindling. But it would reveal their presence, and when the troopers returned they would only move to the next gallery.

He glanced back at Kade and saw she was staying on the edge of the encampment, looking around uneasily. "What is it?"

"There's a great lot of iron in here." She retreated to a marble bench along the wall and began to scrape the bottoms of her boots off on it.

Thomas knelt and brushed gloved fingers across the layer of dust and filth covering the warm butter color of the inlaid wood floor; he found small particles that glinted dully in the light. "Iron filings. They're everywhere." So these men did not quite trust their fay allies. He had wondered if they would find evidence of the human servants of the Host that had led the attack, but they wouldn't be here in the presence of all this iron. They might have been only shock troops, to be expended in the battle. If the siege lasted much longer, the Host would certainly be able to replenish their supplies, when starvation began to drive more people out into the streets.

He dusted his hands off and went back to where Kade waited at the edge of the camp.

"If they stayed here last night—" She swiped at her boot one last time, brushing the last of the dust off. "Where are they now?"

"If we knew that, we'd be a damn sight better off." Thomas considered a moment, weighing the danger against what else they might discover. "We have to go further in."

She gave a half-shrug. "Very well. But I think it's going to get worse."

They followed a lesser-used path toward the center of the Gallery Wing, through a connected row of state dining rooms and smaller pillared halls, and it was there they found most of the dead. Many had died running, caught alone by some creature of the Host with the walls shaking from the explosion and lamps going out in the foul wind that had followed. There were small groups of Cisternan guards and sometimes servants and courtiers who must have tried to band together to escape. Worst of all, they came upon a small room with the remains of a smashed barricade across the door, where a group had held out for a time.

Hours, at least, Thomas thought, leaning against the remains of the door-frame and feeling a rage as cold as the ice outside. *Judging by the condition of the room.* He recognized some of the men, and one of the women. She was Lady Anne Fhaolain, one of Ravenna's gentlewomen, and she clutched a fire-place poker in a delicate hand that had never held anything more dangerous than a sewing needle. He would have to tell Ravenna that Anne had died bravely, trying to swing a weapon. He would also have to convince himself that if he had been here the result would have been the same, only there would have been one more body in the cold little room.

He turned away to find Kade standing behind him. She was trembling in impotent fury. She said softly, "There's nothing that can make up for this. Not if I hunt him all the way to Hell itself."

Somehow he hadn't expected that it would make her as angry as it did him. He said, "You take this all very personally."

After a moment, Kade shook herself all over, like a cat coming out of the rain. "I take everything personally."

There was more evidence of the presence of the fay. Not far from the sad little room, they found a silken web stretched across the width of an arched doorway. Kade examined it cautiously, then detached it from the doorframe. It drifted gently to the floor, all in one piece like a fine section of lacework. So far they hadn't found any answers to their questions. The day was getting on and Thomas's bad leg was aching from walking, and he knew they didn't have much time left here before the danger became extreme. They would have to settle for seeing the Gallery Wing and then making their way out.

They reached the foyer of the Grand Gallery, where there was a heavy foul smell, reminiscent of bats in a deserted cathedral. Thomas whispered to Kade, "They could be in the walls all through here."

She nodded. "Spriggans. They're asleep. I hope." She flitted past him into the archway. He saw her pause there, and as he came up beside her he saw why.

Light from the steps that gave onto the loggia illuminated the foyer, and the arched entrances provided a panoramic view of the Grand Gallery. The floor had been blown up from below and the back wall of windows onto the terraces had been smashed outward. This had to be the source of the explosion the night of the attack. *This was the center of it then,* Thomas thought, and beside him Kade said grimly, "They did a job of work in here."

The orange trees between the pillars were frozen but still green, the cold had caught them so by surprise. Thomas sensed there was something alive here and looked up from the blasted ruin of the floor to the shadowy stillness of the vaults above. But nothing moved in the silence.

In the center of the room, the foundation stones had been pushed up from underneath by some powerful force and scattered on the bare twisted earth visible beneath. But not scattered randomly. Thomas took a few steps into the room, wondering at it, then climbed the dais so he could get a better view. As he had thought, the broken area of the floor was in the shape of a large circle, with an outline too perfect to be accidental. The shattered stones formed concentric circles within it. It couldn't be anything but a fayre ring.

Peasants found them occasionally in the deep country, circles of trampled grass, stones, or strange growth, and avoided them like the signs of a dangerous infestation that they were. Stories about humans who blundered or ventured into them were not pleasant; usually they were found on the edges of the rings as dried withered husks, as if they had aged a hundred years in a moment. Any attempts to recover the bodies caused them to dissolve into dust.

If they were all like this Thomas couldn't imagine someone foolish enough to wander into one accidentally. It felt dangerous, and it was as unmistakable as a sharp drop off a cliff.

Kade stood regarding the ring for a long moment, and now she followed Thomas up onto the dais. She said, "Fancy that." She sounded more satisfied than anything else, as if the sight confirmed some hypothesis of her own.

Looking down at her, Thomas felt the beginning of a new suspicion. He said, "They used that thing to get in somehow, didn't they?"

Still distracted, she nodded. "They came through it. With the wards confused and floating away, and no spells guarding it, it was the easiest way. I mean, not too easy, with the stones on top of it like that, but all of them together could do it."

"Through it?"

"Yes." She glanced at him a little warily, then explained, "It's a doorway."

"A doorway to where?"

"To Fayre, maybe. To lots of places."

He looked back at the ring, its tumbled stones a silent presence in the shadowy room. Kade grabbed his elbow. "Listen."

After a heartbeat, he heard it too. Voices, echoing down through the long galleries locked in cold silence.

Thomas hurried back to the archway, trying to pinpoint the direction. Tracking the sound echoing off so much stone and marble wasn't easy. The men might be in any one of the several galleries and long halls that led up to the Grand Gallery. Neither he nor Kade had spoken in louder than a whisper, and it was doubtful that whoever was coming this way had heard them.

He motioned for Kade to follow and they crossed the spriggan-haunted foyer, and Thomas chose a smaller hall used for diplomatic processions, where the sound had for a moment seemed louder. They went down it, keeping to the partial shelter of its supporting pillars. The voices had ceased.

"I don't think this was it," Kade whispered.

"No, it must be another—"

They both heard the footsteps at the same time.

Kade looked around frantically. "There's not enough glamour in here."

Thomas searched hastily along the wall and found the unobtrusive servants' door that was designed to blend into the paneling. He went to it, sliding his hand down the crack that marked it until his fingers touched the catch. He pulled it open. Inside was a cramped stair leading up into the wall. Climbing it, they came to a landing with a damask-curtained doorway and another broader stair leading down and away from the hall. Thomas pulled the curtain back and saw that the door led to a small musicians' balcony, one of many spaced around the gallery. He put his hat aside and crouched down, crawling out to look down through the balusters. Kade followed him.

Denzil and Dontane walked into the gallery from an archway below. *So the bastard's alive,* Thomas thought, brows lifted. Dontane had been imprisoned in the Cisternan Guard House during the attack, and Thomas had assumed he had been killed with the others. The two men were arguing animatedly; they were trailed by three men armed as common troopers. The Albon knights who had accompanied Denzil at Aviler's house were probably dead; they would not have betrayed Roland, and it must have been obvious at this point that the young Duke's game was more serious than a petty attempt to disgrace the Queen's Guard.

Denzil was dressed for battle, and Dontane still wore black court brocades. He made quick nervous gestures when he spoke, but it seemed to be more from intensity and anger than anything else.

The echoes were now a hindrance rather than a help. The two men were speaking more quietly after the first shouting that had revealed their presence, and Thomas couldn't make out what they were saying. He heard Denzil mention Bel Garde, and he thought he heard Roland's name, but the rest was inaudible.

He edged back and sat up on one elbow, pulling a pistol out of his sash and winding its mainspring. The faint click it made was disguised by the two men's voices.

Kade glanced back at him, raising her eyebrows inquiringly.

He motioned for her to go back through the doorway and she crawled backward out of the way.

The range was not the best; with a pistol, closer was better. Thomas steadied the weapon on his arm and squeezed the trigger. Both men reacted to the sound of the blast; Denzil staggered. Thomas scrambled back out the door, shoving the empty pistol back into his sash. There would be no confusion about where the shot had come from; the white smoke hanging over the little balcony would reveal his presence like a flag.

Kade was already on the landing, and he followed her down the wider stair. It came out through another servants' door in the foyer, and he could hear running footsteps and a man shouting. Drowning it out was a low humming sound that seemed to come from everywhere.

Looking around, Kade gasped, "Damn, but that woke them up."

A gray-skinned spriggan with a face like a melted wax mask dropped out of nowhere to land within arm's length of them; Thomas ran it through with his rapier almost before he realized it was there. It reeled away shrieking and more of the creatures appeared in the doorways, racing toward them down the halls. Something troll-like, squat, and hairy blocked a doorway, snarling at them.

If they could just get outside and out of the things' sight, Thomas knew Kade could hide them with illusion. He thought of the broken expanse of windows in the Grand Gallery. This idea must have occurred to Kade because she was already dragging him in that direction.

They ran under the archway and toward the broken windows that led out to the terrace and the park. Skirting the torn section of floor where the ring lay, they were almost there when one of the clawed demon-horses leapt up the terrace steps. Thomas swore, spun around, and drew his last loaded pistol.

The howling pack of spriggans rushed toward them in leaps and bounds; Thomas fired into the group to make them draw back. They scurried and scattered as the ball tore through them.

Something shoved him from the side and he stumbled, then felt his bad leg give way. Unable to catch himself, he fell over the edge of the broken floor...

...and felt a rush of warm air as he landed in soft verdant grass. He gasped and pushed himself up. He was in a wide open field under a sky of an odd crystalline blue. Nearby Kade rolled to her feet and shook out her hair, dislodging only a small amount of the greenery caught in it. Around them was a ring of stone menhirs, each nearly ten feet in height and weathered by great age. It was warm and the grass was the deep green of spring, touched with splashes of red from poppies.

Thomas stood up, stumbled a little, and looked around. About a hundred yards away the craggy face of a cliff towered above them, dotted with grassy clumps and hung with a thick growth of ivy. In the distance he could see that the ground rose gently up in a gradually increasing grade, as if they were in a deep bowl-shaped valley. "Where in hell are we?"

"Knockma," Kade said. She looked defensive.

He stared down at her. "Fayre?"

"No. Well, yes. In a way." At his expression she burst out, "If you don't trust me I really can't think why, because I haven't done anything deceptive for days."

But Thomas had looked up at the sky, and barely heard her. The deep blue was there, and far above floated drifts of puffy whiteness that were clouds, but there was a barrier that seemed to hang at about the level of the cliff top. It seemed solid and yet malleable, and was transparent, allowing the sunlight in but gently muting it. He felt a soft breeze, stirring the grass with a faint rushing sound, and the barrier shimmered with it as if it were made of the most delicate glass or… He managed to tear his eyes away and looked at Kade. "Is this…the bottom of a lake?"

She bit her lip. "Yes."

He was getting over the shock, and starting to realize exactly how angry he was. "You knew all along how the Host got into the palace."

Kade paced around in a circle, not looking at him. "I knew about the ring. It was how my mother got there in the first place years ago, but Galen and Surete and the others added a spell to the wards that blocked it. The ring could have faded away; sometimes they do." Though he hadn't had a chance to reply, she threw her arms up in exasperation and continued, "All right, and I sent Boliver to fly over the palace last night and he said they must be using the old ring because there weren't any new ones. I didn't say anything because I wasn't sure." She stopped and shook herself. "No, that's not true either. I don't know why I didn't tell you."

"You could have mentioned what you were about to do."

"There wasn't time."

"There was time when we were standing there staring at the ring before we heard Denzil and Dontane." He looked around for his rapier and found it buried in the high grass a few feet away. It and his pistols had come through the ring intact, and he wasn't sure whether to be surprised by that or not. He slipped the blade back into the scabbard and said, "Damn it, woman, I trusted you. I told you something I swore I'd take to my grave unsaid. I let you watch while I shot the goddamn King's buggering cousin. You know enough to get me drawn and quartered a dozen times over." He was shouting at her now. "You could have bothered to mention that you not only had a quick method of escape from the palace, but that it involved taking me into Fayre which I think you realize is not a place where I wanted to go!"

Kade shouted back, "I had to think about it and by the time I did there wasn't time anymore! And this is not exactly Oberon's Court. I mean, I live here and it's not the most dangerous place on the map for humans and you could credit me with some sense." Her smaller lungs gave out and she sat down hard on the grass. After a deep breath, she continued in a normal tone, "…and I'm not used to trusting people either and I find it very frightening, and sometimes I don't know what to think about you."

What she had said about trust being frightening had hit home with more force than she could have realized. More calmly, he said, "Neither do I."

Neither spoke for a few moments. Kade sat in the grass and looked tired. Thomas felt he could hardly argue with her for saving their lives, even if it had involved frightening him half to death. He said finally, "So you live here?"

"Actually, over there." She pointed.

He looked behind them and then up, and thought, foolishly, *No, you haven't seen everything.* More than half the length of the lake away, a small round island was suspended in the crystal surface of the illusory water. On top of the island, stretching high overhead, was a castle. It was ancient, its stones tinted green by moss, its three towers capped with round turrets in a style decades out of date, stairways curving up them like twining vines. What was amazing was that its reflection in the water that was not water was not a reflection.

A second castle grew downward from the island that was the base of the one on the lake's surface, like a stalactite growing from the roof of a cave. It was a mirror image of the castle above, and the sharply pointed top of its tallest, or lowest, turret was gently brushed by a willow tree.

"It's nice, isn't it," Kade said softly, standing at his side now.

Thomas felt he had to agree. "Did you make it?"

"No, it's been here forever. It's a Great Spell, like the palace wards, only more complicated and much older. The people from Merewatch, the village up on the shore, can fish in the lake and row boats on it, and drown in it if someone down here doesn't happen to be watching. But if you know it's a spell, you can walk into it without getting wet." She dragged a foot through the grass thoughtfully, then said, "I'm sorry I brought you here without saying anything first. It was rude."

He looked down at her, admitting, "I overreacted. I didn't know there would be places like this. I thought it was all blood and bogles, like the city is now."

"I hate bogles." She pointed back to the ring marked by the stone menhirs. "That's the Knockma Ring. I think it was here before the lake. With it I can make a ring anywhere there isn't iron or wards or something to prevent it. It's the only ring I know of that can do that, and both the Seelie and the Unseelie Courts want it. I can send us back to the street outside Aviler's house, to see if Lucas and the others have left yet." She hesitated. "Now that Denzil's dead…"

Thomas shook his head. "I don't know if he's dead. I'm sure I hit him, but he might be only wounded."

Kade frowned. "That would be very inconvenient."

"To say the least." Thomas couldn't get his mind off the castle. "When you're inside, are you upside down?"

"No, that would be silly. It's bad enough as it is, with the stairs all funny in some places. In the middle, between the castle on top and the one below, you have to climb a ladder for a bit and no one likes it."

They stood in silence for a time, until Thomas saw something oddly like a large red dog leaping over the grass toward them. "A friend of yours?" he asked.

Kade said with a sigh, "I suppose so. That's Boliver."

By the time Boliver arrived he had managed to become a wizened little man about Kade's height with red hair and an odd peaked hat, and the bluest eyes Thomas had ever seen.

When he had reached them, Kade asked, "How did you know I was back?"

"How could I help but know? They must have heard the yelling in the next century." He jerked his head back toward the castle. "The others are watching with a spyglass from the wind tower, and it fell to me to come out and see just what was doing." He eyed Thomas speculatively.

Kade shaded her eyes and peered at the castle. "Don't they have anything better to do?" She shook her head in annoyance and turned back to Boliver. "Have the Host tried an attack yet?"

He said, "No, but I been to the village and they say they've seen a hag in the pond and there's been odd things setting the dogs to barking and the sheep to running."

Kade winced in genuine pain. "It's what I thought." She nodded to herself, resigned. "The Host will come here soon."

Thomas hated to see her so torn and desperate. "Look, you've done enough. Send me back to Aviler's house and stay here."

She shook her head. "No, that's what they want. If I let them chase me about, then they'll know they can make me do anything they please."

Thomas understood that only too well. It was a damnable trap, one he had been caught in most of his life. He watched her, knowing there was nothing he could do to help her, that his own involvement had made her decision all the more difficult.

She paced and tugged on her hair. "This place is very strong. It can hold itself against them without me for a time. The village... Damn it, the village." She stopped and told Boliver, "Go up and tell them there's going to be a battle; tell them to run."

"Very well, I will." The fay hesitated then and, with what had to be uncanny and devastating perception, said, "So here's your reason. Well he's got my heartfelt sympathy."

Thomas lifted a brow at Kade, though it was a struggle to keep his expression neutral. The look Kade directed at Boliver should have dissolved him into charred coal on the spot. She said quietly, "You're dead."

Boliver shifted uneasily, as though realizing he might have overstepped himself. He said, "I'll just go and have a word with the village, shall I?"

"Yes, why don't you do that."

"Have to be quick, you know. Wouldn't want to be caught by the Host."

"It wouldn't be nearly as terrible as some things I've just thought of."

"Ah. I see. Well, I'll be going now." Boliver whirled around rapidly, becoming a ball of heatless flames. He shot toward the lake surface above like a firework.

"Do me one favor," Thomas said.

"What?" She was blushing furiously and attempting to ignore the fact.

"Don't kill Boliver."

Kade sighed, managing a rueful smile. "I wasn't going to. I just wanted to think about it for a bit." She dug in the pocket of her smock and produced the chip taken from the wardstone. "I can do this now."

She started toward the castle, and still half-unwilling, he followed her.

As they reached the base of the hilly garden, the castle had begun to look almost ordinary, as if it were perfectly normal to hang upside down from an island suspended in glass with its top turret brushed by a tree. If he had ever thought about it at all, Thomas would have expected a place like this to be eerily perfect, without blemish, as if it were carved out of marble, all imperfections smoothed away. This fayre castle had cracked stones where heavy climbing vines had silently invaded, moss growing around its windows, and was crumbling around the edge of its parapet.

Below the lowermost turret, a stone stair curved up the hillside garden to meet one of the windows, and Thomas followed Kade up to the top. The garden itself was a little overgrown, as if it was only tended when someone had the time. The grass was tall, flowers hung out of their beds, and heavy rosebushes had all but taken over the low wall that circled it, but the fountain was running cheerfully.

The room inside the turret was round, taking up the entire top, or bottom, level. It was lined with book-filled shelves, and clay jars seemed to be crammed into every available space that wasn't occupied by the books. It smelled thickly of herbs and flowers, and sunlight from the wide window had faded the once-bright colors of the carpet and the chair covers.

Kade hopped down onto the wide stone window seat and then to the floor. She glanced back at Thomas as he was getting his first bemused look at the room. "Not what you were expecting?" she asked.

He stepped down from the window seat after her. "If I'd ever considered it, I wouldn't have expected to see the place and still be in any kind of condition to comment on it. You were a deadly enemy of the crown not so long ago, remember?"

"I'd forgotten." She crossed over to the shelves on the far wall. "Well, it doesn't look like the abode of a wicked fay sorceress, but this is where it's all done, all the plots, all the nasty little tricks." Kade ran a hand along the shelves, and selected a large dusty volume.

She flipped through the book until she found the page she wanted. He watched her as she stood on the lower shelves to take down several of the clay jars. He asked, "How did you find this place?"

"It belonged to my mother. She had others, but she lived here most of the time. After I left the convent, I looked for her. I looked so long and so hard she eventually had to let me find her."

Kade dumped the armful of jars on the draw table. "She wasn't a very nice person, not exactly what I was hoping for. But she was taken with the idea of having a daughter, for a while at least." She paused in dumping the herbs and powders out of their containers and smiled at some memory. "She gave me a fayre ointment to take the mortal scales off my eyes, so I could see through fayre glamour. She had more people here, fay and humans, all of them bound to her somehow." She went back to her task. "She had Boliver locked up inside a stone in the garden. He's a phooka, and he likes to change into horses and dogs and fool people, but he's mostly harmless, and he wasn't very happy inside a rock. I broke it and let him out, and Moire threw a terrible fit, but she didn't really do anything about it. That's when I realized that I didn't have to do what she said. I knew sorcery, and she was wary of it."

While she tossed ingredients into a bowl and muttered to herself, Thomas paced the room. After a time, she stopped to glare at him and he took the hint and settled into the window seat. He looked out into the bright air of Knockma and the realization of what Grandier and the Host had done to the city struck with renewed force. If Ravenna and the others hadn't reached Bel Garde safely...

It wasn't long before Kade said, "Now we wait until it works." She ran her hands through her hair. "If it does."

"If it does," Thomas said. "The keystone's place was in the largest under-cellar of the Old Palace, in the base of the fourth pillar from the north side on the third row." At her look of surprise, he explained, "I wasn't comfortable being the only one alive besides Urbain Grandier who knew that."

Kade came to stand next to him at the window seat, looking out into the garden. She was blushing, and he wondered why. He said, "What happened after you released Boliver?"

She lifted a corner of the faded gold curtain and looked at it as if she had never seen it before. "I disobeyed her frequently. She pretended not to care. Then the Unseelie Court tricked her and she had to go to Hell, and I inherited everything. Most of her people ran away as soon as she was gone. Boliver stayed because he's feckless and hasn't anything better to do, and a few others stayed because they haven't anywhere better to go." She was quiet for a moment, looking out at the overgrown comfortable garden.

It was hard to believe that Boliver had ever been imprisoned out there, or that anyone but Kade had ever lived in the quiet dusty peace of this room. Thomas said, "Or maybe they liked it well enough where they were, once your mother was gone."

Kade looked down at him, her gray eyes serious. "I think you like me a little bit, even if it would half kill you to admit it."

"It would not half kill me to admit it." The sunlight, muted and changed by the layer of illusory water above, transformed the color of her hair to the same dusty gold as the drape. After a moment, he said, "I know what Ravenna told you, that night in the Guard House. She was oversimplifying the case. She does that when she's trying to get something she wants very badly."

Kade clapped a hand over her eyes, reeled around, and half fell into one of the wooden chairs. "Do you know everything?" she demanded.

"No. If I knew everything, we wouldn't be in this situation." He smiled. "But I suppose I should be flattered that she considers my presence an inducement. I'm old enough to be your father."

"But you're not." She slanted a deliberate look at him. "You're not?"

"No, I wasn't at court then. And I do keep careful track of those things, in the event they become important later." Thomas realized he could hardly be doing a worse job of putting her off if he had actually set out to seduce her.

Kade shifted uncomfortably. "I told her I didn't want the blasted throne."

"I know. If you'd accepted, it would have been a rare disaster. Exciting, but a disaster all the same."

"Well, that's what I thought." She hesitated a long moment, drawing a design with the toe of her boot on the floor. "Do you trust me?"

Tell her no, he thought, *and whatever it is that's happening between us will end.* But he didn't want it to end. He wanted to see what would happen next, to follow it to its conclusion. He wanted it more than anything else he had wanted in a long time. He said, "Yes, oddly enough, I do."

She bolted back across the room, stood for a moment in front of the shelves, then took down a white-and-blue banded jar. She wandered back, and not looking up at him, she said, "This is the fayre ointment my mother gave me. It will let you see through glamour. Not all the time, because fay can use glamour to fool each other, but if they don't know you're there, or that you can see them, they won't know to hide from you. I mean, if you want it."

There's more to this than just that, Thomas thought. *It will make some kind of tie between us, and then what will happen? Anything or nothing.* He pulled off his glove and held out his hand.

ᘉᘉ

The room was cold and still, windowless, a single candle sparking color from the blood red fabric of the walls, leaving all else to fade into the gray-black of shadow. Urbain Grandier sat at the table, the polished wood chill under his hands, his face turned toward a framed parchment map of Ile-Rien. The southern border with Bisra was marked in red, Umberwald and Adera to the north and east in blue, and the compass rose and the faces of the four winds were rendered in precise and loving detail. Grandier could not possibly decipher the ornate script that described towns, rivers, and borders in the wan flicker of the single candle, but his eyes were as intent as if he treasured every faded brown scratch of the artist's pen.

There was noise outside, voices, then an alarmed shout. The door banged open, revealing Dontane and an Alsene trooper, half carrying, half support-ing the young Duke of Alsene between them. Denzil's shoulder and left arm were soaked with blood, his doublet and buff coat torn aside to reveal lacer-ated flesh. There were more troopers out in the brightly lit anteroom, and one of the young lords of Alsene who had arrived with the duchy's troop that day was shouting at them. Grandier rubbed his eyes under Galen Dubell's gold spectacles and said mildly, "Put him on the daybed. And for heaven's sake, shut the door."

Grandier stood and winced. He still felt the old pain; his mind tracing the path of injuries that this body had never known. He lit the other candles in the room as the two men took Denzil to the couch and gently let him down on it. The Duke's face was bleached white, fierce with pain. One of his young pages had followed them in and now knelt anxiously beside the couch. "How did it happen?" Grandier asked, watching them.

"The Gallery Wing," Dontane replied. He stepped back from the couch, breathing hard from exertion, sweat gleaming on his forehead. "Someone was there, and fired at us from cover. It woke the fay sleeping in the walls, and they overran the place so quickly we didn't have a chance to pursue him."

Grandier tut-tutted under his breath, taking his leather-covered apothecary box out of a cabinet. "To be expected."

Dontane stared. "Expected...?"

"Of course. It would be a very great mistake to think our opponents are fools. They were bound to investigate at some time."

"Then they know the Alsene troop is here." Dontane's sharp features were fearful.

"I would imagine so, yes."

Dontane strode for the door, gesturing for the Alsene trooper to follow him. Denzil watched him go, perhaps knowing as Grandier did that Dontane would take this opportunity to order the Alsene troops and officers, using the Duke's authority. Denzil was in no position to object; his blond hair was soaked with sweat, and he was biting his lips until blood came from the effort to not cry out.

And bleeding like a slaughtered pig on good furniture, Grandier thought. After the poverty of his early life in Bisra, the abundance of first Lodun and then Vienne and the palace had astonished him. Ile-Rien had little understanding of its own wealth, of how valuable was the flow of goods from the foreign vessels flocking to its trading ports, of the surfeit of arable land that allowed any peasant with enough coins in his pocket to own it. Of how this wealth would affect those who did not possess it. His voice dry, he told the kneeling page, "You may go. This won't take long, and he can do without the necessity of adoration for a short while."

The boy was too afraid of Grandier to argue. He left without protest but with several longing backward glances. Denzil took a breath, brow furrowed with exertion, and whispered, "Jealous, sorcerer?"

It did not surprise Grandier that the Duke would make the effort to say something vicious despite his agony. Grandier examined the large wound in Denzil's shoulder where the pistol ball had penetrated and frowned at the visible bone splinters. "Oh, yes, terribly," he answered. "It affects my judgment, you see." He turned back to the apothecary box to select the necessary powders. Dontane had been the messenger in the forging of the alliance between Grandier and the Duke of Alsene in Ile-Rien, and that alliance had never been anything but uneasy. And Grandier did not like the accord he saw at times now between Dontane and Denzil.

"Your affectation of superiority is amusing." Denzil gasped, closed his eyes briefly, then continued, "I hardly think you can take the high moral ground in this situation."

"I, at least, am not a traitor. My homeland turned against me long before I returned the sentiment." Grandier came back to Denzil's side. On the panel supporting the daybed's canopy was a painted scene of nymphs, satyrs, and human shepherds enjoying each other's company in several ways that would have been displeasing to the Bisran Church. The casual displays of sensuality and the acceptance of it in Ile-Rien had also been a surprise. Like the acceptance of sorcery. Grandier had heard about it, about the university at Lodun, but he had not really credited the rumors until he had seen the reality. *I wish I had come here as a young man,* he thought. *So much might have been different.*

"And what excuse do you make for your betrayal?"

"Attempting to excuse the inexcusable is always a mistake," Grandier said. "Why not simply admit that greed overwhelms loyalty, affection, and common sense."

"I have no affection or loyalty for Roland," Denzil said, voice grating with pain. "He serves my purpose."

"I wasn't speaking about you," Grandier said. Denzil might have grown to hate the young King because of the power Roland held over him, even though as Denzil's friend and patron Roland had never exercised that power. Grandier understood this all too well. He knew the danger of allowing any individual, any state, any force of whatever kind, to hold one in its power, to control one's actions. "This is going to hurt, but I can't think why you should mind. You seem to enjoy the pain of others."

Denzil's chuckle was weak, but it held real amusement. "You mean that as a taunt, but even you would be shocked at how accurate your assessment is."

For an instant, Grandier hesitated. He knew Denzil to be a smiling killer, as excellent an actor as the hags who lured children to their deaths with their own mothers' voices. No, that was not quite the analogy he was searching for. *He is not a monster,* Grandier thought, *but forces beyond his control have warped him past reason. Even as they have me.* "Perhaps I would," he said, actually enjoying Denzil's presence for the first time in their short acquaintance. "We are both in good company."

CHAPTER FOURTEEN

"ROLAND, I WANT you to come with me." Ravenna stood in the doorway, her look of determination as grim as the faces of the Queen's guards accompanying her.

Her son looked up at her nervously. He sat in an armchair holding a small lapdesk, though the paper on it was still blank. The room would have been light and airy in the summer, but now the wooden winter shutters covered the large windows and the fire in the hearth could not dispel the cold. There was no one with him but his personal servants; Ravenna had made sure she would not have to do this under the eyes of any courtiers or hangers-on.

Roland turned the pen over in his hands and got ink on his fingers. "Why?"

She said, "I have something to show you."

Roland stood reluctantly. "Has something happened?"

Ravenna knew he wasn't interested in anything besides news of Denzil's whereabouts and that he would realize she would not be the one to bring such news to him. "Take your cloak; we'll be going out on the wall."

Immediately an impassive servant brought a thick fur-trimmed cloak from the bedchamber. Roland stood still for the man to arrange it around his shoulders. "Where's Renier?"

"Downstairs, attending to the guard placements."

"Oh." He followed her through the other rooms in the suite and out to a landing on the grand stairwell. Ravenna could tell Roland was uneasy, even though the four knights guarding the door to his chamber followed them and she was accompanied by her gentlewoman Elaine.

They went up the stairs to a lesser-used floor, then waited as one of the Queen's guards unbolted a door and forced it open against the wind's pressure. They walked out onto the wall, which was sheltered by a shoulder-high parapet, and the wind tore through the crenellations like a mad creature.

Ravenna and Elaine each held onto a guard's arm to steady themselves, and Roland forced himself to walk along unaided. Ravenna held her head down and tried to breathe the shockingly cold air, knowing she would pay for this ordeal later with coughing fits. In the face of everything else, it was a minor consideration.

The sun was making a brief appearance, though dark clouds were visibly building up in the distance. To the north, if one could have forced oneself close enough to the parapet to take in the view, were several miles of snow-covered fields and then the rise of the city, like a man-fashioned mountain range. The wind had torn away much of the haze of wood and coal smoke that normally hung over it, and the snow made it appear pristine and empty. The other side of the wall looked down on the inner court, where Denzil had hosted gatherings in the summer and displayed the little fortress's wealth and elegance. When they had arrived yesterday, they had found the usual garrison depleted, and the steward had said that the Duke of Alsene had ordered most of his men to one of his other estates to quell some tenant problems over taxes some weeks ago. Messengers had been sent on to the Granges, a day's ride to the south, to General Villon.

Ravenna wondered if Thomas was alive.

There was no other man she had ever felt closer to, or who had actually understood how her mind worked without condemning her for it. When he had first been accepted into the Queen's Guard it had not been his political astuteness or his wit that had attracted her, though from the occasional flashes of ironic humor she had witnessed, she had suspected that he might possess those qualities. No, most of that she had discovered later, and that discovery had added more meaning to what had been one of the most pleasurable times of her life.

You're getting old, my dear, Ravenna told herself. Old and frail and helpless. It was the constant underground war of intrigue that had beaten her down. She and Thomas had once found such subtle battles exhilarating, but now... Palace power struggles had always been intense, but since Roland's maturity, the battles had escalated into full-scale wars with no clear victors. Denzil had much to do with it, but it was also that the wolves sensed Roland's weakness. And her options to remedy that were severely limited.

She forced her mind back to the present. Grandier had rendered the court's tenuous balance of power a matter for future academics to consider. If

Thomas was alive, he would come to her when he could. If he wasn't... That would be for her to face alone.

They were heading toward the old keep, a rough square tower more than seven stories high. It had been the center of the fortress before the bastion behind them had been built.

They reached the door into the side of the tower, and two of Ravenna's guards split off to post themselves at it. The others went inside, and Ravenna shivered gratefully. The keep felt warm after the wind. A guard stopped to light a candlelamp with flint and steel, and Ravenna saw that the Albon knights were standing stiffly together as if anticipating an attack they could do nothing to prevent. Roland saw it too and said, "What are we doing here, mother?"

Ravenna didn't answer immediately. She started up the stairs, the guard with the lamp going on ahead, and there was only room for Roland to walk beside her. Finally she said, "I've made allowances for you, where Denzil is concerned."

She could see he was slightly shocked that she brought this up in the presence of her guards, let alone Elaine. In an effort to outdo her effrontery, he said, "Allowances? You've been trying to turn me against him with lies for years."

Ravenna stopped and looked at her son for a moment. As always, it hurt that he found her eyes hard to meet. She said, "My dear child, I didn't think you had noticed."

Roland stared at her. "You admit it?"

"Of course. Recent developments have made it possible."

She continued on up the stairs, and Roland followed her, bewildered. He said, "I don't understand."

"That man has made a fool of you."

"He has been my only friend—"

"He has used you to accumulate power and wealth beyond his reach under ordinary circumstances."

"He's been the only one who cared for me; I gave him all those things—"

"Of course you gave it all to him, Roland; that's the way these people work."

Ravenna stopped on a landing and faced him. Roland was out of breath and must have forgotten that he was King and able to order her to be silent, if he could enforce it. He said, "You certainly never showed me any affection. You never gave a damn for me."

"Perhaps you are right," Ravenna said. "You look too much like your father, and God knows I never gave a damn for him." She took a key out of her sleeve and handed it to a guard, who unlocked the door and pushed it open.

"Go in there," Ravenna said.

Roland didn't move. He was trembling, and his eyes were dark with hatred. *He isn't stupid,* Ravenna thought; *he must know his cousin's protestations of eternal love are not sincere. But perhaps he thinks he can earn his respect by doing everything Denzil asks.* It made her feel sick at heart, though her expression betrayed nothing. *The world doesn't work in that fashion, and Denzil is not interested in respecting you, my foolish son.* The guard with the lamp stepped into the room but stayed close by the wall. After a moment Roland went through the doorway.

Inside was a large shadowy room, dark wood a rough veneer over the stone walls. The back half was filled with wine barrels and other boxes stacked to the high ceiling. "You wanted to show me this?"

"Why would anyone store wine here, Roland, away from the livable portions of the fortress, high up where the air is so very dry, in a place more fit for the storing of other things?" Ravenna nodded to one of her guards. "Open one."

He went forward and carefully knocked out the bunghole in a barrel at the bottom of a stack. Something dark flowed out. Roland started toward it, stopped when the odor reached him, but still went to kneel and touch the dark granular substance. "It's powder," he whispered.

Ravenna said, "The four floors above us are as well stocked as this one. The supply does not quite rival the city armory, but I'm told that it approaches it. More than enough to stage a palace coup."

Roland lifted his head, saw the pity on the face of the guard who had opened the barrel, then looked back at Ravenna. She knew her expression showed only weariness. She folded her arms. "Surely you are not going to say we brought it with us."

He shook his head mutely. He stood and walked the length of the row. The lid had already been pried off one of the long boxes, and he lifted the coarse wood to see matchlock muskets packed in heavy cloth.

Ravenna said, "There is another store of powder and shot, a small one, enough to supply the garrison for a few months, set where it should be near the gate. There is only one reason for all this."

Roland began to tremble. "He will have an explanation."

"Undoubtedly."

"I'm going back now." He strode past her and down the stairs.

His knights came to his side, Ravenna's party following. They reached the landing where the door led out onto the parapet, and Roland stopped, waiting. Ravenna reached him and regarded him quietly for a moment, then nodded for one of her guards to open the door.

As the door swung back she caught a glimpse of the sky and saw it seemed inexplicably dark. Then she saw the body of a man lying half in front of the threshold, before the guard slammed the door and braced his weight against it. "Run," he said breathlessly. "Something's out—"

A force struck the door half off its hinges.

Ravenna ran, pushing Elaine in front of her, all thought for the moment purged from her mind. She saw Roland dragged by one of his knights, half flung up the stairs, shoved on when he stumbled.

Below them, the door flew off its hinges and smashed into the wall. Someone fired a pistol and the noise seemed to galvanize Roland and he ran up the stairway with them to the landing. Ravenna grabbed the door there and flung it open, and Elaine stumbled inside. Then Ravenna stopped and looked back. She saw that the guards and knights were trying to hold the stairwell; there was already blood on the floor. There was screaming, and something roared, the sheer volume of sound making the ancient walls tremble.

Roland was standing and watching, blank faced, in shock. He stood there until Ravenna seized his arm and pulled him into the chamber.

Elaine was holding the candlelamp, trembling and wild-eyed with fear. Ravenna shut the door and bolted it, then stepped back, looking around the room and rubbing her hands together. Roland leaned against the wall, watching her helplessly.

There is a way out, Ravenna thought. There was always a way out. She had never been trapped yet, and by God, she wouldn't be now. "This is a corner room," she muttered to herself. "There must be…" She took the lamp from Elaine and set it carefully down near the wall, then went toward the back of the room, trying to make her way past the boxes and barrels of powder. "Roland, damn it, help me."

After a moment he joined her, wrestling a box out of her way but moving stiffly, as if terror had frozen his blood. "What are you looking for?" he gasped.

"This, perhaps." It was made to look like part of the roughly paneled wall, but Ravenna's fingers found the edges and Roland helped her lift it away in a shower of cobwebs and dust. It concealed a small wooden door set back into the stone wall. Roland tugged on the iron handle and it came open with a protesting squeak.

Dank freezing air flowed out. It was a well within the outer wall of the tower, and handholds had been carved out of the stone, leading down into darkness below.

"For sieges." Ravenna nodded to herself. "It will lead all the way down to the bottom floor, with an opening on each level."

Roland looked down and bit his lip. Ravenna knew what he was thinking: it would not be a pleasant climb for him, let alone the two women. He said, "Do you think you can make it?"

"Of course not," Ravenna said flatly. She knew someone would have to stay to close the door and draw the cover over it or the fay would have them within moments. "Go on. You'll have to help Elaine."

"But—" Roland automatically reached for the girl's arm as Ravenna pushed her toward him. "You can't—"

Elaine said, "No, I'm staying with you." She twined her arms around Ravenna with unsuspected ferocity. "I won't leave you."

Ravenna tried to pry her loose. "Damn you, you silly child, I—"

Roland protested, "Mother, you can't stay here, they'll kill you, at least try to—"

The door cracked as something heavy struck it. "Roland, go on!" Ravenna whispered furiously.

He stepped onto the little ledge, then cautiously felt for the handholds. He looked back and said, "I—"

"Climb," she ordered and swung the panel closed. Elaine helped her with the cover, and they wrestled it back in place, moving away from it just as the door gave way.

Ravenna put her arm around Elaine's shoulders and the girl clung to her as the fay poured into the room.

There were a dozen at least of varied shapes, bogles with distorted grinning faces, some hulking things with no faces at all, a delicate winged creature that looked something like both a demon and an angel. One of them had blood spattered on its mouth; Ravenna wondered if it was from one of her guards, and it was rage, not fear, that turned her to stone. They scampered or strode through the room, disarranging the boxes, searching, for the moment ignoring the two women. Ravenna wondered if they would casually toss a barrel onto the lamp; they did not seem to have any fear of the powder.

Another fay entered. This, Ravenna knew, was the leader. He was tall and slight, human in shape but blue skinned, with a face of childlike attractiveness and a horrible leering smile. He bowed mockingly to her. "Greetings, Queen of Nothing. I am Evadne, a prince of the Unseelie Court."

"What do you want?" she asked. She felt cold down to her bones, and it had nothing to do with the temperature of the room, but her voice was still hard.

"Your boy-king; why else would we go to this trouble?" He looked around the room. "You've hidden him, of course."

Ravenna felt Elaine quiver slightly beside her. She said, "He isn't here."

One of the troll-like creatures left off its search and grunted something at Evadne. He glared at it, then said to Ravenna, "We saw him come into this tower. You will tell us where he is."

"He did not come into the tower. You can see that for yourself. Whoever saw him must have been mistaken." She didn't look around at the other creatures but she could tell they had stopped searching. They would have looked harder, she knew, if they had really been positive that Roland had come into the tower. They must have observed from a distance, and Evadne had taken the chance.

Evadne paced across the room, glaring at the other creatures, who shrank back or snarled at him. He stopped and thought for some moments, his smooth brow wrinkling, then leaned down and spoke to the other fay. Ravenna could tell that some of them did not seem happy with his decision, whatever it was.

He turned and came back toward the two women. "You will tell your men to bring him to us, or we will kill you."

How daft, she thought. *This thing doesn't understand us at all, does he?* But it gave her an idea, and she thought she knew how to manage him now. She said, "I can't do that."

"You can. You will."

Ravenna pretended to falter. She thought she did it well; she raised a shaking hand to her brow, and said, "Please…"

Evadne leered at her. "A King or a Queen, what is it to be?"

"I…" She managed a fairly creditable sob. "I'll send the message."

Evadne sneered in triumph. He snapped his fingers and a small winged creature with a hideous face produced a gold-chased quill, inkpot, and a ragged piece of parchment out of the air. It set the things down on the box in front of her.

Ravenna gently disentangled Elaine's hands from her arm until the girl stood alone shivering, and sat down on the box. She picked up the pen and dipped it, then paused to frame her thought. She wrote, *Accede to no demands and keep the men away from the tower. By my hand Ravenna Fontainon Regina.*

She hesitated. The fay didn't ask to see the note and had made no attempt to watch her write. He couldn't read, then. It made sense. Why would a fay read?

Except for Kade, of course. Ravenna would have given quite a bit to have Kade at her side rather than Elaine, whom she had to protect.

But would Renier and the others obey the note? Without Thomas here, there was no way to be sure. How could she make sure they would do it? There wasn't a way.

Evadne snapped, "Hurry, old woman."

Ravenna knew the expected response and tried to compose her features into something like fear. She had spent so much of her life concealing her fear that she had forgotten how to show it. She felt she looked more confused than afraid, but it apparently satisfied the fay. She said, "I'll have to seal it, so they will know I wrote it."

"Go on, then."

She folded the note and Elaine took the candle out of the lamp and handed it to her without being told. Ravenna looked up and saw the girl's expression, and knew she had read the note over her shoulder. There were both fear and trust in her eyes. *She thinks I have a way out of this.*

Ravenna took the candle and dripped the wax onto the paper, then pressed her ring into it. Her personal seal, the crescent moon embossed by the family symbol of the salamander. It was not until then she realized she had signed herself Queen, not Dowager. *Damn. Well, let them put that in their history books.* Elaine reached for the candle but Ravenna set it down on the crate, grinding the base into the wood so it would stay upright. Now for the next part. She handed the note to Elaine and said, "Take this to Renier, dear."

With an awful childlike smile, Evadne said, "I'm not sure I want to part with so lovely a hostage."

The paper crackled a little in Elaine's grip. Ravenna said, "Perhaps you would take the message yourself, then. No doubt my men would like to meet you."

He looked amused, enjoying Elaine's fear. "I suppose you're hostage enough for their good behavior. The girl may go."

And you need no hostage for my good behavior? Ravenna thought. She resisted the urge to kiss Elaine good-bye and merely said, "Go on, dear." Elaine looked down at her, bit her lip, then turned and hurried to the door. *I taught her not to cry before enemies and she doesn't.* Ravenna nodded to herself, satisfied. *That one turned out well.*

Evadne watched the girl go, but made no attempt to stop her. Ravenna waited until she heard Elaine's steps on the stairs, then relaxed a little. She settled herself more comfortably on the box and watched Evadne.

The fay said, "He told me you would be weak. I see he was right again."

It surprised her. "Who told you that?"

"Our pet sorcerer, Grandier. He had leisure to study you."

Your pet sorcerer! Your pet snake is more to the point. She said, "He doesn't like you very well, does he?"

"He is a human, and therefore a fool."

She inclined her head. "I see."

The time passed slowly. Ravenna counted her heartbeats and stared at the candle flame. It kept her mind off wanting something to do with her hands. She saw Evadne grow impatient. He began to pace again, snarling at the other creatures. To distract him, she said, "I thought your kind could not attack during the day, only your servants and the lesser members of your court."

He grinned at her implied insult. "Our sorcerer has made the sky darken for us, made the clouds turn black so the sun does not disturb us. Even now, one of our great ones perches on the outside of this tower, ready to destroy your men in the courtyard." He glared down at her. "Why don't they send out your king, old woman?"

"It will take them some time to persuade themselves that there is no alternative."

Evadne's stare turned curious, and she realized she had spoken with a smile. She thought of trying a fearful expression again, but it was too late for that. *Oh, I'm leaving everything undone. Roland, learn from this if nothing else.* Probably Elaine had unintentionally helped matters by telling Renier that Ravenna had some plan of escape. Roland had had more than enough time to climb to the bottom of the tower. *Or fall to it, God help him*, she thought.

"They take too long. I think I'll tell my friend outside to kill a few men down in the courtyard, to hurry the others along."

Ravenna said, "I think you won't."

Evadne laughed.

She said, "I may be old, but not too old to deal with you." She stood, and before he could think to come at her, she tossed the lit candle into one of the broken barrels of powder.

The blast blew gaping holes in the outside wall, and brought the upper floors and the roof down on top of them. The flying creature perched on the side drifted to the ground in a ball of flame, keening most of the way.

When Roland's reaching foot touched solid stone he gasped in shock, then leaned against the rough wall and sobbed in relief. His arms were shaking and his fingers had begun to bleed. A hundred times he had seen himself falling to the bottom of the narrow well, bouncing off the walls, dying in filth and darkness. But the most painful thoughts did not concern his own death. *He'll have an explanation. Powder and shot hidden in the tower, enough for a small army, and the fay have come and he isn't here, and wherever he is, he's taken Falaise with him... He will have an explanation.* After a moment Roland rubbed his sleeve over his face and began to feel for the wooden door in the pitch darkness.

Roland found a catch but the door was stiff from disuse. He managed to push it open a crack, enough to let in a breath of air, but no further. He hesitated, afraid to make too much noise. If the fay had taken all of Bel Garde, if they had won past the gate Braun's apprentices had said was sealed against them... *Then we'll all die, mother and Elaine in the tower, everyone down here, and when they catch me...*

But then he heard voices, rough human voices, the familiar city accent. A woman asked some inaudible question, and a man's louder tone replied, "That's what I said, but they're looking for the King down here, and why he's down here I—"

"In here!" Roland yelled. "In here! I'm here!"

There was consternation outside, more voices, then lamplight fell through a crack in the top of the door, and Roland looked up into it gratefully. He saw a brown human eye gazing at him in astonishment. "I'm here," he said again.

The eye withdrew, to the accompaniment of profane cursing. Then the door was pried open, the wood bending at the center and cracking under the pressure. Roland saw why he had not been able to push it any further. A wooden floor had been built up to it at about waist-height, probably dividing an ancient high-ceilinged room into two usable compartments. The man outside had to break the wood to get it open, and Roland reached upward and was drawn out by strong arms in a rough homespun shirt.

The man, who was large enough to be a blacksmith, set him on his feet, then steadied him when his legs tried to give way. The room was a storeroom or pantry, shelves on the walls, piled with bags and barrels, and a group of servants and several wide-eyed children were staring at him in astonishment. "God," one woman shrieked, "it's the K—"

She was leapt upon by several of her companions, one ripping an apron off and shoving it against her mouth. "Those demons are in the tower overhead," another woman hissed. "Who d'you think they're looking for?"

"He's all over blood," someone else whispered. "They've tried to kill him."

"No." Roland looked down at his hands and winced. "I was climbing. I have to get to Renier. I have to tell him—"

"I'll go and fetch him, Your Majesty," the man who had pulled him out said. "Best you stay here; the beasts could be anywhere."

"Yes, you're right." Roland leaned against the wall and watched the man pick up a musket and hurry out. A voice in his head whispered, *Denzil lied to you all along. His friendship ended the day they put the crown on your head.* Roland thought, *But he saved my life. He did save my life, that wasn't a lie. But he was a boy then, and he wasn't my heir. He needed a live prince. But a dead king is a different matter entirely.* One of the older women came forward with a scarf and, without meeting his eyes, started to gently wipe the blood from his hands. "Thank you," he said automatically.

The woman who had tried to scream had been released and allowed to take the apron out of her mouth. She said in an audible whisper, "Now he seems a nice lad, not like what they say at all."

Roland started to laugh. He knew they thought he was being brave, or hysterical, but he was laughing at himself. *I must have always known what Denzil was, but I didn't care, I didn't care, and now he's going to kill me.*

Then the door opened again and two of his knights stood there gaping at him.

And Ravenna and Elaine were still in the tower. The memory jolted Roland back into his senses and he started toward the knights. "Where is Renier? We have to—"

The pure shock of the explosion knocked him to his knees. There was screaming, and Roland knew past his own fear that the others in the room were reliving the moment of the explosion in the palace, when the nightmare had started. One of his knights was standing over him, as if the man could shield him from falling stone and timber with his own body. Dust settled around them, but no stones fell.

After a moment Roland caught the knight's arm and pulled himself up. He felt pitifully weak from the long climb, from fear, from everything else. Many of the servants were still huddled on the floor, and he heard a woman weeping. "It's all right," he said, then repeated more loudly, "It's all right." He saw Renier then, standing in the doorway and staring at him. "What was that?" Roland asked. "What's happened?"

Renier came forward and led him out of the room to a narrow passage beyond, out of sight of the others. "What is it?" Roland asked again.

"Elaine said there was a gunpowder store in the tower." Renier's face was so pale he looked sick.

"Yes. Elaine's here, they escaped? Where's my mother?" Roland couldn't understand Renier's expression.

"She was up there with them."

And Roland knew. To the last he had fooled himself into believing he had been sent for help, not sent away from death.

But part of him still failed to comprehend, and that part said, "What was that noise?"

"That was the tower."

ᘛᘚ

The cold was a shock.

Thomas shook his head and blinked hard. It was almost twilight in a gray world of muted color and dim light. They were in an open square in front of Aviler's house. The walls of other town houses rose up around them, and snow had buried the fountain in the center. Around he and Kade the new fayre ring appeared in the snow as a shallow trench in the shape of a perfect circle.

The corner of the house loomed above them, the shingled roof dusted with ice and thin gusts of smoke issuing from the chimneys. It was quiet, the dim glow of candlelight showing through the shutters on the upper floors. Thomas said, "I didn't realize it was this late."

"It takes time to travel through the rings. We've lost an hour or so out of the day," Kade said, but she was looking up and frowning. She folded her arms and shivered. "Though the sky is very dark."

Thomas started toward the house, thinking that one over, and Kade followed him. He supposed it made sense that time would be lost traveling from ring to ring, even if it didn't make sense that one was not aware of that time's passage.

The spell that Kade hoped would show her the location of the keystone had still been inert in its bowl when they had left. Once Thomas found out if Lucas was still here, Kade was returning to Knockma to see if there had been any result yet.

They moved around the side of the High Minister's house to the alley, and there Thomas stopped and loaded his pistols. In making the open attempt to kill Denzil, whether it had succeeded or not, he had crossed a line and there was no going back. As far as the rest of the world knew, he had committed treason, and he had to get to Ravenna and tell her what he had done before Roland learned of it.

There was a servants' door along the alley wall, and someone had taken the precaution of nailing iron cutlery to it to discourage fay. He listened at it for a moment, then tried the handle. It was locked, but the catch was not strong and he drew his dagger to pry at it. In the deep shadow of the alley the cold was far more intense, and Kade bounced up and down with her hands in her pockets in impatience. Thomas didn't comment; after the mild climate of Knockma, he was feeling the cold more as well.

The lock broke, and he slowly eased the door open.

Inside was a servants' passage with doors opening to either side. A candlelamp on the wall was still lit, but the tallow collected in the bottom showed it hadn't been attended to for some time. Kade slipped in behind him and he closed the door silently.

She whispered, "Something's wrong."

He nodded. The house was far too quiet. Aviler might have left the city, though Thomas thought the High Minister had meant to hold out here until the last possible moment. If Aviler had abandoned the place, he had had good reason.

He whispered, "Wait here."

She drew breath to protest and he put his hand over her mouth and said, "Please."

After a moment, she nodded. He removed his hand and she said, "Just this once."

He gave her a smile, then went down the dimly lit passage. He found a half-open door, taking a cautious look through it to see the small room on the other side was dark. There was a curtained doorway on the opposite wall, light flickering just past it. Then he heard the low mutter of voices.

He tried to ease the door open only to find it stuck against something that lay on the floor. He shoved it open enough to see in and stopped. It was Lucas.

Thomas felt the wood of the doorframe crack under his hand.

Lucas lay on his back, and he had been shot in the chest, probably just as he had come through the door. *He walked into a trap,* Thomas thought, *just as I have.*

The hesitation undid him. Armed men burst through the curtained doorway, shouting.

Thomas ducked back out of the room and into the servants' passage, then halted when he saw more men coming out of another narrow hall, blocking his way. In the dim light all he could tell about them was that they were dressed in the ragged buff coats and mixed armor pieces of mercenaries or private troops. One drew a pistol and Thomas ran into a dark scullery and out the opposite door, momentarily losing them. He hadn't seen Kade at the end of the hall behind them; she must have slipped out the door.

They would expect him to stay on the ground level and look for an exit, not to head for the upper floors. He found a narrow servants' stair behind a curtained door and climbed it swiftly. He heard men pound through the passage below, but they didn't come up. He reached the second floor and made his way through a darkened salon and anteroom set, searching for a windowed room at the back of the house. Climbing down the icy stone would be a problem, but he would risk the drop.

There were more crumpled bodies on this floor, mainly city troops. Possibly the civilian refugees had been allowed to escape, though small chance that would be once night fell. Thomas was one room away from the family's private staircase and could see it through the open doorway. He heard voices and stepped back against the wall, half behind an arrangement of heavy drapes. It was shadowy and ill-lit here, where most of the candles had guttered.

The men at the stair paused as someone gave orders, then spread out to the surrounding rooms. The light from the lamp one carried clearly showed Thomas the badge of the Duke of Alsene on their brown soldiers' doublets. It was a troop from one of Denzil's manors.

There was a shout as someone saw him and Thomas turned and slipped back through the salon. The darkness and confusion worked for him, but they knew where he was now. He stopped in a darkened room to wind both his pistols. It would be dangerous to carry them like that but he was past that point now. He checked the doors as he went through and closed the bolts of the ones that had locks.

Thomas paused outside the door of the next chamber. The stairs down into the stable court were just beyond it.

A quick glance showed him two men waiting in the beautifully appointed room, both looking down toward the stairs. He pulled back as one started to turn toward him, and drew his pistol.

Thomas stepped into the doorway and fired as the first Alsene trooper started forward. The ball struck the man in the chest at a range of no more than ten feet, sending him staggering backward into a row of lacquered cabinets.

Thomas dropped the first pistol and drew the other just as the second man reached him. He deflected the thrust of the soldier's rapier by hitting the narrow blade with his forearm and batting it away, almost managing to grab the blade and pull it out of his opponent's grasp. As the man closed with him, Thomas's pistol was knocked upward. It went off, the blast deafening him and scattering burning grains of powder down onto his attacker. The soldier faltered at the pain, giving Thomas time to shove him away and draw his main gauche. As the man rushed him again, Thomas stabbed him under the ribs.

He stepped back as the soldier collapsed, and in the sudden quiet he could hear others breaking through the locked door into the room behind him. He grabbed up his other wheellock from the floor and tucked it into his sash with the second pistol. Drawing his own rapier, he took the dying man's discarded sword and went out onto the landing above the stables. There he shut the door and wedged the extra blade through the catch to keep it closed. It would not hold them for long.

He turned as the carriage doors below were flung open and a large group of Alsene troops burst in. Thomas judged the odds and knew this was it. He stayed where he was, to let the narrow landing guard his back for him.

The first one to the top of the stairs came at him like a madman with something to prove. Thomas parried the first flurry of blows, then took the offensive, driving the man back a step. The lack of room worked to his advantage; with his bad leg he would not have been able to fight as effective a running battle. There were more of them waiting on the stairs below, and he knew he wouldn't have a chance to run.

His opponent tried an unsuccessful feint and Thomas drove his blade deeply into the man's side. The soldier stumbled backward and the man on the step below lunged past him, only to be speared through the neck. He collapsed on the top step, choking and bleeding copiously, and temporarily blocking the landing.

There was a brief moment of respite as the others below tried to wrestle their fallen comrades out of the way and Thomas hung onto the railing, panting. He could hear them battering away at the other side of the door, and it looked as if the thick wood around the wedged blade was beginning to give. The man with the neck wound made a loud strangled cry and stopped moving.

Then Thomas saw a trooper on the stable floor below aiming a musket up at him. He flung himself back from the rail in pure reflex; this left room for another attacker to leap over the body blocking the stairs and come at

him. Thomas parried the blows, letting himself be put on the defensive, trying to maneuver the man between himself and the musket. But moments
passed and there was no impact or even the blast of a missed shot. They were
trying to take him alive.

This realization energized him and he closed with his attacker, bringing
their swords hilt to hilt and trapping the other blade in the quillions to hold
it away from him. Pushed back, the man stumbled on the corpse behind him
and Thomas shoved him down the stairs. He leapt after him into the momen-
tary clear space, slashing at the men below who were struggling to disentan-
gle themselves. He caught one in the face, the point tearing through the
man's eye and cheek before glancing off bone. The soldier fell against the
wall, screaming.

Another struck upward at him, and he felt a tug and sudden pain as the
point punctured his leather sleeve and stabbed into his arm. He cursed and
tore himself free, falling backward on the steps now slippery with blood. The
idiots were still trying to incapacitate rather than kill him. *No matter what
their orders, I've given them enough provocation*, he thought in disgust.

Another man fought past his two fallen comrades in time to be stabbed
in the chest, but Thomas's grip on the hilt was weak now and the point slid
away instead of going deeply into the trooper's flesh. But it was enough to
send his opponent reeling backward into the railing and Thomas struggled
to his feet again.

Then he was struck from behind, between the shoulder blades, knocking
him into the wall with stunning impact. He slid down it, unable to catch himself, blackness flowing in at the edges of his vision.

∾∾

Waiting beside the door in the darkened hall, Kade kept her freezing
hands in her pockets and tried to calm her thoughts. Anything to keep her
mind off the man who had driven her half-mad standing there on the green
plain of Knockma being too much a gentleman to take any notice of what
Boliver had said.

With effort she managed to drag her attention back to the immediate
problem. She didn't think Grandier could really be helping Bisra. *Why not
lure us into invading them?* She could shrug and say it didn't matter; she
would kill him anyway for what he had done to Galen Dubell. *He was so like...*

The soldiers burst out of a door five short paces in front of her. Their
backs were to her, and she instinctively searched for glamour to hide. There

was hardly any in the dark hall, but the candlelight provided just enough for her to slip out the door unnoticed.

Outside she dropped the barely adequate illusion and ran down the alley to the front of the house. She would have to get in another way, use glamour from the snow outside...

The wall just in front of her exploded.

She hit the icy ground, more from surprise than any impulse to duck. When the building did not collapse on top of her she looked up. Several men crossed the square toward her, one of them carrying a musket, the glow from its slow match just visible in the dusk.

Shooting a poor little girl like me with something that large is hardly fair, she thought, dazed by the suddenness of it. At a distance and in bad light her red smock probably looked bloody. It wouldn't fool them at close range.

She dug in her pocket, hiding the movement in the snow, and managed to draw out a piece of guncotton stained with powder she had prepared earlier. She brought it up to where she could see it without having to turn her head and stared at it, trying to conjure a spark. Sympathetic magic, or unsympathetic magic as Galen had preferred to call it, was faulty and difficult to use. She might only burn her fingers. If she could call flame at all. *Damn it,* Kade thought, *a spark, just a little spark.* But she did her best work under pressure, and as the men came nearer, her mind stopped chattering and she reached the right level of concentration. The edge of the cotton began to glow.

Now. Just as the man with the musket suddenly shouted and raised his weapon, Kade sealed the concurrence spell. Every grain of powder within a ten-foot radius ignited.

The musket exploded almost over her head, there were screams and blasts as pistols went off, then a storm of little popping sounds as the scattered grains of powder from the musket's blast ignited.

Kade scrambled to her feet, her clothes dotted with someone else's blood. Three men lay dead or dying on the snow, two more running away around the corner of the house. She bolted after them, down the alley between Aviler's house and the next, into the street where they had fought the battle with the fay the day before.

Kade slid to an abrupt halt as she reached the street. She felt her heart hit the pit of her stomach. The carriage doors stood open and there were armed troops milling in front of them. She could tell by their dress only that they were not city or crown troops. It looked as though there were a hundred of them.

Someone saw her and shouted, she saw the slow match of a musket glow in the twilight; she darted back around the corner and ran.

※

"Where's the girl?" Dontane stood in the carriage doorway.

"Gone," Grandier said. He stood in the middle of the street, wrapped in his scholar's cope, thoughtfully studying the sky.

Dontane strode out and started around the corner of the house. "I sent five men after her. Damn it, she was running."

"Perhaps she wanted someone to chase her," Grandier said, and followed him.

On the other side of the house, they found the remains of the first group in the bloodstained snow. Dontane stared down at them a moment, then looked at the older sorcerer. Grandier was humming to himself and contemplating the sky again. Then Dontane saw what appeared to be a pile of rags on the snow further into the square. He went toward it.

It must be the men he had sent after the sorceress, though all were dead and none was recognizable. They looked like corpses that had been left to mummify in some desert, dry desiccated husks.

Dontane started forward but then stopped, his attention caught by Grandier, who was watching him with a speculative half-smile. Dontane took a step back and said, "There's a ring here?"

Grandier nodded to a faint circular trough in the snow. He said, "It doesn't do to walk uninvited into Fayre. Or run, for that matter."

Dontane looked down at the pitiful remains of the Alsene troopers and wondered if Grandier would have let him walk unknowing into the ring. But he only said, "Good, we're rid of her then."

"Oh, I think not." Grandier smiled and turned back toward the house. "We have something she wants, you see."

CHAPTER FIFTEEN

THOMAS WOKE WHAT must have been only a few moments later, lying on the steps in someone else's blood with one of the soldiers standing over him, slapping him awake. He had been disarmed and his head hurt incredibly, and he made a grab for the man's arm only to miss. They dragged him to his feet and he thought, *It can't last too long.*

He made them half drag, half wrestle him down the steps to the stable floor. Troopers wearing Alsene's badge moved around the enclosed court, stripping the weapons from the bodies of dead comrades as well as from those of the city troops who had tried to defend the house. The outside doors were open and cold air poured in as a smothering blast, temporarily lifting the thick odor of death that hung over the room.

Dontane waited at the bottom of the stairs. He had participated in the battle—the powder-stained buff coat and the pistols proved that—but the pallor of his face made him look half-dead and his eyes were red-rimmed and haunted. He smiled at Thomas and said, "It seems I can now offer you my hospitality."

Thomas looked past him but couldn't see Kade, not as a prisoner and not as a crumpled little body on the flagstones. The pain radiating through his skull made it impossible to concentrate. He managed to focus on Dontane. "Really? And I was given the distinct impression that your position in all this was a subordinate one."

Dontane's expression tightened into anger before returning to the studied look of amused contempt. He glanced toward the open carriage doors where the daylight was beginning to fail, where Grandier must be waiting somewhere out of sight. His self-control had slipped since he had been in Lestrac's house biding his time and waiting for that foolish young lord to die.

He looked back at Thomas and said softly, "It was you who shot at us in the palace, wasn't it? How very foolish of you to go back there. The Duke of Alsene isn't dead, you see. He's very much alive. And you are going to regret that."

If they had caught or killed Kade outside, surely Dontane would brag of it. "I have regrets already. I regret you weren't on our side of the siege doors when the Host attacked, where after sufficient persuasion you would have accused Denzil and informed us of Grandier's disguise. I regret I didn't spare the time today to blow your head off—"

He didn't even sense the blow coming. It rocked his head back and for a moment he sagged in the grip of the troopers as everything went black. He had time to hope that it would stay that way before the world slowly but relentlessly reasserted itself. The stable roof swam into hazy focus, and he swallowed blood and managed to lift his head. He said, "Careful, you might bruise your knuckles."

"Grandier wants you alive." Dontane stepped closer. "What does he want with you?"

Thomas heard the underlying tension in that cool contemptuous tone and sensed a possibility opening up before him. If only he could pull his pain-scattered wits together enough to take advantage of it. "Ask him."

"It's easier to ask you."

"And I had the impression you two shared confidences." Thomas knew he was provoking the other man too much, losing what little control he had over the situation. He had the sudden impulse to goad Dontane further into rage, just because he could, just because it was so easy, no matter what the consequences to himself. It was astonishing how difficult he found it to suppress that urge.

Dontane struggled for calm and managed to lower his voice to say confidently, "Cooperate with me and it will go easier on you. Or do you really want to be handed over to that old madman?"

"If you've taken him as your master, you're far madder than he is."

Dontane snarled, "That's your last—" and Grandier's mild voice interrupted, "That's enough."

Grandier stepped into the circle of lamplight, appearing suddenly out of the dim cold twilight outside. From his tone he might have been encountering the younger man at a promenade or a market square, but Dontane whipped around to face him.

Grandier regarded him imperturbably. Dontane started to speak, thought better of it, and stepped back.

Moving forward, Grandier said, "An unexpected pleasure, Captain." He still wore the baggy black scholar's cope, still wore Galen Dubell's face.

That was the hardest part. *Now that I know who he is, he should look like a monster, not like... Not like an old friend.* Thomas tried to pull free of the troopers and was surprised when they allowed it. He stood on his own, swaying a little. "Are you getting what you want out of all this?" he asked Grandier. About ten of the Alsene troopers were grouped around him; he thought about fighting but his bad leg was trembling, threatening to give way, and the room kept swaying. He thought about attempting it anyway.

Grandier regarded him silently for a long moment, his gray eyes calm as ever. "Not yet. But soon."

At that moment it occurred to Thomas just why Grandier might want him alive.

Grandier turned away, and while the troopers' eyes were on him, Thomas dove sideways and slammed into one of the men, ripping the sword out of his surprised grip and slashing upward at him. But a hilt cracked down on Thomas's head from behind, and in the end they took him alive.

◊◊◊

Roland walked along a colonnaded porch open to the interior court of Bel Garde, his knights surrounding him, feeling as if his mind were a rusty clockwork that hadn't been wound in far too long. Everything felt out of proportion, and time seemed to move in fits and starts. He said suddenly, "The steward of this place must have known about the powder store. Arrest him at once."

"Sir Renier has already done so, my lord."

"Oh. Good." *God*, he realized suddenly. *My mother is gone and there's no one to think of these things.* He looked up, seeing the confusion in the court for the first time, recognizing the figures in the center of the milling crowd of servants and guards. It was Falaise, sitting her horse in her riding clothes with Queen's guards around her, obviously just come through the gates.

Breaking free of his escort, Roland ran across the court to catch her bridle. He had never made the effort to get to know Falaise very well, but he was glad out of all proportion to see that she still lived. It seemed to promise that the world as it was had not been completely destroyed. "Falaise, we thought you were dead! Where were you?"

She looked down at him, startled. Her expression was frightened and there were dark circles of weariness under her eyes. Her horse stamped and tried to nibble Roland's sleeve. She said, "My lord, I must see Ravenna at once. There is something I must...something I must..."

"My lady," he said, not quite recognizing his own voice, "my mother is dead."

Falaise turned white, the blood draining out of her face as if she were dying in front of him. Shocked, Roland called for help. Guards came to help the Queen from her horse; her ladies and servants appeared in the court. An Albon knight urged Roland away, saying, "My lord, you must come inside. It's not safe out here." Numb, Roland let the man lead him into one of the rooms off the court, thinking, *Something has happened. What is she so terrified of?*

The room was long, with many windows to look out onto the garden court, their lace curtains woefully inadequate to stop the drafts. Roland paced tensely, rubbing his cold hands together, ignoring his knights and unsure of just what he was waiting for.

Falaise appeared in the doorway, half-supported by the Queen's Guard Lieutenant Gideon. Past them, Roland could see two of the Queen's gentlewomen waiting outside, huddled together like children expecting punishment. Holding tightly to the lieutenant's arm, Falaise managed to cross the room, then collapsed at Roland's feet. He looked at Gideon in bewilderment, and the lieutenant bent over the Queen, saying, "My lady, you must tell him."

"Tell me what?" Roland said. Sickness hit the pit of his stomach suddenly, and he groped for the table to steady himself. He remembered that Falaise had disappeared at the same time as Denzil.

Falaise looked up at him, her face tear-streaked and frightened, but something in his expression must have encouraged her because she said, "My lord, I should have spoken days ago."

Roland listened in agonized silence to Falaise's story of more treachery, of how Denzil had deliberately kept the Queen from leaving the city so that she would be in his power. "Before this, he had offered me marriage if you were to die, Your Majesty. I...I don't mean to accuse him but..."

"No." Roland had to stop her. He didn't want to hear how she had concealed treason out of fear of him. He understood her reaction to his mother's death now. She had been counting on telling this to Ravenna first, counting on Ravenna to protect her from him. *More nails in my coffin,* he thought. "It's all right, really. I don't blame you. There are... Other things have come to light which... Perhaps you should go to your ladies now."

The lieutenant led her away, and Roland stood at the table, staring at his own reflection in its polished surface. He had never loved Falaise, knew he never would, but this was the first time he had realized that he might have saved a great deal of trouble by simply making a friend of her. *When Denzil is with me it's as if I can't think.* His fist struck the table and the face in the reflection twisted. *Oh God, let him have an explanation.*

۞

Thomas didn't remember much of the trip back to the palace. They bound his wrists and got him on a horse, and he leaned over the saddlebow, unable to sit up. The cold grew intense as night took the city in a dark wave and the freezing air was raw on his throat and lungs. His stomach was cramping with nausea, and dizziness kept overwhelming him.

He came back to full consciousness only when they were passing through St. Anne's Gate. He lifted his head and shook back the hood of the cloak someone had thrown over him.

They were passing between the Cisternan Barracks and the Mews, as he had days earlier bringing Galen Dubell into the palace for the first time. *I couldn't have been more helpful if I'd been in the plot with them,* he thought. He hadn't even been able to get them to kill him.

The barracks were a gutted ruin. The wooden panels over the three arched doorways had been torn open, exposing the dark pit of the interior and the piles of snow that had drifted inside. With the outer gate closed and guarded, the assault from within the palace would have caught the Cisternans completely by surprise. In the narrow corridors of the ancient stone structure the attack by the fay must have had the devastating effect of a hunter blocking all the holes but one of a rabbit warren, and then releasing his ferrets.

The gates into the old siege wall stood open. As they rode through and toward the towering wall of the Old Palace, bogles dropped out of the eaves of the two long stone city armories across the court. Gray-skinned, ugly, distorted creatures, their yellow eyes gleamed in the gathering darkness. Each was short and squat, their arms hanging disproportionately long and their wide mouths grinning with rows of pointed teeth.

Sniggering in almost human voices, the bogles ambled toward them; the nervous horses shied away.

They stopped in the paved court beneath the bulk of the Old Palace, where lit sconces illuminated the high double doors of the westside entrance. Thomas managed to get off the horse on his own without falling. He held onto the saddle a moment while his head and legs became reconciled with the notion of standing. The troopers hung back from him now, watching him warily. He wondered if it was due to his unpredictability or his apparent familiarity with Grandier.

Inside the circular entrance hall the few lamps made hardly a dent in the shadows. This area of the Old Palace seemed remarkably undisturbed, the untouched rooms and short halls leading off into darkness and silence.

Grandier was standing beside him suddenly, and Thomas was too weary to be startled. Grandier said, "This way."

Both Dontane and the sergeant in charge of the Alsene troops turned to look at him, but Grandier ignored their unspoken questions. He said to Thomas, "I want to show you something."

Grandier led the way down a lesser-used series of rooms, lit only by the lamps the soldiers carried, and to a staircase leading down to the lower levels. At the third turn of the stairs Grandier led them into an old stone-walled corridor, and Thomas realized they were going toward the same cellar where the keystone had been concealed. He looked at Grandier walking beside him, but the older man's features betrayed nothing.

As they moved through the cold rooms the flickering light revealed the sheen of sweat on a soldier's face, a white-knuckled grip on a swordhilt or musket that told volumes about the troops' relationship with the fay invaders.

They reached a plain wooden stair leading down, and were now roughly backtracking the route they had taken away from the cellar the night of the attack, but heading toward the lower passageways they had been unable to reach because of the collapsed corridor. The strain of the fight had exacerbated the pain in Thomas's bad leg and it was protesting this treatment, but he managed not to limp too obviously.

The stairs led to an unblocked passage below the storerooms, and the stale air carried the fetid smell of death. Thomas' thoughts kept turning back to Grandier's shape-shifting ability. *Not that way. I don't want to die that way.* He had given up everything else—his honor, his right to say he had never killed a helpless opponent, his claim on his ancestral lands. Voluntarily or pushed to it by circumstance, bit by bit everything had gone to win a few years or a few months or a few days of political stability in a world where so few others seemed to care, and most of them were dead now. He was willing to die for duty's sake but the thought of giving up his identity turned his heart to ice.

There was light up ahead, from a place where there should be stygian darkness. Abruptly raucous noise, growling, and a high-pitched keening echoed off the stone walls. A few more uneasy troopers drew their swords.

The corridor turned, and the first thing Thomas saw was that a large chunk of the stone wall had been knocked out, allowing a view down into the cellar. Grandier moved to the edge, and after a moment Thomas followed him.

The Unseelie Court had found a home here. Fay with long emaciated bodies and huge leathery wings flew in lazy circles over the foul revelry below. There were hundreds of them, bogles, spriggans, formless creatures like the boneless that had attacked them in the street. The mockery and distortion of human and animal forms was endless and infinitely varied. Thomas could see them much more clearly this time, perhaps because they were not troubling to conceal themselves anymore. The light came from a mist that crept up the walls and wreathed around the giant columns supporting the ceiling.

This opening had been made at about the second level of the cellar, and the wide pillars met the ceiling another two levels above them. Below were the remains of two flights of stairs and the narrow well that had enclosed them, now a mound of broken stone and shattered wood. Corpse-lights flitted around the stairs and the tops of the columns.

The unnatural light was bright enough to let Thomas see the dark openings in the ceiling for the air shafts and the doors through which the larger siege engines had been lowered. Chains and frayed ropes hung down from some of those doors, the old system of block and tackle. Thomas said, "They fly up those shafts."

"Yes." Grandier's gaze was on the unholy revelry below. "It protects them from daylight, but gives them access to the surface." He turned back to the others and said, "Dontane, they seem disturbed. Go down and ask them what's wrong."

Dontane moved forward, threw an unreadable look at Grandier, then started the awkward climb to the bottom of the cellar.

"So he is a sorcerer," Thomas said.

Grandier glanced at him. "He's learning. He had been refused admittance to Lodun, and in anger he came across the border to Bisra, and to me for teaching before my arrest. I refused him, because I felt he lacked moral character." He smiled, amused, apparently, by this earlier self who had had the leisure to make such judgments. "Trust was a very important issue, among those of us who practiced sorcery in Bisra. The merest suspicion of necromancy, or anything else the Church could interpret as traffic with demons, was death. But after I escaped from the Inquisition, I sought him out. I had discovered I needed a man who lacked moral character. He was at Lodun with me after I was Galen Dubell, but one of the masters learned he had been across the border, and became suspicious of him. The rumors that I had come to Ile-Rien had already started, you see. So I sent him on to contact the Duke of Alsene for me, which he did through our unfortunate and foolish Lord Lestrac."

Dr. Braun had visited Lodun frequently, Thomas remembered. "You killed Braun because he recognized Dontane."

"I would have had to eventually, anyway."

Thomas watched Dontane pick his way down the remains of the steps and said, "Are you sure he's not the one who turned you in to the Inquisition?"

"Oh, good try." Grandier smiled. "No, that man is dead."

Dontane had climbed halfway to the bottom, and now one of the winged sidhe flew to meet him, cupping its wings to hold itself in midair, gesturing and shouting at him in a high-pitched shriek. Dontane turned and waved at Grandier, his posture betraying irritation. Grandier said, "It appears this needs my attention." He nodded to the Alsene sergeant, then looked back at Thomas. "I'll see you shortly, Captain."

Without Grandier's presence, the troopers muttered nervously as they made their way back, but Thomas was too preoccupied to notice. *Why did he want me to see that? What did it accomplish?* A will-o'-the-wisp followed them part of the way, playing in the unlit wall lanterns and taunting them silently.

Thomas felt each step of the various stairways as a short stabbing pain. By the time they reached the upper floors of the Old Palace he was limping badly. They entered one of the smaller halls that had been set up as temporary barracks, now occupied by a few sullen troopers gathered around the hearth fire, and they passed through it into an attached suite. The last room had been stripped of furniture and wall coverings, and it was dark except for what light flickered uncertainly in from the lamps in the anteroom.

Thomas watched tiredly as one of them pounded an iron spike with a set of manacles attached to it into the wall. With respect for his unpredictability, one held a pistol to his head when they untied him to put the manacles on.

The chains were short but he was able to sit down against the wall. The troopers withdrew into the anteroom to huddle in a nervous knot near the hearth.

He tested the set of the spike in the wall to see if it could be worked loose, but it held firm. *Well and truly caught this time.* He rested his pounding head back against the cold wood, and tried not to think.

"I didn't believe they would let you live." It was Aviler's voice. Between the dim light and the distraction of various injuries, Thomas hadn't seen the other man chained to the opposite wall. The High Minister's dark-colored doublet was torn and bloodied, and from the livid bruises on his temple it seemed he had not been taken easily.

Thomas closed his eyes a moment, damning the fate that had consigned him to be imprisoned with Aviler. Then he said, "Grandier wanted me alive, and if you imply I'm in league with him, I'll kill you."

At the moment it was a supremely empty threat, but Aviler answered, "Don't take me for a fool, Captain."

"I don't know what else to take you for." Thomas sat up and gingerly felt the back of his head. His hair was matted with blood, and there was a sizable lump composed of pure pain.

"You can take me for a man who did not acquire my power in a Queen's bed."

"Yes," Thomas agreed. "In her bed, on the daybed in the anteroom, on a couch in the west solar of the Summer Palace, and other locations too numerous to mention, and if you had the slightest understanding of Ravenna at all, you would know it never made one damn bit of difference as to whether she took my advice or not. And no, your father handed you your power wrapped in ribbon on his deathbed."

The High Minister looked away. After a long moment of silence, he said, "I expect it doesn't matter now."

Already feeling the bite of the manacles on his wrists, Thomas expected it didn't matter either.

Aviler rubbed his eyes, making his own chains jingle slightly. "Galen Dubell really is the sorcerer Grandier, then. Denzil told me something of it when he brought the Queen to me, but under the circumstances I don't place much confidence in his word."

"Dubell really is Grandier. He got a shape-changing magic from the fay, and he killed Dubell and took his place." The stab wound in Thomas's left arm was still bleeding sluggishly, though the pain of it hardly competed with that in his head. The thinner sleeve leather of his buff coat had absorbed some of the force but the blade had still penetrated a couple of inches at least. He tore a strip of material from the tail of his shirt to use as a crude bandage. "Why are you alive?"

"I don't know. No one's bothered to say. What's your opinion on the subject?"

"He wants to keep his options open. He can't stay Dubell forever."

As Aviler considered the unpleasant implication, Thomas tightened the rag around his arm, taking malicious satisfaction in letting the other man in on his private terror. He knew he had more to worry about on that score than the High Minister did. Grandier hardly knew Aviler.

With Lucas dead—he hesitated in tying off the makeshift bandage, wondering who had done it, Dontane or some nameless hireling trooper—there was no one but Ravenna who knew him well enough to realize the deception immediately. He didn't think anyone could find a way through the complexities of his relationship with Ravenna, but that would only mean Grandier would have to kill her, the way he had coldly eliminated anyone who might have noticed that Galen Dubell had changed more than time could account for.

Then there was Kade.

Kade had done well enough leading her own erratic and dangerous life before Thomas had dragged her into this, talked her into staying with them past the point at which she could have left safely. And made her vulnerable. *The little idiot trusts me.* Lucas had been right. And he remembered that the last conversation he had had with his friend had been an argument; stupid thing to do in a war, and he would regret it the rest of his no doubt short life.

Kade was her own woman, and he was too old to bother lying to himself anymore and too young not to want her. But any chance of anything between them was wasted, as pointlessly wasted as Lucas, Vivan, and all the other lives lost and destroyed by Denzil and Grandier.

There was a stirring among the men in the anteroom, and after a moment Urbain Grandier appeared in the doorway, carrying a candlelamp and a short stool.

He set the lamp down on the scuffed floorboards, and glanced once, thoughtfully, at Aviler. Then he looked back to Thomas and said, "I felt I owed you more of an explanation."

Thomas had a sudden impulse to delay whatever the sorcerer had come to say. He said, "You have Dontane fooled. He thinks you're mad."

Grandier shook his head, put the stool he had brought just inside the doorway, and sat down. "I give him what he expects." He sighed, and looked like a tired old man. "He imagines himself to be subtle and dangerous, and I suppose he is, but there are things he fails to understand. Denzil, on the other hand, is rather like an incompetent copyist's version of you."

As the clear gray eyes met his Thomas felt a stab of pure fear. *Worry about it later*, he thought. Grandier had probably noticed but there was no help for that. He said, "Do they know what you're planning? And there is a plan, isn't there?"

"Yes. I first conceived it in my cell in the Temple Prison at Bistrita I had to think about something besides the torturers, and the death by fire that waited for me." He looked down at his hand and stretched the fingers, contemplating the unbroken skin as if he did not quite recognize it as his own.

And perhaps he doesn't, Thomas thought. He remembered the catalog of tortures the court documents had listed. Grandier was driven, dangerous, and intelligent, but not insane. It was almost as if he had passed into another phase of being that was not madness or sanity but some lawless ground in between.

Across the room, Aviler shifted a little, breaking the silence with a faint clink of chain, and Grandier said, "Then an emissary of the Unseelie Court appeared with their offer, which you know about already. Part of a scheme on their part to suborn a human sorcerer, to make the Host more powerful in our world. It's a contest they have with the Seelie Court, their opposites in Fayre. Having a sorcerer at their beck and call would be a coup of sorts." He shrugged. "They thought me a likely candidate."

Thomas realized he was trying to control the conversation out of panic, and that Grandier was allowing him to do it. *Try to be a little less transparent,* he told himself. *You've helped the man enough already.* Grandier seemed to expect a comment, so he said only, "The more fools they."

"I thought so." Grandier smiled a little. "It's not entirely their fault, the trusting creatures. They are accustomed to Fayre, which bends to their will. The mortal world has sharp edges, bends to no man's will, and events occur with fatal finality. Mistakes are not suffered. Evadne was pressing me to give up this game and go on to something more entertaining. He was one of their self-proclaimed leaders, a very annoying character. He's dead now, of course. I rather thought someone might kill him eventually. And I meant to tell you, Kade escaped through the ring and is presumably in Fayre, at the moment."

That's one mercy. Thomas fought not to show relief and asked, "Why are you helping Denzil?"

"The Duke has offered me what I want. A war with Bisra."

"We've had a war with Bisra. It didn't turn out that well for anyone." But things began to fall into place. Ravenna would never have agreed to another war. They had been the victors of the last long conflict with their mortal enemies to the south only by a bare margin. Even if Roland had supported such a suicidal course, Aviler and the other High Lords and advisors would have prevented it at any cost.

"There was a war," Grandier conceded. "But I was not involved. And I have the Host."

Thomas thought of the monstrous turmoil in the undercellars. He said, "If you want to turn them loose on Bisra, be my guest, but why do you have to destroy us in the process?"

"I have no intention of destroying Ile-Rien. But I will have to alter it somewhat. Denzil needs the war to cement his position as usurper. When word leaks out that Vienne is under a virtual state of siege by creatures of Fayre, Bisra will move to take advantage. They need Ile-Rien's wealth to maintain a balance of power with Parscia, on their southern border, and their Church fears any sorcery not under its control. Justifiably so.

"When the landed lords of Ile-Rien realize Bisra is marshalling its forces to attack, they will support any central authority that has a chance of marshalling a resistance. The Duke of Alsene will be that authority. Oh, that won't be all. There is to be some document of formal abdication, signed by Roland. Under what circumstances, I don't know." He looked over at Aviler, who had been listening in a kind of horrified fascination. "That explains your presence. Your position allows you to deputize the King's seal on state documents during an emergency when the King has been removed for his own safety. I doubt the originator of that particular tenet of courtlaw intended documents of abdication to be included in that category, and it would be laughed off if Roland's supporters took power again, but Denzil intends to keep all his options open."

Aviler looked away, his face grim. "I will not sign anything for Denzil, for you, or for the Prince of Hell himself."

"I know." Grandier nodded seriously. He turned back to Thomas. "Once the Bisran army crosses the border, and are no longer protected by their priests' defenses, the Host will help to harry them and they will be driven back. At that time, outrage against the Bisrans will be so high it will not be difficult to turn an army of defense into an army of offense."

Thomas shook his head in disbelief. "The Host participates in this out of the goodness of its collective heart? What did you offer them, the destruction of Lodun? What are they going to do when you don't keep up your end of the bargain?"

Grandier looked up, surprised and pleased. "Oh, very good. Go on."

"Denzil's motive is plain: he has to own everyone and everything around him. The Host wants the death of as many human sorcerers as possible. And you want Bisra. And I'd wager anything that you mean for no one to get what he wants except you."

"And how will I accomplish this?" Grandier asked softly, eyes alight.

"I don't know. But I don't think you'll let them destroy Lodun."

"No, I would not let them do that." For a moment his expression turned abstract. "Evadne was the one demanding I destroy Lodun. He is not a factor anymore."

Grandier hesitated, his face craggy and harsh in the candlelight. "I don't like Denzil; he is cunning and I will need help to manage him. But he will give me what I want, and so I must use him. Bisra will be struck by the might of your armies. Once their priests can no longer defend them from the fay, I can further the collapse. In time, there will be nothing left but to sow salt into the empty fields...and Bisra will cease to be. It will probably take many years, I know, but I have the time." He looked thoughtful, then shook his head. "I regret the necessity of a long war that will have ill effect on this land, but I really can't see any other way to start the process of collapse. You will agree that an all-out conflict can be particularly devastating."

Thomas just looked at him. There was nothing to be said. Grandier was setting forces in motion he couldn't possibly control. The old sorcerer might never see his goal accomplished, but he would see years of destruction.

Quietly, desperately, Aviler said, "What you are planning—dreaming—will never come to pass."

Grandier got slowly to his feet, as if the cold hurt his back. "I have ridden the tide of events for many years. I am quite capable of guiding it now."

Thomas looked up at him, and knew any argument was useless, but he said, "You are mad. You're handing the kingdom to Denzil, and he doesn't give a penny damn for you or your plans."

"That remains to be seen."

In a tone of quiet rage, Aviler said, "I hope you burn in Hell with your damned fay allies."

Grandier chuckled. "I have already burned in Hell. You see the result. Heaven help us all if it happens again."

Thomas said, "Has Denzil noticed that anyone who gets in your way dies?"

"I don't think so. Not yet, at any rate. But then, you're not dead, and you were certainly in my way."

Not nearly enough, Thomas thought. "That's only a matter of time, isn't it?"

"It's what I'm told." Grandier regarded him silently, then said seriously, "There is one more thing. The Queen... The Dowager Queen Ravenna is dead."

Thomas felt the silence stretch, felt Aviler staring at him. Calmly he said, "You're lying."

"Not about this. She was trying to protect Roland. She succeeded and destroyed several important members of the Host in the process."

"You're lying." Thomas tried to stand and the chains jerked him back to his knees. He didn't notice.

Grandier closed his eyes a moment. "No. There are some things I regret, but this isn't one of them. She was too dangerous."

And then he knew it was true. "You fucking bastard!" he shouted at him.

Grandier turned to go and Thomas said, "You are a coward. You didn't have to do this."

His back to Thomas, Grandier paused in the doorway, but then continued out.

Thomas sank back against the wall. Aviler said, "It is a lie, surely."

"No. No, it's not." It was the last thing he said for several hours.

CHAPTER SIXTEEN

KADE LANDED AWKWARDLY in the high velvet grass of the Knockma ring and rolled to her feet. She pressed her hands to her temples and tried to concentrate, feeling the lines of force radiating out from the ring around her. She reached out along them to open a ring in the maze court below the Old Palace. She opened her eyes and saw the green sward of Knockma, the menhirs standing around her in silent contemplation, and in the distance, the mist-shrouded column of the castle and its reflection.

She snarled, shrugged out of her coat, and tried again.

After four failures she knew it was no good; she couldn't form a ring inside the palace. *What did Grandier do?* He would have had to ward the palace against her, that would take... But traveling the rings from the palace to Knockma, to Aviler's house and back here, had distorted her sense of time's passage. By the sky, they had lost nearly an hour on coming to Knockma and returning to the city. Moving from the less powerful ring she had made at the High Minister's house and coming back, she could have lost more than that.

Grandier could have begun the spells against her when he was alerted to her and Thomas's presence in the palace. It would not have taken long if he used the wards already in place. No time at all if he had used another keystone prepared earlier when he had first known she was coming to court.

Kade knotted her hands in her hair until the pain stopped the rise of bile in her throat.

She opened her eyes. Boliver was standing at the edge of the ring, watching her and scratching his bearded chin. He said, "What happened?"

"They have him," she said simply.

His eyes widened a little. After a moment he shuffled his feet, then said, "What are we going to do, then?"

"Wait here." She scrambled to her feet, touched the power in the ring, and took that step that carried her away.

The cold embraced her first. Kade had left her coat in the forever-spring of Knockma. She was outside the palace wall, near the Postern Gate where she and Thomas had got in earlier that day. The square with its broken fountain was still empty of life in the gathering dusk, the buildings staring down at her with gaping dark windows.

Kade stepped out of the newly formed ring in the snow and moved to the gate, and the hair on the back of her neck rose. Cursing, she dug in a pocket for the last of the gascoign powder she had with her and rubbed it into the corners of her eyes.

The wards rose up from the ground in front of her in a corona of light, stretching up and curving over the wall. *He has put the wards back.*

High above, a razor-winged shadow dove out of the clouds, passed unharmed through the corona it could not see, and disappeared among the palace towers. *That was a member of the Host. And it went through the wards.* Kade raised a hand toward the light and saw the gooseflesh spring up on her arm. *And I can't. He turned the wards against me, to let the Host in and keep me out.*

Kade stepped back, and felt the awareness of the wards' hostile presence recede. There was one other way in. She could go through the ring that already existed in the shattered remains of the Grand Gallery. *Yes, that way, the trap.*

Kade went back to the snow ring and took the turn that brought her into the Grand Gallery.

The cold was no less bitter for the shelter of the walls. The huge hall was dark and silent and a wind flung snow through the broken terrace windows.

A winged fay with blue skin and an angelic human face was sitting in the middle of the floor, picking its toes. It glanced up, saw her, and screamed.

As it fled the room, Kade lifted a hand to touch the edge of the ring. Just above the surface, she felt the heat of hostile force. The old ward around the ring was tied to the same etheric structure as the wards around the palace. She could not step outside it.

The floor was piled with chunky broken stone from the foundation, shattered wooden flooring, and dirt. She began to trace the outer edge of the circle, stepping up onto one of the larger pieces of foundation, leaping to the next. It took concentration. A recently formed ring would have hardly any mark on it at all. The Knockma Ring was ancient and well used, but it was a still pool of power. This ring was a whirlpool of conflicting forces, stirred up like a hornet's nest by the Host's recent passage. It had originally been her mother Moire's work and had rested atop the polished wooden floor of the gallery. Dr. Surete had sealed it off with spells long ago, and the pressure of the wards had eventually pushed it down to this level, even with the foundation.

After some moments Kade heard footsteps. She looked up to see Dontane and Grandier standing in one of the archways. Dontane was leveling a pistol at her.

She smiled grimly. He fired, the blast reverberating through the room, echoing off the high sculpted ceiling. Kade didn't see the ball until it entered the ring's sphere of influence, where it veered abruptly from its straight course and began to travel the ring's outer circle, orbiting around her like the philosophers claimed the sun orbited the earth.

Grandier said, "Don't waste your shot." He crossed the room to stand within a few yards of the ring's outer edge, and after a moment Dontane joined him. Kade had already resumed her halting progress around the outer rim. The pistol ball whizzed past her again, starting a breeze that stirred her hair.

To Grandier, Dontane snapped, "What are you waiting for? Kill her."

"She isn't here," Grandier said. "She is a breath away from a thousand other places, aren't you?"

Without interrupting her progress, Kade glanced up at Dontane. "Come and get me."

He took an impulsive step forward, then hesitated, looking at Grandier.

Ignoring him, Grandier said seriously, "I don't have to ask what you want here, Kade."

She had found the ring's pattern now and hoped her slight hesitation at the cardinal point would be put down to reaction to his remark. She said, "I want you dead."

"He's alive."

This time the hesitation was unplanned. She had not allowed herself to think Thomas might be dead, but from the sudden suffocating constriction in her chest, some part of her mind had recognized it as a very real possibility. She forced herself to step to the next rock. *I shouldn't have come.* This was what Grandier wanted, this was why he had not sealed this ring against her. Now he could ask her for anything he wanted, and she would have to give it to him. She thought about fleeing now, but it was too late. She took a deep breath, and continued her progress around the ring. Her head was buzzing, and she was going to have to leave soon to find somewhere private to be sick.

Dontane was watching his master carefully.

Grandier said, "I want you to stay out of this, Kade."

She took another deep breath, but did not look up at him.

"I know it won't be easy—"

All the fear and panic inside her crystallized into an icy knot of pure rage. Without betraying her intentions by the flicker of an eyelash, she tapped the fayre power in the ring and released the orbiting pistol ball. Grandier staggered against Dontane, and the ball struck the far wall with a loud crack and a shower of plaster and dust.

Grandier reached up and touched his right ear, smiling ruefully when his fingers came away lightly spotted with blood.

Dontane had drawn his second pistol. "She missed you by a hair's breadth," he hissed.

"On the contrary, she hit exactly what she aimed at," Grandier answered dryly, straightening up with an effort. "And I'll thank you not to toss her any more shot."

Kade was waiting for him to look at her. When he did, their eyes locked for a long moment. Then Grandier said, "Very well put. I will not patronize you again."

Dontane swore. "Are you going to let this mad creature get away with that?"

"Your appraisal wounds me to the heart," Kade said softly, before Grandier could answer. "Believe me, I shall fall down in agony at some more convenient time."

"She knows my death will not affect the wards that keep her out, or the presence of the Host, or any of the other plans I have set in motion." Grandier was speaking to Dontane, but his eyes went to Kade. "She has no choice but to cooperate."

There was a keening howl from outside the gallery, and a sudden eddy lifted a scatter of ice crystals from the floor.

"The Host is coming," Grandier said. "Perhaps you had better go. They will follow you."

"Will they?" Kade smiled. *No choice,* her thought echoed. *But appearances are everything.*

The Host streamed in through the doorways, the bogles, the grinning mock-human fay, the distorted animals, the hideous inhuman shapes, flying, crawling or running, bringing the stink of death. Dontane wheeled to face them, involuntarily moving closer to Grandier.

Kade waited until the first were almost to the edge of the ring, then stepped back into Knockma.

ဆ

Thomas awoke leaning back against the wall, stiff and freezing. The candlelamp on the floor had burned low, a pool of tallow collecting in its base. An iron brazier had been placed in the center of the room and was putting out just enough heat to keep them from freezing to death. He was surprised that he was alive at all. He had remembered that lapsing into sleep with a head injury was often fatal.

"Are you all right?" Aviler asked, watching him closely.

His head hurt so badly he didn't think he could move it, but he said, "Whatever gave you the idea I wasn't?"

Aviler was not fooled by this sally at all. He said, "Do you know where you are? Forgive my persistence, but we've had this conversation before."

"Oh." Thomas watched the flicker of light over the sculpted ceiling for a moment. He remembered who was dead. "Yes, I know where I am. Unfortunately. How long was I out?"

Aviler tried to shift his own position and grimaced in discomfort. "Several hours. I believe it may be near morning, but it's difficult to say."

Near morning of the third day since the attack. Not much time for travelers or refugees to carry word of the disaster. And if Ravenna was dead, what had happened to the rest of the court? Thomas tried not to care, and was surprised to find it impossible. There were Falaise and Gideon, Berham, Phaistus, his other men. If Denzil realized Falaise had betrayed what little she knew of his plans to Thomas, even if she had done it too late to be of any help...

He saw that Aviler was trying to loosen the heavy iron spike that held his chains to the wall with an air that spoke of several hours' familiarity with the process. Thomas shifted over enough to reach the peg holding him and started to work on it, for all that it felt absolutely immovable.

Another Bisran War. All the heroes of the last terrible years of war were gone. All the famous names that had passed into folklegend and ballads were the names of the dead. Aviler the Elder had succumbed to illness or possibly poison; the Warrior-Bishop of Portier had been thrown from a horse; Thomas's old captain was killed at duty; Desero, who had been Renier's predecessor as Preceptor of the Albon Knights, retired and passed quietly away in the country; and all the others had been killed in later battles or by the weight of years. For the last year or so there had only been Ravenna,

Lucas, and himself, and they had come into the legend only at its triumphant conclusion. Now there was only himself, who had been the youngest of the lot, and who would not live to be executed by Roland for some imagined offense, or to see his skill degenerate from time and old wounds. It was the end of an age.

Then Thomas heard someone come into the anteroom, heard one of the troopers reply to some question. He glanced at Aviler, who looked grim, and he remembered that Denzil had wanted the High Minister to sign a falsified document of abdication.

After a moment Dontane appeared in the doorway. He stood there, smiling down at them coldly. Thomas leaned back against the wall, relieved it wasn't Grandier. He couldn't find it in himself to feel anything but contempt for Dontane, for all that he was a sorcerer. After Grandier's example of how far one man could go for revenge, Dontane seemed nothing but a persistent gadfly of a schemer, not unlike the young nobles Denzil had used as cannon fodder in his plans.

"The Duke of Alsene has much to discuss with you," Dontane said then, and motioned to the soldiers outside. Two entered the room, one standing back with a drawn rapier and the other unlocking Thomas's manacles.

Thomas made no attempt to stand, letting the trooper jerk him to his feet. That was the only way he would've been able to get there; his leg had stiffened up again.

They led him out of the makeshift prison and down one flight of stairs into an area heavily guarded by more of the Alsene troops. Men were crowded into the disordered rooms, and every candle and lamp was lit to fight the darkness and the presence of the fay. The fear was palpable.

Dontane asked suddenly, "What did Grandier say to you?"

Thomas remembered Dontane's persistence in demanding why Grandier should want him alive when he had first been captured. He had suspected then that Dontane felt his position was insecure. Only a sane reaction, considering how many people Grandier had disposed of to further his goals. Thomas said, "He told us all his grand plans. Do you want to know if they included you?"

Dontane did not turn to look at him. Thomas sensed he was struggling to control a bitter anger, which was probably directed at Grandier almost as much as it was at him. After a moment Dontane replied, "If Denzil doesn't rid me of you, I'll just have to think of something myself, won't I?"

Dontane led the way through a suite piled with supplies, to where servants with the Alsene badge waited outside two large double doors.

Inside was a long low-ceilinged council room, decorated in blue and gold with a long draw table across the back wall. Three men stood with their backs to Thomas, consulting a map spread out on the table. Dontane went to lean against the wall, watching with folded arms, but the troopers stayed to either side of Thomas. The men wore the heavy velvet brocades of nobles, and two were blond. Alsene lords? he wondered. A couple of servants waited by the other door, with a dark-haired boy-page. Then Thomas saw that the man in the center of the group at the table had his left arm in a sling, and he forgot about Dontane and the others.

Denzil turned to face him, and Thomas said, "Pity I missed."

"Pity for you," the Duke of Alsene said, smiling as he came forward. "It was a good shot; it shattered the bone, but our fine sorcerer Grandier healed it." Thomas must have shown his disbelief because Denzil added, "Yes, I thought it impossible too, but it seems he's more skilled than most. Quite an advantage for me."

Quite an advantage. If not for Grandier, Denzil would have died, or lost his arm. One of the other nobles, watching from across the room, grinned and said, "So this is the one who gave you so much trouble, my lord; you didn't tell us—"

Denzil spun around and snarled, "Shut up!"

The silence became absolute. Thomas noted he was the only man in the room who hadn't started at the sudden transformation from urbane calm to nearly blind rage. He had always known Denzil was capable of that kind of anger, but that the young Duke had hidden it from his followers came as no surprise.

Denzil turned back to him, again the cool amused young noble. Smiling, he said, "Relatives are a necessary encumbrance."

"For now," Thomas agreed. He could see the family resemblance to Denzil in the other two men's features, the cold blue of their eyes. The one who had spoken looked resentful at being publicly chastened; the other was watching the scene with amusement, as if it were a play put on for his enjoyment. If Denzil succeeded, Thomas wouldn't have bet copper on the chances of either of them living out the year. He said, "Did you get Roland?"

"No." Denzil's eyes were very bright and he was flushed slightly from excitement. Excitement at the power. He was watching Thomas carefully. "Ravenna's dead."

"I know," Thomas said, able to keep his expression neutral and wondering if Grandier had told him first only to spoil his ally's fun.

Denzil was too good at this to betray even a flash of irritation. He only shook his head in mild regret. "Grandier again? And I was so looking forward to telling you myself."

At that moment Thomas knew for certain that Denzil had brought him up here to kill him. He had suspected it as soon as he had walked in, but now it was all there to be read in the younger man's face, the way he carried himself. He said, "You hide your disappointment well."

"Do you think so?" Denzil drew the main gauche from the sash at his back and touched the point thoughtfully. This wasn't the deadly toy with the serrated edge and extra rods for breaking blades. It was an elegant weapon with a long utilitarian blade and a gold-chased half-shell guard. Thomas watched Denzil's opaque eyes and tried to keep his mind blank.

Denzil said, "I don't suppose you're surprised by this," and stabbed him in the stomach.

For the first moment Thomas only felt the force of the blow. It doubled him over, and as the blade pulled free and air reached his sliced flesh, the pain began. A wave of icy cold rose around him, and his legs gave way. He didn't notice that the troopers had let him go until his knees struck the floor. For a moment he supported himself with one hand braced against the wooden planks, the other pressed to his stomach. The blood felt hot against the chill of his skin, and there was so astonishingly little of it at first. He was distantly aware of noise in the room, voices raised, but then his arm gave way and that was all.

⚜

Out of the warm darkness of fevered sleep, he heard voices.

Galen Dubell... No, Grandier said, "I don't have to justify my actions to you."

"Don't you? You're putting me on a throne, and I'm going to help you get your heart's desire, and you don't think you owe me a few words of explanation?" Denzil said, his tone soft and reasonable.

"Correct."

There was silence. Thomas managed to open his eyes. He lay curled on his side on a couch, and a large spot of the heavy damask upholstery was soaked with blood. He knew this because his left hand lay in it. His doublet had been unbuttoned and his shirt pulled aside. It was cold, though not as frigid as the room where he had been imprisoned. His limbs felt too heavy to move, and there was something about the absence of pain that was shocking.

Grandier's back was to him, and he could see Denzil across the room.

Denzil's brows had lifted in gentle inquiry, but when Grandier remained politely attentive, he said, "That man is my enemy."

"That isn't my concern."

Denzil was ominously still for a moment, though Grandier's reply had been in the same mild voice. He said, "Consider that you would do better not to antagonize me."

"Perhaps. But I have already antagonized you, it seems, so I see no point in not continuing on my chosen course."

"Very well. It means nothing then, but..." Denzil shrugged gracefully, only a slight tremor revealing his rage. "Do be more careful in the future."

Thomas closed his eyes, feeling darkness sweep up over him in a moment of dizziness, but he heard Denzil's steps cross the room and a door close.

He opened his eyes again and saw Grandier shake his head and turn around. The sorcerer smiled when he saw him awake and said, "Really, the man is driven mad by anyone who fails to succumb to his particular charm. But then, you are aware of this."

"Intimately." The sarcasm was automatic, and Thomas's voice slow and rusty. He winced at the sound of it.

Grandier turned away, and Thomas managed to lift himself a little on one elbow. Pain seized him for one sporadic moment, doubled him up, and let him go, leaving him breathless. His fingers found the small web of tight white scar tissue about five inches below his heart. That was all that was left of the puncture wound where the blade had entered, but his body remembered its presence all too well.

When he looked up, Grandier was watching him with a puzzled frown. "You are fortunate," Grandier said. "He could have injured you in a way less easily remedied."

Thomas took a deep breath, but the pain didn't return. The stab wound in his arm had stopped its insistent ache as well. He said, "You don't think he knew that?"

Grandier shook his head. "He was angry because I did not allow you to die."

"He was angry because you were so calm about it. Before he did it he was very careful to tell me how you healed his arm after I shot him."

Grandier hesitated a moment, eyes thoughtful, then he said, "A valuable insight."

He sent Dontane to contact Denzil for him, Thomas thought. That had undoubtedly gone well for Denzil. *Might as well send sheep to bargain with wolves.* Grandier had crossed the room to a round table that held a number of jars and bottles, probably apothecary powders. He was tightening the stoppers and putting them back into a leather case. Thomas wanted to ask why Grandier wanted him alive, but he suspected he would find that out anyway in a moment or two. He wished the damned Bisran priest who had heard Grandier's confession in prison had asked for more specifics about the shape-changing magic. How a potential victim could escape it, for example. But there was one thing he wanted to know regardless of what happened to him next, and he asked, "How did Ravenna die?"

Grandier paused, without turning, and said, "Evadne and a band of fay had trapped her in the tower at Bel Garde, and attempted to exchange her for Roland. She fired a powder magazine Denzil had hidden there, killing Evadne and the others. A few fay who had clung to the outside of the tower survived; I had the story from them."

Firing a powder magazine. God, woman, did you think about what you were doing to yourself? No, probably not, even if she could have considered it as anything other than a means to an end. She would have given her own life the same weight as anyone else's, done her best, and then proceeded on her course with style. *Oh, but the bastards must have been surprised.*

When he looked back, Grandier was watching him thoughtfully. "You wondered why I felt the need to show you the Dark Host."

"Yes."

"It was not intended as a threat. It was a test."

A test I failed, Thomas thought suddenly.

"There was no light in that cellar," Grandier continued. "Or no light visible to mortal eyes. The men with us heard strange cries and laughter, and caught brief glimpses of foul things darting out of a wall of darkness. I could see the Host, as could Dontane, because we have been touched by their power. How was it that you saw them?"

Coming out of a wall of darkness, like the attack in the Old Hall. Wary, Thomas answered, "If you knew enough to perform the test, then you must already have a theory."

"She took you to Knockma, didn't she?"

Thomas watched him, saying nothing. Kade's Fayre kingdom had been like an island of calm reality in the midst of a nightmare. It had been easy to forget that the pact he had made with her there would have an effect in the violent whirlwind of the present.

Grandier said, "The change is noticeable, to those who know what to look for. Perhaps even to those who don't. But she did more than take you there, I think. She has opened the Otherworld to you."

"And what does that mean to you?"

"I could use your help. With the Duke of Alsene, for one example. As you have pointed out, my understanding of the way his mind works is woefully incomplete." Grandier closed the leather case and leaned back against the table. "Ravenna is gone, and Roland is alone. Even if you could free yourself and reach him, he wouldn't listen to you, not about Denzil's involvement. Those who might have organized resistance to the Duke's bid for power are either dead, scattered, or will not learn of it in time." He shrugged. "I agree with you. Denzil is dangerous, unamenable to my influence, and too clever to control. It will be a battle to make him carry out my wishes, at least until I no longer need him. You could help me win that battle."

Thomas's first impulse was to play for time. He knew what a flat refusal to cooperate might get him, and he wasn't willing to give up yet. He asked, "What about Kade?"

"She can no longer enter the palace, as I have turned the wards against her, but I spoke to her some time ago through the ring in the Grand Gallery. She is somewhat angry with me."

"You've tried to kill her at least twice."

"And was unsuccessful. You helped her in the Old Hall, and she handled my golem herself without much trouble." Grandier smiled a little, almost in pride, as if he'd been the one to teach her and not Dubell.

And Thomas thought, *I wonder if sometimes he thinks he is Galen Dubell...*

But the smile faded and Grandier said slowly, "He would never talk about her. How much he had taught her, what fay powers she had, where she was likely to be... He kept all her secrets, even at the end, when he became confused and told me what I needed to know about the palace wards."

Thomas thought of Dubell, who had been so trusting despite his occasionally acerbic wit. He had known him only through the faulty mirror of Grandier's imposture. But that imposture had fooled Kade who had known the old man better than anyone, so much of it must have been accurate. He said, "Is that how you do it? Get someone's confidence, earn their trust, learn their secrets, and gradually draw every scrap of information out of them until there's nothing useful left?"

"Yes, in a way. It is a domination of the personality."

"You sound like Denzil."

"Perhaps I do."

"Don't pretend to delude yourself," Thomas said, too angry to stop the words, to play the game safely. "You're not like Denzil; you're not blinded by self-absorption or maddened by what the Bisran priests did to you, however much you'd like us to think so. You've calmly made the decision to take your revenge this way, and you're aware of exactly how much pain you're causing."

"Perhaps that is a sin of which we are all guilty. We sane men who participate in insanity for reasons of our own." Grandier was silent for a moment, then he said, "But you are wrong about my intentions. I do not mean to take you as I took Dubell. Your cooperation is more valuable to me than your body, for the moment. I don't suppose you will care to give me an answer yet. But I suggest you come to a decision soon."

కుళ

Different troopers brought Thomas back to the makeshift cell and replaced his manacles. Aviler was still there, still relatively unhurt, except for the lines of strain and fatigue on his face, briefly visible in the light of the guard's lamp.

When they had gone, Aviler asked, "What happened?"

Thomas leaned back against the wall. On the walk back, he had discovered that the only wound that hadn't yielded to Grandier's unwanted healing had been the hole the elf-shot had left in his leg. He said, "I was offered a place in Grandier's glorious revolution."

Aviler considered that, then asked softly, "And where did all the blood come from?"

"Denzil stabbed me, and Grandier took care of the damage. Denzil intends to repeat the performance later. I could see him thinking it." Thomas looked away, glad of the darkness in the cold little room. He hadn't meant to say quite that much.

Aviler was silent for a time. Thomas wondered if he was thinking about the document he was supposed to sign. Then Aviler said, "An interesting demonstration of the consequences of refusal. What answer did you give Grandier?"

"I didn't give him any answer. It's called stalling for time."

"I see."

కుళ

Kade sat down hard on Knockma's thick grass. She hoped the entire Host had flung itself into the ring after her, but she knew better than that. She had connected one cardinal point of the ring to the other, and any of the fay who followed her into it would find themselves caught in the ring's maelstrom, flung around and around until the connection broke, which it would do fairly soon. Rings were difficult to tamper with at best, and always sought to return to their original state.

Boliver was still waiting for her. He had settled on the grass outside the circle of menhirs and was smoking a white clay pipe. "No more than an hour," he said, answering her unspoken question. "Did you discover anything useful?"

Kade stood and stepped out of the ring so she could think without it singing in her ears. "Yes, but I made a mistake. I shouldn't have gone." She sat beside him and put her head in her hands. "Grandier was waiting for me. He knows that I— He told me Thomas is alive, and that I am to stay out of the way." She felt her mouth twist into a sneer. "He knows it will be difficult for me."

"Yes, you made a grand cock-up," Boliver agreed.

She rubber her eyes and said sourly, "Your confidence in me is overwhelming."

Boliver sighed. "Is your Thomas that important to you, then? Has he said anything of the kind to you?"

She looked up and saw he was watching her gravely. She stilled the quick flare of anger. "Yes, he is important to me. And if he's dead I'll never know what he thinks about me." *And I wouldn't care if he hated me as long as I knew he was alive somewhere...*

"Then stop rushing about like a daft-headed chicken and do something," Boliver said suddenly, scattering her thoughts.

"I am not rushing about like a daft-headed anything," she said through gritted teeth.

He pointed the pipe at her. "Oh, you're not weeping or fainting, but you're running about in circles, letting this damned human wizard point you any way he wants you."

"I am not—"

"By Puck's pointed ears, woman, you're the Queen of Air and Darkness. Act like it!"

Kade was on her feet and Boliver was scrambling for cover when it occurred to her that Thomas had said much the same thing to her. He had said it on that cool rainy night on the loggia, when they had listened to Denzil twist Roland's friendship into slavery.

She supposed she should feel like dying. What she felt was a cold numbness centering around her heart, as if she were already dead. Kade turned away and started to cross the field toward the castle. Reaching the edge of the garden, she climbed the steps and entered her turret workroom. She stood for a moment in the quiet with the sweet smell of herbs and flowers. Then she saw that the bowl on the table was glowing softly. It was the spell she had tried to make to reveal the location of the keystone. She had forgotten it.

Holding her breath, Kade went to the table. The water at the bottom of the bowl had formed an image: a hazy translucent image of a room. And she recognized the room.

"Gods above and below take that canny old bastard," she whispered, almost reverently. "It was there all the time."

Then she had an idea.

CHAPTER SEVENTEEN

THE SUN WAS shining here, too.

Kade and Boliver stood in an open court, bordered on all sides by a low wall and a sheer drop to the sea. The wide blue vault of the sky stretched over them, and the stiff breeze had the tang of salt and dead fish. Kade went to the edge of the ring, which resisted her for a moment before she stepped free of it. The power swelling it had almost the same force as the Knockma Ring, but it was far more turbulent. But then, this ring saw a great deal more use.

She went to the wall and looked down. They were atop a pillar of rock that stood a hundred yards or so above the sea that tore at its base. Leaning out, she could see the stairs that climbed it, leading up from a bare stone dock, and the stern of the fantastically painted ship that was moored there.

On the opposite side of the court, two identical fay with golden skin, red-pupiled eyes, and long amber hair guarded an archway twined with carved oak leaves leading to a narrow delicate bridge. It led from their pillar over the channel of gray-green churning water to the cliff tops of a rocky section of coast. A massive structure grew out of the end of the bridge, with heavy octagonal towers the warm brown of sandstone from the faraway deserts of Parscia. Squinting at it in the afternoon sunlight, Kade saw that light glittered off it at regular points, as if it were adorned with a pattern of jewels, or small round windows. She looked back at Boliver, who was watching the bridge guards warily and cleaning out his pipe onto the immaculate flagstones. "This is the place."

She went up to the guards, who were dressed in cloth of gold and glittering gems and armed with slender swords of silver. They were both watching Kade and Boliver with disinterested amusement, and one said, "Your name and your errand, fair lady, before you pass."

The words "fair lady" had no doubt been applied facetiously. She answered, "I'm Kade Carrion, the Queen of Air and Darkness, and I'm here to see Oberon."

The two exchanged an opaque glance that might have concealed more amusement, or surprise, and the other said, "Then pass gladly, lady."

She walked down the bridge, Boliver padding behind her. Ahead they could see two large wooden doors surrounded by stonework carved into waves and bubbling seafoam. Closer, and the sun brought out the faint tint of rose in the brown stone; closer still, and she saw that the small round windows that studded the tower were not windows but eyes, with dark iris and blue pupil, and that some were watching them, others staring off to sea.

Boliver stage-whispered, "We're being watched!"

Kade ignored him.

Another fay guard, identical to the two at the bridge except for the graceful amber-glazed wings on his back, pulled open one of the heavy doors for them.

Inside was a high stone gallery, floored with white tile, airy and cool. They went down it and into the perfect silence of the place. Corridors branched off at intervals, but they might have been the only living creatures inside.

Thinking over what she had to do—what she was forced to do—Kade was conscious of a curious numbness that might be shock. She was beginning to recognize it as the feeling of anger taken to such a level it was no longer possible to separate it from any other emotion or thought. In a way, it was a liberating sensation. The attitude of the fay guards, or what she suspected was their attitude, would have bothered her very much under any other circumstances; now it seemed the most minor of considerations. Anger this intense defined everything into the goal, and the obstacles that must be overcome to reach the goal, and it would make it very easy to make the decisions to dispose of those obstacles.

It was probably quite close to how Urbain Grandier felt when the Bisran Inquisition had finished with him.

As they neared the end of the hall, they could hear a thread of harp music, and voices and laughter.

"We're going to be roasted," Boliver said, with gloomy relish. "And eaten."

"Stop sniveling," Kade muttered. Boliver had driven her out of her despair with arguments that she should do something constructive; now that she had embarked on a plan, he was arguing against it. Typical fay perversity.

The hall made an abrupt turn, and stairs spilled down into a large roofless court that must be at or near the center of the fortress. More of the amber-skinned guards lined the porticoes, lazy but watchful, armed with gold-bladed pikes.

Most of the Seelie Court was gathered here.

Lake maidens dripped water and glamour from their gowns like pearls. Beautiful ladies wore clothes of flowers, gossamer spangled with dew, silvery gauze, or were covered only by their long hair. There were men of the same ethereal beauty as the guards, in velvets, fine lace, and gold-shot brocade. Here and there a wing as delicate as a butterfly's and more beautifully hued rose above the crowd. The bright sunlight in the open court made so much glamour the air glowed, and a troupe of gaily dressed fay tumblers performed feats impossible for humans. Most of those here were shape-changers.

Kade went down the steps and through the crowd.

They parted for her. There was no stink of unwashed flesh under the perfumes, as there would be in any human gathering. Her faded and dirty smock, her dragging petticoat lace, her page boy's boots, were violently out of place here, and she caught many sidelong glances. She could have used glamour to make herself more pleasing to the eye; several here had done so. But she didn't need to be told that that would have been a mistake.

Titania lay on a leopard-skin couch under a canopy of ostrich feathers, cool shade under the bright light. A small woman, smaller than Kade, the fayre queen wore a mantua heavily laden with pearls and silver embroidery, and her hair was the color of gold, true gold, and her features were much more beautiful than even Queen Falaise's. But Falaise's face had been touched by fear, worry, and care, and Titania's was as perfect as a carved goddess's; Kade suddenly preferred Falaise, for all that lady's wavering will.

Two fay pages with the appearance of fair young boys waited on the fayre queen, one holding a wine carafe, the other her fan. They watched Kade with matched expressions of sly mockery. But seated at her feet was a human boy with skin the color of chocolate and dark curly hair, whose gaze remained locked on the tumblers.

Kade did not curtsey to Titania. She was a queen here in her own right.

Titania's shrewd sapphire eyes considered her. She held a silver wine goblet beaded with moisture, and ran a thoughtful finger over the rim. "Oberon is not here, my sister." Her voice was like harp strings stirred by the wind.

"But you are." A few days ago Kade would have replied *I am not your sister*, but she couldn't afford to be driven now.

Titania laughed. "And what have you come for?"

"A favor." Kade looked down at the human boy, and when his brown eyes met hers curiously, she asked him, "Do you want to go home?"

There was an almost soundless gasp from the assembled fay, the music ceasing and the tumblers staggering to a halt.

The boy smiled and shook his head. "No, lady," he said into the silence. His voice was a little husky, but still a child's.

Kade looked back at Titania, who smiled. "I love him," the queen of fayre said.

"The sad thing is," Kade found herself replying, "you probably do."

Titania shook her golden head in irritation and set the goblet down on a low jade table. "You always ruin our pastimes, Kade."

"Good." Kade paced a few idle steps away from the bower, to avoid showing her rabid impatience, to keep Titania from knowing how every passing moment grated. She saw the smaller sprites at the edge of the crowd back hastily away. She was hardly surprised; she probably looked like she should be standing over a battlefield piled with corpses with a raven on one shoulder. She had been right not to try to put on a pleasing appearance with glamour; that would have been catering to their whims. She looked like herself, fey and eldritch even in this company.

Watching her with perfect brows lifted archly, Titania said, "I only tolerate your interference because of my affection for your mother."

Words, no sentiment. Copied from some human. Kade smiled at her feet. She couldn't think why she had ever feared Moire, or Titania, when she had spent much of her early life sparring with Ravenna, who could have effortlessly handled both fay queens were she blind, deaf, and lame. Kade said, "I am the Queen of Air and Darkness."

Titania accepted a fan from her page and drew the delicate ivory construction through her fingers. "You do not know what that means."

"Someday I'll find out." Kade looked up and smiled. "And here you will be."

"And what must I do about that?"

"Make me happy."

Titania laughed again, this time in genuine amusement. Or at least genuine for her. She waved the two fay pages away, but let the human boy remain. "What do you want?"

Kade sensed the crowd behind her begin to relax. The clear note of a harp sounded, and the jugglers began to perform again. The boy's eyes strayed in their direction. Boliver was around somewhere; she could smell his pipe. "The first, the power to shape-change."

"Ah." Titania must know every movement of the Unseelie Court, and she did not ask why. "Best tell me what else you want, for I cannot give you that."

"You mean, you won't give me that."

Titania's perfect brow creased in annoyance. "Words. I am not a fool; I can't hand you that much power."

Kade knew it would come to this. "What if I were to offer you a power in return?"

Titania shook her head, consideringly. "You are very desperate."

"Yes. And I am very dangerous, when I am very desperate." That was as close to a threat as she wanted to come. Threats she did not have time to make good on. Kade was at a severe disadvantage and knew it. All she had was bluff and Titania's greed.

"What would you offer?"

Kade felt as if she were about to step off a precipice. After this, there was no going back. She took a deep breath, and jumped. "Knockma." Somewhere in the crowd, she heard a thump: Boliver hitting the floor. He had known what she meant to do, but his sense of the dramatic had gotten the better of him.

Titania stared, honestly shocked. Kade waited, forcing herself to smile lightly. Then Titania shook her head, her expression of honest consternation making her look more human, and, Kade thought, more beautiful. "I cannot do it, not even for so great a prize. I cannot give you that much power."

Kade sighed. *I know. If I were you I wouldn't do it either. But I was hoping you'd be too blinded by greed to care. So forget the first plan and try the second.* With Knockma dangling before her like a diamond in the sun, Titania would break down eventually. "We can bargain."

Titania tapped her fan on the fur couch, watching her. "Bargain. Very well. But why are you doing this?"

Kade smiled and met Titania's eyes. "For love." The queen of fayre looked frankly disbelieving, but the human boy grinned up at Kade.

᙭

Kade met an anxious Boliver at the portico above the court. "How went it?" he asked, nervously hopping from foot to foot.

"Not as good as I hoped; not as bad as I feared." Out of her pocket, she drew one of the concessions she had wrested from the fayre queen. It looked like a well-crafted glass ball, only a few bubbles marring its perfection. Boliver peered at it closely, and she turned it in the light to show the lines of fire glowing ghostlike within. "It will turn a shape-changed being back to its original form." She pocketed the powerful little construction carefully, and they started up the hall toward the entrance.

"Is that all? What will you if it doesn't do its work?"

"What will I? I'll die, that's what will I. Gods below, Boliver, don't ask me these questions at a time like this." Kade had hoped to get the power to shape-change at will from Titania, hoped to get it without having to kill people right and left as Grandier did, but the fayre queen had refused her and she would just have to do it the hard way. *It's the only way to get anything done lately.*

"I'm sorry, lass. But one transformation is not much. And you'll need that to get in. You'll be going against all the Host."

"Yes." She hated to lose Knockma, but it was a tie to the past, to her mother, and to the Seelie Court and all their wrangling. And if the Host did cross into Knockma, she would never be able to defend it and find Thomas at the same time. Titania would defend it now, with every resource at her disposal, and the Unseelie Court would never have it.

It was also the only home she had ever had. Besides the palace, and that had been taken away. But Knockma had not been taken away, she had given it up, and the difference was important.

And if it would help her destroy Grandier and Denzil, then it was well given.

Kade put a hand in her pocket to touch the glass ball. No, losing Knockma she could live through. It was the next part she had doubts about.

Thomas had worked steadily at loosening the spike in the wall and was rewarded by feeling it begin to shift a trifle. If it wasn't his imagination; his hands were numb with cold. "Any luck?" he asked Aviler.

"No." Aviler left off his own efforts and leaned back against the wall. "I think you should accept Grandier's offer."

Thomas kept working on the spike, without answering. He supposed he should be flattered that Aviler had not automatically assumed that he would leap at any way out.

If he did... Grandier would not let him interfere with his plans to start a war. And once that war was started, Thomas would have no choice but to do his best to help win it. Grandier was well aware that Thomas would not be a willing participant, and Grandier had a talent for influencing people, working his way into their thoughts, bringing them unwillingly over to his side. It was how he wrested the needed information out of his victims before he killed them and took their shapes. There was the possibility that after a year or two of helping Grandier, Thomas would find that he no longer wanted to oppose him.

And then there was Denzil.

Movement out in the anteroom jolted Thomas out of his thoughts. Aviler looked up, puzzled, and they both listened. It sounded as if the troopers who were guarding them were gathering their weapons and leaving. After a long moment of silence, there was a faint shuffling sound from outside the door, and a low deep snarl.

Dontane had said he would have to think of something else. Aviler swore softly, looking around hopelessly for something to use as a weapon. Thomas gathered himself to move, watching the lighted doorway.

A fay appeared in the doorway, the torchlight gleaming from its jaundiced yellow skin. It was perhaps five feet tall, human shaped but with clawed hands and long powerful arms dangling almost to its knees. Its mouth had a wide evil grin revealing far too many sharply pointed teeth, its face distorted by round red eyes and a nose that was an ugly ragged hole.

It sprang at Thomas too quick for thought. He threw himself sideways as far as the chains would allow, flinging up an arm to shield his face. He felt the hard grip on his wrist, the claws tear through the leather of his sleeve, a pressure that nearly tore his arm from the socket. Then its hand came in contact with the iron manacle around his wrist and it shrieked and leapt away.

He rolled over and looked back. The fay staggered, keening in rage, its hand dripping burned flesh, the stink of it filling the room. Thomas's shoulder felt dislocated but as he tried to push himself up he realized the chains had far more slack now. The spike holding them to the wall had been pulled half out by the force of the fay's grip.

The creature turned on Aviler, snarling, and he scrambled back against the wall, swinging a loop of his chains at it. Thomas stretched and hooked the brazier with his boot-heel, bringing it closer with a frantic kick and grabbing the handle. He flung the brazier at the fay's back just as it leapt again at Aviler.

The iron struck the fay and it staggered.

Thomas got to his feet and leaned his whole weight on the chain in one solid jerk. With a spray of wood chips and plaster, the spike came out of the wall.

He grabbed the spike just as the fay reached him again. Its claws sank into his shoulder and it hauled him up and almost off his feet before it felt the tip of the iron in its chest. It tried to shove him away, its other hand finding his throat. With instinct greater than sense, he grabbed its arm and fell against it, driving the iron spike through its thick skin. It fell backward, dragging him down. From the blood on his hands he knew he must have given it a killing blow, but it still had the strength to snap his neck.

Then Thomas fell against the wooden floor. The fay had vanished. He tried to sit up, looking around, braced for it to appear somewhere else. Then he saw the heavy gray dust that covered the floor, the spike, his hands, and that even the creature's blood had disappeared. It had vanished, but in death, dissolving into dust.

His buff coat had protected his shoulder, but his neck was covered with shallow scratches from its claws; he was lucky it hadn't managed to tear his throat out. Aviler started to speak and Thomas shook his head hastily. Dontane would not have sent all the guards away, only those not bribed to silence.

After another moment, Thomas managed to stand. He gathered the chains up and quietly moved along the wall to the door and stood beside it, waiting tensely. Without having to be told, Aviler slumped against the wall, trying to look like a corpse. In the dim light, and for a few moments only, it would fool someone; Thomas would not have long to move. Moments crept by, and Thomas thought impatiently, *You can't sit out there forever; you have to see what happened. Come on, damn you.* There had to be at least one man out there, to make sure that the fay had done its work. The difficulty was that the one last guard didn't have to sit out there forever, only until Dontane returned with reinforcements.

Then Thomas heard a low scuffling in the anteroom, someone cautiously approaching the door. He flattened back against the wall and stopped breathing. The swordpoint came first, and there was a hesitation; the trooper had seen the spilled and battered brazier, and Aviler's apparently lifeless form. He stepped inside, and Thomas slipped the loop of chain around his neck.

The trooper made the mistake of dropping his sword to grab onto the chain. He staggered forward, trying to slam Thomas against the wall. Thomas held on grimly, feeling the strain in his shoulder. The man fell to his knees abruptly, dragging Thomas with him. He felt something give way under the chain and the trooper collapsed. Thomas held on long enough to make sure the man was dead, then glanced back to check the anteroom. It was empty and the fire was guttering in the hearth.

He searched the trooper's corpse thoroughly and savagely, keeping one eye on the door. Besides the rapier, the trooper had a main gauche with a half-shell guard and a small dagger. He would be armed again at least. After more searching he angrily shoved the body away. "It would be the one without the goddamn keys."

"What now?" Aviler asked, grimacing.

Thomas took the trooper's narrow-bladed dagger and began working at the lock of his manacle. *It's been a long time since I've done this,* he thought. After a long tense wait, the manacle gave and he shook it off and started on the other.

The chains holding Aviler were of slightly different make and took longer to open. After Thomas had worked over the first one for some time unsuccessfully, Aviler said grimly, "It's not working. Get out of here before they come back."

"I," Thomas said through gritted teeth, "do not have time for theatrics."

Aviler stiffened, but didn't voice any more objections.

The manacles came free finally, and Aviler got to his feet in relief.

Thomas slipped the plain leather baldric of the trooper's rapier over his head and handed Aviler the main gauche. They passed through the anteroom quickly, hesitating only to make sure the troopers had left behind no other weapons.

As Thomas stepped out the doorway onto the landing, he knew he had made a mistake. He heard Aviler gasp an incoherent warning and Thomas dove forward, rolling. This didn't help any of his various bruises and when he came to his feet, he staggered. But Aviler was struggling with the trooper who had waited for them beside the door, and as Thomas reached them, Aviler managed to plunge the main gauche up into the other man's rib cage. The soldier collapsed with a choked-off gasp and Thomas and Aviler rolled the body back into the anteroom. Breathing hard, Aviler explained, "He moved just as you went out and I saw him. Was he there all along?"

"No, he could have easily taken me when I was strangling the other one. Probably came looking for him when he didn't come back for the others." Thomas cast a look back to check the landing, which stretched quietly into darkness in either direction, doorways leading off it and the staircase opening directly in front of them.

Aviler stripped off the soldier's baldric and tossed the extra main gauche to Thomas. The High Minister slung the baldric over his shoulder and picked up the trooper's fallen rapier. Something that jingled as it hit the floor fell from the trooper's baldric and Aviler nudged it with a boot. "This was the one with the keys," he said, with an ironic lift of an eyebrow.

Thomas snorted. "My luck."

They stepped out onto the landing. Hesitating a moment to get his bearings, Thomas saw the bob of lamplight on the stair below. "This way," he said, and led Aviler down to another doorway. It opened onto a progression of rooms that, if Thomas was where he thought he was, would eventually give onto another staircase. The rooms were as dark as the pit, but they had been meant to be viewed as a set, so the doors were all in the same position on the left-hand side of the hearths and were unblocked by furniture, making it relatively easy to cross them even in almost complete darkness. They had made it through the third room when they heard a shout of alarm and running footsteps from the landing.

They stopped to listen, but no one came in their direction. Aviler whispered, "I don't suppose they're going to think that thing ate both of us, killed the two guards, then wandered off."

Thomas smiled grimly. "They could try to tell Denzil that, but I don't think it would be very well received."

They came to the last room, and through its open door, Thomas could see the landing of the other stairwell, lit wanly by one candle in the silver and rock-crystal chandelier hanging above it. Across the threshold was the body of a young woman, the gray and brown of her skirts marking her as a servant. Thomas stepped over her without bothering to pause. He was growing used to seeing dead women and had stopped looking for familiar faces; since it was likely he would be killed at any moment himself, it hardly seemed to matter. After a moment he heard Aviler follow him.

Just as they came out onto the landing, the muffled explosion of a pistol shot destroyed the silence. They both instinctively dove for the stairs. They reached the landing below and cut through another dark suite back the way they had come. The first room was unlit and crowded with dark shapes of furniture. Soldiers were pounding down the stair behind them and Thomas could not find the doorway. He stumbled on a low table, then turned and put his back against the wall. The men coming after them would have oil lamps, and the light would be momentarily blinding. Then there was a muffled thump and Aviler gasped in pain, then said harshly, "Over here, a door."

Thomas made his way toward Aviler's voice and found the edge of a narrow door. Aviler whispered, "It's a servants' stair." He climbed down a few steps, and Thomas stepped inside, closing the door after them.

In the unfamiliar room, it was doubtful the Alsene troopers would find the stair, which had a door meant to blend into the paneling, but Thomas didn't breathe easily until he heard them clatter through the room, cursing and knocking things over, then retreat. After some moments of silence he said lightly, "I won't comment on your clumsiness since it saved our lives."

"Someone else wasn't so lucky," Aviler replied out of the dark. "There's a body down here."

Yes, there would be fay roaming here. *This is not going to get any easier,* Thomas thought, straightening up and feeling for the wall to guide him down.

"He didn't come down here without a lamp," Aviler was muttering. Before Thomas could point out that he might very well have, Aviler said, "Yes, here it is."

After more fumbling, Aviler found the man's tinderbox and managed to light the lamp. "Good God," he said softly, standing up and looking down in disgust at the corpse the wan light revealed. "What could have done that to his head... No, don't speculate; I'd rather be surprised."

They heard footsteps in the rooms overhead and voices from below, and moved a few steps down the narrow stairs. But the door with its heavy covering of carved paneling and flocked paper cut much of the noise from outside.

Aviler looked around, lifting the lamp high. The original stone of the wall was to one side, radiating cold like a block of ice, and the wooden bones of the lath and plaster facing to the other. The air was stuffy and thick with dust. This was technically a servants' passage, though it had probably been installed more with an eye to moving about quickly and unobtrusively in the event of a palace coup. The years before the reign of Ravenna's father had not been calm or untroubled.

"We're on the west side of the Old Palace," Aviler said quietly. "We could get out through the siege wall into the Old Courts..."

Thomas sheathed the rapier and drew the shorter main gauche, which would be more effective in these close surroundings. "If we can get there. The King's Bastion is probably still sealed off from the other side. Most of the troops are quartered right below us." He took a soft step down the narrow stairs, careful of the creaking boards that would betray their presence.

The bogle dropped from above. It landed on Aviler, knocking him forward. He dropped the candlelamp and the flame guttered wildly, threatening to leave them in darkness. Aviler stumbled into Thomas, who caught himself against the wall. He turned, getting a grip on the thing's greasy skin below its neck and dragging it off the other man. It turned on him more swiftly than a cat, claws flailing, and he stabbed it with the main gauche. It dropped and he saw that Aviler had gotten it from behind with their late guard's dagger. It struggled wildly on the steps, its claws scrabbling on the wood, a random swipe of one long arm sending Thomas staggering back into the wall. Then it froze into immobility.

They stared at one another, breathing hard, then Aviler wiped the blood from the scratches on his forehead. He said softly, "That was rather a noisy episode. Do you think anyone heard?"

After listening for a moment, Thomas shook his head. "No, they'd be hacking through the wall by now." He leaned back against the stone, considering their options. They would have to make for one of the rooms along the outside wall. And they could go no lower than this floor: the levels below had no windows. And what was Kade doing now? That she was planning something he had no doubt. Fortunately Grandier would have as little chance to guess what it was as he had. Kade made her strategy on the run, which was poor planning in a chess game, but in real life tended to make opponents waste time bumbling around wondering what in hell she was thinking. The only problem was her inclination to the dramatic. Would Grandier consider that?

He looked up to find Aviler watching him narrowly. At his look of inquiry Aviler said, "You haven't yet pointed out that I was wrong about Denzil and you were right."

Thomas said dryly, "I thought the consequences so obvious that calling further attention to it was unnecessary."

Aviler snorted and shook his head. "Even though you've saved my life, I can't seem to bring myself to like you."

"That's probably just as well." Thomas was thinking of ways to rooms with outside windows, and that the nearest could only be reached by using this wall passage to travel directly through the part of the palace Denzil had made his stronghold. *And why not? They won't be searching for us there. And there's less chance of running into more fay.* There was also another possibility in that direction to be explored. "Did you know about the spyhole near the third-floor council chambers?"

Aviler's eyes widened. "No, I did not."

"Denzil doesn't either. When Dontane took me to those chambers, they had their maps laid out, so it must be where they plan their troop movements at the very least."

He could tell the notion appealed to Aviler. "You think it would be worth it, for what we might hear?"

"Perhaps not, but it is on our way."

There were voices coming from the direction of the faint glow of light. "Why you?"

It's my plan, Thomas started to say. Instead, he put a properly sardonic note in his voice and said, "Another noble impulse? You're the only one who has a chance of convincing Roland of any of this; don't you consider that a little more important than your pride?"

They were crouching in the narrow darkened wall passage, beside a gap in the baseboard just large enough for an agile spy. But someone had been through this servants' passage at some point strewing the floor with iron filings, so they couldn't afford to waste time here. The hole in the baseboard had an extra helping of iron sprinkled around it, but there was no sign that its real purpose had been discovered.

Aviler glared, and gestured reluctantly. "All right, damn you." As Thomas bent to scramble under the lintel, Aviler added, "Eventually that little tactic is going to fail, then what will you do?"

Thomas grinned to himself. "Hit you over the head."

From inside the cramped spyhole, he could see the gap carefully cut into the planks below the wall, leading into a narrow crawl space below the first council room. They were there, right enough. He recognized Dontane's voice, but it was impossible to distinguish individual words. He would have to try to get over to the next room.

The crawl space was perhaps two feet high, the bottom made of planks supported by the thick wooden rafters of the room below, lit by soft candle-light finding its way through the cracks in the floorboards above. On the far side, where the wall of the second council room had been erected, another hole had been torn in the baseboards, allowing access to the crawl space below the next room. That was where the voices were coming from. *Well, it would be*, Thomas thought. He sat back, pulling off and laying aside the baldric and rapier, which would be far more trouble than it was worth in the narrow space. He hesitated over the main gauche, which would be equally unhandy at his back where it could catch on things or in the front of his sash poking him determinedly in the stomach. He settled for wedging it down into his boot, though he knew if he encountered anything more hostile than a rat, he was a dead man.

He worked his way slowly across the crawl space, trying to keep from choking on the dust, gasping in pain when his bruised ribs encountered the sharp corners of a rafter.

About halfway across, something sharp bit through the leather of his glove and he jerked his hand back. It was only a nail loose on the planks.

Then he took a closer look and saw the boards of the crawl space were sprinkled with them. They must have fallen down through the cracks from above. Denzil did not trust his fay allies at all.

Thomas edged closer to the gap. The voices were distinctly louder here. And louder. *Damn them,* he thought; *they're coming in here.* There was no time to move as a door squeaked open nearly overhead. He froze as heavy footsteps sounded on the floorboards of the room above and Denzil's voice said, "God, you're such a fool."

"I didn't have to tell you," Dontane replied, his tone surly.

You prick, you've been so splendidly stupid, why did you have to ruin it by thinking? Thomas had counted on Dontane being fool enough to try to hide their escape from Denzil as well as from Grandier.

"You did if you wanted to live. You idiot, I would have gotten rid of him in time." Footsteps paced overhead, a long winter cloak brushed the floor. Thomas winced as Denzil came to stand by a dark area that must be a cabinet or other large piece of furniture, the Duke's boots almost directly over his hiding place. He was cramped and his shoulders were aching, but he dared not shift his position.

"They can't escape," Dontane protested.

"Of course they can. Boniface knows the palace very well; he's been spying on everyone in it for years."

"I'm not a fool, damn you, I was—"

"It doesn't matter, not at this point." There was a hesitation, then Denzil asked softly, "What position do you want when I take the throne? Court Sorcerer?"

Ah. I should have known Denzil would contrive to sell everyone to everyone else, Thomas thought. *He's lured Dontane away from Grandier, that was why our mercenary friend was so afraid.*

"Will the nobles accept me?" Dontane spoke slowly, diverted by visions of the future.

"They will if I order it."

They might at that. Anything to keep Denzil away from home and family.

The door opened again, and a young man's voice, shy with hero worship said, "My lord, there's a message."

"Thank you." Denzil's voice warmed, probably out of habit. He would keep no one close to him who was not his absolute slave. How it must gall him that Grandier remained his own man. Dontane had probably been an easy conquest.

Paper crackled, then with a smile in his voice, Denzil said, "Villon has reached Bel Garde."

Thomas caught his breath.

"No." Dontane sounded horror-stricken. "The cavalry—"

"The siege engine cavalry," Denzil corrected gently.

"How could he get here so quickly?"

"If the messages went to the Granges yesterday, if Villon left his Train of Ordnance behind and traveled through the night, it could be done easily."

"Without Grandier's help I couldn't possibly hold him off."

"Yes, if Evadne hadn't failed I'd have Roland by now." Denzil was silent for a moment, possibly calculating the time as Thomas was. It would have been impossible to conceal the cavalry's movement up the plain to Bel Garde; they would have been spotted easily from the city wall. But it would have taken time to send the message through the dangerous snow-choked streets. And Villon was a cautious general, preferring maneuver and siegecraft to pitched battle. He had taken Bel Garde as a base from which to stage his attack.

Denzil said, "It's unfortunate. If I can't keep Bisra from attacking us in what they will perceive as our weakness, Lord General Villon would be useful. But he won't deal with me. I hope he has more amenable officers. You'll have to send the Host against him."

"Grandier won't allow it. He's counting on Villon to help lead the attack against Bisra."

"And counting on me to convince Villon to support my claim to the throne. But I can't... I won't do that. He is an old friend of Ravenna's, you see."

Denzil was not going to allow a war with Bisra. He wouldn't want a kingdom locked in struggle, war torn and poor. And he really didn't need a war to put him on the throne; he only needed the threat of it. *He's going to hold Bisra off somehow. If he can. If he gets past Grandier,* Thomas thought.

"I want you to speak to your friends in the Host and persuade them to attack Villon tonight," Denzil said.

"I'll go now, but—"

"Don't go now; wait until dusk. I don't want Grandier to learn of it. We can scarcely ask him to arrange the cloud cover for us, so they will have to wait until dark anyway." Footsteps crossed the floor to pause near Dontane. "Take care. Everything depends on you."

Does it? Thomas thought. *Does it really?*

He heard them move toward the door. As soon as it closed he rolled away from his painful position over the rafter and began to work his way back toward the hole in the baseboard, half-formed plans turning in his head. He had almost reached it when there was the thump of a chair pushed aside, hurried steps crossed the floor, and the door banged open.

Thomas swore and scrambled through the opening into the spyhole. Dontane and Denzil had departed, but he had never heard the messenger boy leave. He grabbed up his sword and baldric and ducked under the lintel back into the passage.

"Well?" Aviler demanded.

"Move. Someone heard me."

They made their way through the twists and turns of the passage and up a narrow flight of rickety stairs. "Villon's reached Bel Garde," Thomas said.

"Thank God. The court got through."

"It's not over yet. Denzil's sending the Host against him tonight—despite Grandier's orders to the contrary. Villon will have to be warned."

They came to a door with a thin line of chill daylight leaking under it. Thomas listened at it, then carefully prized it open. The room outside was a long formal dining room lit by slanting gray morning sunlight from tall windows opening onto a portico. It was undisturbed except for a little snow that had blown in through a window left carelessly open; the scene had the strange still quality of a painting.

Thomas crossed the room and opened the window further, stepping out onto the portico. The tiled floor was heavily laden with ice, and he held carefully to the light railing and looked out on a view of the garden courts and the siege wall, the bastion rising up beyond. To the north was the open land of the park, and cut off from sight by the side of the Gallery Wing would be the Postern Gate. The ground was two stories down from the bottom of the portico. He stepped back through the window to lift a heavy velvet drapery cord. "Think you could make it?"

Aviler nodded. "Of course."

They started to tear down the drapes, pulling loose the cords and discarding the ones that had gotten wet from the open window and had stiffened with ice.

Aviler tied off a section and tested it, then said, "We can secure it to the table. It's heavy enough to support a dozen men, so—"

"It won't have to. Just you. I'm staying here."

Aviler frowned at him. "What do you mean?"

Thomas tied off two cords and reached for another. "There's barely enough time for you to make it across the city to Bel Garde by nightfall on a good day. I'm going to try to stop them here."

Aviler looked incredulous. "How?"

"I don't know," Thomas snapped. He didn't want to give Aviler the chance to talk him out of this. He controlled himself with effort and said more calmly, "Apparently Dontane's the only one who can talk to the Host besides Grandier. If I can stop him—"

"That would help immeasurably, of course, but Villon is hardly going to be unprepared for an attack by night. That he's here now means he knows what's happened. He will realize the danger."

"And with Ravenna dead you're the only one who knows for certain that Denzil is a danger. Even if the attack on Villon fails, all Denzil has to do is ride up to Bel Garde tomorrow and ask to speak to Roland alone."

Aviler hesitated. Thomas could see him turning over that image and not liking what he saw. But Aviler shook his head. "Outright assassination would hardly serve his purpose—"

"It wouldn't have to be that. But it's hardly politic to allow the man who's near destroyed a city so he can usurp the throne unlimited access to the King."

"All right, all right." Aviler shook his head impatiently. "I'll go on. But I think you're only going to succeed in killing yourself."

"Probably," Thomas admitted.

They finished the makeshift rope and tied it off, and Thomas told Aviler the way over the canal and through the Postern Gate that he and Kade had used.

They secured the rope to the table, and with Thomas to hold it steady, Aviler started to climb. The High Minister disappeared over the portico with no more than a whispered "good luck" and Thomas was grateful, loath to countenance any attempt at sentimentality at this point. When Aviler had reached the snowy ground and vanished into the shelter of the garden walls and frozen hedges below, Thomas pulled the makeshift rope up and bundled it into the bottom cabinet of one of the sideboards. With luck the tangled draperies would look like an aborted attempt at looting. He closed the window and slipped quietly out of the room.

CHAPTER EIGHTEEN

ROLAND COULD NOT stop shivering. He sat near the fire in a windowless interior chamber at Bel Garde. A salon meant for entertaining, its walls were softened by cloth-of-gold draperies and the overmantel and borders delicately painted with black grotesques on gilt backgrounds. Fretfully looking around the room, Roland's eyes lit on a silver and gold filigreed perfume burner he had given Denzil some months ago, and it occurred to Roland just how isolated he had become from the others in his court. He had no other close confidant or advisor but Denzil; most of those who had surrounded him were his cousin's companions, not his, and he had no wish to see any of them.

Lord General Villon had arrived with his men not long ago, and the walls of the little fortress had almost trembled from the cheers of the other guards. After Ravenna's death their situation had seemed hopeless, and now for the first time there was a chance for revenge and victory. Roland had been just as glad as the others to see them, but he was nervous of Villon, knowing the General's opinion of him was not a high one. And having to greet the old warrior with news of the Dowager Queen's death...

Behind Roland, in the center of the room, Villon and his officers, their cloaks still steaming from melting snow, met with Renier and the Queen's Guard lieutenant who had brought Falaise. They were talking intently, pointing to the maps laid out on the round table, making some plan. Roland had no wish to join in their council. They all thought him a coward, or a fool, and perhaps they were right.

A new voice made Roland look up, and he saw that Elaine had been brought in again. The hem of her skirt was torn and dirty, and her face was a pale oval in the candlelight. Her only companion was an Albon knight standing at her elbow as if she were a prisoner, and Roland wondered if she had been left to sit in some cold anteroom, without even a maid to accompany her. Such treatment suddenly reminded him of one of Fulstan's more subtle tricks, when Roland had been left alone in a bare room to contemplate his fate for hours, only to discover later that the King had left the palace and that there would be no punishment after all.

"Hasn't anyone even sent for a lady to care for her?" Roland interrupted. All heads turned toward him, and he wished they would stop looking at him as if he were mad, or had just grown an extra limb. "God, just let her alone. Your damned questions are worthless."

"At once, m'lord," someone said. Roland found himself meeting General Villon's expressionless gaze and quickly looked away. Elaine still stood shivering in the center of the room and he motioned her to come over by the fire. She came obediently, taking a low cushioned stool near his chair, moving stiffly as if the cold and shock had solidified her muscles. Roland felt more at ease in her presence. Here, at least, was someone who knew he could not have disobeyed his mother's order, who did not think him a coward. If he had stayed in the tower he would be dead as well, or Bel Garde overrun by fay and they would all be prisoners. But he wondered if he would have had the courage to order his own son or daughter to safety while he met death. *I will never know, because we'll all die here and I will never live to have a son or daughter...*

There was more quiet talk, but the council seemed to be over. Roland stared into the fire, trying not to see images it hurt to think about. Since hearing Falaise's tale, he had sunk deeper into grief and pain, and he felt powerless to help himself. He heard Renier move up behind his chair, and he said the words he had been living on since that moment in the tower. "He will explain himself. There will be some reason."

"Yes, my lord," a soft voice answered. "But if he meant to betray you, wouldn't he also have a reason, a clever lie?"

Roland looked down at Elaine, startled, and heard Renier gasp. He glanced up and saw that his Preceptor looked as shocked as if a pet cat had spoken. But Roland knew that his mother would not have had women close to her who were fools; they had been at the focal point of the court with her.

Renier stepped forward to take Elaine's arm and Roland motioned him away, irritated at the interruption. He wanted to talk, and the young woman's eyes were red and bruised from crying and the expression in them anything but cruel. "If he loved me how could he betray me?" he asked, hearing the tears in his own voice.

"If he loved you, he couldn't," she whispered.

Roland hesitated. If his mother had asked it of her, this woman would have flung herself off the roof of the highest tower in the city. She would believe whatever Ravenna had told her to believe. But Ravenna was not here to tell her what to say now. If Elaine was repeating his mother's views, it was only because she believed in them herself.

"You were close as boys," Elaine persisted. "I remember it. But didn't he change?"

Didn't he? Roland asked himself. Had the teasing turned to mockery? *I know he has a cruel streak. God, he could hardly hide it.* "That was because..." Roland began, and thought, *because after I tried to die, he knew how much I needed him, and he thought me pathetic, and it made him feel powerful.* He felt anger stir in him, old tired anger. "Yes, he changed."

They sat in silence for a time, until a matron who had been one of Ravenna's gentlewomen came for Elaine. She let the older woman lead her away, but reluctantly, with a worried glance back at Roland.

ката

The frigid wind tore at Kade's hair, blowing it into her face, and she shook it away irritatedly. "You'll be ready?"

The gold and amber fay leaned on his pikestaff and looked down at her with a smile. "If you can flush the birds, my lady, we can chase them."

It was late afternoon, the sky a low solid gray like the polished surface of an ancient shield, the housetops around them still sheathed in ice and snow. Kade had left Boliver at Knockma, to help the others pack what was necessary and to take them through the ring to Chariot, another of her mother's enchanted castles. She hadn't been to it for years, so it would not occur to the Host to search for her there. She had little memory of what it was like, except that it was big and old, and hidden rather prosaically in the hills of Monbeaudreux, a province in the south. It was protected from the Bisran border by steadily rising mountains that were too high and rugged to cross except on foot. The summer and spring lasted longer there, and they grew olive trees. At the moment it sounded like heaven.

The fay from the Seelie Court, with his white blond hair, delicate features, and the embroidered satin of his doublet and cloak, was unreal in this world of gray and white. "Chase them far," Kade told him. "I don't want them turning back on us. I've paid enough for it."

"To the ends of the earth, and that will be a pleasure." The fay swept a bow to her, and suddenly a golden hawk glittered in the air beside her, and with a powerful sweep of its wings, it shot toward the sky.

Kade watched him until he disappeared into the clouds. She couldn't afford mistakes, and she wasn't at all sure of herself. She had been lax over the last few years, using what she could of the swift instinctive fay magic, depending on glamour and illusion. Swift, and in the end ineffective against the sorcery that was practiced so painstakingly, using as poor a tool as letters from a dead language's alphabet to symbolize concepts that passed understanding. With fay magic it was impossible to attempt something beyond one's skill; with sorcery it was all too possible, and all too deadly.

Kade hugged herself and shivered. She hadn't given sorcery the long hours of study it needed. Her efforts seemed so ungainly compared to the elegant and involved work of sorcerers like Galen Dubell and Dr. Surete. *Both of whom are dead now*, she thought, savagely, *and at least I'm alive.* But it all came home to rest in the end, and she had taken the easy way out far too often.

Kade knew she should have returned to make up with Roland at once after their father had died. She would not have had to stay long, and it might have made the difference in so many things. If she went to him now to tell him about Denzil, he would never believe her.

The glass ball Titania had traded her was in a deep pocket of her smock, and when it brushed against her she could feel the warmth radiating out of it even through all her layers of clothing. *God, I hope it's contained*, she thought. *I hope it's not sapping my strength or power, or leaking something into the ether that's going to interfere with the spell.* She was not at all sure that what she was attempting would work. She had bought the Seelie Court's help with Knockma, and they would hound the Host from the city, but she would have to stir the creatures out of the palace herself.

Kade heard something at the edge of the roof, then saw a small fay with ugly wizened features and cornflower blue hair peering at her over the edge. Its narrow eyes widened at her, and she snarled, "Bugger off." It vanished, and she stretched, easing the tension in her tight shoulders. She was a little shocked to realize it was not the cold that was making her tremble. *It's going to work*, she told herself. *It's not going to work*, a little voice answered. *I'm going to die.*

She took out a pinch of the gascoign powder and rubbed it into her eyes. Looking toward the palace's towers, she could now see the corona of shifting light that played over them, colors touching and fading into one another.

There should still be gaps between the wards high in the air above the palace; there hadn't been time for them to draw all the way together, and the higher they were in the air, the slower they would move. *Here I go*, she thought, and flung herself into the sky.

Kade had wings, and for a moment only, an unfamiliar instinct told her to use them. Colors changed; blurred outlines in the distance became sharp and clear. Her vision was incredible. Shadows had edges like razors, and her eyes found movement—the flutter of a curtain's edge through a broken window, the slight rustle of a frost-covered tree's branches in a garden court— that she would never detect with human sight.

Kade realized she was gliding in a circle over the High Minister's house, then she realized she was flying. For a moment human thought and hawk instinct clashed, and her wings flapped frantically. She dropped like a stone. Kade forced herself to let go, to let the unfamiliar senses guide her, and her wings made the correct angle and she caught the wind again.

She thought she had the trick of it now. One had to exercise enough control to keep one's memory and purpose, but had to give the hawk enough rein to control the body. She made a slow circle to face toward the palace, watching the ground rush by below in impossibly fine detail and trying not to think about what her wings were doing.

Kade had not taken this form lightly. She knew that hawks, who could dive from hundreds of feet in the air and pluck a mouse off a forest floor, would have good eyesight and that with the gascoign powder she would have a chance of finding the gap in the wards. The smaller body would make slipping through easier as well. Also, if she failed, this wasn't a bad way to spend one's last hour. But she had chosen better than she could have guessed. She could see the wards as fine shadings of gray mist moving almost imperceptibly above the walls.

And just a moment ago I thought gray a dull color, she thought, amazed. Who had known that one bland color would have so many distinctions?

A few powerful strokes of her wings took her higher and she flew toward the palace, astonished again at the power and strength of such a small body. She had risen above the wards and almost overshot the palace before she caught herself and turned back. It was no wonder human sorcerers lost themselves when they changed shape. If her sense of urgency hadn't been so strong, it would have been easy to play on these wind currents until she forgot who she was. *Is that what happened to all the human sorcerers who tried the shape-changing experiment? Did they keep saying, "I'll just stay out a little longer," until all the words faded from their minds?* If only she could afford that kind of self-indulgence.

Kade found the gap close to the high point where the edges of the wards met above the palace. It was an irregularly shaped hole, a bare four feet wide at its largest... And closing fast. Hawk instinct seized her and pushed on by her fear she dove for the gap. She had forgotten how fast she could move if she tried, and found herself safely through and frantically cupping her wings to slow herself as the sloped roof of the Queen's Tower rushed upward at her.

Elated, Kade controlled her dive and slipped sideways, catching the wind current around the tower and letting it steer her toward the North Bastion. She hadn't felt a thing when she had rushed past the wards, and now she knew she was going to beat that Bisran bastard at his own game.

Kade made one slow circle above the King's Bastion for curiosity's sake. Along the top level, she could see the staining on the stones above the windows where smoke had poured out from the sporadic fires there the night of the attack. Then a play of light over the dark tiles of the multipitched roof caught her attention. It looked almost like a ward.

Yes, it is a ward. She didn't think it was a new one of Grandier's design; it lay on the roof like a discarded scarf. Kade circled again, losing altitude in her effort to see it more clearly. It could be Ableon-Indis, the ward she had called to route the Host in the Old Hall. Her spell might have pulled it out of the etheric structure entirely, and that was why it was still here instead of with the other wards above. It might not have been affected by Grandier's conversion of the other wards at all.

Kade saw the black shape out of the corner of her eye, and her hawk's body twisted away, reacting before her human mind had grasped the danger.

It was a black spraggat, its leathery wings stretched above her, claws raking. She dove again, slipping in and out of the currents, but it followed her, its stronger wings overpowering the wind and forcing itself closer to her.

Kade slipped sideways and it overshot with a scream of rage. She flapped her wings frantically, trying to gain height and take advantage of its mistake, then she heard its screaming turn from anger to pain. She risked a look and saw it was rolling and scrabbling across the roof of the King's Bastion, its leathery wings smoking and bursts of flame appearing over its dark body. It had fallen into Ableon-Indis. *I'm right*, she thought with great satisfaction. *But it's much weaker than it was without its keystone, or it would have burnt that thing up at once.* She had one ward on her side, and she would have to think carefully about the best way to use it.

She turned, making for the North Bastion. Then claws raked her back, and the force of the blow sent her tumbling, her wings frantically beating the air. The second black spraggat dove toward her again and struck at her. She wheeled and turned desperately to escape. The wall of the North Bastion seemed to spin, all the while rushing closer and closer.

The instincts Kade had fought off earlier took over in force, letting her right herself and fight her way toward the flat mountain looming in front of her. Her claws grasped stone, and there was a rush of air behind her as the spraggat stooped for the kill. She felt herself fumbling, trying to remember what she had to do now, her thoughts overwhelmed by the hawk's fear and its terrible desire to turn and throw itself at the spraggat in a hopeless attack. With the last bit of herself, she stretched out with her mind and touched the spark of light within her feathers that in another existence was a fayre queen's glass ball. She shattered it.

Then her fingers were digging into the chinks in the stone face, her boots slipping on the ledge. The spraggat screamed its confusion, suddenly confronted with a human larger than itself and the bright painful backwash of a powerful spell. It swung away in fright, and half sobbing with exhaustion, Kade clung to the stone and kicked at the catch of the window. Once, twice, then it sprang open and she fell through.

She lay on the wooden floor of a cold empty room, gasping, then reached into her pocket. Titania's glass ball was in shards, still faintly warm with the force of the contained spell. *Well, I'm not doing that again soon,* she thought, sitting up awkwardly. The fay's claws had torn through her coat, leaving two long tears in her back that sluggishly leaked blood. Her shirt and smock hadn't been torn, only snagged aside, and distractedly she searched her pockets for a pin to pull the fabric of the coat back together. Then Kade saw where she was: the walls covered with gilt-trimmed bookshelves, the large windows, the beautifully carved partners desk still piled with paper, more books, and an upset inkwell.

In her confusion Kade had all but forgotten which room she was making for. She had meant to approach cautiously and make sure the rooms were empty first. She climbed to her feet, inwardly cursing herself and listening hard for any sign of occupation. *Stupid, stupid, have you ruined it all now? Is he still using these rooms? Did you go through all that just to be caught?*

She steadied herself against the wall because her legs were still trembling, and crept to the door. But the next room, a small parlor with furniture buried under more books, was cold and unoccupied as well. She ventured through the rest of the suite, feeling her heartbeat begin to steady. She could hear nothing but the wind against the windows, and the rooms were cold, the candles and hearths unlit. Grandier had not come back here, then.

Kade returned to the study and started her frantic search. The simplest hiding places were the best. It seemed like a year ago, but the morning that she had stood on the windows and spoken to him, he had been planning to let the Host in that very night. *It wasn't Galen who betrayed you*, she reminded herself. *It was Urbain Grandier the murderer.*

She went to the desk and opened all the drawers and looked through the first layer of papers. They were covered with crabbed half-completed calculations, none of which she could follow for more than a few steps. The books on the desk were *Theater of Terrestrial Alchemy* and *The Black Keys*; nothing illuminating there.

She moved around the room, scanning the shelves, shifting books, looking under chair cushions, then turned to the leatherbound chest on the floor. It had books stacked atop it but not much dust compared with the rest of the room, and she remembered that he had just finished putting something in it when she had come to the window the first time.

Kade kneeled beside the chest and lifted the books from the top. It wasn't even locked. She opened it and was disappointed by the sight of perfectly ordinary folded linens and fustian blankets.

Then she moved the top layer aside. It lay on a bed of cloth, a stone from the bottom of some streambed, rounded and smoothed by water, small enough to fit comfortably in her two cupped hands. The keystone was inert and silent now.

She picked it up, marveling at the symbols, letters, and equations incised into its surface. They started out blocky and large enough to read, then shrank as they wound around the stone, some obviously formed by different hands, becoming so tiny they might have been carved with a jeweler's knife, ultimately shrinking until they disappeared from sight. Kade blinked and shook her head, dizzied. She could follow the sense of it for no more than a few turns of the stone, if that.

Well, Kade thought, rolling it from one hand to the other. *So I've got it. Now find Thomas, and take this down to its place in the cellar.*

She bundled the keystone up in the bag she had brought in a pocket and tied it securely around her waist, then started out of the suite.

Kade listened at the heavy wooden door a moment, hearing no betraying sounds, then opened it cautiously. The next room was dark, but she had expected that. There was the smell of must and dampness and, far away and barely detectable in the frozen air, of death.

Kade hesitated, one hand on the doorframe. The hackles on the back of her neck lifted.

If the black spraggat outside had been a guard, there would be a guard inside, as well.

She crossed the anteroom in three light-footed leaps and reached the opposite door. Let whatever it was come for her then; she had found the keystone. She could do anything.

Stretching before her was a suite of rooms, filled with silent shapes, distorted by shadows.

Kade slipped through the first room, sweat freezing on her back, the heavy lump of the keystone bumping her familiarly in the leg. In the second room she stopped. The cold had changed consistency. She felt it moving over her like a mist, clinging to her face and hair, her clothes. *There is something here.* She touched the wall to keep her orientation, straining her eyes in the darkness and slipping the bronze knife out of the scabbard at her belt. Then something moved. She couldn't tell if she was seeing it with her eyes or inside her head.

Kade eased back against the wall, her heart pounding. Whatever it was would attack her in a moment. She didn't want to give it an advantage by bolting out of the room screaming.

The whisper almost made her jump out of her skin. It came from across the room, and she tightened her grip on her knife. The voice was low and harsh, and she couldn't make out the words.

Kade hesitated, aware of precious time passing. Sweat was freezing on her forehead and she didn't know whether to be afraid or angry, to try to push her way past the thing or retreat. Maybe that was its purpose, to keep her here while something else—

The voice was getting louder, and though she still couldn't make out the words. It trembled on the edge of her memory, recognition barely a breath away.

Then she remembered that *The Black Keys* contained spells for necromancy.

Her father's voice said, "Little bastard, why did your bitch of a mother bother to drop you? She didn't have to leave you to devil me."

Kade didn't remember running; she wasn't aware of anything until she was slamming the door of Grandier's study behind her and leaning against it, shuddering. Her knees hurt and one of her gloves was ripped, and the burn in her palm had torn open. She must have gone over or through a piece of furniture, though she didn't remember it.

Kade went to the desk, picked up the book on necromancy, and slung it through the window. It hit the open casement and smashed the glass, then tumbled out of sight. It was the first time in her life she had ever mishandled a book.

She paced the room because the liquid fire of fear and anger was in her veins and it hurt to stand still. She smashed an astrolabe and turned over the globe, and dug her fingernails into the open wound on her hand until she stopped sobbing. Then she asked all the old pagan spirits to visit their curses on Grandier, and the Church God to strike him down.

Kade stopped in the middle of the room finally, pressed her hands together, and thought. It was a test, a trick, a challenge. Grandier meant her to fail. Had he set the ghost here outside these rooms, or had it wandered the palace, to be drawn to her presence if she won a way inside?

The latter made more sense. But then... *But then it could come in here.* Kade was at the window in a moment.

She climbed out onto the sill, then stepped to the broad ledge. The black spraggat was no longer in sight though it might come back at any moment. She was in a poor position to defend herself.

The frigid wind tore at her, tearing the air out of her lungs. Kade edged her way along, fingers clinging tightly to the chinks in the stone. She hadn't pinned her coat together again and the cold air poured down her back. She would have to cross the siege wall to get to the Old Palace anyway. *Can I do it from the outside?* Another laborious ten feet and Kade saw that she couldn't, not without falling to her death. She would have to enter the North Bastion to reach the walkway along the top of the wall.

Finally Kade could stand the cold no more. She reached a set of windows she could push open, then almost fell through them onto the floor of a small bedchamber. Sitting up on the rug that was stiff with frost, she realized she had not even bothered to glance in first to see if the room was unoccupied. She could have landed headfirst among a whole tribe of spriggans, or a troop of Alsene soldiers.

She buried her head in her hands. *He has you on the run. You're playing into his hands again.*

Kade pushed to her feet and went through the doorway to the next room. It was a beautifully arranged parlor, the wallpaper and upholstery of rose and gold. She didn't know who this suite had belonged to or where she was, except that she was near the corner and would have to find the stairs that let out onto the siege wall. The light from the window in the bedchamber made no inroads on the shadows in the corners. The next room would be dark as pitch.

Kade dug in her pockets and finally came up with a tinder-box. She would light one of the candles in here and take it with her. She would have to do that anyway if she didn't want to be running into walls and stepping on bogles. *Coward,* she thought as she fumbled with the flint. *Bloody coward.*

It refused to catch, and she pried the candle out of the lamp, sat down on the floor with it, and tried to light it with a spell. Her heart was pounding too fast, distracting her, but finally the wick began to glow gently with spell light. It was beginning to yellow to real flame when it went out, as if invisible fingers had snuffed it. "What?" she said aloud, and looked up.

It was there, in the darkest corner, looking at her. She could feel its gaze with the inner eye of her own sorcery. Her skin turned to ice and sweat dropped into her eyes. Then it whispered, "I could have you killed tomorrow and no one would notice. Perhaps I will—"

Kade was through the bedchamber, slamming the door behind her, and poised on the windowsill like a bird about to take flight before her wits caught up to her. She made herself stop, grinding her injured hand against the frozen metal of the casement, forcing herself to think. She could climb out and enter through another window, go around it. But it had taken so little time to find her. It would just follow her again. How could she find Thomas with the damn thing following her and freezing her blood—

Had it gone after Thomas too? He had helped Ravenna kill Fulstan. But Thomas had never been particularly impressed with Fulstan when the old king was alive; Kade thought it unlikely that he would be concerned about him now that Fulstan was dead.

It was coming after her because it could make her afraid.

Kade hesitated, considering the idea. Fulstan had been nothing in life and was even less in death. Thomas and Ravenna had disposed of him with less regret than a peasant would feel when putting down a mad dog. Kade nodded to herself.

That was the key to it.

She had not let the old bastard stop her from living her life. She was not going to let him stop her from finding Thomas.

Kade pushed away from the windowsill and crossed the cold room to the door. Her legs were trembling; her hand on the doorknob trembled. That was all right. She could shake, cry, scream, as long as she didn't break and run. There was no one who mattered here to see her.

Outside the door she could hear the muttering of the voice. She opened it and stood on the threshold.

Light from the room behind her fell only a short distance, then seemed to hit a wall of blackness and stop. The voice rose, ranting at her, words of darkness forming all the old terrible nightmares she remembered. "Little lying bitch, my punishment from God for my sins."

Anything to stop that. She said, "You're nothing."

It had no effect. The voice rose in volume. "Do you think your pathetic little brother could help you? He'd kill you himself if I ordered it—"

Roland do something you ordered? Kade found herself thinking. "Who's the liar now?" she said. "He hates you more than I do." And suddenly the words were just words. They hurt, but not with the sting of truth. They were the same words Fulstan had always flung at her, but she was not a child now. Perhaps she had not needed to return to the city of her birth to face her brother. Perhaps she had needed to return to face this. Her voice gaining strength, she shouted, "You're nothing! Galen Dubell was more a father to me than you ever were. Thomas is more a husband to Ravenna than you ever were." The voice went on, louder, and Kade's voice rose to a shriek, drowning it out, all thought of concealment forgotten. "You were nothing to her, you're nothing to me! She killed you because you got in her way and she wouldn't put up with your stupidity anymore. Roland's King now and he curses your memory whether he admits it or not. You're nothing and you always were!"

On the last word she stalked forward—not running, not blundering in the dark—until she barked her shin on a chair. Cursing the pain, she fell against the other door, opened it, and stumbled through into the next room.

It had an open door leading into the stairwell, and wan yellow candlelight came down through it from somewhere above. The silence was complete.

She looked back and could see the gray daylight from windows of the bedchamber through the open door of the salon. It was just a room, cloaked in shadow, no colder than the stairwell.

"And don't come back," Kade muttered, leaning against the doorframe. Then she heard heavy footsteps from the floor above, and she started hastily down the stairs. If there had been anyone or anything in the bastion, her idiot screaming would bring it running.

In the next hour Grandier or the Host or Denzil could kill her. But Kade had never felt more free in her life.

CHAPTER NINETEEN

THERE WAS A clank somewhere in the passage below, as if hollow metal struck stone. Thomas paused on the edge of the gap in the floor and thoughtfully fingered the hilt of his rapier. He had seen Dontane come down the stairs from the council rooms, and he had taken the chance on going ahead into the lower passages and catching him here.

This was the large passage Grandier had shown him yesterday, the only unblocked way to the cellar where the Unseelie Court had established itself. Thomas had found a spot where a weak place in its ceiling had partly given way, spilling some debris down onto the floor and creating a hole into the space above. Climbing up through the gap, he had found another narrow corridor which was blocked on one end by a collapse of its own. It led only to more disused rooms and a now-rickety stairway up to the floor above.

A dim light fell down the stairs, slightly alleviating the darkness. Moving silently, Thomas poised on the edge of the gap, listening as the faint noise below became the footsteps of at least two men. Then Dontane passed below, with two Alsene troopers trailing reluctantly behind him. Thomas felt a rush of both relief and tension; he hadn't been certain until now that he would have his chance. Dontane could have brought twenty troopers with him, but the need to conceal his activities from Grandier must have won out over caution.

Thomas quietly stepped down to a fallen rafter half blocking the gap, then leapt onto the back of the second trooper.

His weight slammed the man into the hard stone floor. He rolled off the inert form and came to his feet against the opposite wall, ducking the flailing sword of the other trooper. Thomas parried the second wild blow, feinted, and put his point through the man's neck. The trooper sunk back against the wall, clawing at the wound and gasping, then slid to the floor.

Dontane had turned, whipping his sword free of the scabbard. He recognized Thomas and stopped, eyes widening in disbelief. "You still here—"

Thomas moved toward him, making it look like a casual stroll. He doubted he could catch Dontane if the sorcerer bolted toward the cellar. "Afraid of Villon? Things not going quite according to plan?"

He saw the realization of where those things had been said pass over Dontane's frozen expression, and an awareness of just what else had been said. "So that was you. I thought the boy dreaming when he said something had moved in the floor."

Dontane rushed forward. Thomas started to bring up his sword to parry but saw the blue flame of spell fire flickering down Dontane's blade. Instead of locking their weapons together he swept his sword around, deflecting the deadly blade and disengaging. Even then the shock of contact with that power was enough to send a jolt down his arm.

Dontane laughed, but sweat was running down his face and he held his sword en garde, not pressing the attack immediately. Thomas steadied himself against the wall. He thought, *Damn, this could finish me.* It had taken a moment or so for the blast of power to travel down the long rapier blade to his hand, long enough for him to parry and break contact. If he had connected with the shorter blade of a main gauche he would have a useless arm now. Stupid not to realize that the young sorcerer would have an arcane defense against attack. But Dontane had seen the battle at Aviler's house and knew he was outclassed in swordplay; Thomas could almost smell the fear on him.

Thomas eased away from the wall. "I hope that isn't all you've got," he said softly. "It's not going to be enough." He circled to the side, trying to get between Dontane and the cellar.

Dontane backed away, preventing him from blocking the passage. Thomas lunged, pulling the tip of his sword up and over Dontane's parry, nicking him in the opposite shoulder. Dontane cried out and his blade swung wide, the flat of it catching Thomas's sword arm. The force of the spell fire on the blade sent Thomas staggering. Dontane stumbled back and lost his grip on his sword. Pressing a hand to his wounded shoulder, he turned and bolted down the passage.

Cursing at the pain and forcing his almost-numb fingers to hold onto his swordhilt, Thomas ran after him.

Around the corner he could see the gap in the wall. The unearthly light of the Host had faded, leaving a well of darkness in the old cellar. With the waning daylight outside, the Host must still be quiescent. But Dontane was just disappearing down the stairway and would have every intention of waking them.

Thomas plunged down after him. Dontane was moving more slowly, still holding one hand pressed to his bleeding, shoulder. He turned as Thomas reached the landing and swung a fist at him. They grappled, struggling across the narrow landing. His sword arm pinned, Thomas forced Dontane toward the edge, then felt the stone give way under his boot; the next instant they were both falling.

ॐ

Kade had found enough glamour to make it difficult for human eyes to focus on her and had made her way silently through the cold dark rooms to the Old Palace. Now she crouched in the concealing shadows beneath one of the grand staircases, watching the Alsene troops rush about. Most carried lamps and all seemed to be shouting at each other. They had sprinkled more of the cursed iron filings around the areas on the third and fourth floors where they seemed to have made their main encampment. It was the place where Thomas was most likely being held, but Kade's glamour wouldn't last there, not in such close quarters with the lights and so many wary men.

Kade was torn between staying here to look for Thomas and continuing on her way to replace the keystone. Frustrated, she gnawed on her thumbnail and tried to consider her options rationally.

Spells might alert Grandier or some member of the Host. The ether was disturbed enough as it was; Kade didn't want to stir it up further and give them the idea that she was about somewhere. She couldn't afford to be caught until she had at least replaced the keystone and driven the Host out of the palace to the waiting Seelie Court.

A page boy in a slashed doublet and heavy fur cloak came down the stairs and stopped a few feet from her hiding place. He rested one small hand on the newel post and watched the frantic activity of the other men.

Kade's ears pricked. She needed information. Here was someone to get it from who was small enough for her to overpower.

For a moment the landing was almost empty. She waited for the last trooper to step through an arch into the next room and then darted forward.

Kade wrapped her wiry forearm around the page's throat and dragged him back into the shelter of the darkened stairwell. His choked cry broke off as she put the tip of her bronze knife below his jaw. She hissed, "Be quiet."

She pulled him further into the shadow and whispered, "Quietly now. Grandier has a prisoner, the Captain of the Queen's Guard. Where is he?"

She eased the pressure off the boy's windpipe enough to allow him to talk. He drew breath to scream and she pressed the knife down just enough to draw a bead of blood. After a moment the boy whispered, "The prisoners escaped."

Well, that's just fine, Kade thought in irritation. *How am I going to find him now?* "When?"

"Earlier today, sometime, I don't know exactly—" His voice was rising, and she prodded him with the knife again to remind him to be quiet.

There was no way to tell if Thomas had left the palace yet or was still trapped inside. Kade decided she would just have to replace the keystone and improvise the rest.

The page was trembling under her arm, but Kade sensed he was angry enough to try to come at her when she released him, instead of the far more sensible act of running away and shouting for help. She shoved him away. As he turned back to lunge at her, she threw a handful of glamour into his eyes. He gasped and stumbled to a halt, staring at her, his eyes widening until they were almost all pupil. She said, "You had a dream. A confusing dream. A jumble of images."

He was still staring straight ahead when Kade slipped around him and started down the stairs. That should confuse his story long enough for her to accomplish her goal. It would only take a few moments to replace the keystone.

ऌ

Thomas lay facedown, cold gritty stone against his cheek. He levered himself up a little and shook his head, too stunned to think. He caught his breath at the unexpected pain of a hundred new bruises. Then memory returned. He was on the flagstone floor of the cellar. He had fallen down the last flight of stairs.

Thomas rolled over and sat up. His sword was near his hand; he must have held onto it in instinctive reflex until he struck the pavement. Dontane lay sprawled perhaps twenty paces away.

And the Host was stirring around them.

Thomas looked back to the stairs. A dark winged fay with a sleek narrow dog's head had settled on the landing. It was looking down at them with brilliant red eyes. The cellar's soft light grew brighter as corpse-lights climbed the walls. Creatures slunk from under the piles of discarded wood and trash, or seemed to rise out of the floor. All were uniformly hideous but no two were alike, with grotesquely distorted heads, jagged teeth, long clawed hands, ratlike tails, or bat's wings. One of the columns looked as if it had grown fur; Thomas realized it was covered with a troop of brown and dun-colored spriggans. The smell of the place was as foul as the bottom of a bog, and the creatures were still coming out of hiding.

Three misshapen bogles leapt to the ground between him and Dontane, drawn by the smell of blood. Thomas looked for cover, or something else to use as a weapon. To his right he saw a long heap of broken wood, an old scaling tower lying on its side. While its supports and platforms had been made of wooden beams, the pulleys and chains that extended them and the plates that had protected the troops manning it were of iron, and there were no fay near it. While their attention was on Dontane, Thomas snatched up his sword and ran to the broken tower. He crouched next to it, his back against a large rusted iron plate propped up by the rotting wood.

As more fay gathered, the growling mutter of their talk growing louder, Thomas scraped up the bolts and metal scraps scattered nearby into a handy pile. Most of the creatures were moving toward Dontane, drawn by the blood and possibly by the young sorcerer's magic. But one small fay covered with fiery red scales and straggling hair crept toward Thomas. He waited until it was close enough, then used the tip of his sword to flip it back and away.

Incredibly light, the creature sailed back a good twenty feet before bouncing against the flagstones. It leapt up and yelled, "Hey, 'e saw me!"

Hell, now they know, Thomas thought. The Host could conceal themselves from him now that they knew he could see through glamour. *Idiot.* It was the second time he had betrayed himself that way.

But the fay were distracted again as Dontane stirred. The sorcerer rolled over, moaning, and the Host began to draw around him. A chorus of hags, their emaciated bodies barely recognizable as female, strands of grizzled hair clinging to their skulls, gathered around, laughing at Dontane's efforts to stand.

Dontane staggered to his feet and looked around, realizing he was trapped. He had lost his sword in the corridor above, and Thomas could tell from the way the blood drained from his face that he knew his danger. But with more bravery than Thomas would have given him credit for, Dontane said hoarsely, "Listen to me! We have more mortals for you."

The stubborn bastard still means to send them after Villon. Thomas knew his chances of reaching Dontane now were poor at best. Still he had to try. He gathered himself to move.

The assembled fay seemed to be listening, or at least they hadn't attacked Dontane yet. Dontane pivoted, watching them warily. He licked his lips and said, "An army is outside the city gates—"

Screeching from up in the ceiling drowned out Dontane's voice. Thomas looked up as with a clatter and bang several fay tumbled out of one of the air shafts. They drifted or cartwheeled to the floor, one landing on the far side of the cellar with a fatal-sounding splat. The odor of burning meat and peat moss descended with them.

One of the drifting forms reached the floor, landed lightly, and strode toward Dontane. Its tall body had a human shape but that was where the resemblance ended. Its skin was black and rough, and as it moved closer Thomas could see that it had been burned. It still carried raw red wounds in its flesh.

As it neared Dontane, a smaller fay with a flattened head and limbs with too many joints hopped out of the watching crowd to greet it. The little creature danced around the large wounded fay, singing in a piping, clearly audible voice, "He's here, we told! The human wizard! He's here!"

The tall fay watched this performance, then leaned down and slapped the little creature out of the way.

Dontane took a few stumbling steps backward as the fay came toward him. It looked down and said in a harsh croak, "You don't know me? Surely you must. I'm Evadne."

"But—" Dontane stared up at it, growing fear in his eyes. "The others said you didn't come back, there was an explosion in the tower—"

"Yes, I saw the explosion. I saw it from the inside. I have only just returned with these few, for it took us this long to drag our poor selves back." The hissing voice rose to a shriek. "Your master sent me to my death, you lying human fool!"

"No, he couldn't have, he knew Denzil wanted to take the King prisoner—" Dontane said, taking another step back. He halted in confusion when he realized the other dark fay were creeping closer to him.

He sees it now, Thomas thought. Grandier hadn't trusted Dontane and Denzil either.

Evadne moved nearer to the sorcerer, and Dontane begged, "Wait—"

The fay prince paused, staring down at Dontane with burning eyes in a ruined face. The others had gone silent in anticipation.

Dontane hesitated, then with fatal desperation in his voice, said, "I didn't know—"

"You admit it," Evadne snarled. Dontane clapped his hands together, shouting something. A blue glow of sorcery grew over his head just as Evadne lunged forward.

One long clawed hand caught the front of Dontane's doublet, jerking him up off the floor. The sorcery evaporated harmlessly as Dontane panicked, struggling to break Evadne's grip.

Evadne threw Dontane down, slamming him into the hard stone floor. Thomas started at the dearly audible crack of breaking bone.

Dontane twitched once, then lay like an unstrung puppet.

Evadne stared down in satisfaction at the silent form, then slowly lifted his head. My turn, Thomas thought, and shifted his grip on his swordhilt. Evadne's hot eyes found him and the fay grinned. "You are human as well, but you see through glamour. What are you?"

"Does it matter?" Thomas answered. He heard something move behind the heap of wreckage and gathered the bare handful of iron scraps he had collected.

"Perhaps not." Evadne shrugged, strolling toward him.

The dark fay were gathering again, drawn by this new promise of entertainment. This is not going to be pretty, Thomas thought. Then something slammed into the rotten wood of the tower behind him. Before the heavy mass could come down on top of him he rolled forward, then he was in the midst of them. Thomas flung the handful of bolts at the closest, momentarily clearing himself a path. He made it almost ten paces toward the stairway before a pack of bogles blocked his way. The others closed around him again and he swept his sword around, scattering them back.

A squat troll creature leapt at him wildly and he lunged at it without thinking. It fell on his sword, ripping the weapon out of his grip. He was struck from behind and he staggered forward, caught himself, and turned around, waiting to die.

ਾ

Kade had arrived at the top of the stairway down into the cellar in time to watch the burned fay kill Dontane. She hadn't recognized Evadne until he spoke and his appearance shocked her. What happened to him? I hope it hurts as *terribly as it looks.* Then she saw Thomas trapped against the broken siege tower and panic sent every other thought out of her head.

She started forward to the steps, about to plunge down into the cellar. She caught herself, one hand on the wall, and forced herself to be rational. *This is no time to be an idiot.* The Host was in force here and it would be a fight to the death she could not win.

Kade knelt on the cold stone of the passage floor, ripped a piece of fabric from her skirt, and shook out the handful of ash she had collected from one of the fireplaces, thinking, *I only need a little time, just a little time; don't get yourself killed.* She had already gotten the candle lit before coming down here, thinking the cellar would be dark, and that saved precious moments. Dripping the wax onto the fabric and ash, she whispered the powerful words and begged Ableon-Indis to listen.

She completed the spell and hesitated. If Ableon-Indis had drifted farther away or dissipated... There was no time for that. Kade leapt to her feet and stepped out onto the stairs, shouting "Evadne!" at the top of her lungs.

All eyes turned to her and the various voices of the Host stopped their singing and howling. They had forced Thomas away from cover and surrounded him, but he was still on his feet. He looked toward her, but she bit her lip and didn't betray any sign that she had seen him. If Evadne had any idea she meant to help him, then they were both dead and that was that. She reached the first landing, and the large flighted fay that squatted there edged away from her, angling its narrow head to watch her surreptitiously. From below Evadne called out, "What are you doing here, sister? Have you come to join us?"

"I..." She spoke slowly, and wondered if it was as obvious as it seemed that she had no idea what to say. Inspiration struck and she finished, "I lost Knockma to Titania, and I want your help to get it back." She started down the last flight of steps, holding the scrap of spell-patterned fabric behind her back. The creature on the landing could see it, but it would have no idea that it was anything but a rag.

Evadne turned suddenly to look down at Thomas. "It wouldn't be because of this human, would it?"

"No." Kade sounded shocked that he would even think such a thing. Her heart wasn't pounding quite so hard now, and it was a little easier to think.

"That isn't what I was told," Evadne said slyly.

"Told by whom?" Kade pounced on the admission. "By Grandier? By Dontane?"

Evadne hesitated, his eyes bright in the dusky cellar, contemptuous of her but growing doubtful.

"Do you think that was the only lie they told you?" Kade persisted.

"I don't think it is the only lie you told me."

She was almost to the bottom of the steps. *Where is the damn thing?* she thought desperately. The sweat from her hands was soaking into the scrap of fabric. *Why is it taking so long?* She had to get closer to Evadne. "But you expect that from me. I never pretended anything else. I never sent you off to your death with a false promise." *I am, however, about to destroy you now if I can just get this damned ward to—*

Behind her the fay who had guarded the stairs shrieked in agony. Kade turned as if she were as surprised as the others. The creature staggered and tried to leap into the air, its flesh melting away like hot wax.

Ableon-Indis had finally arrived.

The ward had grown weak, and Kade thought her spell would only hold it for a few moments before it drifted back up from the cellar. More of the Host screamed and fled as the ward fell among them. A burst of hot air from the motion of their wings struck her and Kade stumbled and sat down hard on the bottom step. As the nearest gang of bogles burst into flame, a roar of mingled disbelief and fear from the assembled creatures deafened her. Kade clapped her hands over her ears. The fay remembered the battle in the Old Hall too, and now they realized what she had done. Evadne charged toward her, his mouth open in a silent scream, but he was swept away by the rush of his fleeing companions.

Kade got to her feet and ran into the chaos.

༺༻

Thomas took advantage of the confusion to recover the rapier from the body of the troll that had taken it. He turned around as Kade reached him. She shouted, "Are you all right?"

"I'm better," he told her. One of the flighted creatures flew low over their heads, howling, and Thomas caught Kade around the waist and pulled her to him.

She had never stopped talking. "I found it! The keystone. Look." She struggled to unwrap a round stone covered with delicate carving. "It was right there in his rooms."

By God, now we have a chance, Thomas thought. He saw that Evadne was fighting his way free of the milling fay, coming toward them. He said, "I'll distract him, and you put it back in its place."

Kade shook her head, adamant. "No, you have to do it. You couldn't hold him off long enough and I can."

He stared down at her. Other fay were joining Evadne, and there was no knowing whether the fay prince realized that they had the crucial keystone, or was only coming after them in a blind rage. Kade shrieked, "There's no time! Go on. I'd do it for you!"

She was right. He said "Damn you," took the keystone out of her hand, kissed her hard on the mouth, and ran.

Thomas ducked around the milling creatures still panicked by the ward, forcing himself not to look back. He found the right pillar in moments and saw that the clay seal a foot or so above its base had been recently replaced. He reached down just as something struck him from behind. Claws dug into his back, parting the leather of his buff coat. He spun and slammed the creature and his full weight into the stone pillar. Its hold loosened and Thomas wrenched away. Turning, he stabbed the dazed spriggan and shoved it out of the way.

Dropping to his knees, Thomas broke the clay seal with the heel of his hand. He dug into the soft dirt and his fingers found the stone buried within, but it seemed to slip away as he tried to get a grip on it. He swore, and shifted against the pillar to reach deeper into the niche. Finally he caught the stone and pulled it out. Flinging it away, he shoved the old keystone into the niche, wondering if it was going to struggle to escape too. But it seemed to slide out of his hand and into the proper spot of its own volition. Thomas sat back, breathing hard. Then he realized that the entire room had gone silent.

He looked up. In that whole great chamber it seemed that not a single fay moved. All were arrested in midaction by a sound or a sight only they could hear. All except one.

Evadne was coming toward him, shoving his motionless companions out of the way.

Thomas picked up his rapier and stood.

ﻬ

Kade had led Evadne and the others in a chase toward the opposite end of the cellar, stopping only when she could put one of the pillars at her back. She had felt Ableon-Indis's withdrawal and knew she hadn't much time. She threw a handful of glamour at the nearest snarling bogle to give herself room, then whispered a spell of blinding. The sorcery had greater effect on the creatures of Fayre than it did on humans, and the nearest of the Host screeched and stumbled away as the mist of sightlessness settled over them.

The mist dispersed rapidly. As a large and hideous water-fay bore down on her, Kade thought frantically for another spell.

Then her ears popped and she felt the ether tremble around her. The nearest fay were staring at her, the others gazing about in astonishment. *He did it*, she thought in relief. The old keystone was taking control of the wards, and the Host could feel the enmity in the etheric structure re-forming around the palace. To those nearest her, Kade said, "You'd better leave, before you're trapped here forever. If you aren't already."

The dark fay erupted into sound and motion as one, plunging away from her, taking to the air, running screaming across the floor toward the steps. Kade leaned against one of the pillars, weak from relief, then realized Evadne was nowhere to be seen.

෨෬

The Host was dispersing in panic. Some charged up the stairs while the flighted fay rose into the air, running into the pillars and each other in their confusion.

Thomas couldn't see Kade. He put his back against the pillar. If Evadne tore the keystone out this would all be undone.

Evadne broke through the milling fay, charging at him, his long arms reaching. Thomas ducked and swept his sword up. Evadne was too quick and dodged back, aiming a fist at him.

The blow caught Thomas in the shoulder and knocked him sprawling into the pavement. He rolled over, tasting blood, dazed for a moment. Evadne was standing over him. The fay's burned flesh hung in ribbons and the death's-head grimace of his mouth below the childishly petulant eyes was terrible. Evadne hesitated, obviously torn between the desire to kill Thomas immediately and the need to rip the keystone out of its niche. Thomas struggled to stand and got no further than his knees.

Something distracted Evadne. He cocked his ruined head, then turned in a crouch. Urbain Grandier stood at the bottom of the steps. Thomas had not seen him come down either; the old man might have materialized out of the air.

Evadne straightened his tall frame slowly. "You betrayed me, sorcerer."

Grandier started toward them, his steps unhurried. "Did I?"

"But I betrayed you."

Grandier stopped. His expression had not changed, but something in the very stillness in which he stood there was daunting.

Evadne's grin was terrible. "I bargained with your creature Dontane to destroy you. The human prince you sought to put on the throne would have given me everything I wanted."

Grandier sighed. "That hardly surprises me."

Evadne's look of disappointment would have been comical on any creature less maimed and ruined. Thomas crawled back to the pillar and leaned against the niche concealing the keystone. Grandier would have no difficulty in killing him and taking it away, but he meant to keep it in place as long as he could. If Kade hadn't managed to kill herself for him, it would give her more time to escape. The fay wheeling around in the air overhead were moving with purpose now. At the far end of the great cellar they were whipping themselves into some kind of frenzy, flying in a great circle around one of the pillars. A wind was rising out of nowhere in the chamber.

Grandier shook his head, his features twisting for a moment in disgust. He said, "And what has your scheming gotten you?" His voice rose. "There is an army at the gates! A human army with iron and sorcerers to destroy you, and an army of the Seelie Court waits for you in the air."

Thomas realized it was the first time he had ever seen Grandier show anger. Evadne snarled, "They cannot destroy—" The pillar the fay were circling on the far side of the chamber suddenly shattered into dust. More fay were joining the circle and others on the floor below were swept up into it. And disappearing. The Host was forming a ring, Thomas realized, and remembered the broken foundation in the Grand Gallery. *They're going to bring the ceiling down.*

"Command your Host then; gather your court!" Grandier gestured contemptuously at the fleeing creatures, at the ring forming in the air. "Could you not control your greed for a few days? Could you not have waited until we won to betray me?" He turned his back, as if he were unable to look at the product of his own folly anymore.

He's speaking to Denzil, Thomas thought. Denzil, who was very good at causing chaos but not so practiced at bringing order out of it. Grandier had betrayed Evadne as well, or tried to; he must know he had no right to expect loyalty from a prince of the Unseelie Court. It was the defection of his human allies that maddened him. And if Thomas was correctly interpreting the expression on the fay's ruined face, Evadne didn't understand one word in three.

Evadne shook his head, "Lies again. I made you, sorcerer." His voice dripped contempt. "And I'll destroy you."

Evadne started forward. Grandier turned, his hand moving suddenly. Evadne started back in surprised anger, raising his arms to protect his face. Yes, Grandier still kept his pocket of iron filings.

Then Grandier raised his hands, speaking softly.

Evadne shook his head and raked a hand across his face, leaving bloody streaks where the filings had touched him. He sneered, "And what do you intend to do to me, old man?"

This creature has no sense of self-preservation, Thomas thought in wonder.

"I'm going to turn your blood to iron," Grandier told him, and his voice held no anger. "It's a spell I prepared for just such an occasion as this, a derivative of a common alchemical process, which you would know if you studied sorcery."

"I gave you your power," Evadne said. He smiled at the old man. "Destroy me and you will lose it. You will be trapped in this shape forever."

Grandier hesitated. Then just as Evadne made to move forward, Grandier gestured sharply. Evadne froze. Grandier walked toward him, and as he moved past the silent fay, he pushed Evadne's arm. The corpse toppled and fell, breaking into dust as it struck the floor.

The Host was disappearing rapidly now, the ring a wild circle of airborne stones, splintered wood, mangled fay bodies, and other debris. Thomas leaned back against the pillar and looked up as Grandier reached him. "Well," Thomas said, "What now?"

"I still have no regrets." Grandier smiled. His seamed face showed all the weight of his own years as well as Galen Dubell's. "Except perhaps my choice of allies."

"And your choice of enemies?" Kade was leaning next to the pillar at Thomas's side. He hadn't seen her approach and felt a surge of relief so intense it was painful.

Grandier watched her a moment, then said gravely, "Yes, that as well."

"So Villon's troop is here," Thomas said. Trying to keep his attention on Grandier, he didn't look up at Kade.

Grandier nodded. "Denzil thought the General would hold Bel Garde and attack from there. He did not. He entered the city late this afternoon and is now attempting to force St. Anne's Gate."

Aviler got through, and Villon decided to risk an assault rather than be trapped in Bel Garde, Thomas thought. *And you think he's forcing St. Anne's Gate, but Aviler can tell him that with the Gate House unmanned, the Postern is indefensible.* Raising his voice to be heard over the howling wind, he said, "Why aren't you trying to stop him?"

"I came to stop Kade from replacing the keystone, and to summon the Host." Grandier could still take the keystone, but he made no move to do so. The wind was tearing at their hair, taking their breath away. Grandier squinted into it, then shook his head regretfully. "I fear you and the High Minister were correct. Despite all my experience with violence and treachery, I am still politically naive."

Thomas couldn't see Galen Dubell in that lined and weary face anymore, as if it were no longer a disguise. As if Grandier himself was actually completely present in that shell for the first time.

Kade eyed him, unimpressed. "You killed one of my only friends, and I'll never forgive you."

Grandier's calm gaze went to her. "I cannot argue with that sentiment."

Still wary, Thomas asked, "What will you do now?"

Grandier looked startled. Then his knees buckled and he started to collapse, his thin form giving way like an empty sack. Thomas caught him as the old man sagged against the flagstones. As Grandier slumped over forward he saw the bloody gaping hole in his back.

He looked up, automatically tracing the line of fire. Denzil stood on the second tier of steps, handing a smoking musket to an Alsene trooper. They had heard nothing; the musket's blast had been carried away in the wind caused by the ring and the Host's departure.

Kade crouched beside Thomas, her face white and drawn in the rapidly shifting light. The trooper handed Denzil another loaded musket. Thomas pushed Grandier's body aside and stood, dragging Kade with him, putting the pillar between them and Denzil's line of fire. "They'll come after us. We have to—"

Kade shook her head. "It's too late." He could barely hear her over the growing roar of the wind.

There was a crash that reverberated through the stone beneath them. The swirling mass of the ring seemed to lose its structure as the last of the Host winked out of existence. It flung out a deadly hail of rocks and splintered wood, then it drifted crazily, moving sideways toward them across the large chamber. The troopers on the stairway panicked, bolting back up to the entrance. Looking back around the pillar, Thomas saw Denzil hesitate, cradling the fresh musket, before the rain of debris moved nearer and he too retreated up the stairs.

They couldn't escape that way without being felled by the flying rubble. Even the keystone pillar was no longer providing decent cover. Thomas winced as a stinging deluge of splinters struck them. He pulled Kade closer and felt her arm go around his waist.

A section of the ceiling collapsed almost above them, and fell into the ring, pulverized into dust instantly. The pillars shuddered as the ring brushed against them, the forces that drove it pressing outward at the stone, and chunks began to fall out of the far wall. The ring tilted on its axis, falling toward the cellar floor, directly over their heads.

Then they were in the empty cold silence of the Grand Gallery. Thomas stumbled and caught himself on one of the broken boulders. He would never get used to this form of travel. He let Kade steady him, and they made their way to the edge of the ring and climbed out onto the cold dirty tiles.

Kade sat down abruptly, as if her legs had suddenly given out, and after a moment Thomas sank to the ground beside her. Out the broken windows of the terrace they could see Alsene troops running awkwardly in the deep snow across the park. There was a burst of pistol fire and two of the men spun and fell, roses of blood growing around them in the snow.

Thomas looked at Kade, sitting so close, with her hair in wild disarray, and wondered what it would be like to kiss her when he didn't think he was going to die. So he took her chin gently and turned her face toward him and did.

He had started to draw back when her hand in his hair stopped him. Her mouth stopped his chuckle.

There were shouts and musket fire from somewhere inside the Gallery Wing now.

Kade jumped to her feet. "Come with me."

Thomas looked involuntarily toward the silent fayre ring in the Grand Gallery's floor. He decided that with sufficient motivation he could grow used to anything. Then he noticed that his hands were still speckled with Grandier's blood and thought of Denzil, and Ravenna. *Not now*, he thought. For a moment the words stuck in his throat, then he said, "I can't."

He hadn't expected her to react like anyone else, and she didn't disappoint him. She smiled. "It's not that easy." And she stepped back into the ring and disappeared.

CHAPTER TWENTY

THE WIND HAD changed direction and emptied the night sky of clouds; stars were visible for the first time in days.

Lord General Villon had set up a command post on the siege wall of St. Anne's Gate, under the light of lamps and torches placed all along the high crenellated battlement. Thomas leaned on an embrasure and watched as the old General paced up and down, consulting with his officers through the couriers continuously reporting in. The snow and ice were melting rapidly and it was warmer now than it had been at twilight.

Villon had wanted to bring Roland back into the city as soon as possible. His men were clearing the palace of any remaining fay and Alsene troops, with the help of the sorcerers from Lodun who had arrived at nightfall just after Villon. It was Grandier's manipulation of the weather that had drawn their attention and brought them to investigate. Lodun had never received any of the messages Ravenna had sent out before the attack.

Thomas didn't know where Roland was and hadn't asked. He knew the young King had been taken to some secured place inside the city wall. Falaise was at the Bishop's Palace; he had approved Gideon's suggestion that she be taken there a few hours ago. Some of the court at least had returned, and the rest of his own men and the Albon Knights were here helping to hunt down the last of the Alsene troops.

Fire occasionally blossomed in the dark canyons that were the streets of the city below: the lamps and torches of patrols or of townspeople hesitantly venturing out. They expected reinforcement in the form of the royal garrison at Portier to arrive sometime in the morning. Villon had learned that frantic messengers from the mayor of a village on the trade road had been sent there and to the Granges, bearing confused tidings of a massive attack.

Thomas had deliberately removed himself from the action. He had been with Villon for the past few hours, answering questions and directing him to the areas where Denzil's men might be concealed. Now he was merely waiting.

Recently he had noticed that time seemed to be passing in short stretches bordered by periods of less-than-coherent thought, and that his only support was the rough stone of the battlement. At one point he noticed that Berham was standing next to him, and had apparently been there for some time.

There was a new flurry of activity along the wall as Villon's cornet officer arrived with Dr. Conadine, one of the Lodun sorcerers. After a long consultation with them, Villon turned and came toward Thomas. The General was a small man, half a head shorter than Thomas, with graying dark hair. He had been one of Ravenna's oldest friends, having grown up with her on her father's country residence. Villon said, "They've taken our good Duke of Alsene. He's confessed to Aviler."

Thomas was not so far gone that he misinterpreted the General's expression. "And?"

"He's embellished somewhat, trying to make it look as though it were a misunderstanding." Villon's expression became deeply ironic. "That's to be expected. But he also says he killed the sorcerer Urbain Grandier. Conadine truth-tested him, and he's not lying."

Thomas looked at the night-shrouded city that was slowly creeping out of hiding. "I know."

Villon nodded, letting out his breath in resignation. "Of course, we look at it and say he's cutting his losses. It's only sense for a man to dispose of his confederates when a plot like this goes wrong. But the boy won't see it that way."

Roland had always been "the boy" to Villon. Still looking out at the city, Thomas said, "Denzil sent the Unseelie Court to take Roland prisoner and kill Ravenna."

"No, Grandier did." Villon was not arguing the point, but stating the facts as Roland would see them. "But he made a mistake in not killing Aviler. There's no getting around the point that Denzil brought a private troop into Vienne for the purpose of forcibly removing a High Minister from his home, killing a number of city guardsmen engaged in their rightful duty, not to mention a great lot of folk who were driven out into the street and killed by those demon creatures. And he didn't put that troop at the King's disposal, but used it for his own business which involved imprisoning warranted officers of the crown." Villon shook his head. "If Ravenna were alive I'd order the scaffold built. As it is... There was only one hope, but too many people saw us take him alive. He made sure of that."

Thomas felt Villon expected a response, so he said, "He would."

Villon's gaze went to the city. "You can't help us anymore tonight. Go back to the Guard House."

After a moment, Thomas smiled. "You're bringing Roland back to the palace and you want me out of the way."

"She taught you everything she ever knew, didn't she? Everything the boy should have learned." Villon sighed. "Do you think you can control your desire for martyrdom and let me manage this?"

Desire for martyrdom? Thomas thought. "I don't have to be here, you know. I had two better offers."

"That's not an answer."

"Of course it is." Thomas pushed away from the wall and turned to leave.

"The boy won't think so," Villon called after him.

Thomas decided to walk along the wall as far as he could before going down to the courts below. The sky was beautiful. Berham was following him, and Thomas noted the servant still had the two pistols he had given him the night of the first attack. When they had walked awhile Thomas said, "I'm going to send you and Phaistus over to Renier."

"Respectfully, Sir, I'm a forgetful man, and I don't think I could re-member that I was Lord Renier's servant after all the years of being yours, so if I were asked—" Berham shrugged. "I would just have to speak my mind."

"That was a very gentle threat." Thomas smiled to himself.

"I don't know what you mean, Captain."

The wind picked up, cool but without the frozen edge that took the breath away. They walked along in silence for a time, then Thomas sug-gested, "You could get yourself up as a highwayman and terrorize the trade road."

Berham chuckled. "There's a thought; there's a thought indeed."

గా

Even though the Old Courts had been taken over by the Host shortly af-ter the evacuation, the Queen's Guard House had not been much disturbed. Thomas wondered if the sigils Kade had put on the cornerposts had been more effective than she had realized. As he came into the entryway, he could see that the lamps were lit in the practice hall, and there were Queen's and a few of the remaining Cisternan guards there. Out of the original hundred and twenty men in the Queen's Guard, over seventy had survived, and that was more than he had expected. Deciding to avoid the occupied areas of the house, Thomas trudged wearily up the side stairs.

Phaistus was in the anteroom, building up a fire in the hearth. The bed-chamber beyond was musty and cold. Thomas stripped off his buff coat and what was left of the doublet beneath, left them in a ragged bloodstained pile, and sat down on the bed. After a moment he fell over backward and stared at the underside of the tester.

He fell into a kind of half-conscious doze, only dimly aware of Berham and Phaistus rustling familiarly around the room and laying a fire in the hearth.

He said "ouch" quite distinctly when Berham pulled his boots off. The servant leaned over him a moment, then said, "Is there something you want us to see to?"

Thomas shook his head. He heard the door shut as the two servants left, and in moments he was asleep.

It must have been hours later when he opened his eyes and Kade was kneeling on the bed, leaning over him. She grinned. "Surprise."

Eventually Thomas brushed a tendril of hair back from her forehead and said, "It's a long time since I've been with a woman who giggles."

Despite the awkwardness of mutual bruises, cuts, and claw-marks, they were good together. There wasn't any other woman he would have felt com-fortable making love to in this condition, but there wasn't any other woman who would have pounced on him like that either. He had been trying to de-cide what would be worse: a taste of what the next twenty years could have been like, or never knowing at all. He was glad she had taken the decision out of his hands.

"Don't brag," Kade said, smiling. "I know there have been hundreds of others."

"Not quite hundreds."

There was a scratch at the door and Berham's voice whispered harshly, "Captain, there's a couple of Albons downstairs. They were sent to tell you the King's giving an audience and he wants you there."

Couldn't he have waited one damn day? was Thomas's first thought. Reluc-tantly, he rolled off the bed, found his clothes, and started to dress.

Kade sat up and pulled her smock on over her head, then watched him quietly. When he sat down on the bed to get his boots on she said, "Leave with me."

One boot halfway on, Thomas stopped. The words "all right" were on the tip of his tongue. "I can't."

"Ravenna's gone. There's nothing left for you here."

"I have that lovely offer from Falaise."

She grimaced. "Listen to yourself. You know she's afraid of you."

He finished pulling his boots on. "That makes the situation perfect then, doesn't it."

"That's not what you want."

He couldn't ask her how she knew what he wanted, when it was all too obvious that she did know.

After a moment, Kade said, "I don't know exactly what I'm going to do, after giving up Knockma. I have other places and my household—well, you met Boliver; they're all mostly like that, except some of them are human. We argue sometimes but we never try to kill each other and no one's terribly ambitious, which is why they live with me, I suppose. What I'm trying to say is it wouldn't be like here at all, if you're as sick of this place as I think you are, and I hope you are, because I think I'm going to have some difficulty living without you."

"I'm not going to make any promises I can't keep." There was a muffled crash from the next room. Thomas grabbed the scabbarded rapier hanging over the bedpost and went to the door. He opened it a crack and saw Berham and Phaistus looking out the far door onto the landing. Thomas stepped out. "What is it?"

"Nothing, nothing." Berham looked back. "One of the Albons thought he should deliver his message in person, Sir, but some of the men pointed out that he was mistaken."

"Did they throw him down the stairs?"

"A little, yes."

Thomas shook his head, stepping back into the bedroom. Kade was gone, and one of the high windows was open, the morning breeze stirring the curtains.

❦

The court was held in a hall on the ground floor of the King's Bastion. It was relatively undamaged, except for marks of smoke and water where the walls joined the high sculpted ceiling. Massive paneled paintings hung on the walls, views of the canal city of Chaire. Standing in the center of the room was like standing on the Mont Chappelle and looking down at the beautiful ancient city.

The audience was small: Villon's officers, and men from the city troops that had come out of hiding, the courtiers who had returned from Bel Garde with Roland. Thomas was glad to see the Count of Duncanny in attendance. His party had not been able to make it out of the city, but had taken refuge in one of the fortresslike great houses and survived almost intact.

Albon knights lined the walls and were posted next to the doors. Thomas went to join Villon. Without looking at him, the old General said, "Don't expect much."

A worn and haggard Aviler was pacing in front of the chair prepared for Roland. Falaise was already present, seated in an armchair near the front of the room but to one side, so the focus was on the tapestry-draped chair waiting for the King. That was Aviler's touch, Thomas was sure. Renier would not have thought of it.

Gideon and Martin and several other Queen's guards stood around the Queen's chair. Thomas knew from the way Gideon kept trying to catch his eye that they were wondering why he didn't join them, but he was not going to unless Falaise ordered it.

The door at the front of the room opened and Roland and Renier entered, followed by more Albons. Thomas was surprised to see Ravenna's gentlewoman Elaine in the King's entourage, but only for a moment. She had learned survival from the best.

As Roland took his seat Aviler stepped back to the side, waiting with folded arms. At the King's nod, he motioned to one of the knights.

Roland's eyes were dark hollows in his drawn face. He held his cloak pulled around him tightly, though the hall was almost warm.

There was a stirring at the back of the room, then the crowd parted for a group of Albons. Thomas felt his nerves go taut.

The knights were escorting Denzil, of course.

They crossed the room in silence except for the click of their boots on the parquet floor, stopping before Roland's chair. The Duke of Alsene wore a court doublet in somber colors, and his arm was no longer in a sling. He looked less weary than Roland, but then, after his capture, Denzil had probably been able to sleep through the night.

Surprisingly, Roland spoke first. He said, "It was all true." His voice was soft, but clearly audible in the room so silent a loud heartbeat could have been heard.

Denzil said, "My lord—"

"I did not give you permission to speak."

Denzil waited, watching Roland.

"You plotted with the sorcerer Urban Grandier." Roland closed his eyes. "Against me."

The gesture might have looked theatrical, to someone who didn't know the actors. Roland was in real pain. He looked up suddenly. "My mother was killed."

For the first time there was a response from the crowd, a low whisper of comment that was hardly more audible than a wind stirring summer leaves. Thomas knew they were thinking that it had broken Roland. Aviler swayed as if to move forward, then stopped himself. It was a curiously moving gesture of restraint; the High Minister was going to trust that Roland hadn't gone mad, and would not attempt to control what the King said in an open audience.

Roland fingered the carved chair arm, and his eyes went to Denzil. "Many people were killed. Someone should die for that."

Thomas realized he was holding his breath.

Denzil was as still as a statue, and almost as pale, but he didn't look away from Roland's hollow eyes. Thomas knew that people were remembering the two had grown up together, though Denzil was older.

Roland shifted in his chair suddenly, looking away. "The sorcerer Grandier is dead. Most of the traitors are dead. The charter of the troop of the Duchy of Alsene is to be torn up, the survivors disbanded, their arms taken, and they will not be allowed to form again under those colors on pain of death. The men who hold Officers' commissions in the Troop of Alsene will be ordered executed as traitors, for the act of treason against the crown and the Ministry. Any of the lords of Alsene found in the palace taking part in the conspiracy will be ordered executed as traitors, on the same charge. Denzil Fontainon Alsene, Duke of Alsene, is...is ordered..." Roland did not look at Denzil, or anyone else. His gaze was locked on the pastel haze in a painting of a harbor skyline. The silence stretched, but no one in the crowd made the slightest sound of inattention. Roland closed his eyes to shut out some vision other than the painting. "Is ordered banished from our borders—" He hesitated again, as if he heard himself speaking and wondered at it. Then he continued, "Forever. On pain of death."

Thomas realized that Villon had moved to his other side and was now companionably holding his sword arm. It wasn't necessary. He didn't move.

Roland stood and left the room in a flurry of robes, his attendants closing in around him. The crowd began to talk and mill around, speaking softly at first and then more loudly as tension began to ease. Villon said, "For a moment I thought—" He shook his head, wry bitterness in his eyes. "My days of service won't last much longer, and I can't say that I'm sorry."

Villon had released of Thomas's arm, so he started making his way up toward the front of the hall. Halfway there Aviler met him. The High Minister looked haggard but also energized. He had probably done more of his life's work in the past day than he ever had since first taking office. He said quietly, "Denzil has three days to leave the city. That's not much time. We need to talk."

"No," Thomas said.

Aviler looked blank. "You mean, not here?"

"I mean, not at all." Before he could move on, he saw Renier coming toward them, using his bulk to part the milling crowd.

He reached them and said, "The King wants a private audience with you, Thomas."

"Good." He followed Renier to the front of the room, conscious of Aviler and Villon watching him.

The door at the back of the hall led to a short maze of old council rooms, all crowded with Albon knights, servants, and court functionaries. Thomas recognized no one, conscious of them only as blurs of color and noise. Eventually they reached a chamber with wide double-panel doors standing open and another contingent of knights guarding it.

Thomas followed Renier inside. It was a large parlor with arabesque wallpapers, thick carpets, and heavy brocaded furniture. There was a fire in a hearth with a mantel supported by two carved-marble nymphs, and all the candles were lit. Roland sat in one of the armchairs, staring unseeing at the far wall.

Renier said, "My lord."

Roland looked up, his eyes focusing. "Thank you. Everyone else go."

Some of the knights stepped out immediately, but the others lingered, looking to Renier for direction. Thomas knew they were not easy with the idea of leaving him alone with Roland, and was almost amused to see that Renier apparently shared their opinion. What surprised him was that Roland realized it as well.

As Renier started to speak, Roland stood suddenly and shouted, "Get out!"

The other men moved reluctantly, and Roland crossed the room and flung the heavy carved doors shut after them. The sudden movement seemed to almost exhaust him, and he dropped into the nearest chair and buried his face in his hands.

Thomas simply stood there, not discomfited by the display, and waited for Roland to recover himself. He looked around the room and was startled to notice a portrait of Fulstan in the far corner. It was a good likeness of Roland's father in his early middle age, and it had probably been moved from some other more prominent location and buried away here, as all the portraits of Fulstan were eventually buried away somewhere.

Roland looked up and noticed what had caught Thomas' attention. He stared at the portrait for a long moment himself, then said, "He hated you."

"He hated everyone," Thomas answered.

Roland sat very still for a time, then looked away. He said, "My Queen has given me to know that she wishes you to remain as Captain of her guard. I agree."

Roland would allow Denzil to return. Not today, or this month, but perhaps before the year was out. If Denzil had killed Ravenna with his own hands, if Roland had actually seen him casually ordering the destruction of Villon's troops, then it might have been different. But the ties between them were too strong, Denzil was too seasoned a manipulator, and Roland was still too enmeshed in self-hatred to break the link for good. The boy had proved that to himself and everyone else in the audience hall. But now he knew what his lifelong friend was capable of, and in time he might manage to break free.

But Roland was a King, and could not be allowed the time.

"That won't be necessary, Your Majesty," Thomas said. "I'm resigning my commission."

Roland's head jerked up. His hands trembling on the arms of the chair, he asked sharply, "Why?"

Thomas needed to get away now, before Roland changed his mind. He said, "Your mother would have wanted it this way," bowed, and went out, closing the door behind him. Roland made no attempt to call him back.

Thomas passed Renier without speaking and made his way back through the passages. Roland already knew what was going to happen. The only one who thankfully hadn't realized it was Kade. She had been away from court too long and must have believed that Denzil would die for his crimes. *And so he will*, Thomas thought. *So he will.*

Denzil was still in the hall. The knights were grouped loosely around him, and he was watching the crowd with folded arms, smiling faintly.

Thomas went up to him, ignoring the knights who tensed watchfully and the stares from the others in the room. He said, "We have a long-delayed appointment." All Denzil had to do was refuse. Refuse and walk away alive, free to use all the persuasive powers at his command on an oversensitive boy-king who had lost his only companion and his mother in one blow, to trade on old love and loyalty to work his way back into Roland's trust. *But he has always been greedy*, Thomas thought, *and he wants me badly.*

Denzil hesitated, watching Thomas, weighing chances, opportunities, desires. If Roland could have seen that look in the eyes of a man who should be nearly broken by the sentence of banishment from a childhood friend... But that was something Denzil would be far too clever to allow. He nodded. "Is that how it is?" he asked lightly. "Do you want to challenge me or should I challenge you?"

The room was silent now. "It doesn't matter," Thomas said, and thought, *Now I've either gotten what I wanted or handed him the pleasure of killing me on top of all his other victories.*

"Very well then. Now, no seconds, and out in the court."

"Agreed."

Thomas started for the double doors at the end of the room without waiting to see what Denzil did. There was a rising murmur of comment among the people still in the hall. Gideon caught up with him on the steps and said, "Captain, what's—"

Thomas interrupted, "The Queen will give you the appointment. You know as much as I can teach you now; the rest you'll do on your own. Just be careful and don't trust anyone, especially Falaise."

He went out into the wide paved court between the bastion and the Mews. The clouds had drawn over the sky again and it was raining a light drizzle. It slicked the paving stones and covered everything with a fine coating of moisture.

Denzil and his escort came out into the court, but they still had to wait while Denzil's swords were sent for. Thomas paced to keep bruised and strained muscles loose and felt a tense excitement building in him.

He thought of Roland sitting alone in that beautiful unused room, waiting for the news. The young King would not stop the duel. But if Thomas won, and that outcome was much in doubt, he would not forgive him for it either. *Burn the bridges after you cross them, not before*, Ravenna would say. He had lied to Roland; he didn't know if Ravenna would have wanted it this way or not. To the end, she had always been capable of surprising him. But with Kade or without her, he couldn't live with himself if Denzil survived this.

A crowd was gathering of Albons, Villon's men, Queen's guards, the servants and courtiers who had returned with Roland and Falaise. A servant brought Denzil's weapons finally, a swept-hilt rapier and main gauche. Both were utilitarian dueling weapons, with silver-chased hilts and no ornamentation.

Thomas waited while Denzil examined the blades, then drew his own weapons and moved out into the open area of the court. Denzil wore a tight smile; he had nothing to lose by this and he knew it.

They circled each other. The first exchange of blows was light, testing. Denzil was strong and quick, and he had excellent instincts.

And excellent training. Thomas countered a feint and lunge that should have punctured his shoulder and left his sword arm useless. Wanting to see if something unorthodox would rattle the younger man, Thomas parried the next thrust with a broad sweep of his rapier and stepped in to attack with his main gauche. It surprised Denzil but he recovered in time to parry with his own offhand weapon.

They were both more careful after that, and in the steady exchange of blows that followed, Thomas felt the duel taking on a rhythm. They were evenly matched, but he was feeling the fatigue of the past four days, and the knot of scar tissue the elf-shot had left behind in his leg was starting its persistent ache. If Denzil felt any lingering effects from the pistol wound in his shoulder that Grandier had healed, he didn't reveal it.

Denzil made a hard lunge and Thomas struck the blade away. He realized an instant later that the parry had not been strong enough as he felt the steel slip past his right side. Denzil whipped the forte of the blade against Thomas's ribs and pulled sharply back. Thomas felt the cut opening in his side even as he stepped away and brought his sword up in a thrust.

In his eagerness Denzil had overbalanced himself and stumbled, his parry turning into a desperate block with the hilt. The tip of Thomas's rapier caught in the bars of the swept hilt and was trapped for an instant. Thomas slipped on the wet cobblestones and fell as Denzil wrenched the hilt free. Denzil recovered first and lunged at Thomas's chest as he was trying to stand. Thomas twisted away and the point struck the ground behind his back. He rolled back onto the blade, jerking it out of Denzil's grip, his weight snapping it.

Thomas rolled to his feet. Denzil backed away, wiping his face with his sleeve, then he looked at the watching crowd and yelled, "Another sword!" His glove was torn and his hand bled from where the point had caught him.

Thomas picked up his own rapier and saw that the tip was broken off. He walked back toward the crowd, shaking the rain-soaked hair out of his face, trying not to press a hand to his side where he could feel the blood soaking through his shirt. The blade hadn't bitten too deeply, but it was more than enough to slow him down.

He handed the broken weapon to Berham and took the cup-hilted rapier Gideon was holding out to him. Their stricken expressions said it all.

There was some movement in the crowd, someone pushing through the group of anxiously watching guards. Then suddenly Kade was standing in front of him. She was barefoot again, and with her ragged dress and disarrayed hair, she could have been some wilder variety of nymph. Except her gray eyes were too human, angry and afraid at the same time. Thomas said, "I thought you'd gone."

She said, "I'm half fay, but I'm not a fool. I've been up on the roof of the Guard House. I was going to wait you out, but Phaistus came and told me."

Thomas glanced up in time to see the young servant quickly retreating behind Gideon. He looked back down at Kade.

Almost pleading, she said, "Can't you just let me kill him, or have someone shoot him, and then we could go?"

"No. I have to do this."

"But I could—"

He put a finger over her lips. "No. It has to be this way. You said you'd do it for me, remember?"

She shook her head, anger temporarily winning out. "Fine. If I'd known you were going to do something like this, I'd have let you stand there and take on all the Unseelie Court and be killed."

"Fine. But if he wins, I want you to hurt him very badly before you kill him."

"I will. Very badly."

He turned and walked back to the center of the open area. Denzil was waiting for him with an unguarded expression of grim rage. *Good*, Thomas thought. *He's angry; that'll help.* Thomas was only exhausted and bleeding. Denzil had probably never faced an opponent in a serious duel who was as good or better than he was, and the young Duke was responding to it with anger. Falaise had come out onto the steps of the bastion and was watching with her ladies, her guards around her. She lifted a hand to him, and Thomas saluted her with his sword, then turned back to Denzil.

Denzil came at him furiously, but was not foolish enough to leave himself open. For a time Thomas was aware of nothing but his screaming muscles, of the flickering danger of the blades, of the blood pounding in his ears. He could see that Denzil's face was white and strained, that he was tiring too. The rain was coming down harder now and they were both slipping on the wet stones; Thomas knew another fall would finish him.

Then they both lunged at the same moment. Thomas disengaged and circled his rapier around Denzil's blade, twisting his wrist as he sent the point home with his remaining strength. He felt the point of the other rapier graze his arm even as he moved, felt it open a line of fire across his biceps as it went toward his chest; then it dropped away. It wasn't until he stumbled back and felt the resistance on his own blade before it came free that he realized what had happened.

Denzil was on his knees, one hand pressed to his chest with blood spreading between his fingers. Thomas stepped back, waiting.

It had been a clean blow, right to the heart. Denzil tried once to take a breath, his cold eyes fixed on nothing and already going blank, then he slumped forward onto the wet pavement.

Thomas dropped his sword and walked back to where Kade and the others waited. He stopped in front of her, trembling with exhaustion and feeling cold and empty. She shook her head, ran a hand through her tangled hair, and looked up at him. Meeting her eyes, the feeling of emptiness fled.

Impatient, her voice weak with relief, Kade said, "Now can we go?"

"Yes, now we can go."

CPSIA information can be obtained at www.ICGtesting.com
Printed in the USA
LVOW06s1543080514

384967LV00003B/631/A